W9-BYA-329

What the critics are saying...

ଛ

Bloodlust – Conquering Mikhel Dumont is the winner of a CAPA award

"Ms. Lee has excelled herself...Bloodlust: Conquering Mikhel Dumont has sizzle, chemistry." ~ *Just Erotic Romance Reviews*

"THE TALISMAN is a great paranormal erotic story."~ *Sensual Romance*

"Ms. Lee has a riveting and wonderful story in Bloodlust: Conquering Mikhel Dumont." ~ *Just Erotic Romance Reviews*

"This was a very good romance, with a plentiful amount of sexual content." ~ *Sensual Romance*

Destiny's
SLAVES

MARILYN
LEE

ELLORA'S CAVE
ROMANTICA PUBLISHING

An Ellora's Cave Romantica Publication

www.ellorascave.com

Destiny's Slaves

ISBN 9781419955426
ALL RIGHTS RESERVED.
The Talisman Copyright © Marilyn Lee 2002
Conquering Mikhel Dumont Copyright © Marilyn Lee 2004

Edited by Martha Punches
Cover art by Syneca

Excerpt from *Bloodlust II – The Taming of Serge Dumont* Copyright © Marilyn Lee 2002

With the exception of quotes used in reviews, this book may not be reproduced or used in whole or in part by any means existing without written permission from the publisher, Ellora's Cave Publishing, Inc.® 1056 Home Avenue, Akron OH 44310-3502.

This book is a work of fiction and any resemblance to persons, living or dead, or places, events or locales is purely coincidental. The characters are productions of the authors' imagination and used fictitiously.

Content Advisory:

S – ENSUOUS
E – ROTIC
X – TREME

Ellora's Cave Publishing offers three levels of Romantica™ reading entertainment: S (S-ensuous), E (E-rotic), and X (X-treme).

The following material contains graphic sexual content meant for mature readers. This story has been rated E–rotic.

S-*ensuous* love scenes are explicit and leave nothing to the imagination.

E-*rotic* love scenes are explicit, leave nothing to the imagination, and are high in volume per the overall word count. E-rated titles might contain material that some readers find objectionable — in other words, almost anything goes, sexually. E-rated titles are the most graphic titles we carry in terms of both sexual language and descriptiveness in these works of literature.

X-*treme* titles differ from E-rated titles only in plot premise and storyline execution. Stories designated with the letter X tend to contain difficult or controversial subject matter not for the faint of heart.

Contents

Also by Marilyn Lee

ଛଇ

About the Author

&

Marilyn Lee lives, works, and writes on the East Coast. In addition to writing erotic romances, she enjoys roller-skating, spending time with her large extended family, and rooting for all her hometown sports teams. Her other interests include collecting Doc Savage pulp novels from the thirties and forties and collecting Marvel comics from the seventies and eighties (particularly Thor and The Avengers). Her favorite TV shows are forensic shows, westerns (Gunsmoke and Have Gun, Will Travel are particular favorites), mysteries (she loves the old Charlie Chan mysteries. Her all time favorite mystery movie is probably Dead, Again), and nearly every vampire movie or television show ever made (Forever Knight and Count Yorga, Vampire are favorites). She thoroughly enjoys hearing from readers.

Marilyn welcomes comments from readers. You can find her website and email address on her author bio page at www.ellorascave.com.

THE TALISMAN

Chapter One

ဆ

Aware that the moonlight shining in through the open bedroom window cast a pleasing glow over her body, Cassy Thompson slowly turned, her arms extended so that every inch of her tawny body was clearly visible to the man standing scant inches from her. She knew her breasts, which were large and firm, were one of her best assets, so she came to a slow stop in front of him, fully exposed to his gaze.

His face was in shadows, but his breathing was fast and labored. And a quick glance down at his dark trousers told her all she needed to know. The sizable bulge resting against his thigh was clear evidence of his state of arousal and added to her own rising excitement. This time she was going to get what she wanted. What she'd wanted from the moment she saw him.

"Well? What do you think?" she prodded, her voice husky and a little anxious. "I hope you like what you see."

"What's not to like?" he asked, his voice thick with desire. "You're as beautiful as I knew you'd be. Every lovely, dusky inch of you."

Smiling, she undulated her body suggestively in time to the soft, hypnotic jazz playing in the background. She thrust her breasts out and slowly rotated her hips from side to side. "I showed you mine, now it's your turn," she teased. "Let's see what you're hiding in those pants."

He quickly discarded his tie and shirt. She watched with heightened anticipation as he kicked off his shoes, pulled off his socks and scrambled out of his pants. Finally, he removed his briefs.

When he stood nude before her, she stared, her lips parted in silent wonder and delight. His tall tan body was absolutely gorgeous. His shoulders were broad, his chest almost hairless, his abs tight and sexy. His hips narrow but powerful and his thighs, strong and muscled.

But it was his cock, jutting out from his hairy crotch, that made her gasp in eager expectation. She'd seen larger erections, but size wasn't everything. And he was thick and hard. She stared at him, slowly licked her lips, certain that just feeling the head of that delicious-looking weapon sliding into her body would be enough to drive her insane with desire.

"Well? Do I disappoint?" he demanded in a confident voice.

"No. Oh, no!" She held her arms out to him. "Oh…Chandler! Chandler!"

He quickly closed the distance between them and drew her slowly into his arms. She closed her eyes and slipped her arms around him, savoring the feelings rushing through her. The feel of his chest crushing her breasts, of his shaft pressing hot against her stomach, made her shudder helplessly.

"Oh! Chandler! Chandler!" Cassy turned her head and rained a series of quick kisses against his shoulders. His skin was smooth and warm under her lips, too delicious to resist gently nipping at. The sucking in of his breath drew a delighted smile from her. She gradually moved her hands down his back to his buns. The twin mounds were hard and tight. Touching a man's butt had never turned her on so much. She loved the sensations coursing through her as she rubbed her eager palms against his behind.

"Very nice buns," she whispered trying to force his body closer to hers.

In response, he gripped her hips and ground his shaft against her aching body. The resultant sensation caused a rush of moistness between her suddenly trembling legs.

Cupping a hand behind her head, he brought his mouth crashing down onto hers in a kiss that ravished and plundered. She moaned as he sank his tongue deep between her parted lips at the same time as one big hand cupped and massaged her breasts.

"Hmm," she gasped, stretching on her toes to wrap her arms around his neck and return the hungry pressure of his mouth. "Chandler! Oh, Chandler! Please. Please. Now. I need you now!"

Pulling back, he trailed a hand along her body, over her breasts, down over her smooth stomach to palm her mound. She thought she'd die of pleasure when he gently inserted two fingers inside her. She gasped and pushed her hips down against the digits of delight moving slowly inside her. Laughing softly, he pumped his fingers deep in her and urgently rubbed the ball of his thumb against her swollen clit.

She shuddered helplessly, in the grip of mindless pleasure. "Oh! Yes! Yes, Chandler!"

He blew gently into her ear. "You like that, baby?"

"Yes! Oh...yes!"

"Oh yeah, you like it. I can feel you overflowing. You want more?"

"Yes!" The word rushed out in a breathless, senseless whisper.

He increased the motion and speed of his fingers inside her. She whimpered and felt herself creaming around his fingers. "Oh! Please...you're torturing me...now...now."

"Yeah, baby. You like that. You're ready. You're ready. You want me? You want me inside your sweet body?"

Her legs buckled and she clung to his shoulders. "Oh yes! Please!"

He lifted her off her feet and carried her across the moonlit room. He lowered her onto his big brass bed and stood looking down at her.

His gaze lingered on her breasts before trailing down her body to rest on her dark, hair-covered mound. "That's a pretty pink pussy," he murmured.

Feeling totally shameless and loving it, she smiled and deliberately parted her legs, giving him a better view of herself. Reaching down with a trembling hand, she parted herself so he could see all of her. "What about this view?"

"Oh God!" He groaned, then he pinned her to the bed with his big hard body.

"Please. Now!" she begged, reaching between their bodies to clutch the object of her desire in greedy hands. He felt hot and silky against her fingers. She shoved her hips up and rubbed the head of his hot dick against her hardened clit. A white-hot bolt of lust thundered through her vagina. "Please! Now."

"Now!" He echoed in a strained voice. He lifted his body slightly off hers, braced his weight on his knees and finally, blessedly, placed his hot flesh at the entrance of her quivering mound. She lifted her hips eagerly and moaned as he began to press the big head of his shaft between the lips of her heated sex.

She bit her lip and sucked in her breath. The pulsing head of his dick began the slow, exquisite journey into her hot, wet body. "Oh…yes…yes! God, yes!"

She closed her eyes, lifted her hips and…

Bbbrring! Bbbrring!

Cassy kept her eyes tightly closed in an effort to hold onto the dream, while she wildly reached out a hand to shut off the alarm. But by the time her desperate fingers located the button to silence the offending buzzer, the dream…her lovely, sexy dream had vanished like a light breeze hit by a blast of summer sunlight.

"Oh no!" She rolled over onto her back and allowed her eyes to open. She lay in her own bed, in her own bedroom, with an empty dampness between her legs. She turned her head to look at the undisturbed pillow bedside her. Alone. He hadn't been here, except in another of her inexplicable, shameless dreams.

Of all the Saturdays to forget to disable her alarm. If it hadn't rung, she'd now be in heaven. Granted it would only be a dream, but having Chandler Raven make love to her was a fantasy and a dream she'd been having with increasing and disturbing frequency.

She turned and buried her face in her pillow, rubbing her aching mound against the rumpled sheets. Her body quivered and pulsed for relief from the tension and desire created by her erotic dream.

She had as much chance of sleeping with Chandler Raven as she had of starting the upcoming football season as the Philadelphia Eagles quarterback—unless she used The Talisman.

She could still recall her mother, Ida, refusing to accept the small gold figure from her own mother. As her Grandma Maud lay dying, just after Cassy's eighteenth birthday, with her own mother sobbing softly in the background, Cassy had reluctantly accepted The Talisman.

"Cassy, you're a woman now...old enough to own The Talisman," her grandmother had said.

"No, Mama, she's eighteen, but she's still just a baby!" her mother had whispered. "Don't ask her to take that thing."

"She's old enough to make her own decision, Ida. Just as I let you make your own not to take possession of The Talisman, let her make her own." Grandma Maud had gripped her hand and looked up at her with dark brown eyes full of pain and worry. "Will you take it, Cassy?"

She had stood by the bed, holding Grandma Maud's hand, tears streaming down her cheeks. She was losing her grandmother and inheriting the small figurine that her mother had always warned her to avoid. Although she shared her mother's fear of The Talisman, she'd felt unable to refuse her beloved grandmother's only request.

"Yes, Grandma Maud. I'll take it."

"It has the power to bring you love, but there is a price to pay if you use it too often and unwisely. You must use it sparingly and carefully. Make sure that the man you use it on is the man you'll want forever. Never use it otherwise. Used properly, it'll bring you a love like no other. Used improperly, it will bring you a lifetime of grief."

"I promise…to be careful with it."

Grandma Maud had then pressed the small cool charm into her palm and closed her hand over it. "Remember, Cassy, you must not follow the ritual unless you're absolutely sure of the man."

"I promise."

Grandma Maud had sighed deeply then, as if a weight had been lifted off her. "Go now. I need to sleep."

"Cassy, why did you take it?" Her mother had sobbed as they'd sat in the back of a cab being driven away from the hospital together. "You know your Great-granny Marie was a Creole and brought it with her when she left the Louisiana bayou. It has powers that you can't control and don't need. You're a lovely girl, Cassy. You won't need it to find love."

Cassy had shivered, the small gold figurine clutched in the hand where Grandma Maud had placed it. Her hand felt hot and yet cold. She was scared because the tighter she held The Talisman, the more it seemed to vibrate in her hand. Her mother was right. She shouldn't have accepted it.

"I had to take it, Mom. I couldn't let her die worrying what would happen to it when she was gone."

"She's my mother and I love her, but I'm afraid what's going to happen to you if you ever use it. Oh Cassy! You must never, never use it."

Alone in her room, Cassy had locked the door and only then did she dare open her hand. She bit her lip and pressed her free hand against her lips as she stared down into her palm.

The Talisman, approximately one and a half inches high and an inch wide, depicted a couple. Although small, the gold carving clearly showed the firm contours of the nude couple. The woman faced away from the man, revealing the outline of her body, including her hair-covered mound. The man, muscular and aroused, stood behind the women, clutching her breasts in his palms, with part of his cock buried in the woman's body.

Always the copulating twosome, were frozen in that erotic position. Now, to Cassy's startled dismay, the golden couple moved. She could actually see the small, golden dick moving in and out of the woman's body. After a moment, Cassy realized that instead of being in the woman's cunt, as she'd assumed the few times she'd seen the charm over the years, the man's cock was actually tunneling back and forth in the tiny woman's anus. They couple were having anal sex!

That night Cassy had lain awake for hours, holding the couple in her hands, watching the endless mating. When she finally fell asleep, it was only to dream of some faceless man having anal sex with her, bringing her to a climax with several fingers thrusting into her pussy as he came in her bottom. In the morning, tired and ashamed, she had promised never to watch the unnatural coupling again.

In the intervening ten years, she had kept The Talisman in a small jewelry box in the back of her underwear drawer. Although she had occasionally been tempted to take it out and watch the couple having sex, she had resisted the urge. Still, as she lay in bed, alone and lonely, she often thought she heard low moaning in her room. Once, when she dared to look in her underwear drawer, the tiny dick pounded the tiny behind ruthlessly.

Watching, she'd become aroused. Unable to stop herself, she reached out and touched the clenching behind of the male. A shock radiated up her arm when the small, golden dick came all the way out of the woman's anus and her finger touched it.

"Oh God!" It was warm and hard, like a real penis. It had taken all her will power to put the couple back in the box and close the drawer.

She'd never taken the time to really find out about The Talisman. The next morning she'd gone to her mother and learned as much as she knew about it.

"Your Grandma Maud said she'd followed the ritual with the wrong man and was never happy. My father was a good man, but because she'd used The Talisman unwisely, Mother was never happy with him. If you want to avoid the heartache and misery your Great-granny Marie and my mother faced, don't ever follow the ritual, Cassy."

"I won't," she'd promised.

After that, she'd decided that although she couldn't bring herself to destroy it as her mother urged her to, she would not fall into the trap of allowing it to ruin her life.

So using it to lure Chandler Raven was out of the question. If she were to attract him, it would be the old-fashioned way and not by means of the power of The Talisman.

She had always admired women with enough courage to go after the men they wanted. She'd often thought it must be wonderful to be a forceful, uninhibited woman, who didn't wait to be asked out. One who not only asked the man of her choice out, but then went on to seduce him. Maybe do a sleazy striptease for him that left him panting for her before giving herself wantonly and uninhibitedly to him.

That's exactly what she wanted to do the first time she met Chandler Raven. One look into his deep smoky gray eyes, and her heart pounded and her knees shook. Shortly after their first meeting, she found herself daydreaming of lying naked with him on a beach, making love while the waves crashed at their feet. Other fantasies included lying nude under his big, sweaty body in some rose-scented garden while he rapidly pumped his hot cock in and out of her greedy, aching tunnel.

She felt her face burn at her crude thoughts. What was wrong with her? At twenty-eight, she'd only had two lovers. And she never discussed sex with anyone other than her best friend, Derri Morgan. An attorney for a prestigious Center City law firm, Derri was completely no-nonsense. Currently involved in an ongoing, long-term relationship with another lawyer, Derri seldom shared her own sexual fantasies. Which, in turn, made it difficult for Cassy to discuss her own in graphic detail or in a vulgar way. She wondered uneasily if her mother was right. Was The Talisman affecting her, even though she had never followed the ritual?

Was that why her dreams of Chandler Raven had become increasing graphic and crude over the last few weeks? As if creating sexual fantasies around a man who didn't even know she was alive wasn't bad enough, she never thought in terms of making love in her dreams anymore. Now it was always fucking—like the small golden couple who fucked endlessly in her panty drawer. In her dreams, she begged to be fucked and Chandler obliged. In her dreams, he sometimes fucked her missionary style, sometimes doggie style, sometimes up her anus.

What was it about him that made her think such thoughts? Want such treatment? Especially when she knew there would never be anything between them, not even mindless sex. And certainly not anal sex. There was no way she'd ever engage in anal sex.

She sighed. Like she was going to get the chance to say no to a bottom reaming from Chandler Raven. He was the owner of the computer company where she worked. Much to her surprise, she'd landed the job just two weeks after graduating from college.

Competing against a bunch of twenty-one-year-olds who'd gone to college straight from high school, she hadn't been too sure of her chances of getting the one opening at Raven Electronics. Forget catching the eye of the tall, athletic, dark-haired Chandler Raven.

While waiting in the reception area for her turn to be interviewed, she'd seen the two women he'd interviewed before her, both twenty-year-old beauties who could easily have graced the cover of a *Sports Illustrated* swimsuit issue.

She was already mentally running down the list of other job prospects when the office door opened. She looked up and saw a man standing in the door, who, although a stranger, looked hauntingly familiar to her. He might have stepped off the cover of *GQ*. He was tall and well built with short dark hair graying at the temples. One look at him and she found herself thinking of his white penis plunging into what one lover had called her pretty, pink vagina. Again and again. Over and over until she came in a frenzy of lust and passion.

His voice had startled her out of her unexpected erotic thoughts. "Ms. Thompson?"

She looked up into his gray eyes and felt as if they were alone in the room...in the building...the galaxy...a dark, overgrown swamp. They'd been alone before. She could be quite happy to spend the rest of her life in the world with this man alone for company.

"Ms. Thompson?" he asked again.

"Oh!" She blinked and nodded, her face heating with embarrassment. Thank God he couldn't read her shameless thoughts. "Yes."

"This way, please." He pushed the door of his office open wider and stepped back. She was aware of the subtle cologne he wore as she moved passed him into a big office with cream-colored walls. He motioned to one of two dark red leather chairs in front of a large mahogany desk. "Please, sit down."

When she had, he lowered himself into the chair behind the desk. "Miss Thompson." He glanced down at an open folder on his desk. "Miss Cassy Thompson." He looked up at her. "Or is it Ms?"

"Either one is fine."

"But which do you prefer?"

"Miss is fine."

He smiled, giving her a glimpse of even, white teeth. "Miss it is. So Miss Thompson. I'm Chandler Raven," he told her.

She blinked at him. "You're Mr. Raven?"

"Yes." He smiled. "I believe that's what I just said."

She digested that news in silence. He was the head honcho. She wasn't used to presidents of companies who did their own initial interviewing. Now she was doubly nervous.

"So. Miss Thompson. Tell me about yourself," he invited.

"What would you like to know, sir?"

"Everything," he said, his voice cool and professional.

"Everything? You want to know my grade point average and where I went to school?"

"No." He smiled briefly. "That's not what I meant." He tapped a finger against an open folder on his desk. "Those details are in your application folder. I want to know about you, Miss Thompson. About your background. If you have a family. What your values are. If you're superstitious. What your goals— long and short term—are, professionally and personally. Why you studied electronics. Why you want to work for Raven Electronics. What you expect to bring to our firm and what you expect from us."

"Oh," she said. "Everything."

"Yes." He nodded. "Everything. We invest a lot of time, money and resources in our employees. We like to know our investments aren't going to be wasted."

After the interview, she couldn't remember what she'd said, but it must have been adequate because the next thing she knew, he was smiling at her and offering her the job.

"Really?" She blew out a breath she hadn't realized she was holding. "The job is mine? You're offering me the job?"

He nodded. "Yes. It's yours if you want it, Miss Thompson."

"Of course I do! Thank you, sir."

He sat back in his chair, his gaze locked on her face. "You seem surprised."

"Well...I am. A little." She nodded toward the closed office door. "I saw the other two applicants and I really didn't think I stood much of a chance."

His gaze flicked slowly over her face. "Why not? Your work history is impeccable and your resume is impressive."

"Thank you."

He looked at her with raised brows, clearly expecting an explanation.

"Well, the other two applicants were younger for one thing," she began reluctantly. She didn't want to comment on her other concern.

"They were that, Miss Thompson, but your working your way through college at night while working full-time impressed me. That couldn't have been easy."

It had been difficult, but her goal on landing her first job at seventeen had always been to help her mother pay off the mortgage on the house where she and her younger siblings had been raised.

He studied her face for several moments in silence before speaking again. "But I think there's something else you'd like to say. Here at Raven Electronics, we take a very hands-on approach to employee relations. That means we're all encouraged to speak our minds. Speak your mind, Miss Thompson."

"Okay. As you said, I worked hard to earn my degree. And I do think I deserve this job."

He shrugged. "Clearly, I agree with you. So why don't we cut to the chase. Say what's on your mind, Miss Thompson."

She sucked in a breath. "I guess I'm a little afraid that my new coworkers will think I got the job as a result of some type of affirmative action."

His eyes narrowed. "Why would you imagine that anyone would think that, Miss Thompson?"

She shifted in her seat and resisted the urge to look skyward. If he called her Miss Thompson one more time, she'd scream. "Well, you have a reputation as an employer who goes out of his way to hire minorities. And being a black female, I'm certainly a minority."

His lips twitched and his eyes twinkled. "I guess you are at that. Nevertheless, I almost always say what I mean and mean what I say. Rest assured that I'm offering you the job because you have the qualifications and because you've demonstrated a willingness to work hard that I admire in and demand from my employees.

"I think you should understand that I do not hire unqualified people for any reason. If you were not amply qualified, I wouldn't have offered you the job. Now, would you, or would you not like the job, Miss Thompson?"

Feeling as if she'd been put firmly in her place, she nodded. "Yes. Yes, I would like the job. Thank you, sir."

He rose, smiling again, his hand extended. "Welcome to Raven Electronics."

She rose also. Her hand was engulfed in his and a tingle danced along her nerve endings. Confusion filled her. Never had the touch of a man's hand affected her this way. She pulled her hand away so quickly that he stared at her with his dark brows elevated.

"Is there something wrong, Miss Thompson?"

"No. No, sir. Thank you, sir."

"It's really not necessary to call me sir with every other breath." His smile turned into an engaging grin. "You make me feel like an old married grandfather."

She stared at him in bewilderment. The gray at his temples notwithstanding, his face, with its slightly crooked nose and firm lips, was attractive without being handsome. It was also unlined. He appeared to be in his late thirties or early forties. And he did not look like anyone's grandfather. But was he anyone's husband or significant other?

For a moment, with him standing there grinning down at her, she felt the urge to ask him how old he was. And if they had ever met.

"Sorry," she said instead, only just stopping herself from adding 'sir'.

He nodded and moved across the room to the door.

She followed him slowly, her gaze locked on him. He had a long, graceful stride. She found herself wondering if he'd been an athlete in college. Under his pants, his thighs would be strong with well-developed muscles that rippled when he walked. His chest and shoulders would—

She became aware that he was standing at the door watching her with raised brows and a speculative look on his face. Oh no! He'd caught her staring! Filled with embarrassment and shame, she averted her gaze and hurried across the room.

"If you'll call my secretary tomorrow, she'll make all the necessary arrangements with personnel."

"Thank you, s—"

"Mr. Raven will do." He smiled briefly and opened the door.

"Mr. Raven," she repeated and hurried from the office, her heart thumping with excitement, her nostrils filled with the faint scent of his cologne.

Remembering that day now, she sighed. She rolled onto her stomach and buried her face in her pillow. Soon, she would get up, but for now, she just wanted to lie there, thinking about Chandler Raven and wondering if he ever thought about their first meeting. It was strange but sometimes she felt as if their thoughts and feelings were intertwined.

Chapter Two

Chandler Raven came awake abruptly, his immediate thoughts centered on Cassy Thompson—again. He glanced at his beside clock. 6:20 a.m. Damn, he thought angrily. This was getting ridiculous. Instead of sleeping late on a Saturday morning before he spent the day with Julie, he woke early—horny and wanting one of his employees.

As happened with increasing frequency, once he thought of Cassy Thompson, he remembered their first meeting—still fresh in his mind after several weeks.

Yielding to the inevitable, he lay back, a slight smile forming on his lips as he recalled how shaken he'd been after his first meeting with Cassy Thompson...

After she'd left his office, he'd sat with his head back against his chair, his eyes closed. He'd told himself for the third time that he had made the right decision.

Cassy Thompson *did* have the right qualifications. She *had* demonstrated a willingness to work hard. She *did* deserve the job. His hiring her had nothing to do with the shock of desire he'd felt when he'd found himself staring down into her bottomless, liquid brown eyes. The fact that she bore a startling resemblance to the exquisitely sculptured ebony figurine that had haunted his dreams for years had not factored in his decision. Except for the fact that Cassy Thompson had short hair and the statuette had long, wavy hair, she might have modeled for it. Of course he was speculating. He had no way of knowing if her body was half as exquisite as the curves and lines of the foot high statuette his grandfather had given him on his thirtieth birthday.

He had not made a success of his company by hiring people who were not amply qualified. Okay, so maybe the other two applicants had slightly higher grade point averages. But neither of them had much work experience, he told himself. For all he knew one or both the other applicants might have proven to be lazy and unproductive.

The fact that he had not been physically aware of either of the other two applicants had *not* factored in his decision. Still, there was no denying the fact that the touch of Cassy Thompson's long fingered hand in his combined with her shy, but sweet smile had sent him straight to sexual fantasyland. Just as the nude ebony figurine on his desk at home did.

It had been a long time since he'd been so attracted to a woman. And, his appreciation for The Ebony Venus notwithstanding, he'd never been particularly attracted to black women, at least not consciously. Serge Dumont, his college roommate would have been quick to point out that Chandler was finally suffering from what Serge called his southern roots.

Serge was of the firm opinion that most southern white men harbored secret passions for black women. Chandler had learned that it was a waste of breath pointing out that both he and his father had been born and raised in the north.

"Ah, yes, but you've got that hot Cajun blood running through your veins," Serge would retort. "And one day it'll stir you toward one of the many lovely ebony beauties you've spent years dissing."

Serge's theory notwithstanding, Chandler preferred slender, blue-eyed blondes. Like Jane Gardner, a petite blonde beauty he'd met a year earlier at a party given by his sister-in-law, Ellen.

His relationship with Jane had progressed slowly. He'd wined and dined her for three months before they slept together. Once they had, his interest had quickly waned. She hadn't been very responsive to him physically and they'd drifted into a casual friendship. He still saw her and when his body dictated, occasionally slept with her.

Their relationship held very little physical challenge or excitement for him. He had to work hard to arouse her and harder still to maintain control long enough to satisfy her. He got the feeling she found their sex life as unrewarding as he did. But they'd grown used to each other and had learned to settle for less than they both wanted or needed sexually. And there was the comfort of knowing she wouldn't demand more of him than he wanted to give.

Jane was his 'type'. So why did just the thought of seeing the statuesque, brown-skinned and brown-eyed Cassy Thompson again make him so damn hard?

Remembering his last conversation with his nephew, Steve, he frowned. Steve was his late brother's oldest child. At nineteen, Steve's hormones were in full bloom and he couldn't seem to keep his pants up. Within the last five months, his mother, Chandler's sister-in-law, Ellen, had caught Steve sleeping with three different girls.

Just three weeks earlier, Ellen had called Chandler in hysterics, screaming that she'd caught Steve with yet another girl — this one eighteen and black.

He'd promised to talk to Steve and he had. He and Steve had met for lunch at a downtown sports cafe, where Steve had sat sipping a cola. He had listened in silence to Chandler's spill about how going to school full-time and dating was traumatic enough without the added burden of crossing the racial dating line.

"I guess you're right, Uncle Chandler," he said when Chandler fell silent.

He'd been surprised at how easy it had been to reason with Steve. "So you'll stay away from her?"

Steve had looked at him with gray eyes very like his own and shook his head decisively. "Not only am I going to go on seeing her, but I'm going to fuck her as often as she'll let me," he'd said.

Chandler had stared at him in silence, wondering how to make him understand how messy dating the girl could get.

"Have you ever fucked a black woman, Uncle Chandler?"

The abruptness and the crudeness of the question had rattled him. He'd answered cautiously, uncertain where Steve was headed.

"No."

"Have you ever wanted to?"

At the time he hadn't found that question hard to answer. "Not particularly."

Steve stared at him, a skeptical look on his face. "Are you telling me you've never seen a black woman you found attractive, Uncle Chandler?"

He'd thought briefly of the many black Greek frat parties Serge had dragged him to. "That's not what I said," he pointed out. "As a matter of fact, I've seen many black women I found attractive...breathtaking even."

"Then?" Steve challenged.

"Then what?"

"Then why haven't you ever dated one?"

"Because there's an equal number of white women that I find just as attractive and breathtaking, so why give myself the grief still associated with interracial dating?"

"Because the woman in question was worth any amount of grief," Steve said promptly. "Like Tia." Steve had leaned across the small table then, his eyes gleaming. "They're incredible!"

"They're? You mean you've dated black girls before her?" He'd asked, surprised, not only because Steve was sleeping with a black girl, but because he'd had so many lovers. At his age, Chandler had only had one lover. That had quickly changed once he met Serge. It had been difficult not to be horny as hell sharing an apartment with Serge who ate, drank and lived to have sex. He'd spent many sleepless nights in the room next to

Serge's listening as Serge satisfied his rapacious sexual appetite, sometimes with more than one woman at a time.

"No, but I've fucked five other girls. But Uncle Chandler, Tia is fantastic. She has the best pussy I've ever had. It's tight and hot and she has a nice round ass that jiggles like crazy when we fuck each other. I'm telling you, Uncle Chandler, you don't know what you're missing!"

Chandler had realized that trying to talk Steve out of seeing this Tia would only make him more determined to see her. So, instead he'd talked to him about protection.

"Steve, I hope you're taking the proper precautions. If she ends up pregnant, we'll see how good you think her pussy is then," he said wearily.

Steve had just grinned at him. "It's more than good! It's fantastic. And we do use protection—both of us. She's on the Pill and I use condoms. We're horny, Uncle Chandler, not stupid! Don't worry. I won't give Mom a heart attack by bringing her a half-black grandchild."

Chandler frowned. "Steve, I hope you're not misunderstanding," he said slowly. "We are not a prejudiced family. If you know our history, you know that."

Steve had held up a hand. "If you're going to give me the 'my great-great-grandfather fell in love with a black woman' spiel, I've heard it a dozen times. That was a long time ago in the bayou and that didn't exactly work out well for the old man or his Creole lover, did it?"

"No, but if you read the letters he wrote her, you know he never stopped loving her."

"Yeah, right. He was so in love with her that he let his family separate them."

"Come on, Steve. It was a different place and a different time."

"Whatever. I'll bet she could do without that kind of love. Besides, Uncle Chandler, that story only serves to prove that this family *isn't* color blind."

He couldn't deny that Steve had a point there. "That was a different time and place, Steve," he said again. "This isn't Louisiana and your mom and I are *not* prejudiced."

"I know you're not, Uncle Chandler."

"You do? How?"

Steve had given him a sly grin. "Come on. I've seen her, you know."

"Who?"

"Her."

"Her, who?"

"The Ebony Venus on the desk in your office at home. Any man who has that on his desk can't be prejudiced. Doesn't looking at her make you want to get with a real live black woman? That's what made me want one—seeing her."

Great. That was all he needed—for Ellen to find out that his statuette had been responsible for sending Steve into this Tia's arms.

"I can see why Mom wouldn't let Dad have her. How could a guy not want a black woman after looking at her?"

He'd frowned. "So you only want to date this Tia because she's black?"

"No! At first that was my reason, but not now. Now that I've gotten to know her. She's funny, sweet, warm and pretty. But most of all she makes me feel special."

He sighed. "I didn't really intend for you to see The Ebony Venus, Steve."

"Why not? Want to keep her all for yourself?"

"Steve, it might interest you to know that I've had the statuette for nearly ten years now and it has yet to drive me into the arms of anyone. So let's get back to the fact that your mom is not prejudiced."

"You know, Uncle Chandler, I'm not so sure about that. I know she makes all the right politically correct noises, but the first time she finds me dating a back girl, she loses it. How prejudiced is that?"

"Oh, come on, Steve," he said impatiently. "You were doing more than dating her. Your mom caught you sleeping with her!"

Steve grinned unrepentantly. "Mom always did have bad timing. She came home at a bad time. Tia is an incredible person with the most amazing pussy. She has a way of squeezing my cock with it that drives me wild. I was balls-deep in that sweet cunt of hers, about to blow my load when—"

Chandler held up a hand, hoping that his face wasn't as red as it felt. "Look, Steve, I know I said you could tell me anything in any way and I mean that. But do you have to be so graphic?"

Steve looked at him in surprise. "Graphic? Are you embarrassed, Uncle Chandler?"

"No!" He hadn't heard such crude language since the last time he'd talked to Serge. "Well...maybe a little with all this talk of cocks, pussies and cunts."

"You want me to say penis and vagina?" Steve sounded surprised and amused.

To his annoyance, Chandler felt the heat rising up the back of his neck. "Say whatever you like, Steven, but that kind of talk tends to make it sound as if you don't really care about this girl. As if you're only interested in sex."

Steve shook his head. "Oh no! It's not just sex. That's what Mom would like to think, but she's wrong. And so are you, if that's what you think. I like Tia...a lot. More than any other girl I've ever met. It's almost as if we were meant to be together. She knows how deeply I care about her. That's why she's still seeing me, even though her parents don't approve."

"Why don't they approve?" he asked, curious.

Steve grinned at him. "Because they're a proud black family with lots of money. Her father expects her to marry well to a black man and give him a couple of all black grandchildren. No white guys need apply."

"Are you saying her father is prejudiced?"

He shrugged. "Not according to him. Like, Mom, he says his objection to me has nothing to do with the fact that I'm not black. Yeah, right."

"Steve, isn't the fact that your mom and her parents object to your relationship reason enough to tread lightly with this girl?"

"No. I'm nineteen and she's eighteen. We can see and sleep with who we like. And that's each other."

With that he'd dropped the subject.

He shook his head. He found himself in the same position—that of getting big-time horny over a black woman. A woman he'd just hired. He considered again Steve's question about his ever having wanted to "fuck" a black woman. His reaction to Cassy Thompson had been disturbing, to say the least. He *had* found her attractive, but he had *not* thought in terms of "fucking" her. Kissing her full, luscious-looking lips until they were both breathless? Yes. Sliding his aching, throbbing rod deep in her willing body until they both came? Absolutely. But fucking her? No.

He didn't want to fuck her. He'd done enough of that in his college days. To him fucking implied a sexual act devoid of tenderness and consideration for the other person. A man interested in fucking had one thing on his mind—getting his cock into a woman and shooting a load of come in her as quickly as possible. If the woman managed to find satisfaction before that happened, fine. If she didn't, well, what did she expect from a fuck?

He wanted to make love to Cassy Thompson—slowly, sweetly—all night long, night after night.

Of course that was also out of the question. He sighed. It was that damned statuette. He'd looked at it too long, developed hidden passions he hadn't even been aware of. He'd have to make sure that he stayed well away from Cassy Thompson.

When he got home the Ebony Venus was going into the nearest closet...

Now, lying in bed, Chandler frowned. After he'd stopped reminiscing about his conversation with Steve, things had only gotten stickier. Closing his eyes and settling back against his pillow, he let his thoughts drift back to the day he'd met Cassy Thompson when his secretary had questioned his quick hiring of her...

He'd looked up as his office door opened after a cursory tap. Jennifer Johnson, came in. She carried several folders and a cup of coffee. She sank down into the chair in front of his desk and put her cup down. "You look lost in thought."

"I suppose I was."

"Pleasant ones?"

"Not entirely, no."

"Hmm. So, who looks good?"

"What?"

"Which applicant do you want to discuss first?"

"What applicant..." Damn! How could he have forgotten? For the last four years, after each interview, he and Jennifer, who'd been with him since he started the company twelve years earlier, discussed the merits of each applicant before he made the final decision.

How was he supposed to tell her that one look at Cassy Thompson and his whole procedure for interviewing had been tossed out the window? That all he'd thought of was giving her the job so he could occasionally see her?

"Chandler? What's wrong?"

He ran a hand through his hair. "Ah...nothing. It's just that I offered the job to Miss Thompson."

She blinked at him, her green eyes wide with surprise and ran a hand through her short, gray hair. "You already offered her the job?"

He nodded. "Yes."

She sat back in her chair. "She must have been very impressive, indeed." She glanced through the folders in her lap. "Any special reason why you choose her over the other two so quickly? Ms. Wilder's grade point average was 4.0 and Ms. Dilworth's was 3.9." She'd paused, looking at him over the tops of her glasses.

"And Miss Thompson's was 3.7. I know, but she had other qualities that compensated for the lower grade point average. And really, Jen, you'll have to admit that 3.7 isn't too shabby." He flicked through Cassy Thompson's application folder on his desk. "And her current employer gave her an outstanding performance report. In fact…" he'd trailed off, abruptly aware that he was protesting far too much.

Jennifer took off her glasses and looked at him. "Chandler?"

During the last four years, Jennifer had become his confidant and sounding board. She knew him better than he was comfortable with. Now she clearly knew he wasn't being straight with her.

"She went to school at night while working full-time as a domestic and being a Big Sister." That had impressed him since he'd spent several years as a Big Brother. "I thought she demonstrated a willingness to work hard and she deserves the job."

Jennifer tilted her head to one side and studied his face. "Chandler, your face is red," she said lightly. "And you sound like you've been rehearsing that spiel."

He stared at her in silence, wondering if she knew the effect Cassy Thompson had on him. But she didn't. She couldn't.

Some of his discomfort must have been obvious because she looked worried. "You want to talk about it, Chandler?"

"No." He spoke more sharply than he'd intended. He took a deep breath before going on. "No because there's nothing to talk about. She deserved the job. I offered it to her and she accepted. She'll call you tomorrow to make the arrangements."

"Okay." She flashed him the cool, professional smile that signaled he'd offended her, gathered her folders and cup, and left the office.

He'd sat back in his seat, feeling like a fool. He was worse than Steve. At least Steve was young enough so that being ruled by his hormones was understandable. At thirty-nine, Chandler himself had no such excuse. And these days, he wasn't a man given to allowing his dick to dictate to him. He'd learned the folly of that in his last year of college when he lived in fear that he'd have to get married before he was ready when a female he'd had a one-night stand with told him she might be pregnant. After several weeks of sleepless nights, she'd found out she wasn't pregnant.

Then there was his miserable excuse for a marriage. He'd married Karen because she'd had the best pussy he'd ever had and she'd given it to him just enough to get him thinking he couldn't live without it. When she'd cut off the sex, he'd proposed. It had taken a full year before he admitted that maybe it had been a mistake to marry a woman with whom he'd shared nothing more binding than a raging desire. Yet, one look at Cassy Thompson and he was feeling horny as hell.

He resisted the urge to slip his hand inside his pants and palm the bulge hardening against his thigh. That was all he needed — to have Jennifer walk in and catch him playing with himself like some desperate teenager who couldn't buy himself a date. But damn he needed a woman.

Still lying in bed, Chandler gave a shake of his head and decided to get up, shower and get his Saturday morning started. As he headed for the shower, he wondered briefly what Cassy Thompson was doing. Was she awake already? Maybe thinking of him and the day they met? Or did she still sleep? Maybe dreaming of him?

Yeah, boy, in your dreams, he told himself and let the cool water of the shower wash over him in an attempt to clear his head. It didn't help much. He couldn't shake the feeling that she was somehow thinking of him.

* * * * *

Their thoughts and feelings were intertwined? *Cassy, girl, you are living in fantasy big-time. The man doesn't even know you're alive, for heaven sakes.*

Cassy rolled onto her back, frowning. It was the damned Talisman. If only she'd tossed it the day she met Chandler Raven, she wouldn't now be so obsessed with him. Moving restlessly, she allowed her thoughts to drift back to that day...

The first thing she'd done when she got home was to look into her panty drawer. Pausing to take a deep breath, she opened the jeweler's box and gasped. The copulating couple was no longer golden. The tiny figures were now flesh colored. Which she had half expected. After all, that was one of the signs her mother had warned her to watch out for. What she didn't expect was that they were no longer the same color. The male now plowed his tiny pink cock between a pair of ebony cheeks to reach the woman's anus.

She reached out a trembling hand to touch the tiny buns. As before, his cock came out of the small hole and hung in front of him. The small white drops hanging from the tip of his dick were a new wrinkle. Feeling her twat moisten, Cassy touched the tip of the tiny rod. The small dick began pumping and her finger was covered with cum.

Oh Lord, she was losing her mind. She slammed the drawer shut and leaned against the dresser, breathing hard and fast. Unable to stop herself, she lifted her fingers to her lips and licked them clean. Then, ashamed that she felt no shame, she stumbled over to the bed and lay facedown.

She would not take the next step. She wouldn't.

Lying in bed now, unable to clear her thoughts of the day she and Chandler Raven had met, Cassy knew she'd made a grave mistake in not getting rid of The Talisman. She had a feeling that it was too late to do it now. She had a feeling now that with or without The Talisman, her destiny was somehow linked to Chandler Raven's. Rather that was a good or bad thing, time would tell.

* * * * *

Settling into her new job was easier than Cassy had expected. Her immediate supervisor, Mai Lee, was professional, but approachable and the other employees were quick to invite her to join them for lunch whenever their schedules permitted. Her only regret was that she rarely saw Chandler Raven. She sometimes caught sight of him in the employee dining room or walking across the parking lot to his car. If they came face-to-face, he always nodded politely but looked as if he weren't quite sure who she was.

The certainty that he didn't even remember her name didn't stop her from weaving romantic fantasies around him. She often wondered what it would be like to be kissed by him; to feel his hands caressing her face, stroking her body, holding her close as he made love to her.

She'd been on the job for a month when Chandler Raven's secretary called and said he wanted to see her.

She panicked. Her last job, her biggest to date, had been repairing the mainframe of an office supply company. Granted the job had taken longer than she'd expected, but not so long that the owner had complained to Chandler Raven. At least she hoped he hadn't.

"Is everything okay, Mrs. Johnson?"

Jennifer Johnson's voice was soothing when she replied. "I'm sure this is just routine. Mr. Raven likes to keep in touch with new employees to make sure everything is proceeding as it should. Come along as soon as you can. He doesn't like to be kept waiting."

Ten minutes later Cassy found herself sitting in Chandler Raven's office facing him across his desk. Today he wore a dark gray suit a few shades darker than his eyes and a smile that was so warm it seemed to seep into her pores and spread heat through her whole body. Damn, but the man was sexy as hell.

She swallowed several times. Did he smile at everyone that way? And if he did, did it have the same affect on others as it did on her? Did his smile make other women fantasize about long nights of endless lovemaking?

Aware that her face was burning, she bit her lip and lowered her gaze so that she looked at the knot in his silk tie instead of at his smiling face.

"You…you wanted to see me, sir," she said.

"Yes," he agreed.

She waited for more. When he remained silent, she reluctantly lifted her gaze to meet his.

"That's better. I dislike talking to the tops of heads."

The smile he flashed at her mitigated any sting his words might otherwise have had. She relaxed and tentatively returned his smile. Maybe this was routine after all.

"You've been with us for a month now, Ms. Thompson. I just wanted to see how you're making out."

"Oh." The final bit of tension left her and her smile this time was warm and genuine. "I'm still getting my bearings, but I find the work interesting and challenging."

"And your coworkers?"

"They've been great—friendly, helpful and supportive."

"You're one-sixth through your probationary period, Miss Thompson. Miss Lee tells me you're punctual and that you complete each assignment in a timely and professional manner. Tell me, has this job met your expectations?"

He sat forward in his seat, his gray gaze locking with her brown one. "Can we expect you to remain with us, Miss Thompson?"

It was a perfectly innocent question without hidden meanings or innuendoes, but Cassy found herself feeling that she'd just been propositioned. She wasn't sure why. Maybe it was the way he looked at her, his gaze intense, his smile sexy and intimate. It was the look of a familiar lover.

A fresh wave of heat flooded her cheeks and she resisted the urge to avert her gaze. "What...what do you mean?"

He sat back in his seat, his gaze widening. "What do you mean 'what do I mean'? I'm asking if you intend to stay with us, Miss Thompson." He smiled suddenly. "I'm not asking for the soul of your firstborn, just the answer to a simple employment question."

Feeling like an idiot, she smiled and relaxed. "Yes. Yes, I do. Thank you, sir."

"Good."

She told herself she was imaging things in thinking he sounded and looked relieved by her answer. Why would he care either way?

He got to his feet. "If you have any problems or concerns, Miss Thompson..."

He paused and she looked at him, waiting for him to tell her to bring them to him personally. "Yes, sir?"

"Feel free to discuss them with Ms. Hanks in Personnel."

She nodded and turned away so he wouldn't see her disappointment. "Thank you."

A moment later, she found herself standing outside the closed door of his office.

That night she dreamed of him making love to her in such graphic detail that when she woke, she found that her panties were wet and her whole body ached with wanting him. She could hear soft, muted moans coming from her panty drawer, but she didn't give in to the temptation to watch the tiny couple. If she did, she would come closer to surrendering to the talisman.

It took her a long time to fall back to sleep that night. In her dreams, she became the tiny woman in the drawer being endlessly fucked in her behind by a hard pink cock. In the ensuring weeks, her dreams became more erotic and frightening. What was even more frightening was the fact that anal sex no longer seemed unnatural to her. She could see that given the right man, having her bottom drilled might be quite a turn-on. With each night, she moved ever closer to taking the final step her mother had always feared she would take—at least in her dreams.

While awake, she still determined never to surrender to the power of The Talisman. She did not intend to be unhappy like her grandmother or her great-grandmother Marie Savoy, who'd never quite recovered from her ill-fated love for her handsome but forbidden Cajun lover.

Her letters told of long nights of endless love. Sweet, wonderful kisses, hungry, passionate caresses and a hard cock filling her forbidden hole with her lover's seed.

Chapter Three

ЮCO

"I didn't know you were into white guys," Derri said when Cassy finally confided in her regarding her incessant dreams of Chandler Raven one night as they shared dinner at Derri's apartment during the weekly girls' night out.

Her face burned. "I'm not!"

Derri gave her a strange look. "Hey, don't misunderstand, Cassy. I'm not passing any judgments. Whatever floats your boat, or in this case, eases your itch, is fine by me. There's nothing worse than needing a man and not having one."

"Needing a man? Wait a minute, Derri! You're making me sound like a nympho. I don't *need a man.*"

"You can say that with a straight face after the dreams you've been having? Get real, girl. Rather you're willing to admit it or not, you *need* a man. But why a white one?"

"I didn't think his being white would bother you, Derri. I mean before you started seeing Karl regularly, you dated a couple of white men."

"Dated, yes, but never slept with."

"Never wanted to?"

Derri paused, her dark eyes sliding away from Cassy's gaze. Now that was un-Derri-like. She was usually very forthright, never skirting the issue at hand. "Yes."

"Then why haven't you ever slept with a white man?"

Derri shook her head. "Why should I when I intend to marry and settle down with a black man? I'll admit I've thought about sleeping with some of the guys I dated, but..."

"And here I've never even dated one." She leaned forward across Derri's dinning room table and stared at her friend.

"What was it about sleeping with a white man that excited you?"

Derri hesitated again and Cassy knew that when she did speak, she wouldn't be giving her the whole story. "I don't know…maybe the thought of looking down our bodies as we made love and seeing the contrast of our skin colors. But what's going on with you all of a sudden?"

Derri would understand if she told her about The Talisman, but somehow she couldn't. She recalled licking her finger after watching the couple from the box and knew she wasn't prepared to share her shameful secret with anyone — even Derri.

"I'm not 'into' him."

Derri laughed. "Oh girl, give me a break. The man's smiled at you a couple of times and you're having wet dreams about him. I'd call that being 'into' him and wanting him into you. What you need, pronto, is a man. Get yourself a man, Cass. A man in your bed is the quickest and surest way to chase one out of your dreams."

She shrugged. "Okay. I admit it. You're right. I need a man."

"Immediately," Derri added.

"Soon," she countered.

"And badly."

"Not so badly," she denied, feeling her cheeks heat up with the lie. "Okay. Soon and badly, but not before I go shopping."

Derri grinned. "Now that's what I'm talking about, girl. Get yourself a minuscule, strapless red dress you have to pour yourself into and a pair of three-inch heels that'll show off your legs and you'll have to beat the men back."

She forced a smile at the picture Derri painted. It sounded great, as long as Chandler Raven was the man she was supposed to beat back.

Derri tilted her head to one side. "You remember the party I told you me and Karl were invited to?"

She nodded. "What are you going to do now that he's out of town with his mother?"

Derri shrugged. "I'm going to the party. Why don't you come with me?"

Cassy frowned.

"Why do you look so surprised?"

"Well, for the last two and a half years, you and Karl had been inseparable. I can't remember the last time you went to a party without him."

Derri shrugged. "Well maybe it's time I stopped planning my life around Karl and his schedule."

"Whoa! Derri, is everything all right between you and Karl? I mean you used to say he was your Ebony Knight."

"Cass, Karl is still a very sweet man and a fantastic lover."

"Okay. But?"

"But, I'm thirty-two years old."

"And?"

"And time's running out for me."

"What?"

"There are things I want to do before I settle down. I'll never get to do them if I marry Karl."

Cassy thought of the tall, dark, mouth-wateringly handsome Karl. He had a big hard body that screamed *I can love you all night every night if you want me to* and a deep voice that sent chills down her spine when he said hello. How could Derri possibly want more than that man had to offer?

"What kind of things?"

Derri shook her head. "Things that... I'm just not sure where our relationship is going."

"Has he asked you to marry him?"

"Not yet. I think he's been close to proposing a few times lately, but I've always headed him off at the pass."

"What are you going to say when he finally asks you?

"I don't know."

"Derri, don't you love him?"

"I don't know that either. I know he's a great lover, but...I have sexual fantasies he can't fulfill."

Personally, Cassy couldn't imagine what sexual fantasy Karl couldn't fulfill. She knew from the outline of his cock that she'd seen once against the inside of his leg as he'd looked at Derri, that he didn't lack for size. And Derri had just admitted he was a great lover. "How can that be, Derri? The man's a bona fide hunk. A nice hunk."

"Don't worry about me and Karl," Derri said quickly. "We were talking about you. You'll come to the party with me?"

She nodded absently. "Yes, but Dare, if you need to talk, I'm here for you."

"I know. Look, Cass, don't worry about me. I'm fine. You're the one we have to get a man."

She decided that Derri was right. But after years of spending every penny she earned on tuition and bills, she needed a new wardrobe before she went looking for love, or more exactly, a lover. When a local department store had a going out of business sale, she was there when the doors opened at eight that Saturday morning. Around three o'clock, she struggled out of the doors and right into a man walking past the store.

Her bags spilled onto the sidewalk. The man reached out in an effort to steady her. She felt big palms brush against the sides of her breasts before hard fingers closed on her arms. But the momentum carried them both to the ground, on top of her bags. She ended up with her breasts smashed against his chest, her legs intertwined with his. Instead of immediately struggling to her feet, she stayed as she was, enjoying the sexy cologne he wore and the feel of his arms cradling her. And the feel of a suspicious lump at the top of his legs—his cock. The thought that just bumping into her was enough to arouse a stranger like this sent a thrill of feminine satisfaction through her.

He didn't seem any more eager than her to move, but they could hardly lie on the sidewalk much longer with her sprawled between his legs.

"Are you all right?" He finally asked.

"I'm sorry! Yes. I'm fine." She forced herself out of the man's arms. After a slight hesitation, he drew his lower body from hers and they both scrambled to their feet. "I didn't...oh!" Her voice trailed off as she found herself staring into a pair of intense smoky gray eyes. "Mr. Raven!"

She wasn't sure what she expected him to say or do. But she definitely didn't expect the slow, intimate smile he turned on her. "Miss Thompson."

For a moment, she didn't know what to say. She stood in front of him, mesmerized by the look of unmistakable desire in his eyes. But the look was gone so quickly that she might have decided she must have imagined it, if she hadn't felt his cock. Still she wondered why he would look at her as if he was attracted to her when he so clearly wasn't. He oozed sex appeal from every pore. He must have to fight off the women. Okay, so she had felt his cock, but for all she knew thoughts of his woman might have aroused him.

"You've been shopping," he said, amusement in his voice. "Big-time." He bent and began picking up her bags.

"Ah, yes." She was so flustered, she hardly knew what she was saying. He began piling the bags into her arms and hands. When there was no more room, he still had three bags.

"You seem to have run out of hands," he said.

"They can fit," she told him. "Just pile them on, please."

He looked doubtful. "If I do, you won't be able to see where you're going. Which is why you ran into me," he reminded her.

She stared at him in dismay. Was he annoyed? Not if the wide grin on his face was an indicator of his mood. "I'll be fine," she assured him. "And I'll make sure to pay attention where I'm going."

"I don't see how if you can't see who you're about to knock off their feet. I think I'd better help you to your car."

She blinked at him surprise. "You do?"

"Yes. Strictly in the interest of public safety, of course."

"Of course," she echoed flatly.

He glanced around. "Where are you parked?"

A car was one of the "necessities" she planned to acquire after her probationary period was over. "I don't have a car."

"Oh?" He glanced down at all her bags. "How did you plan to get home with all these bags? A taxi?"

"No, actually, I'm taking the bus."

"With all these bags? What if you have to stand up? How did you plan to hold on?"

She hesitated a moment, then grinned up at him. "Oh, I know I don't. I thought maybe I'd just smile at some kind gentleman on the bus in the hopes that he'd offer me his seat."

Their gazes met, locked, and he nodded slowly. "Oh. I see what you mean."

"You do?"

"Oh yeah. I'm thinking that'll work, all right."

"Excuse me."

They both stepped aside to allow several women to enter the department store doors and to allow several women to stagger out, laden with bags.

"Where's your bus stop, Miss Thompson?"

"Not far." She paused, wondering what he'd say if she asked him to call her Cassy.

"How far is not far?"

"A couple of blocks."

"That can be a long haul with all these bags."

"It can," she began hesitantly. She bit her lip, then remembering that look of desire in his eyes and the feel of his cock, she went on in a rush, "I don't suppose you could...walk me there?" She peeked up at him. "Could you?"

She didn't know where she got the nerve to ask him that. Any minute now his eyes would turn cold and he'd look at her as if she'd lost her mind. Which she clearly had.

She felt a sort of stunned amazement when he smiled and nodded. "Sure. Why not?"

"Yes? Did you say yes?"

He grinned down at her. "Is there something wrong with your hearing, Miss Thompson?"

"No. It's just that...no. Thank you, si—"

"Please," he interrupted. "Don't sir me to death."

She flashed him an uncertain smile and felt the breath catch in her throat when he responded with that slow, sexy smile of his that made her of think of lying with him in a scented bubble bath while he slowly slid his shaft in and out of her body.

Feeling the heat rise up to her cheeks and her body quiver, she averted her gaze.

"Let me help you with those." As he reached for the first bag, his fingers brushed against the side of one breast and she sucked in a breath.

"Sorry," he muttered. He was careful not to touch her breasts again as he lifted most of the bags out of her arms until she was left with one bag in each hand. "Okay. Lead the way."

She nodded, and still not looking at him, she turned and headed for the bus stop.

"How far did you say?" he asked halfway through the second block.

"Just a couple of blocks."

He turned and looked down at her, his brows raised in that quizzical way of his. "Okay, it's actually five blocks," she admitted.

He stopped suddenly. "Five blocks? How in the world did you expect to carry all these bags five blocks?"

She shrugged. "They're not heavy and I had them all arranged. I could have managed...if you hadn't knocked them out of my arms," she pointed out, smiling at him.

To her surprise, he returned her smile. "Really? Well, you're right."

"I am?"

"Sure. I make it a point never to argue with attractive women armed to the teeth with dangerous bags." He inclined his head in the opposite direction from which they'd been walking. "In any case, Miss Thompson, my car is closer. I'll drive you home."

"You will? All the way?"

His eyes twinkled. "If I were you, Miss Thompson, I'd really look into having your ears checked. You seem to be having some difficulty hearing."

She laughed, feeling, suddenly, inexplicably happy. Five minutes later, she sat beside him in the plush, contoured leather seat of his Lexus, wondering what they'd talk about on the thirty-minute drive to her apartment.

She needn't have worried. He put a CD in his compact disc player and concentrated on driving. She stole frequent, sidelong glances at his profile. He kept his gaze on the road ahead and evidenced no interest in looking at her. Which didn't stop her heartbeat from pounding at the thought of just how close he was.

He was close enough for her to see how his dark hair curled against the back of his neck. And because he was dressed in casual slacks and a short-sleeved shirt, she could see his biceps. They were very nicely muscled. He must work out regularly.

She shifted her gaze to his hands resting on the steering wheel. They were big and long fingered. She knew his palms were smooth, but not soft. What would his hands feel like on her bare skin? On her breasts? Her thighs? Cupping her rump? Palming her mound?

She felt her face burning at her thoughts. With an effort, she made herself think of other things. Like the party she and Derri would be attending that night. Where, hopefully, she'd meet some ebony hunk who would knock thoughts of Chandler Raven out of her head once and for all. Once that happened, The Talisman would have to go.

She felt like one big bundle of knots and was relieved by the time he pulled the car into her parking spot in her apartment building. "Thank you. If you'll open the trunk, I'll get my bags out so you can get on your way." She released her seat belt and reached for the door handle.

"Hey, wait a minute."

She froze in her seat when he leaned over and covered the hand resting on the door handle with his. "You're obviously interested in getting rid of me as soon as possible, but hold on a sec. You're going to need help with all those bags."

"Thank you, but I can manage." She just wanted to get away from him as quickly as possible before she said or did something outrageous. Like allowing him to see how his nearness affected her.

His gaze met hers briefly. "I'm sure you can. You're obviously very resourceful, but I'm here and it's not necessary for you to struggle with the bags on your own."

Anxious for him to just move away, she nodded and released a slow breath when he pushed open her door and finally withdrew his arm and moved away.

They were silent as they carried the bags to her first floor apartment. She opened her apartment door and he deposited the bags he carried just inside her doorway before turning to look down at her. "There you are."

"Thank you."

He nodded. "No problem. I'll ah…be on my way."

His gaze was so dark and intense it would be very easy and pleasant to lose herself in its depths…in him. "Ah…would you…would you like to come in?" she asked impulsively.

"Come in?"

"Yes." She nodded. "I…you know. For coffee or…something."

His gaze locked with hers. "Excuse me? Something? What kind of something did you have in mind?"

That's when she crossed that line she'd never had the nerve to cross before. "I don't know exactly…what did you have in mind?"

"What did *I* have in mind? I wasn't aware that I'd indicated I had anything in mind, Miss Thompson. I think we're getting our signals crossed. You needed a ride home. I offered you one and you accepted. End of story."

The lingering gaze he cast at her breasts mitigated his cool tone. Although the heat flooded her cheeks, she didn't look away from him. She even managed to conjure up what she hoped was a vampish smile. "The story doesn't have to end there. Would you…like to come in? For coffee or tea? We could discuss…the something."

For one heart-stopping moment, his gaze moved to her lips and she thought he would accept her invitation. The look in his eyes made her catch her breath and bite down on her lower lip. She could almost feel the sudden tension between them, a passion born of a long denied desire.

She was sure he felt it too. But did he want or intend to do anything about it?

He abruptly lowered his lids so she couldn't see the expression in his eyes. "I wonder if you know how…tempting your invitation sounds."

Her throat felt dry. "Tempting enough to accept?"

He shook his head slowly, almost reluctantly. "Yes, but that would definitely not be a good idea."

"Actually, I think it would be a great idea," she said, trying to hide her disappointment. "But if you don't agree…well, thanks for the lift. It was a real lifesaver."

He nodded slowly, lifting his eyelids and locking his gaze with hers. "No problem. Giving you a lift was my pleasure, Miss Thompson."

"Yeah?"

"Oh yeah," he nodded, smiling. "It was an undeniable pleasure. You can run into me with a zillion bags any time you like."

"Really? And you can...sprawl between my legs in the middle of the sidewalk anytime you like."

"Actually, you were the one sprawled between my legs," he pointed out. "But either way, the thought holds definite appeal."

"Yeah? Then maybe you could come for coffee and we could discuss another accident." The moment the words were out, she could happily have bitten off her tongue. Here she was coming on to him after he'd already refused her! He must think her desperate for a man.

Those gray eyes of his flicked slowly over her heated face, settling briefly on her lips. She knew she wasn't Vanessa Williams beautiful, but men, black men anyway, generally thought she was worth a second look. And judging by the way he looked at her, he must think so too.

"A bed would be a nicer place to have a second accident."

Her heart thumped in her chest. "Funny you should mention a bed." She pointed a finger over her shoulder toward her open door. "I just happen to have one inside. It's big and very comfortable. Would you...like to see it?"

He licked his lips. "You have no idea how much I'd like to see your bed...your floor...your anything."

Oh God! He wanted her too. "Then step right in and—"

He ran a hand through his hair and looked away. When he spoke his voice was so low, she barely heard it. "I...ah, I'd better go. Now."

"Now?"

"Now."

"But what about—"

"Goodbye."

She watched as he left, leaving her full of frustrated desire.

* * * * *

Chandler gripped Jane's slender hips and bent to kiss her neck as she bounced up and down on his lap, grinding her petite butt against his naked thighs. Jane was gasping and making little sounds. Her small breasts brushed against his chest and he could feel her begin to contract around him. She was almost there, about to come. She just needed a minute more of firm sure strokes and she'd have an orgasm.

"Chandler…Chandler," she whispered. "Chandler."

That was about as excited as she got—at least with him. And it wasn't enough. He wanted more. He needed more. Was it too much to expect his woman to writhe on his cock like it was the best she'd ever had? A fleeting memory of a long night spent fucking Serge's sister teased him. He pushed it away.

He couldn't expect Jane or any human woman to be as wild and lusty as Katie, but he did need a more responsive woman. It was all he could do to keep his cock from wilting inside Jane's quaking body. He settled back against the chair, continued the steady rhythm inside her and gave his imagination free rein.

With his eyes closed, the woman on his lap was transformed. She was more voluptuous. Her legs were longer. Her breasts were bigger, fuller. Her buttocks more deliciously rounded, fitting into his palms as if they had been molded for his hands alone. The outer lips of her vagina were dark. Inside, between the pink inner lips was an irresistible sweet heat that clung to and welcomed his raging hard-on.

And when he looked into her eyes, her smile would be shy, but warm. A sensuous combination of passion and intriguing reserve. Her golden gaze would be like liquid fire as she sensuously slid her sweet, brown body along his aching cock all the way to his balls.

Her voice would be husky and full of need for him as she gasped his name. She would tell him in terms that made him rock hard, how good his cock felt in her. How much she needed to feel it buried deep within the depths of her body, her dark heat.

"My God, Chandler! That's so good! I love it! I love it! I love your cock! I love your balls! Fuck me, Chandler! Fuck me hard!"

"Oh God!" Cassy! Her name and her dark, sensuous image filled his mind and overwhelmed his senses. A vision of his cock gliding deep into her was all it took to make him lose control. He groaned, gripped her hips tighter and pumped furiously into her until he finally exploded into her convulsing body.

"Chandler!" Jane spoke his name in a small, shocked voice.

Oh God, he'd done it now. He groaned silently and reluctantly opened his eyes. Had he actually said Cassy Thompson's name out loud while having sex with Jane? "Look, Jane, I'm...I'm sorry," he began, but trailed off. How could he expect her to forgive the unforgivable?

Jane's blue eyes were slightly glazed as she looked up at him. "You're sorry? For what, Chandler? Chandler, that was absolutely incredible." She sounded both surprised and embarrassed.

He felt his face flush. It had been incredible, but only because he'd pretended she was another woman, a woman he couldn't have. Not only because she was black, but because she was also one of his employees. He could not get involved with her. He would not get involved with her.

Still fully seated on him, Jane ground her hips against his and linked her arms around his neck. "What's the matter, Chandler?"

"Nothing."

She reached a hand back and palmed his balls. "That was nice."

"Yes. It was."

Still holding his balls, she leaned forward and kissed him. "Then what's wrong?"

"Nothing's wrong." But he didn't want her arousing him again. If they had sex again, he might actually call out Cassy's name. He pressed a quick kiss against Jane's mouth. She responded quickly and leaned forward to deepen the kiss, but he lifted her off his fast deflating shaft and set her on her feet. "I just have to use the john."

She ran a hand down his abdomen to his cock. "Hurry back."

In her bathroom, he stared at his reflection. His face was flushed and he looked guilty as hell. Jane was happier than he'd ever seen her and all he wanted was to get away from her ASAP so he could go home and fantasize about Cassy Thompson.

He sighed and raked a hand through his hair. If he were going to develop the hots for a black woman, it could not be Cassy Thompson. *If?* He'd already developed the hots for her and what's more he'd been foolish enough to let her know it. But he could not afford the luxury of a relationship with her, no matter how alluring or irresistible he found her. If he went down that path and things went wrong between them, he could find himself slapped with a sexual harassment suit.

He turned around when the bathroom door opened behind him. Jane stood there, naked and smiling almost shyly at him. Her cheeks were flushed, her eyes radiant. She looked completely satisfied. He realized with a shock that she was not unresponsive. It had only seemed that way to him because he hadn't worked hard enough to really turn her on before.

She would be as responsive as he made her. But he realized that he no longer had any wish to make a wild woman out of her in bed. How the hell was he going to tell her that without hurting her?

She crossed the room and slipped her arms around him, grinding her hairless mound against his flaccid shaft. She reached a hand down to cup him. "Chandler? You're soft. Come back to bed and let me harden you," she said softly. "Let me suck you."

"What? Let you what?"

"I want to...taste you."

He stared at her in surprise. Jane had always been shy. Though he'd frequently fantasized about her behaving this way, she'd never once initiated their lovemaking. And now that she had, he was no longer interested.

He gently lifted her hand away from his shaft and stepped back. "That sounds very exciting."

She smiled confidently up at him. "Yes. It does. I want to feel you in my mouth, taste you, have you come in my mouth."

"I'd like that too," he lied. "But unfortunately, I have to go. I have an early day tomorrow."

She closed the distance between them and rubbed her small breasts against his chest. "But tomorrow's Sunday," she protested. "And I really want you to stay the night. Or at least for another few hours." She reached a small hand down to palm his cock and balls. "I have plans for these bad boys."

"And I'd like to stay, Jane, but there are things I need to take care of to be ready for Monday. I really need to hit the road."

"Oh." She sighed. "Well, when will I see you again? When can we get together again? When you can stay the night?"

He lifted her hand to his lips and kissed it gently. "Jane, we agreed to be friends," he reminded her.

Even as he spoke, he felt like a heel. He had come to her straight from Cassy Thompson's apartment. To sleep with her. Being with Cassy Thompson had left him far too horny to masturbate. He'd needed a woman and he'd come to her.

Having assuaged his physical hunger he longed to get away from Jane. He didn't like the sudden adoring look in her eyes.

"You didn't come here tonight looking for a friend, Chandler," she said, sounding testy. "You came to share my bed. Now that you have, you want to go back to being friends?"

"That's all I can handle right now," he said, knowing he sounded as lame as he felt.

"When you were thrusting into me like a wild man a few moments ago, it felt like you could handle more. Why did you come here and…and do this, if all you want is friendship?"

"Jane…I'm sorry. I shouldn't have come."

"Maybe not, but you did come and you did sleep with me." Her eyes narrowed. "Or should I say you fucked me? Because that's what this was all about, wasn't it, Chandler? You didn't want to make love, you wanted to fuck."

He bit back the urge to remind her that judging by her response, she had apparently wanted the same thing. "I'm sorry," he said again.

She pulled away from him, her pretty face flushing. Glancing around, she yanked a towel off the towel rack and wrapped it around her body, sarong style. "Is that supposed to make me feel better because you're sorry, Chandler? Well, it doesn't. It just makes me feel cheap!"

"Look, Jane, you know there's no reason for you to feel cheap, as you call it. We're two consenting adults who've enjoyed a pleasant physical relationship. There's nothing wrong with that."

"Nothing wrong with that? You come here and treat me like some hussy you found in a back alley and I'm supposed to be okay with that?"

"It wasn't like that."

"Oh, yes it was, but guess what, Chandler? It's not all right. *I* am not cheap and I will not let you treat me like I am!"

He stared at her wearily. Why did women always insist on overreacting and clinging like a damned leech when it became clear that a relationship was over? "I'm sorry you feel that way, Jane. It certainly wasn't my intent to —"

"Oh, to hell with you and your intent, Chandler! Why don't the both of you get the hell out of my life and my apartment?"

He had wanted it to end. But not like this. "Jane, I—"

"No, don't say anything else, Chandler. You wanted mindless sex and that's what you got. Now please get out. And Chandler, don't bother calling me and I sure as hell won't call you."

Later, lying alone in his bed, physically satisfied, but still aware of a longing for Cassy Thompson, he found sleep elusive. And that annoyed him. Why was he allowing thoughts of Cassy Thompson to haunt him? She wasn't the only woman in the city. Hell, she wasn't even the only black woman in the city. Damn if he was going to lose his head over her. She was just one woman in a city full of willing and available women, and he wasn't going to waste any more of his time lusting after her.

He sighed and turned his head. In the moonlight shinning into the room through his open curtains, he could see the outlines of the Ebony Venus. Staring at and caressing it each night before he went to sleep only served to feed his hunger for Cassy Thompson. What he needed was to get rid of the damned thing.

The thought of trashing the statuette both his great-grandfather and grandfather had cherished went against his grain. Tossing it in the trash was not an option. He frowned. He supposed he could pass it on some other sucker. That too went against the grain. How could be subject someone else to the same dilemma he was trying to escape himself?

He couldn't do that—unless, of course, that someone was perfectly capable of taking care of himself. He thought immediately of Serge. He was out there enough not only to want the statuette, but also to actually follow the ritual. And with Serge he wouldn't have to worry about the possible consequences. It was settled. He'd give Serge the statuette.

Chapter Four

🕉

Cassy stared up at the man smiling down at her. Talk about tall, dark and handsome. An undeniable tingle of excitement danced through her at the thought of dancing with him. He was the proverbial ebony knight if ever there was one. And to have him single her out from all the other women in attendance at the party was a thrill.

"What's your name?" He had a deep, warm voice.

"Cassy Thompson."

He took her hands between his. "Frank Wilson." Still holding her hands, he glanced around them to the large room where couples were dancing and talking. "Please tell me you're here alone."

"I am." The look of interest in his dark brown eyes sent a spark of warmth through her. "At least, I'm here with a female friend, but—"

"Glad to hear your friend's female." He smiled down at her. "I'm hoping we can get to know each other tonight."

She smiled silently up at him.

"Let's start by dancing, Cassy."

She nodded and went willingly into his arms. They danced several times, each time, slow and close together. As they moved around the floor, a bulge developed against his leg. She overcame the urge to press close to it to gauge its size. Later, they found a small table in a darkened corner of the patio and ate dinner.

"So you're an electronic technician, Cassy?" He sipped his drink and looked at her. "What exactly does an electronic technician do?"

"Oh, lots of things. Mostly I repair electronic components in cash registers, ATMs and computers."

"Do you enjoy it?"

She nodded. "Oh yes. I've always been curious about how things — electronic things work and getting to fix them at my own pace is great. What about you?"

"Me?" He leaned across the table and smiled at her. "I'm an accountant, who would very much like to get to know you. Is that possible, Cassy? Are you seeing anyone?"

She shook her head, not allowing herself to think of the man she'd like to see. "No."

"Then I'd like to see you."

"I'd like that, Frank."

She told herself she really liked Frank and was having a great time. Still when he bent to kiss her as they said good night, she closed her eyes and found herself pretending the lips kissing hers belonged to Chandler Raven.

"I'll call you," he whispered, running the tip of his tongue along her closed lips as he kissed her.

She gasped and slipped her fingers through the short hair at the back of his neck. "Yes. Please do."

His arms tightened around her and he kissed her again, full on her mouth. This time, she allowed her lips to part and fought hard not to think of Chandler Raven. The tips of her breasts tightened against his chest as his cock hardened against her. For one insane moment, she toyed with the idea of inviting him to spend the night with her. She had needs and she ached to have them assuaged. But she'd never been a one-night stand kind of woman. And until she was certain she wanted a relationship with him, she wasn't about to sleep with him.

It was clear he knew of her desire, when he tightened his arms around her waist and whispered in her ear, "I sure hate saying good night to you, Cassy. You feel so good."

As did he.

"I know we've just met Cassy, but I wish we could — "

"I know, Frank. I know, but we can't. I can't."

"Oh baby." He rubbed his lower body sensuously against hers and she shuddered. "Are you sure?"

"Yes." She pulled away from him, trembling. "Good night."

She found Derri standing alone on the patio. "Dare? Are you all right?"

Derri turned to look at her with a slight smile. "Yes. I was just thinking."

"What about?"

She shrugged. "Me and Karl and where, if any place, we're going." She smiled suddenly. "You're leaving?"

She nodded.

"Alone?"

She nodded again.

Derri frowned. "But you and Frank at least exchanged numbers, I hope."

She grinned. "Oh yeah."

"Good. Then I'll talk to you in a day or two."

They exchanged hugs and Cassy left the party. She spent the entire ride home, wondering if she'd made a mistake in not spending the night with Frank. All those slow dances with him, combined with her frustration at her failure to turn Chandler Raven on sufficiently to get him to stay with her, had formed into a knot of tension and need in the pit of her stomach.

At home, she headed for her bedroom and her panty drawer. She removed the small couple from the jewelry box, half hoping that the male would have changed colors again. Hopefully, the male would now be black. He was not. She sighed and put the couple back in their box.

She then stripped and took a long cool shower. With the water pouring over her head, she began to fantasize about sex. She started off thinking about it with Frank. He would be a hot, insatiable lover who would probably take her to places she'd never been. She dried her body slowly, pulled on a sheer nightgown and slipped into bed. By the time her head hit the pillow, Chandler Raven was again the focus of her sexual fantasies.

Angry at her inability to stop thinking about him, it took her a long time to fall asleep. Before she did, she found herself wondering how she could possibly face him again. He probably thought she was a shameless hussy. What was she supposed to say to him the next time they met? She punched her fist in her pillow and decided she was worrying needlessly. They probably wouldn't even have an opportunity to speak to each other again. She'd be very surprised if he didn't look right through her the next time they encountered each other.

She found out on Monday morning. She was late and taking the shortcut across the parking lot, when she saw his car pull in just ahead of her. He got out and he reached the door a little before she did.

"Good morning, Mr. Raven."

He didn't speak. He didn't even nod. He just held the door open without looking at her. It was hard to believe that this grim looking man was the same one who'd flirted with her just two days earlier.

He clearly had no intentions of flirting with her today or even being friendly.

"Thanks, sir," she muttered as she slipped passed him.

This time he inclined his head slightly, still without meeting her gaze.

Feeling a ridiculous degree of disappointment, she turned and hurried down the hallway, aware that he followed much more slowly.

By the time she saw him again in the dining room on Friday, she'd had plenty of time to regret her behavior and to convince herself that his interest in her wasn't serious, nor was it ever likely to be.

Although he didn't wear a wedding ring, he might be married. But even if he weren't married with a couple of kids, he surely had a supermodel-type lady friend to keep him company and share his bed. It was sheer insanity on her part to imagine that he was attracted to her just because he'd been kind enough to give her a lift home and had flirted with her a little. As for his shaft hardening...well some men got hard just looking at a woman—any woman.

* * * * *

"She wants you, you want her. You'd be a fool not to go for it."

Chandler glanced at the tall, dark man standing next to him at the stadium bar, sipping a beer. Serge Dumont looked much the same as he had twenty years earlier when he and Chandler had shared an apartment in a frat house on the Temple University campus. While Chandler's hair had begun to gray, Serge, with his dark head covered by a Phillies' ball cap and sporting a diamond stud in his left ear, still looked like a fresh-faced college sophomore.

When Serge had called to tell him he was flying in from Boston for the Phillies' home opener, Chandler, although not a baseball fan, had gladly accepted the invitation to join him at the stadium. He and Serge didn't often see each other and he welcomed the opportunity to discuss his growing obsession with Cassy Thompson with someone who would understand.

"Why did I know you'd say that?" he asked.

Serge grinned. "Come on Chan, you know how I like my ladies. It's about time you finally let that Cajun blood of yours have its way."

Chandler accepted his beer from the vendor and walked back toward their seats on the third baseline with Serge beside him. "My attraction to her has nothing to do with Cajun blood."

"Then what has it to do with?"

He sipped his beer and shrugged. "I don't know. It must be that damned statuette."

They sank into their seats. "If it's the statuette, Chan, why has it taken you nearly ten years to be attracted enough to a black woman to want to do something about it? It's not the statuette, exquisite though it is. It's your nature, what you were born for. Don't fight it, go with the flow."

He took several swallows of his beer and watched the players begin to return to the field. "Is that what you do? Go around dating your employees? I'm sure Mikhel loves that," he said of Serge's older brother who he'd met several times.

"You know Mikhel, he's a bit of a stuffed shirt. He talks big, but you can bet that if he finds his bloodlust partner in the company, he'll toss his high ideals to the wind and bury his incisors in her neck in a Philly second."

Chandler swallowed the last of his beer and slowly turned to look at Serge. He'd known since their senior year as roommates when Serge had invited him home to Boston over the Christmas Holidays, that Serge and his family were vampires. Now, nearly twenty years later, he still vividly remembered his shock on going into the family room one night and finding the whole Dumont family and several of their friends, not only naked, but engaged in a lustful orgy.

The smell of the blood and the sex had acted like a drug on Chandler. He'd seen sexual positions that only vampires could possibly achieve or enjoy. Without quite knowing how he'd let it happen, he'd stripped off his clothes and joined in. His out of control behavior that week still bothered him. He'd gone from one female vampire's arms to another and come within an inch of being drained.

There had been one particular woman, Deoctra, small, dark and exquisite, who'd sucked his cock until it was sore. They had spent their days and nights fucking anally. She had refused to allow him to fuck her pussy. She would frequently interrupt their fucking to insist he suck her bloody finger. After a day or two, he'd developed a taste for her blood and had sucked it every chance he got. One night, near the end of his stay, as he eagerly sucked her blood, she'd leaped on him and sank her incisors in his neck.

Although he'd been aware that she meant to kill him, he'd been strangely unable to protest. It had been Serge's sister, Katie, who had first noticed his distress. Unable to get Deoctra off him, she'd summoned her brothers. It had taken both Serge and Mikhel to pull Deoctra off Chandler. He'd developed chills and a fever. He'd spent the next three days in bed, delirious. Katie had climbed into bed with him to hold him.

Even with the fever raging in him, he'd wanted her.

When he'd awakened one night to find her naked body pressed against his, he'd had her—over and over. As he'd plunged his cock in her pussy, he'd greedily sucked her blood from her finger. They had spent the remaining four days and nights of his time in Boston fucking almost nonstop. It had taken years to forget those lustful nights with her. She had wanted a relationship with him, but with his return to Philly, had come his sanity. Telling her he did not want a vampire for a wife had been one of the most difficult things he'd had to do.

Serge and Mikhel, both protective of their younger sister had been furious with him. Strangely enough, it was Katie who held their rage in check.

He and Serge had slowly mended their friendship and he had never gone back to Boston. Over the years he had almost convinced himself that he had never spent those wild two weeks with the Dumonts.

When he and Serge got together, they rarely mentioned his family. Now, Chandler felt some of the old guilt returning. "How is Katie?"

Just for a moment, Serge's gray eyes darkened dangerously, then he smiled. "She's well. Everyone's well."

"Good." He swallowed. "Is she...has she found her...someone special?"

Serge's eyes darkened. "That would be extremely difficult given her line of work."

"You mean she's still…?"

"Yes," Serge said shortly. "No matter what we say."

"Oh." He ran a hand through his hair. "So do you want the statuette?"

Serge grinned, his mood lightening. "Absolutely, but not just yet. You keep it for a while, Chan, and you go give that woman want she wants most—a good, hard fuck."

Serge's clavier attitude about women and sex still annoyed the hell out of him. "I don't fuck women I care about," he said coolly.

Serge leaned forward, baring his teeth. "Is that why you fucked the hell out of my little sister because you didn't care about her?"

Chandler had quickly discovered two residual effects of his near brush with death at the hands of the female vampire and all the vampire blood he'd ingested—his cock stayed harder much longer than it used to and the almost hidden fear he'd had of Serge had disappeared. While he knew he could not take Serge, he was no longer afraid to try. Now, he resisted the urge to shove Serge out of his face. "I didn't intend to touch her, Serge. You know that."

Serge slowly relaxed. "Yeah. I do. It was losing so much blood and ingesting Deoctra's putrid blood. I know. So did Mik, which is the only reason we didn't kill you." Serge tossed off the last of his beer and leaned forward in his seat. "The game's about to start up again."

Chandler settled back in his seat, breathing slowly and deeply. One of these days, he was going to have to stop associating with a man who was half human and half vampire.

* * * * *

As if to underscore Chandler's lack of interest, Cassy didn't see him again for two weeks. When she did, she was working late, servicing two of Raven's own computers. It was well after seven before she left work that night. "Darn it!" she murmured when she saw the rain.

She stood in the lobby looking out into the dark, wet night. Although it was early July, the night was unseasonably cool. By the time she walked the three blocks to the bus stop, she'd be cold and wet. But it couldn't be helped.

"Nasty night, huh?"

She cast a grimace over her shoulder at the guard sitting behind the desk in the lobby. "Tell me about it."

"I wish I had an umbrella to offer you."

She smiled at him. "Thanks, but it's only three blocks. I'll be okay." Squaring her shoulders, she pushed open the door and stepped out of the building. She paused under the building canopy as a cold gust of wind-driven rain chilled her. Clutching her briefcase and shoulder bag in preparation for a mad dash through the rain, she heard the door behind her open.

"Can I give you a lift?"

Startled, she swung around to find Chandler Raven coming through the door, carrying a big umbrella. He pushed a button and held the umbrella over both of them as he waited for her answer.

She was tempted. Riding home in his car would be a lot more pleasant than traveling on the bus, after getting drenched. But the bus was safer. Being in close proximity to him, would only serve to provide fresh fuel for her endless fantasies. Even though she'd been out with Frank twice since they'd met and they'd come very close to going all the way, she was still dreaming of Chandler Raven repeatedly, ravaging her in graphic and shameless detail.

"No, thank you." She ducked from the shelter of his umbrella and sprinted down the street.

She'd only covered half a block when she realized she was no longer being pelted with rain. Chandler Raven ran beside her again, holding the umbrella over her head.

She stopped and looked up at him silently.

"Can I offer you a lift, Ms. Thompson?" he asked, just as though she hadn't already refused.

She shook her head. His coolness toward her the last time they'd met made it clear to her that he regretted having been anything less than formal with her. Well, she regretted putting herself in the position of being on the receiving end of his coldness. And she wasn't about to go down that path again. He didn't want to be bothered? She wouldn't bother him.

"Thanks, Mr. Raven, but—"

"My name's Chandler."

Like she didn't know that.

"And my car is that way." He pointed back the way they'd come.

"Well, yeah, but—"

"You'd rather be drenched?" He sounded amused.

"No, of course not, but—"

"Good. Then come along."

She shook her head. "I don't understand you, Mr. Raven. One minute you're friendly, driving me home and telling me to call you Chandler and implying you might like me personally But the next time we meet, you look at me as if I'm something that crawled out from under a rock."

She shrugged, staring up at him and trying to read the expression in his eyes. "And you know what, Mr. Raven? I'd rather be drenched then accept a ride with you and then have you look through me as if I'm not there the next time we meet."

She saw his lips thin and his eyes narrow. "You're making too much to this, Miss Thompson. It's cold, it's dark and it's pouring. I'm offering you a lift. Period. Take it or don't. It's your choice."

She nodded and thinned her own lips. "Thanks for the newsflash, Mr. Raven. I'll pass." She ducked from under the shelter of the umbrella.

As before she didn't get very far before he was beside her again. "Wait a minute," he said. "This is ridiculous. It's just a lift."

She titled her chin and stared up at him. "It's a lift I'd rather not accept, Mr. Raven, sir."

"Why? Because I didn't accept your invitation to come in your apartment for the 'something' you offered?"

The question sent a flash of embarrassed heat up her neck into her cheeks. "No! Because I don't know what you want from me, Mr. Raven!"

"At the moment, I want to give you a lift." He ran a hand through his hair and shook his head. "This doesn't need to be that difficult. Just let me give you a lift."

She looked around them. It was still raining hard. And she was cold and wet. And it was just a lift. She shrugged. "All right, I'll accept the lift. Thank you. Sir." She added the sir, knowing it would annoy him.

She smiled in the darkness when she heard the small, exasperated sound he made, as he nodded. "Fine. This way."

Once settled in his car, she had to admit to relief at being out of the rain. After closing her door, he slipped inside into his seat and adjusted her heat register. He glanced at her. "Is that better?"

She shivered and nodded. Aware that her nipples had suddenly hardened, she turned to look out the passenger side window. "Yes. Thanks."

He fastened his seat belt and drove the car out of the parking lot. He was silent for several moments before he sighed deeply. "Look, I'm sorry. Can we just agree to start over?"

She should say no and ask him to just please take her home. But she nodded instead. "Okay."

"And you'll call me Chandler when we're not at work?"

When they weren't at work? Was he implying that there would be other times when they'd be together outside of work? She felt excitement building at the thought. "Yes."

"Yes? Good. Great."

He sounded pleased and she cast a quick glance at his profile. He was smiling.

To her surprise, he began to talk about himself. She listened in silence, just enjoying the sound of his warm, deep voice. "I'm the youngest of five boys."

"No sisters?"

"No. We're all boys."

"Tell me about your brothers."

"Two of my older brothers were doctors and the other two were lawyers. Since I didn't want to be a doctor or a lawyer, I kind of felt pressured to succeed in electronics."

The warm, dark interior of the car, along with the soft jazz coming from the stereo, combined to create an intimate atmosphere between them. She turned her head to smile at his profile. "Well, you did it. Raven Electronics is successful."

Before he could respond, his car phone rang.

He lifted one hand from the steering wheel to answer it. "Hello. Julie! Hi, honey. No. Of course I didn't forget you."

She saw him glance briefly at the clock on his dashboard. "Yes, of course I'm still coming...in half an hour...no...not before then..."

She felt his eyes on her and turned to find him looking at her. "No, I'm not alone. Yes I'm with a woman and no, you don't know her...Julie...honey...no... I won't be long... No...that's out of the question...fine..."

He made a sound of exasperation. He held the phone against his chest, but kept his gaze on the road ahead. "Would you mind very much if I made a quick stop before I took you home?"

This Julie honey must be his wife or at the very least, his woman. And she wanted him home with her, not out driving some wannabe lover home. She felt a wave of shame wash over her that she had entertained such erotic fantasies about another woman's man.

She peered through the windshield and saw they were only a few blocks from a train station with a stop just a block from her apartment building. "We're nearing the Fox Chase train station. Why don't you just drop me off there," she suggested. "It's only a block from my apartment. I'll be fine."

"No. That won't be necessary. I can drive you home. It'll be a very short stop."

"Okay, if you're sure this isn't inconvenient for you."

"It isn't."

Although he didn't look directly at her, she saw his smile. It radiated such warmth that the breath caught in her throat and she was suddenly aware, that wife or no wife, Chandler Raven was interested in her! But she was not about to get involved with a married man or even one who was involved with another woman.

He lifted the phone back to his ear. "Julie, I'm on my way. Yes." He laughed. "I love you too, honey."

She was convinced that she was about to meet his wife or his girlfriend. It had stopped raining by the time he pulled into the driveway of one of the new town houses on the outskirts of the city.

A small, blonde child of approximately seven or eight rushed down the driveway and wrapped her arms around his legs.

"You came! You came!"

Laughing, he swung her up into his arms. "Of course I came, honey."

The child peeked at Cassy over Chandler's shoulder. "You didn't come alone."

"No. I told you I wasn't alone." He turned to look at her. "Cassy, this is Julie, my niece. Julie, this is Cassy Thompson."

A wave of relief washed over her! Julie honey was a little girl and his niece.

Julie smiled shyly at her. "Hello."

She smiled. "Hello, Julie."

"Who are you?"

"I told you who she was," Chandler said and started up the driveway with Julie still in his arms. "Cassy Thompson."

"Is she your woman, Uncle Chandler?"

The blood rushed up Cassy's neck and into her face.

Chandler turned to look at her. "Why do you ask that, Julie?"

"She's pretty and she's looking at you the same way Tia looks at Steve. And Tia is Steve's woman."

Cassy cringed. Was she so transparent that even a child could see through her?

Chandler responded to Julie without looking at her. "I didn't know you'd met Tia, Julie."

"I have. I like her and I think she likes me. She and Steve are always together. Are you and her always together, Uncle Chandler?"

Chandler's gray eyes searched Cassy's hot face, seemingly unaware of her embarrassment. "No, we're not. And I told you her name is Cassy Thompson. Miss Thompson to you."

"But Uncle Chandler, you haven't told me if she's your woman," the child protested.

This was too much for Cassy. "I'll wait in the car," she said and would have turned away, but he reached out a hand to catch one of hers in his. An electric shock shot up her arm at his touch.

He released her hand so abruptly she knew he'd either felt that electric charge also or he was aware of the effect his touch had on her. "That's not necessary," he said in his usual cool, controlled voice. "Come meet my sister-in-law, Ellen."

"Thanks, maybe another time. If you don't mind, I'd just as soon wait in the car," she said, backing away from him.

"Fine. Have it your way." He took the car keys from his pocket and handed them to her. "I won't be long."

She nodded and hurried back to the car, her heart pounding so fast, she was nearly breathless. Why couldn't she stop reacting this way to this man? Why did everything about him attract her? His voice, his smile, his walk and the way he looked at her as if she were the most attractive woman he'd ever met? More, as if they'd known each other intimately.

She took consolation in the assurance that The Talisman was responsible for her behaving like an alley cat in heat. Was it possible that even though she'd never followed the ritual, it was also affecting him?

She wasn't sure of anything except the fact that she had to get a grip on herself. This incessant fantasizing about Chandler Raven had to stop. She made a silent promise that the next time she and Frank went out, she'd sleep with him. That should be enough to rid her of thoughts of any man other than Frank. It should also cause a change in The Talisman.

Chandler joined her in the car fifteen minutes later. "I was longer than I expected to be. Sorry."

She'd used the time to compose herself. "It's all right. Ah, I haven't eaten yet."

"Oh? Is that a hint for me to invite you out to dinner?"

"No!" She spoke quickly, then realized she'd overreacted. He was teasing her. "Sorry," she said, her voice more normal. "I just wanted to tell you I used your phone to order Chinese. I'll pay for the call."

"Not necessary." He fastened his seat belt. "Pick up or delivery?"

"Pick up. It's only a couple of blocks from me." She swallowed several times then spoke in a rush. "I thought…if you hadn't eaten, you might like to share it with me."

He started the car and pulled onto the road before he answered. "An invitation to dinner?"

He didn't sound overly pleased and she bit her lip. Why had she asked him to join her? Now he was going to think she was coming onto him. Again. "No, it's not an invitation to dinner."

"No? Then what is it?"

"Okay." She licked her lips. "Okay, it was an invitation. Will you come?"

"That depends."

"On what?"

He laughed. "On what you ordered, of course."

His laughter was infectious. She laughed too, feeling happy and daring. "So. You want to share?"

"Yes." He glanced briefly at her. "As a matter of fact, I do."

"Don't you want to know what I ordered before you commit yourself to coming?"

"It doesn't matter," he admitted. "I'm coming even if you ordered dog food."

"Oh. Well. Good. And I know you'll be pleased to know I ordered egg rolls with the dog chow."

He laughed. "Good," he said quietly.

At her apartment, they sat cross-legged on the carpeted living room floor.

"You know, I'm a little old for this floor bit," he told her.

She glanced over her shoulder at the dining room table in the adjourning dining area. "We could sit at the table if you like."

He shook his head. "I was just joking." His gaze met and locked with hers. "Relax." He spoke in a soft voice. "I hardly ever bite."

She bit back the urge to exclaim, *What a shame.* "Ah, are you hungry?"

"Starving. What have you got?"

"Shrimp fried rice and chicken and broccoli with noodles." She licked her lips. "I noticed that you had chicken and broccoli in the café once."

"Ah." He grinned at her and her heart thumped. "You've been watching me."

"No! Yes! Oh…"

He laughed. "It's okay. Actually, I like your choice."

They ate directly from the boxes, using chopsticks. Since neither of them was proficient, they'd soon made a mess.

"Sorry," he said, laughing as he looked around him at the small bits of rice and noodles on the carpet.

"It doesn't matter." She waved a hand to dismiss his concern. "It's stain-resistant carpet. You were saying? Your family is from Louisiana?"

He nodded. "Well, my great-grandfather was at any rate. My grandfather was born here, but went to live in Lafayette, Louisiana, when he was five. He didn't return north until after he graduated from high school. My father and I were both born here. What about you?"

Cassy paused. "It's strange. My great-grandmother was born and raised in Louisiana. The bayou. Not far from Lafayette, in fact."

His gray eyes flicked with tiny lights. "Really? Then you and I have a common background—several times removed. I wonder if she was as…superstitious as they tell me my great-grandfather was."

"Superstitious?"

"Yes. My great-grandfather was Cajun. He believed in the supernatural...charms and such. There's this one particular charm that a woman he fell in love with gave him that's been passed down through our family."

Much like The Talisman had been passed reluctantly down through her family. She resisted the temptation to ask him about his charm. If she did, he might want to know about any charms in her family. There was no way she could tell him about The Talisman. He might want to see it. Then he might think she was trying to use it to attract him.

She shrugged. "I never knew her, but I know she had an unhappy life."

"Why?"

"She...circumstances kept her from being with her one true love. My grandmother, who died ten years ago, used to talk about her all the time and how sad her life was. And yes, I guess she was superstitious. She believed in the old ways, as my grandmother called them."

"So did my grandfather. He was the one who left me the...charm."

She had to ask. "What kind of charm?"

His cheeks reddened. "Just a charm. Nothing special."

Then why had he mentioned it and why was he embarrassed? "You were telling me about starting the company."

He nodded, clearly relieved at the change of subject. "I started Raven Electronics with a fifty thousand dollar loan from my parents. The first five years were really rough. Sometimes I was sorry I hadn't studied law or medicine."

"But you succeeded."

He nodded. "I did, but I worked sixty hours a week for years to break even and pay my parents back. And then—"

She put down the chopsticks and looked into his eyes. "That's all very exciting, but are you married?"

The abruptness of the question didn't appear to surprise him. He shook his head. "No. If I were, I wouldn't be here with you."

"But you've been married though, haven't you?"

"Yes, but that was before I started the company."

"What happened?"

He shrugged. "She wanted more than I could give her."

He sounded bitter. She paused before pressing on. "Financially...or emotionally?"

"Both, but most of our arguments centered around money. I had to get a second job just to pay for all the clothes she kept buying. We got married when we were both twenty-two. We were divorced by the time we were twenty-six."

"Did you have any children together?"

"No. I wanted a few, but she didn't."

"And since your divorce? Are you...seeing anyone special now?"

There was a rather long, disconcerting pause on his part, then, "No."

"No? You don't sound very certain. Are you sure?"

He laughed, shaking his head. "I think I'd know if I were seeing anyone special."

"Well yeah, but...I've seen you with a very pretty blonde in the cafe on at least two occasions. The two of you looked like a couple."

"You *have* been watching me."

She grimaced. "You're making me sound like a stalker!"

He laughed. "A stalker, huh? I can imagine worse ways to spend my time than being stalked by you, Miss Thompson."

She sucked in a breath. "That's very flattering, sir, but what about that blonde?"

"What about her? We…we were close for a while, but we're not now. It's over between us. What about you? Are you seeing anyone special?"

"There's no one…special."

"But you are seeing someone?"

She thought of Frank. On their last date, a week before, she'd come very close to letting him spend the night. But two dates did not constitute special or even exclusivity. "Not really…no. There's this man I met at a party a couple of weeks ago. We've been out twice since then, but there's nothing special there. I mean I don't feel the earth shake or fireworks bursting in the air when I'm with him."

He studied her face. "So that's a definite no? You're not seeing anyone special?"

"No, but I'd like to."

He put down his chopsticks. "Anyone in particular?"

She bit lip. It was now or never. "You…you have gray eyes."

He laughed. "Yes. I know. And you have beautiful brown ones." He shook his head suddenly and ran his fingers through his hair. "Oh man! I can't believe I just said that."

"Why not? It was really sweet."

He shrugged. "Maybe so, but…it was better left unsaid."

"Why? If you meant it."

"Oh, I meant it all right."

"Then what was wrong with saying it?"

He shook his head. "I'd better go."

He started to stand and she saw her chance to make love with him vanishing. She reached out to clutch his hand. "Wait. Please. Don't go."

"I have to."

She stared up at him, making no effort to hide the desire in her eyes. "Why?"

"This is not a good idea."

"Why not? If we both want it." She squeezed his hand. "It's not just me. You want it too. Don't you?"

"Yes," he said in a low voice, as if the word had been forced from him against his will. "I shouldn't, but I do."

"Then stay. Please."

After a moment, his fingers linked with hers. Locking his gaze with hers, he sank back down beside her. "This is crazy. I can't believe I'm doing this."

"Why not?"

"Why not? We have to work together for one thing. You're one of my employees, for God's sakes. We need to maintain a professional relationship."

She squeezed his fingers. "We'll be very professional at work. But when we're alone…when we're just Chandler and Cassy, it can be different. Don't go. I want you to stay."

"I know and I want it too." He took a deep, gulping breath. "If we're going to do this, we need to set some ground rules."

"Okay. Whatever you say." She just wanted him to take her in his arms and kiss her senseless.

"You're sure you want to start this?" He pulled away from her touch and stared at her. "I haven't put any undue pressure on you in anyway, have I?"

"No! You haven't put any pressure on me at all. I want this. I want you!"

"I want you too, but I'd hate to get slapped with some type of sexual harassment suit later."

Her cheeks burned. "You don't have to worry about that."

He touched her heated cheeks gently. "Actually, I do. If we start this and things go wrong, I could really live to regret this night."

"No! You won't! What do you want? You want a guarantee?" She rose to her knees and deliberately pressed her breasts against his chest. "If you like, I'll fill out an affidavit to that effect and have it notarized."

He stared at her for a moment before laughing. "Not necessary. I just want to make sure you understand the implications before we go any further."

"Of course I understand. I'm not a child or an idiot. I understand and I still want it...I want you. Now. Please."

His eyes seemed to darken and he extended a big hand to her. "Then come get me, *chère*."

"*Chère*?" She stared at him.

He blinked at her. "I...don't know why I said that. It's not another woman's name. It's—"

She shook her head. "I know." She knew what the word meant. She had seen it in the letters her great-grandmother's forbidden lover had sent her. She had never expected to hear it from the lips of a man about to make love to her. "It's all right. I like it. It sounds strange, and yet it feels right."

He nodded. "It does. Being here with you like this feels right...like coming home."

A combination of eagerness and anxiety filled her as she leaned forward and brushed her mouth against his.

Chapter Five

ɛ⌀

The moment their lips touched in a series of teasing little kisses, Cassy felt a delicious shock of pleasure and astonishment radiate all through her body. It was as if she'd never really been kissed before, as if she'd spent her entire adult life waiting for this magical moment with this particular, special man. It was as if that first sweet electrifying touch of his lips against hers made her whole and complete, filled an endless aching need in her. It felt like coming home after a long perilous trip.

It seemed he needed more. She heard his indrawn breath. Then he cupped a hand behind her head before he brought his mouth forcefully down on hers. His arms were around her and he was kissing her. Really kissing her. Long, moist kisses that made her body burn with desire and need and washed away what little inhibitions she had left.

She had visions of other, long-ago kisses, in the shade of the bayou in a forgotten time. Other hands touching another body. Black and white coming together as one. Together again—at long last. Philippe. Philippe, *mon cher*.

She kissed him back, loving the feel of his thick, silky hair under her raking fingers. She enjoyed experiencing the texture of his skin. His lips were so warm, so insistently sweet that she found herself licking and nibbling at them like they were chocolate ice cream. She couldn't get enough of him.

Before she had time to have second thoughts, he undressed her. Her last lover had frequently ripped off buttons and destroyed zippers in their haste to disrobe her.

Chandler did it slowly, as if he wanted to savor the experience; as if he knew he could only undress her for the first time once and wanted to fully enjoy it. He kissed her deeply before he began to unbutton the tiny buttons on the white silk blouse she wore. He was just as patient when he unzipped the matching skirt.

When she stood before him in red lace bra and thong panties, he stared at her; his gray gaze flickering with a multitude of tiny silver flames of desire. His hands shook when he slowly peeled her panties over her hips. He paused with the thong poised at the top of her vagina. Then with a quick intake of breath, he kneeled and planted a soft kiss against each thigh. Her own breath caught in her throat when he brushed his mouth against her mound as he continued to push her panties down her thighs until she finally stepped out of them.

He rose to his feet and unhooked her front fastening bra. Her breasts bounced into view.

"God," he said softly. He lowered his head and showered her breasts with small, biting kisses. "You're...breathtaking. Beautiful. You're beautiful." He pulled her into his arms. He didn't kiss her. He just held her, appearing to delight in the feel of her naked body molded to his. "I've waited forever to be with you like this again, *chère*."

She was so excited, her breath came in deep, gulping gusts. She'd never felt this way. Never had the feel of a fully clothed, aroused man caused such havoc in her. Such need. Such delight. And yet she had felt this way before — and with this man.

"You feel so good," he told her. "So delicious. I've wanted to hold you like this almost since the moment I first saw you."

"Oh...I wanted it too," she said in an awed voice. She wasn't sure how much of what she was feeling was her own desire or how much was a result of The Talisman's influence. She didn't much care. Whatever it was, it felt good. She wanted it to continue.

She gasped when he began kissing and sucking on her breasts. He caressed her with those big, exciting hands of his. She trembled uncontrollably.

"I want...I need to be inside you," he told her.

She must be dreaming. She couldn't believe that her fantasies were finally coming true. At long last, he was going to make love to her. The sweetness of it overwhelmed her with a pleasure that was almost painful.

"Oh…please…please…" she begged, cupping his face in her hands. "Please. I need you."

Standing on her toes, she kissed him and began unbuttoning his shirt. His fingers brushed hers aside. He pulled away and quickly shed his clothing.

When he was nude, she ogled him, eagerly comparing the reality with her fantasies. His shoulders were indeed broad, but his chest was covered with a mass of fine dark hair. Her hungry gaze moved quickly over him. There wasn't an ounce of excess weight on his tall, muscular body. He was beautiful. He was also already fully aroused.

She was especially pleased to see that in addition to being thick, his erect cock was much larger than she'd dared hoped. By several delicious inches. As in her imagination, the head was helmeted.

She stared at it, licking her lips in anticipation. The thought of the pleasure it would bring her when it was propelled into her body by the force of his lean, powerful hips, made her stomach muscles churn. "Please." Philippe. *Mon cher.*

"Yes." He moved quickly, taking her into his arms. She'd never been easily stirred sexually, but just the feel of his nude, aroused body pressed tight against hers, was enough to bring her to the brink of ecstasy.

She clenched her hands on the taunt muscles of his buns. "Oh…Chandler. Chandler!"

"Cassy…oh God! You have no idea how good this feels." He lifted her off her feet. She wound her arms around his neck and pressed her mouth to the hair on his chest as he carried her to her bedroom.

He stretched her out on the bed. As in her fantasies, he stood over her, staring down at her, his breathing deep and ragged.

She touched the thigh nearest her, it was hard and corded. "Are you going to just stand there looking or are you going to eat?"

"Oh, I am definitely going to eat!" He spread his big body on top of hers. They both trembled at the longed for contact. Murmuring, he buried his face against her breasts. "Oh, Cassy. I've wanted to be with you like this for so long. I can't believe it's finally happening. You're finally going to be mine again, *chère*. I get to kiss you…make love to you…"

She parted her legs and cupped his buns in her hands. "Now that you've got me where you want me, what do you plan to do with me?"

He responded by rubbing his thick length against her damp mound. "Does this give you any ideas?"

She shook with need.

She felt him press something into her hands. "We'll need this, sweet."

He rolled off her and she scrambled to her knees and opened the small foil packet. She sat back on her heels, feeling a rushing dampness between her thighs as she slowly rolled the condom over his shaft. Covering his cock was an incredibly erotic experience.

When she finished, he gripped her by the waist and lifted her body on top of his. He rolled them over until she came to rest on her back. He was above her, resting his weight on his arms and knees.

Leaning down, he kissed her gently, allowing her to feel the pulsing weight and heat of his shaft against her thigh. It was too much for her. She'd waited too long. With a small cry of frustration, she grasped him in her hands and lifted her hips. The head of him throbbing at her entrance was so luscious, she found herself wishing she could taste him…lick him…suck him until he gushed in her mouth.

He had other ideas. He lowered his hips onto hers.

The breath caught in her throat. She nearly stopped breathing. God almighty, it was happening. The big head of his shaft began to push slowly between the lips of her sex and into her wet, aching passage. She felt her body opening to accommodate him as he worked the full length of himself into her. The resultant sensations were utterly delectable. Philippe. *Mon cher*, welcome home.

When he'd bottomed out inside her, she shuddered, already on the verge of a fall into the paradise that belong exclusively to sated lovers.

"You like it?" He whispered the question against her breasts.

"Yes…oh…yes…Phil—Chandler…oh, yes."

"Tell me how much you like it," he encouraged, beginning a slow, steady rhythm deep inside her. "Tell me you like having me inside you as much as I love this. Oh God, Cassy! I can't begin to describe how good being inside you feels. You feel so…good…so tight…so hot…I've never…it's never been this way with anyone else. God, this is good."

The words flowing from him made her stomach muscles tighten. She wrapped her arms around his neck and her legs around his waist. "Oh, Chandler…please. No more talking. Just please give me more…please…harder, faster…deeper…I've waited so long for you to come back to me. Please."

In response to her pleas, he increased the speed and length of his cock inside her until she could barely breathe with the waves of pleasure washing over her. Tossing her head from side to side, she cried out and clung helplessly to his fast pumping hips. With her eyes closed, she remembered another time…hot, dark nights lying on her stomach in the bayou with her lover, her Philippe above her, his cock sliding ever-so gently in and out of her butthole, his whispered words of love filling her ears as he came.

The first wave of bliss thundered through her, making her toes curl and her back arch as her world shattered around her. He pushed her gently back to the bed and continued with the relentless assault on her senses, kissing and holding and thrusting into her until she again felt the sweet fire of ecstasy burning in her drenched channel. She was on the verge of peaking for a second time when his big body began to shudder. Moaning, he cupped her rump in his hands, lifted her body and pumped his cock deep in her in a mindless frenzy. The speed and force of his thrusts sent her over the edge just as he came in an explosive burst of satisfaction.

He collapsed on top of her, buried to the hilt in her, his arms wrapped around her. Feeling languid and completely satisfied, she stroked a hand down his back.

Still breathing hard, he slowly pulled out of her and discarded the condom. Then he cradled her in his arms and held her close to his damp body. "*Merci, ma chère!*"

Ma chère. There it was again. And she had thought of him as Philippe. Philippe had been the name of her great-grandmother's Cajun lover. It was The Talisman. Oh God, it was taking over.

She shivered and pressed close against him.

He held her, whispering softly to her in a mixture of English and French. She responded with a blend of the two languages.

After he drifted to sleep, she quietly climbed out of bed and went to her undies drawer. She took the box into the bathroom and closed the door. When she lifted the top off the box, she gasped. Instead of the male thrusting into the female from the rear as usual, the couple now faced each other. When she lifted the charm out of the box, the minuscule rod, still dripping, came out of an equally small vagina. The outline of the tiny cock might have been a carbon copy of Chandler's. Or was it Philippe's? Or did it even matter anymore?

* * * * *

It was still dark outside when Chandler woke. He was immediately aware of Cassy beside him. He turned his head. She lay on her stomach. The cover he had pulled over them before he fell asleep tangled in a knot at her feet.

He studied her body through the moonlight shinning in the room through the open windows of her bedroom. Her face was turned away from him and her breasts were hidden from his gaze. But he admired the lines of her smooth dark body. From the curve of her back to the delightful twin mounds of her rounded behind. Her legs were shapely and slightly parted and delightfully big.

He felt himself hardening as he looked at her. She was absolutely perfect in every way. Even more perfect than his Ebony Venus. Hell, she *was* an Ebony Venus. No, damn it! She was Cassy. This was not early twentieth century Louisiana. He was not his great-grandfather and she was not his forbidden and lost love. It was perfectly acceptable for him to be Cassy's lover.

He was her lover. What had happened was between he and Cassy. He sighed with remembered pleasure as he recalled how naturally his cock had fit into her sweet body. Slipping his aching dick inside her heated tunnel for the first time had given him an incredible thrill. He'd felt as if he was where he'd always wanted to be—where he needed to be. He didn't linger on the realization that sliding into her had felt more like coming home than making love to her for the first time. Granted he had called her *ma chère*, but it had been him, Chandler, making love to Cassy. Not his great-grandfather making love to his Marie Savoy.

He'd found her appetite for him equal to his for her. She had wanted him and hadn't been afraid of letting him know how much he was pleasing her. He'd finally found his wild woman. He should have been happy and carefree. And he would have been, if not for the fact that she was one of his employees and he wasn't so sure he and Cassy had been in bed alone. If nothing else, his experience with Serge and his family had taught him the folly of dismissing the supernatural.

"That was really good, wasn't it?"

At the sound of the voice, Chandler jackknifed into a sitting position. "What the hell?" But he knew who it was even before his eyes searched into the darkest corner of Cassy's bedroom and encountered the dark gaze.

"Damn it, Serge!" he hissed angrily, gingerly slipped out of the bed, being careful not to disturb Cassy, and pulled the sheet over her. "What the hell do you think you're doing?"

Ignoring his indignation, Serge moved silently across the room. Too quickly for Chandler to intercept him, he pulled the light sheet covering Cassy aside and stared down at her naked body. "Damn! What a body! No wonder you've been fantasizing about her. Her breasts are nice and that pussy. Now that looks like a sweet treat."

He rushed to the bed and tugged the sheet back up over Cassy's body. "What are you doing here?" he demanded softly. It had been years since Serge had come uninvited to watch him make love.

Serge turned to face him, his eyes dark with lust and desire. "You'll finally hit the jackpot this time, Chan. She's gorgeous. I don't suppose I could spend an hour or so with her?"

"No!" The days when he and Serge had shared their women had ended with their college days. There was no way he was going to share Cassy with another man. "Will you kindly get out of here?"

Serge shrugged. "Okay. No fucking. How about I climb in bed and get just a taste of her pussy with my mouth? Damn it looks and smells good enough to eat." Serge grinned at him. "Have you tasted her yet?"

"Serge, get the hell out of here and don't come back uninvited!"

As silently as he'd appeared, Serge left. Chandler stood near the bed for several moments to make sure Serge really was gone before he slipped back into bed.

Ignoring what felt like a *need* to reach out and touch Cassy, assuring himself that she belonged strictly to him, he rolled onto his back, staring up at the darkened ceiling.

He should go before she woke and they both had to face the consequences of their night together. But now that Serge had seen her naked, he didn't dare leave. Serge wasn't above waking her and compelling her to sleep with him. Still, part of him wished he could leave. No matter how good he felt now, he was already beginning to regret having slept with her. It was going to create so many problems. More problems than sex with her was worth.

So why was he still lying here, waiting for her to either wake or just turn in her sleep and snuggle against him? He wanted that close, personal and emotional contact he'd experienced during their lovemaking.

More surprising and disturbing, was the tenderness he felt for her now — *after* the sex. Telling himself that it was desire didn't help, because he knew it was far more than desire. Sleeping with a woman shouldn't have had this effect on him. It never had before — not even with his ex-wife Karen, in the early days of their relationship when they'd lived to make love to each other.

He wondered uneasily if the statuette was somehow responsible for his feelings. After all, all his brothers had refused to accept it for one reason or another. Jason, five years his senior had urged him not to take it.

"Chan, you know Great-granddad was into some strange things when he lived in Louisiana. I wouldn't have that thing in my house for a million bucks."

He had laughed. "Come on Jace, you make it sound as if you think it's cursed or something."

"I don't know about its being cursed, but you know there's talk that he was sent North because he fell in love with a black woman and got her pregnant. Before they were forced apart, they were supposed to have exchanged charms and promised to one day find each other again."

"And you think if you have the Ebony Venus, you'll be forced to fall in love with a black woman? Come on, Jace, your Cajun roots are showing."

"Maybe so, but if I fall in love with a black woman, I want it to be me falling in love with her, not some long dead ancestor trying to recapture what he lost through me."

Was that what was happening to him now? Was it he who wanted Cassy or was it his great-grandfather who wanted what Cassy represented? Whoever wanted her, she was definitely wanted and adored.

Unable to suppress the urge any longer, he turned onto his side, gently pulled the sheet off her and drew her back against him. The feel of her rounded buns resting against his thighs felt right. He slipped one arm around her waist, cupped the other over her big breasts and nibbled at her neck.

"Chandler." She murmured his name and settled her buns more firmly against him. Chandler. He smiled, pleased that even half asleep she thought of him and not of some other long dead man. This was Chandler and Cassy. "I'm here. Go back to sleep, sweet."

Instead, she turned in his arms. She rubbed her breasts and her bushy mound against him and his cock hardened.

A shudder ran through him when she reached between their bodies to cup him in a warm, soft hand. "Chandler?"

"You shouldn't do that...not unless you're prepared for the consequences," he warned. "I'm already hard."

Her low suggestive laugh sent a shock of lust careening through him. "So I've noticed." She peppered his mouth with soft kisses. "You want to do something about it, *cher*?"

"And how!" He reached for a condom, sheathed himself, eased her onto her back and sank balls-deep into her sweet heat with one lusty thrust.

She began moving her hips, but he grabbed them and held them immobile while he just lay on her, in her, enjoying the heady feeling of being surrounded by her moist, heated tunnel. Her body felt tight and right, as if her pussy had been custom made for his aching cock. They had done this before—a long, long time ago. He had lost her then, but he had her back. Now. She was finally his again. He would never ever lose her again.

He buried his face against her neck, lowering his weight onto her. "I can't believe how good making love to you feels."

She wrapped her arms and legs around him. "It feels good for me too."

"No." He lifted his head and looked down at her. "No. I mean this is good. Really good. Special."

She smiled and lifted her hips against his. "Oh, Chandler! I'm so glad you feel it too. It's not just me."

"No." He stared down at her. Her short, natural hair gave way to long, silky dark tresses that he'd loved to bury his face in as they made love. Only, because she was afraid of getting pregnant, he usually took her dark, sensuous rump. It had been ages since he'd sank his aching cock into her tight, hot, bottom.

"It's not just you, *ma chère*. It was never just you. I've missed you. I never forgot you. Never. But now you're mine again."

"Chandler? What…what are you talking about?"

He blinked down at her, shaking his head slightly. "What? What did I say?"

"You…you were talking as if we've been lovers before and calling me *ma chère*."

"Does it bother you?"

"Yes. I'm Cassy, Chandler."

"I know who you are. Please don't think I'm thinking of another woman. I'm not." At least not consciously.

"Just as long as you know who you're with."

He kissed her. "I do. I know it's you, Cassy."

She stroked her fingers through his hair and he fought hard to think only of her. "Chandler? I want you to...fuck me, long and hard."

He lifted as far away from her as her legs would allow, then he shoved his hips forward, sending his shaft plunging deep into her again. "Oh, sweet, that's the plan!"

In just a matter of moments he was lost—in her. Lost in a world of lust, desire and tenderness that obliterated all thought. Inside her, he had no identity, no purpose other than to please her.

He trembled with the need to keep stroking and loving her until he felt the wild tremors in her pussy that signaled her fast-approaching climax. Only then did he allow himself to come in her in a blissful explosion of pleasure.

He rolled over onto his back, carrying her with him so that she lay sprawled across him. He curled his fingers in her hair and kissed her lazily. "Oh, sweet. That was..."

"Fantastic," she gasped, still breathing deeply.

"Yes," he agreed. "It was."

❊ ❊ ❊ ❊ ❊

Cassy woke suffused with a warm, wonderful inner glow. She lay with her eyes closed for several moments, hugging her pillow. She felt marvelous. She stretched and immediately realized that she was naked. She turned her head and looked at the pillow beside her. In the early morning light, she saw that it, like the other side of the bed had been occupied.

She felt the difference in her body. Her breasts were sore. He'd spent a fair amount of time sucking them. And the ache inside her had been satisfied. This time he'd really been with her.

She sat up and looked at her bedside clock. It was seven-thirty. She looked around the room and sighed. He'd been there, but now he was gone.

Some of her joy evaporated. She fell back against her pillow, pulling the cover back over her. As she did, she heard a sound from the living room. He was still here. She was out of the bed like a shot.

At her bedroom door, she paused and looked down at herself. Deciding that she'd been shameless enough to last a lifetime, she opened a dresser drawer and took out an oversized nightshirt. She pulled it over her head, raked her fingers through her short, dark hair and hurried into the living room.

He stood looking out the French windows. He turned as she paused uncertainly in the doorway. "Hi."

She hesitated. Although he smiled, he seemed somehow withdrawn. Remembering how uninhibited she'd been with him, she flushed and averted her gaze. She'd actually begged him to fuck her. And he had, hard and relentlessly until she'd exploded into a blistering climax that had left her sobbing with pleasure.

He crossed the room and put his hands on her shoulders. "Hi," he said again.

She looked up at him, her face still heated. "I...I thought you'd left."

He brushed the back of his hand against her cheek. "I'm not much on lying around in bed once I wake up."

She pressed her face against his hand. "You're fully dressed. Are you leaving?"

"I can stay...if you want me to."

If she wanted him to? "What about you? What do you want?"

He cupped her face between his palms and kissed the end of her nose. "What I wanted last night—you."

The knot of tension that had began to form in her gut, loosened. She smiled and leaned into him. "Oh, Chandler."

He hugged her to him. "I know this is crazy, but I can't help wanting you." He buried his face against her neck. "Would you like to go out to breakfast?"

She shook her head. "Maybe later. Right now what I'd really like is to go back to bed."

He lifted his head and grinned at her. "Great minds think alike," he said and swept her into his arms.

Later, lying in bed in his arms, with her head pillowed on his shoulder, she marveled at how good she felt. She'd never imagined sex could be so totally fulfilling. Her body felt good. She'd expected that. But more she felt a sense of contentment that she hadn't expected.

She loved the way he continued to kiss and caress her after their lovemaking, whispering softly to her. Just hearing his voice and feeling his big hands shaping and holding her created a sense of delicious after-delight in her.

Chandler was her third lover. No matter how aroused she was, she'd never been able to initiate lovemaking with either of her other lovers. She lost track of how many times she and Chandler had sex that weekend. Every time was better than the last. Sometimes they made love, taking the time to explore and savor each other's bodies fully. Other times they fucked like animals in heat until her bedroom was redolent with the smell of sex. But what really shocked Cassy even more than the many times she initiated sex, was how often she encouraged him to fuck her quick and hard after a tender, leisurely lovemaking session.

Each time they made love, they both whispered in a combination of English and French. And it had taken all of her willpower not to bare her rump and ask him to fuck her there. From the way he fondled her behind, she knew he would have welcomed the chance. But she did not do anal sex and damn if she'd let The Talisman drive her into doing something she'd always thought of as definitely not for her.

Chapter Six

ဢ

Cassy practically floated to work on Monday morning. Chandler had awakened her in the middle of the night to make love one last time. Sex that time had been hot, explosive and quick, with her sitting on his lap in a chair, slapping his thighs and riding his cock until he began to shudder.

"Oh damn, *chère*! I'm coming! I'm coming!"

Acting quickly, she lifted her hips, drew his cock from her body and ripped off the condom. She rapidly pumped his cock, keeping it aimed toward her body. Groaning, he splattered her stomach with come before falling back against the chair. "Oh God, you are so sweet."

Smiling, she leaned forward to kiss him. "You're pretty sweet yourself, lover."

He picked her up and carried her back to bed where they lay together, caressing and kissing tenderly for half an hour. Finally, he pressed a long, lingering kiss against her mouth. "I have to go, *chère*."

She'd panicked and reached out to grab him. "But, *mon cher*, you promised you wouldn't leave me again!"

They'd both frozen, staring at each other wide eyed. Finally, after what had seemed an eternity, she'd found her voice. "I'm sorry. I don't know where that came from. I...I'm really not the clinging vine type. I don't cling. I know you have to go."

He'd sighed. "We both have bayou blood running through our veins, Cassy. One of these days we're going to have to talk about what that means. There's something else going on between us. Something we may have little control over."

She'd shaken her head. "No! There's nothing going on except what we want to go on."

"Cassy, my great-grandfather and grandfather spoke French. I don't, but last night, I called you *chère*. And you called me *mon cher*. Several times. I know I spoke French to you and I know you understood what I was saying. On your application, you said you didn't speak any foreign languages."

"I…I don't."

"But you understood everything I said to you in French. Didn't you?"

"No!" But she had and she knew what it meant. She just didn't want to deal with it.

Long after he kissed her goodbye and left her apartment, she lay in bed, a little frightened; the pillow he'd lain on clutched against her breasts. She knew now, without a doubt that The Talisman was driving her. Maybe driving Chandler too. But she didn't care. It felt right and anything that felt so right couldn't be bad.

She cast her doubts aside, refused to look into the jewelry box in her underwear drawer and left her apartment. She hummed all the way to work and couldn't stop grinning.

"Somebody had a great weekend," Derri said when they met for lunch.

She nodded. "Derri, you have no idea."

"I know, so tell me. What happened? You got a little loving, huh?"

She thought of her weekend. "Oh Derri, I had a lot of loving and it was so…incredible."

Derri leaned forward, her dark eyes centering on Cassy's face. "So he was a good lover, huh?"

"He's a great lover."

She nodded. "I thought he would be. I mean with feet that big, his other…equipment had to be wicked in size."

She stared at Derri. "His feet aren't that big." But his cock was and boy did he know how to use it.

"What are you talking about? He wears a size thirteen at least."

She blinked at Derri. "A thirteen? His feet are not...who...who are you talking about?"

"Who am I talking about? Who are *you* talking about?"

"Chandler Raven. Who else?"

"Chandler Raven!" To her surprise, Derri frowned. "You slept with him?"

"Yes."

"Yeah? So? What was he like? Did you enjoy it?"

She blushed. "Yes! Oh Derri, there is nothing in the world quite as wonderful as a handsome man with a big dick that he knows how to use."

"Big dick he knows how to use, huh?"

"Yes. It's big and he knows how to use it." She felt her twat convulse just thinking about him.

"Cass, I'm glad you enjoyed yourself, but do you think that was a good idea?"

"What? You mean because he's white?"

Derri hesitated and she frowned. Something was bothering Derri big-time. She was not given to all the hesitation and uncertainly she'd displayed lately. "Well, mostly and because he's your boss. Cass, I thought you liked Frank."

"I did...I do, but...I do. But Derri, Chandler makes me so hot. And he's...sweet."

"Sweet? Cass, get a grip. Will you? He's a man with a hard-on. That makes for lust, not sweetness."

She shrugged. "Whatever you call it, I like him. A lot."

"Fine. Like him a lot, if you insist, but don't lose your head or your perspective, Cass. It's sex. It might be good sex. Hell, if he has a big dick and knows how to use it, it's probably great sex. But it's still just sex. Don't start thinking anything else is going on."

She remembered Chandler's tenderness after lovemaking. He'd held and caressed her until she fell asleep. She loved that he didn't just sex her up, roll off her and go to sleep. For her the aftermath of lovemaking was almost as important as the actual act itself. And she'd never been with a man who handled it better than Chandler.

"Okay, Derri. Give it a rest already. I'm not falling for the guy. I have the hots for him. It's sex. Not love. Okay? Happy?"

"Okay. As long as we know what we're dealing with."

"You say that as if we can't have a real meaningful relationship. We can."

"Yeah?"

"Yeah! Why not? This is not twentieth century Lafayette, you know."

"Twentieth century, where?"

Cassy swallowed, realizing what she'd said. "Lafayette, Louisiana. My great-grandmother Marie was born and raised there."

"Ah huh. And what has that got to do with you and your boss playing jungle fever?"

"Nothing! It's just that…she…my great-grandmother fell in love with a white man, which was a no-no."

"You never told me that."

She shrugged. "There was no point. Their story had a sad ending. She got pregnant, but lost the baby and he was sent North and they never saw each other again. But she never forgot him. I have letters that they wrote each other that my grandmother Maud passed down to me. There are letters that great-grandmother Marie wrote to him that she could never send because she didn't know where he was. She died loving him, Derri."

About to tell Derri about The Talisman, she paused. This was crazy enough without telling Derri that she was afraid that she was reliving part of her great-grandmother's ill-fated romance with Chandler Raven. Derri would probably think her elevator wasn't going to the top floor. And maybe it wasn't. Maybe it was all in her mind.

She gave her head a small shake. "But what about you, Derri? What's going on with you? I've never seen you so restless."

Derri shook her head. "I have issues that I need to address and handle before I can settle down."

"You want to talk about them?"

"Yes, but not just now."

"Is Karl going to wait for you?"

"I don't think so. I guess I could ask him."

"But?"

"But I'm not going to."

"Why not?"

"Cass, even if he agreed to wait, which I really can't see him doing, it would create problems between us that our relationship probably couldn't recover from." She shook her head. "Don't worry. I'm fine. Really."

She headed back to work worried both about her relationship with Chandler and the issues Derri didn't want to discuss.

After her last service call, she resisted the urge to rush back to the office. It was after five and Chandler wasn't likely to be there waiting for her.

She fell asleep soon after she went to bed that night, certain she would see or hear from him sometime during the next day. But when she left work on Friday, she still hadn't seen or heard from him.

Just as she was deciding if she should be depressed, her phone rang. She kicked off her shoes and curled up in her favorite chair. "Hello?"

"Cassy, this is Chandler."

She felt the nameless something that had constricted her insides loosen. "Hi, Chandler."

"Ah, I know it's short notice, but I was wondering if maybe I could see you."

"Yes. When?"

"Tonight. Now?"

"Yes!"

She pulled off her clothes, took a quick shower and slipped into a sleek, silky blue dress that clung to her body in what she knew Chandler would think was all the right places. The dress highlighted her breasts and her rump, two parts of her body Chandler like to fondle endlessly. Staring over her shoulder into the mirror on her closet door, she smiled. "You'll knock his socks off. He loves you in blue," she told her reflection.

Chandler took one look at her and whistled. "Wow! You…ah, look great. That dress…that color blue on you…wow!"

She grinned and took the bottle of wine he'd brought with him. "Thank you." She allowed her gaze to move leisurely over him. He looked good in the dark suit that clung to his shoulders and molded to his thighs. "You look pretty good yourself. Have you eaten?"

"No."

She frowned. "I could thaw a couple of steaks and do some potatoes and vegetables. Do you like steaks?"

He linked an arm around her waist and drew her body against his. "What I would like, *chère*, is to make love to you." He tipped up her chin and kissed her slowly. "Unless you're hungry, we can talk about food later."

She slipped her arms around his neck and offered her lips. "Much later, *mon cher*."

Arms wrapped around each other, they went into her bedroom. This time he practically ripped off her clothes in his haste to disrobe her. His clothes came off even quicker. Then, kissing and fondling each other, they tumbled onto her bed.

He rolled her onto her back and quickly mounted her. "Oh, sweet, I've been thinking about you and this since I left you last week."

"That makes two of us, lover." She closed her eyes and clung to his shoulders. He covered her lips, face and neck with heated, frantic kisses, while he pushed relentlessly into her body. She gasped as the first delicious waves of pleasure radiated through her.

The first time that night was quick and devoid of tenderness. But she gloried in his frantic movements and the hands that clutched her so tightly she wondered if she'd have bruises the next day. Their next time, was a slower, tender session that left them both moaning and shuddering in ecstatic delight.

He brushed his mouth against hers. "You make me feel so good...so happy. When we make love, nothing else matters. Nothing but you...nothing but making you happy."

Lying on top of him, she stroked her hands down his body and peppered his chest and shoulders with kisses. "You do that and more, *mon cher*."

They made love until they were both fatigued. Drowsy and completed satisfied, she curled her body against his damp one and drifted off to sleep with his cock still inside her, his murmured words of desire, whispered in her ear in the beautiful language of true and eternal lovers — French.

They spent the weekend inside. They went at each other in bed, in the shower, on the kitchen table and even on the balcony under the stars. As she lay on the blanket on the balcony on her stomach with him taking her from behind, the desire to shove her butt at him and wait to have him drill her bottom was almost unbearable. Once, almost as if he sensed her need, he pulled out of her twat and rubbed his hard length along her crack.

"It's been so long *ma chère*," he'd whispered and lapsed into French, telling her how much he'd missed her. He'd parted her cheeks with his hands and she'd tensed, but after a long moment, he'd slipped his cock between her cheeks and back into her vagina.

Each time they made love, she fell a little more in love with him. Sunday night, after eating the dinner they'd had delivered, they made love one last time. He kissed her buttocks, parted her cheeks and rubbed an exploring finger against her anus, tentatively pressing the tip of a finger inside her hole.

She felt something warm and soft enter her anus—his lubricated finger.

She froze. "No, Chandler! I...I don't do that."

He planted a warm kiss against her back. "Yes, you do, *ma chè*re. You've always loved having my cock buried deep inside your warm, sweet ass."

She twisted away and turned to stare at him. "No, Chandler. There is no way you're sticking your cock up my butt. You're too big! And I'm not the one who likes anal reaming. That's her! Not me!"

He sat up slowly, turned on the light in her bedroom and they faced each other. "Her who?"

"You know 'her who'! Marie! Marie Savoy! She liked anal sex, not me! Not Cassy!"

"So you're finally ready to admit we're not the only ones in this bed?"

"No! Yes! Oh, I don't know anymore what's going on. But I don't have anal sex! If you think I'm going to let you put your cock in my behind, you can forget it! I don't care what she liked and what she let him do to her!"

"They both enjoyed it."

"Well, I don't !"

"Okay. Not a problem." He turned off the light and gently drew her back onto the bed. He placed her on her stomach and his lips and his tongue replaced the finger he'd inserted into her. He licked and kissed her butthole before turning her onto her side. He moved behind her, lifted one of her legs and slowly slid his dick into her wet, ready tunnel. He put one hand between her legs to tease and rub her clit and the other across her breasts.

"Don't worry, *ma chère*. If you don't like that, we don't need to do it. Being inside you is more than enough to keep me happy and satisfied."

"Are you sure?"

He nibbled at the side of her neck. "Yes, sweet. I'm sure." He trailed a finger down her bottom to her puckered opening. "But if you change your mind, *ma chère*, I'm ready to please you just like he pleased her."

"Is that what you what to do to me, Chandler? He wasn't as big or as thick as you are and there was a reason they had anal sex."

He licked her neck and pressed deep into her, making her gasp with pleasure. "If I recall correctly, it didn't work. He wanted her pussy and one of the few times she let him fuck her pussy..."

"She got pregnant," she finished, suddenly feeling that other woman's pleasure and anguish when she realized she was pregnant with her lover's child so long ago.

"What happened to our baby, *ma chère*?" The voice whispering the anguished question against her ear was no longer Chandler's. It was Philippe's.

And she was no longer Cassy. She was Marie. Philippe's Marie. His *ma chère*. "She died, *mon cher*. She died."

He whispered to her in French; sweet, wonderful words of pain, regret and undying devotion. And she, the young Creole girl who'd fallen for the handsome Cajun the first time she saw him, responded as she always did to her lover's insatiable need for her body—

She pulled away from him. Putting a pillow under her body, she lay on her stomach with her bare behind raised to better facilitate his entrance. "I'm yours, *mon cher*. Do with me as you will."

She felt his lips and his tongue moving against her butt and tensed her whole body. She knew that the first few times would hurt like hell. But even through the pain she would know she was loved and cherished by this big, sweet Cajun. And it would gradually get better until she enjoyed it enough to thrust herself joyfully back at him, taking his whole length deep within her bottom hole, while he fingered her slit and the small knob between her legs that drove her crazy with love and need for him.

Then to her surprise, he pulled the pillow away and turned her back onto her side. He curled his body against her back. Holding her and caressing her breasts, his cock plowed into her cunt and he buried his lips against her neck. "I'm not him, Cassy. This is Chandler, who never intends to do anything to you unless you really want him to."

She was no longer sure who he was or who she was. It didn't really matter—not then. Not when everything in her world…her worlds felt right. Whether she was Marie with Philippe or Cassy with Chandler, it didn't matter. She just knew this was right.

She reached down to cup his balls and turned her head, seeking his mouth. "Chandler, *mon cher*. Kiss me."

He found her mouth and they had a sweet, erotic fuck. Afterward, in the shower, he impaled her on his cock and they enjoyed a quick, hard fuck with the water cascading over their heads.

"I love you, *mon cher*," she whispered.

"*Je t'aime, ma chère*," he repeated, allowing his big cock to surge deep into her pussy.

By the time he finally left, she collapsed on the bed and immediately fell asleep for the few hours left before morning.

In the morning when she looked in the jewelry box, the couple was frozen in the initial position with the male buried in the female's bottom. What did it mean? Should she have insisted that Chandler take her behind? She shuddered thinking how painful it would have been trying to take his thick width into her tiny hole. She loved him all the more for not having taken advantage of her moment of weakness. Even though she knew he or at least Philippe had longed to drill her bottom. Or would it have been Philippe drilling Marie's bottom?

She shook her head. It was all so confusing and more than a little scary. And yet, it was also wonderful and exciting at the same time. How could she begrudge her long dead great-grandmother one last chance to find happiness with her beloved Philippe? Especially when it didn't hurt her or Chandler? When it felt so very good?

* * * * *

"I just don't know what I'm going to do with that boy! I found him in bed with that...that girl again!"

Chandler watched Ellen pacing the length of her living room floor, her body tense, her face averted. She was clearly uncomfortable discussing having walked in on Steve having sex with his Tia again.

She turned to face him. "I thought you said you had a talk with him."

He decided to ignore her accusatory tone. "I did, Ellen, but he's not a little boy anymore. He has a mind of his own. I can only talk to him, I can't tell him what to do or make his decisions for him."

"It's not his mind that worries me, Chandler! It's his hormones and his bad judgment. They were in this house...carrying on like two dogs in heat. I walked into the rec room and all I heard was grunting and groaning and her screaming at him to...to fuck her harder!"

Chandler felt the heat rush up the back of his neck as he recalled Cassy demanding the same thing of him just the night before. He had eagerly complied, as Steve would no doubt have done, had Ellen not interrupted.

"What can he possibly see in that cheap little hussy?"

"Ellen, there's no purpose served by calling her names."

"Oh really? Well you wouldn't be so quick to say that if you'd walked in on them—again. That…hussy was lying naked as the day she was born on the pool table with her legs splayed like a bitch in heat while he rutted into her like…and he wasn't even in the right hole if you know what I mean!"

Oh, he knew what she meant all right. Now he knew why Steve wasn't worried about his Tia getting pregnant.

"Chandler, I am sick of that…cheap tramp corrupting him!"

He got up from his chair and walked over to the French windows. He took several deep breaths before he turned to face her. "Ellen, don't you think you're overreacting because she happens to be black?"

"No, I do not!" She shook her head, sending her dark hair cascading around her flushed face. "How can you even suggest that when you know very well that I am not now, nor have I ever been prejudiced?"

He shrugged wearily. While not wanting to further distress Ellen, he found her attitude annoying. If she thought Tia was a cheap tramp, she would think the same of Cassy.

"Ellen, you've found Steve with other girls…white girls. I don't recall you calling any of them cheap tramps."

"They didn't behave as that one did! Decent women do not let men near their rear ends."

"No?"

"No, Chandler! That's why women have vaginas! It's not natural to let a male use your rear end for sex."

He remembered how close he had come to anal sex with Cassy. Resisting the temptation to sink his cock into her beautiful brown bottom had taken all his willpower. Only the sure knowledge that she didn't really want it and the certainly that he would hurt her, had stopped him.

But memories of how sweet anal sex with a cherished lover could be had taunted and teased him. Only they weren't his memories and he wasn't in love with Cassy. It was Philippe in love with Marie. It had been Philippe who longed to ravish his beloved Creole's behind, not him. His one experience with anal sex had left him longing for his lover's pussy. Cassy hadn't wanted it and neither had he. Damn if he was going to let some long dead relative dominate his sex life.

"Chandler! You're not listening!" Ellen snapped.

He blinked rapidly and had to take several moments to gather his thoughts. "I am listening. Tell me Ellen, weren't the other girls you caught Steve with naked with their legs splayed open? And wasn't Steve rutting into them too?"

The angry flush on her face assured him that he'd accurately interpreted her motives. "They weren't screaming to be fucked in the behind at the top of their lungs! Chandler, I didn't ask you to come here to listen to you defending that...girl. I want you to talk to him! Tell him to get himself a nice..."

"White girl?" he suggested coolly when she allowed her voice to trail off.

"Chandler! You're trying to make me out to be something I'm not! What's wrong with my wanting him to date a...okay, I'll say it—a white girl?"

"I didn't say anything was wrong with it."

"Then why the attitude? What's your problem?"

"I don't have a problem, Ellen, but you do. Steve happens to be hung up on Tia."

"I guess he is, considering the way she behaves—like an alley cat in heat! The little tramp!"

"Ellen!"

"Don't Ellen me, Chandler. You can't deny she's a little shameless tramp."

"Yes, I can."

"No, Chandler. No! What would you call her? Decent women do not go around asking men to fuck them!"

What would she say if he told her that was exactly what Jane had begged him to do the last time he saw her?

"Chandler, are you going to talk to him or not?"

He shook his head. It would be the height of hypocrisy for him to attempt to talk to Steve about sleeping with a black woman when he was sleeping with one himself. "Ellen, I think you just need to leave them alone. If it's nothing but sex, it won't last. If it's more, you're only going to push him into her arms."

"Chandler!" She rushed across the room to grab his arms. "Please! I need your help with him. He looks up to you. He'll listen to you."

"I've already talked to him and it didn't help. I'm not going to talk to him again."

"Why not?"

"Because I don't happen to agree with you that his seeing Tia is a problem, Ellen."

"What?" She recoiled as if he'd attempted to strike her. "You don't see a problem with him seeing that girl?"

"As a matter of fact, Ellen, no I don't. She seems to make him happy. Isn't that important to you?"

She stared at him, her gaze narrowed. "So it's true."

"What's true?"

"Julie said you had a woman with you the last time you stopped by. A black woman."

He felt the heat rushing up the back of his neck again. He narrowed his own gaze. "So?"

"So maybe Julie was right. Maybe she's your new girlfriend. Maybe that's why you're so tolerant of Steve's behavior."

He shook his head. "Let's get something straight here, Ellen. I did not come here to discuss my personal life. My personal life is off limits."

Her mouth parted in a soundless circle. "So you are seeing a black woman!"

He was surprised at the almost instinctive desire he felt to deny that he was seeing Cassy. He fought off the urge and remained silent.

Ellen's eyes widened and she backed away from him. "Are you...sleeping with her, Chandler? Rutting in her rear end? Or should I saying fu —"

"You shouldn't say anything! Who I'm seeing is none of your concern!"

"What is it with you Raven men that you can't stay away from black women?"

"What?"

"Don't hand me that. You think I don't know about your whoring great-grandfather and his black lover? Now you and Steve? Is it something in the damned Raven genes that make black women so irresistible to you?"

It wasn't in the genes. It was that damned Ebony Venus that was somehow manipulating his will and his desires. Without the damned statuette would he have even given Cassy a second look? He was no longer sure. But he was sure of one thing, he wasn't willing to allow even a small part of his life to be taken over.

"Chandler! Will you listen when I'm talking to you?" Ellen demanded.

He stormed over to the sofa and grabbed his jacket and briefcase. "Just leave them alone, Ellen, or you're going to be sorry."

"When I want advice from a man who's sleeping with some cheap—"

"Don't you go there!" he snapped. "I am not your son and you do not dictate who I see! And you sure as hell don't use disparaging language to describe anyone I may or may not be seeing."

"What's the matter, Chandler? White women aren't good enough for you anymore? You like your women with gutter morals?"

The venom in her voice and gaze shocked him. "I'm outta here before I forget that Jace loved you!"

"That's right, go Chandler. I don't know that I want you here anymore."

He turned at the door. "What?"

"You heard me, Chandler. Don't bother coming back. If you want to see Julie, I'll drop her off at your place, but I don't want to see you again."

He resisted the urge to tell her to go to hell and left the house. In his car, he sat behind the steering wheel, staring through the windshield without actually seeing anything. How could he have known Ellen for so long without really knowing her? He didn't know what bothered him more, her disdain for black women or the sudden, sure knowledge that she wasn't the only person he knew who would find his sleeping with Cassy unacceptable.

He needed to talk to Cassy. He paused with his hand hovering over his car phone. What would he say to her? What did they have in common except a shared physical desire for each other? They'd spent the last two weekends having sex almost every waking moment. They hadn't talked much or even eaten. His failed marriage had taught him that sex, although powerful and pleasant, was not a strong enough foundation on which to build a real relationship. To make matters worse, he wasn't even sure half the time if it was really him and Cassy having sex or his great-grandfather Philippe and his beloved and unforgettable Marie.

He and Cassy could not have a real relationship. How could they when they were both being used? And he was unwilling to hurt her as he had hurt Jane. Hopefully, he hadn't done too much damage. He withdrew his hand and started his car. He headed home.

In his bedroom, he lifted the Ebony Venus from his bedside table and stared down into the features that were now virtual mirror images of Cassy's. He reached out a hand and touched the dark breasts. Although made of carved wood that his great-grandfather had covered with a preserving liquid, the statuette's twin mounds felt warm and firm under his finger, just as Cassy's beautiful breasts felt when he touched and kissed them.

He lifted the statuette to his mouth and pressed his lips against the behind. The flesh was soft and yielding like Cassy's sweet brown bottom. God, he had to stop this before he lost track of who he was and became Philippe Raven.

Running his lips over the breasts one last time, he felt the small nipples harden against his mouth. "No! Damn it, no!" He walked quickly through his apartment to the kitchen and tossed the statuette into the trash can.

There. It was done. He stood staring down at it for several minutes, fighting the need to retrieve it and return it to his bedside table. He had reached the kitchen door when he heard the voice.

"Philippe. *Mon cher*! Don't leave me again! Please. *Mon cher*! Come back!"

He clenched both hands into fists at his side and kept going. In his bedroom, he closed the door, undressed and lay staring up at the ceiling. It was done. He was through being manipulated. If Serge wanted the damned thing, he'd have to rescue it from the trash.

He lay sleepless for hours longing for Cassy. But it was time to end that too. His love affair with Cassy was as ill-advised as had been his great-grandfather's with his beloved Marie. Then why did it feel like Chandler was slowly losing his beloved Cassy?

* * * * *

Cassy waited a week for Chandler to contact her before she began to suspect he might not want to see her again. The reservations he'd expressed before he slept with her had obviously returned. And just maybe he resented her having refused to give him anal sex. There were lots of women who would willingly give him any kind of sex he wanted. Maybe he had decided to find one of them.

She spent the next weekend alone and miserable. She couldn't stop thinking about him. The remembrance of his lips, hands and body on hers sent tantalizing shivers of delight through her. How could something that had and did mean so much to her, mean nothing to him?

When she woke in the middle of the night to a series of soft, persistent sounds, she found that the tiny couple had turned back to gold again and now they lay back-to-back, clear lines of dejection in their small forms. That's when she knew it was over between her and Chandler.

He'd decided he'd made a mistake and she was supposed to just pretend he hadn't slept with her and rocked her world on its foundation? Was she supposed to go quietly into the night and disappear just to please him? Well, she wouldn't. She had no intentions of making discarding her as easy for him as Marie had made it for Philippe. If it was over, she was going to make him be man enough to tell her so to her face.

She punched a fist into her pillow and burrowed her head in the resultant dent. Maybe poor Marie had had no recourse when her fickle, spineless lover had allowed his family to drive them apart, but she had options. "You haven't heard the last of me, Chandler Raven."

Willing herself not to lie awake thinking of him, she closed her eyes and eventually slept. The next morning, after checking the assignment board for her list of service calls, she headed for the executive offices.

The receptionist looked up and smiled as she stopped at her desk. "Good morning. Cassy, isn't it?"

She nodded. "Yes." She glanced at the name on the desk. "Good morning, Becky. Is Mr. Raven in? If he is, I'd like to see him."

Becky looked surprised. "Now? Is he expecting you?"

"No," she admitted. "But would you ask him if he could spare me a few moments?"

Becky frowned and nodded her head toward the closed door behind her desk. "Why don't you go in and ask Mrs. Johnson?"

"Thanks."

Mentally squaring her shoulders, she went through the door into the inner office.

Jennifer Johnson looked up as she approached. "Good morning, Cassy. What brings you here?"

"Good morning. I know I don't have an appointment, but I was wondering if I might see Mr. Raven for a few moments."

"Is there something I can help you with?"

"Thank you, no. I need to speak with Mr. Raven. May I see him?"

Just for a moment, the older woman stared at her and Cassy wondered if somehow she knew that she had slept with Chandler.

"I'll see if he's available." She picked up the phone on her desk. "Chandler, Ms. Thompson is here to see you, if you can spare her a few moments."

Cassy, suddenly sure that he would refuse to see her, turned and headed for the door. She'd behaved like the fabled village idiot since she met him. It had been foolish to start daydreaming about him, foolish to have slept with him, and foolish to try forcing a confrontation he didn't want. And even more foolish to blame all her irresponsible actions on that damned silly talisman.

"Cassy, where are you going?"

With her hand on the doorknob, she turned, and faced Jennifer Johnson. "I know, he's not available."

The other woman's eyes softened. "Actually, he is. You can go through."

"Oh. Thanks." She swallowed slowly and moved across the room. She tapped on his door, and then without waiting for a response, she stepped into his office.

He rose from his seat as she closed the door. The cool look in his gray eyes chilled her. Why had she come? It would have been better to just pretend the previous weekends had never happened. But how could she do that when she wanted him more than ever? She knew suddenly, that she was in love with him. Not Marie in love with Philippe, but Cassy in love with Chandler.

He gestured toward the chairs in front of his desk. "Have a seat?"

She shook her head and leaned back against the door. "I'd rather stand."

He shrugged and remained standing behind his chair. "You wanted to see me?"

That was all he had to say to her? She bit back the urge to dissolve into helpless sobs. Men didn't like women who cried. She didn't like women who cried. She lifted her chin. "I thought you might have wanted to see me," she challenged. "At least that's the impression you gave me when you kissed me goodbye Sunday before last."

To her surprise, he sighed audibly and nodded. "Oh, I want to see you all right."

"Then why haven't you called me?"

"What would have been the point? We're both adults, Cassy. We both know those weekends, delightful though they were, shouldn't have happened."

"Shouldn't have happened?" She recalled the tenderness of his kisses after they'd made love, the gentle way he'd caressed her and told her how sweet and beautiful she was in English and in French. Even their fucks had been sweet with an underlying tenderness under the heat. And he'd always been considerate of her needs and pleasure. He had *not* been motivated solely by lust or passion. Tenderness didn't spring from those emotions. It sprang from real feelings that involved more than just sex. And all those sweet, powerful emotions had not come from Philippe. Some of them had been from Chandler for her.

"They shouldn't have happened," he repeated. "Look, I don't blame you for being angry, maybe feeling as if you were used, but...that was not my intention."

"What was your intention?"

"To sleep with you," he said bluntly. "I wanted to sleep with you. You're beautiful and sweet and I loved making love to you."

And she'd been only too willing to accommodate him. Now that she had, he had no further interest in her. "But it's only making love if you're *in* love, Chandler. Everything else is just sex, no matter how good it is."

"Whatever you choose to call it, Cassy, you wanted it too," he reminded her.

"And so that makes this all right?"

He sighed. "I'm sorry if you misunderstood and thought I wanted something more...permanent. You must have known that was...impossible."

Despite her best efforts, her eyes welled with tears. She wanted to be angry with him, but all she felt was an incredible ache that seemed to encompass every microscopic part of her. This was how Marie had felt when her Philippe had left her nearly a century earlier—lost with no hope for future happiness.

It was happening again. He was leaving her again. Tearing her world apart, but this time it wasn't necessary. This time he was leaving because he didn't love her. He had never loved her.

"Oh, must I? Let me guess why—because my skin isn't pale enough to suit you in the light of day? Like that other coward from another century, you love sex in the dark with no strings attached and no feelings involved. No, you're not like him. At least he loved her and he was young and afraid."

His lips thinned. "Are you implying that I'm a coward and prejudiced?"

"Are you implying that you're not?"

"Did you think I was prejudiced when we were together?"

"We've never been together! All we've ever done was have sex. That's not being together! They were together!"

"They are dead, Cassy. Long dead and while you may be content to let them live again through you, I am not! I'm through being used. I will choose my own lover on my own terms."

"And I obviously don't fit the bill?"

"Please, *ma chère*, don't misunderstand. You are a beautiful woman. Any man would be honored to have your affection and the privilege of sharing your bed."

"Any man, but you? Well, at twice his age, you're nowhere near the man he was at twenty. At least he loved her. He made love to her and he wasn't ashamed to admit he wanted something more than sex from her."

"Let's not forget that he got her pregnant and then left her to face the music by herself!"

"He didn't know she was pregnant!"

"The hell he didn't! Why do you think he can't rest now? He knew and he still left! It haunted him for the rest of his life because he knew. The only thing he didn't know was what became of their baby. So don't compare me unfavorably to him. I haven't done that to you. I wouldn't do that to you. And another thing, I don't recall you complaining at the time we made love."

How could she argue with that? She turned and fumbled for the doorknob.

Before she could get the door open, he was behind her, holding it closed and pressing against her. She hated that her treacherous body immediately responded to the feel of his hardening cock against her buns.

"I shouldn't have said that. Forgive me, *ma chère*." He whispered the words against her ear. "Don't go angry."

How did he expect her to go—happy? She shoved an elbow back against his body. "Get away from me and don't ever call me *ma chère* again!"

He immediately retreated. She jerked open the door and walked out of the office.

Feeling an unexpected weakness in his legs, Chandler sank down into his chair, closed his eyes and leaned against his headrest. His heart thumped painfully in his chest and he felt...an emptiness he couldn't deny. Was this how Philippe had felt when he'd allowed his family to force him away from Marie so long ago? Had he felt this sense of distress and despair because he knew he was leaving the one true love of his life to face the consequences of their love alone? Never to see his sweet, beloved Marie again? But never to forget her? He'd had to live with the shame and pain of knowing he'd hurt her beyond repair.

As he had hurt Cassy. Why had he succumbed to the urge to sleep with her when he'd known all along that it was a bad idea? He'd known that he didn't want a relationship with her. So why had he slept with her? Why had he allowed himself to fall under the spell of the Ebony Venus Marie had carved and given to Philippe so long ago as a token of her eternal love?

He suddenly knew why Cassy had succumbed to him so quickly. It was because she must have the talisman Philippe had given to his Marie so long ago. Together the two charms had driven him and Cassy into a relationship neither might have sought or wanted on their own. Maybe, given time, she'd realize that she didn't really care for him.

Recalling the tears filling her brown eyes, he doubted that. He felt a particular ache inside him. He had never intended to hurt her. He'd just found it impossible to resist his growing attraction and need for her. Even now, knowing how much damage he'd caused, he couldn't deny that his yearning for her was as strong as ever. He shivered as he recalled the taste of her sweet lips under his, the feel of her soft supple body shuddering against and under his, the exhilarating feel of her hands stroking his body and holding him as he came. The sound of her quiet voice whispering loverlike nothings in his ear until he felt fully sated — happy and fulfilled. Content with the knowledge that he was capable of satisfying all her needs and desires.

God, what if he were wrong? What if it wasn't all Philippe and Marie? What if some of the passion and devotion had been Chandler for Cassy alone? What if it had been Cassy who had offered him the sweet gift of anal sex, even though she didn't want it? He had felt Philippe, eager and anxious urging him to take her. But it had been Chandler who'd refused because he knew Cassy didn't want it. It had been Chandler, afraid of hurting sweet Cassy who'd taken her vagina instead. What if, like Philippe, he'd just hurt and turned away his one true love?

"You want to talk about it now?"

His eyes snapped opened. Jennifer stood in his door, a worried look in her eyes.

He sighed. "Ah Jen, I screwed up big-time."

She closed the door and sat in one of the chairs in front of his desk. "You're having an affair with her."

That was putting it kindly. Having an affair implied he'd romanced her. But he'd never sent her flowers or called her just to say hi. He'd never taken her out to dinner or danced with her. All he'd done was sleep with her and then told her he didn't want a relationship with her. As he'd done so long ago with Katie. God, he was a real bastard.

"Chandler?"

"Nothing as grand as an affair."

"Then what?"

He hesitated, then told her.

"If making love to her made you feel all that, why don't you want a relationship with her?"

"Because...she's so much younger than I am. She's one of my employees..."

"She's black?" she prodded.

He sat up in his chair. "That is not a problem."

"Are you sure? She's not so much younger than you are that it has to be a problem. And with her resume and skills, she could very easily find another job. That just leaves the black part as an obstacle. Chandler, are you sure you're not pulling back because she's black?"

"I told you—"

"I know what you told me, Chandler. But let's face it, not every man has Steve's guts."

He stared at her. "Steve's guts? What's that supposed to mean?"

"It takes guts to follow your heart when everyone around you is telling you not to."

"It's not his heart he's following. It's his penis!" he snapped, stung by yet another implication that he was too cowardly to follow the dictates of his heart.

"Whatever you choose to call it, Chandler, it takes guts to proceed with a relationship when you know everyone who's close to you will disapprove."

"So what are you saying?"

She smiled. "That you should follow his example, Chandler and your desires and your heart. If you want a relationship with Cassy Thompson, pursue one with her. And if your sister-in-law and others disapprove, too damn bad."

He shook his head wearily. "You're jumping to conclusions. I didn't say I wanted a relationship with her. I certainly never said anything about my heart being involved."

"You wouldn't say that if you could see your face. Or come to that, Chandler, hers. Did you see how she looked when she left? Even if your heart's not involved, hers certainly is."

"She's a grown woman," he said angrily. "She can't expect every man who sleeps with her to want anything more than just to sleep with her. And before you give me that disapproving look, no one forced her." Well, at least no one who could be held accountable.

"Oh, Chandler! Don't talk that way. I know you don't mean it. It just underscores my conviction that she's more than just a one-night stand."

"Actually, it was a two weekend stand."

"Oh, Chandler!"

"What do you want me to say, Jen? I wanted to sleep with her and she wanted to sleep with me. So we slept with each other. Period. Now we both know where we stand. It's over."

He held up a hand when she opened her mouth. "I know you mean well, Jen, and I value your opinion, but I do not want to talk about this anymore."

She sighed. "Fine, but if you change your mind—"

"I won't."

"If you do, I'm as near as the phone."

"I know. *Merci.*"

She blinked at him. "What?"

"I said thank you."

"No, actually you said *merci.*"

He shrugged wearily. "Same thing."

"Since when do you speak French, Chandler?"

"I don't speak French, Jen. I know a few words. After all, my great-grandfather was from Louisiana and my grandfather grew up there. It's not a big deal."

She gave him a long look. "I wonder."

"Don't. It didn't mean anything."

Chapter Seven

ဆ

"Hello. It's been awhile. How have you been?"

Chandler stared. The last person he expected to find on his doorstep was Jane. No, actually Cassy was the last one he expected to seek him out. Cassy, at least would be welcome. Which was probably why he'd rescued the Ebony Venus from the trash can before trash day. And not for Serge's sake either. Although he had gladly turned it over to him.

"Jane! This is a surprise."

"A not unpleasant one I hope. Can I come in?"

He hesitated, then shrugged, stepping away from the door. "Of course. What brings you here?"

She came into his foyer and opened the white, car length jacket she wore to reveal her naked body. "You—or more directly your dick. That last time we had sex was wonderful. I can't stop thinking about it. If you don't want a real relationship, fine. Just let me feel that lovely dick of yours pounding my pussy again."

He felt his cock stir as he looked at her firm petite body. His gaze lingered on her mound. To his surprise, she had allowed her pubic hair to grow. One of the many things he'd liked about Cassy was her bushy mound. He loved the experience of working his cock through the hair covering a woman's vagina to discover the delights within, especially when that woman was sweet, sexy, passionate Cassy.

He wanted sex, badly. His cock ached to slide into a warm, welcoming woman. But he wanted that woman to possess a moist, heated body that hugged and massaged his pumping cock like a vise while driving him to one incredible climax after another.

"Well? I need your dick, Chandler. In me. Now."

His licked his lips and spread his hands helplessly. "Jane, I'm flattered. I really am."

"It took a lot for me to come here, Chandler. Please. Stop talking and drop your pants. I just want your dick."

"I'm sorry, but—"

"You're sorry? You mean you're not going to..." Her face flushed. She snatched her jacket from the floor and put it back on. "What are you sorry about, Chandler?"

"Jane, I don't want to hurt you anymore, but—"

She blanched. "You mean you don't even want sex with me now? Is that what you're telling me, Chandler?"

"I'm sorry," he said again.

"Is there someone else sharing your bed?"

"No."

"Then what's the problem?"

His temper began to rise. Why the hell wouldn't she allow him to be tactful? "There is no problem. I'm just not interested in resuming a sexual relationship with you. I'm sorry to be blunt, but..."

"Oh, to hell with you, Chandler Raven!" As she left, she slammed the door so hard that for a moment, he thought the stained glass panels on either side of the door would shatter.

This seemed to be his month for breaking hearts. Way to go, Chandler. Real smooth.

* * * * *

"Of course you know what this means, don't you?"

The cool, impersonal tone sent a chill through Chandler and enraged him.

"You bastard! You stay the hell away from her!" He snatched up the baseball on his desk, spun around and hurled it across the room straight into the face of the man who lounged against his office door. In college, his fastball had been clocked at ninety miles an hour. He'd lost a bit of his speed, but he could still hurl a baseball much faster than a man could dodge it.

Lucky for his intended target, he wasn't completely human. "Why? If you don't want her, what's it to you?"

Serge didn't even bother to duck. He simply reached up a hand and caught the ball within an inch of his face. Grinning, he tossed it back across the room with much less force.

Chandler caught it and took several deep breaths before throwing himself into the chair behind his desk. "You stay the hell away from her, Serge!"

"You know, Chan, I begin to despair of you. You meet a beautiful woman who loves to have you fuck her as much as you like to fuck her. And what do you do? You send her packing because you think it might not be you lusting after her. Trust me, Chan. It's you. You threw that ball faster than you ever have before. Its speed was propelled both by your jealous rage and the lingering vamp blood running through your veins. But I think you should know that if you're finished with the sexy Cassy, I intend to get some of that sweet smelling pussy of hers for myself."

He shot to his feet and crossed the room. He stared into Serge's eyes, gray eyes to gray eyes. "I suggest you take your greedy ass back to Boston while you're still in one piece, Serge. I swear that if you hurt her…"

"What's with this hurt? I have no intentions of hurting her."

"If you touch her…"

Serge arched a brow, an amused smile on his face. "You'll what?"

"I will kick your ass all the way back to Boston," he threatened.

Serge's smile vanished. "You mean that."

"Damn straight I do."

"You mean you'll try," Serge said coolly. "Don't let that vamp blood go to your head, Chan. You don't have enough of it to take me on."

"Don't you fuck with me, Serge!" he snapped. "I am not afraid of your greedy ass. For God's sake, how much pussy do you want?"

"As much as I can get," he said suddenly, relaxing his body. "But if you want to control who she sees, you'd better get your sorry ass back in her life ASAP." Serge gave him a light shove. "Now get out of my face before I kick your ass. I'll give you a few weeks to get your act together, for friendship's sake. After that, all bets are off." He glanced at his watch. "I'm going back to Boston. I'll give you five or six weeks, Chan. Get your ass in gear before then."

Long after Serge had gone, Chandler sat in his home office, fighting against his growing rage. One of these days, he really was going to kick Serge's ass. He approached him as a friend, telling him of his breakup with Cassy, and right away he wanted to move in and fuck her.

Damn him. But for all his faults, he knew Serge wouldn't attempt to seduce Cassy before the time he'd specified. That was little consolation since he'd never seen Serge fail to score with any woman he set his sights on.

* * * * *

"Forget the creep and move on."

Cassy put her glass of wine down untouched. Derri sat across from her in the booth of the restaurant where they'd met for dinner. Forgetting Chandler was easier said than done. She felt as if she'd been branded by the taste of his lips, the feel of his cock buried deep inside her. She missed the sound of his voice, whispering to her in French, *Je t'aime*...I love you. But of course he didn't love her. That was the problem. She was in love alone. Worse, she was afraid, that like her poor great-grandmother, she was in love for life alone.

"Cassy, you didn't forget the game plan, did you? I mean you haven't fallen for the creep, have you?"

She shrugged. "Derri, he's not a creep. It's not as if he mislead me. He didn't even seduce me. I came on to him and he finally responded. Now he's had enough. How can I blame him?"

"I can blame him! He made sure he was saturated before he decided he'd had enough, didn't he? The jerk. And what do you mean by falling for him anyway? Frank wouldn't have treated you so shabbily."

She sighed. "And I guess the implication being Chandler treated me badly because I'm black?" But remembering his tenderness, she couldn't believe that. He just wasn't in love with her.

Derri eyes widened and she shook her head. "That's not exactly what I meant."

"Then what did you mean?"

She shook her head. "Cass, I honestly don't know. This is really not a good time for me."

"Why won't you talk to me about your…issues?"

"I will…as soon as I can get some kind of handle on them. In the meantime, I'm more worried about you and this jerk you've fallen for."

"Derri, he's not a bad guy. I went into this with my eyes open. I can't blame him just because I feel more than he does."

"Well, what are you going to do?"

She sighed. "What can I do?"

"You can show the creep that he's not the only fish in the sea."

"You mean make him jealous?"

"No! Later for him. Cass, you have got to get him out of your system. Get yourself another man and another job."

"I'll get another man, but not another job. I like the one I have," she said stubbornly. "You can't stay there, Cass. He can make things very difficult for you there."

She shook her head. "He won't."

"How do you know that?"

"I don't know how I know. I just do." She couldn't very well explain that when they made love and she shared memories with the other couple, she knew things not only about Philippe, but things about Chandler too. Unless she told Derri about the talisman.

"Derri, there's something I need to tell you. Something I've never told anyone else."

Derri tilted her head to one side. "What is it? What's wrong, Cass?"

She couldn't very well expect Derri to confide in her, if she held back secrets of her own. "I'm not sure. This is going to sound a little crazy, so hear me out before you ask questions or threaten to call the men with the white jacket."

"I'm listening."

She sighed and told Derri everything. "So you see why everything is such a mess? When I thought Chandler was falling in love with me, it was really Philippe in love with his Marie."

Derri shook her head, looking dazed. "Cass, I'm not sure I can buy into this talisman…nonsense."

"It's not nonsense, Dare."

"You really think that when you and your knucklehead boss were in the sack, two long dead lovers were there with you?"

"I know they were, Derri. Neither Chandler nor I speak or understand French. But when we make love, we both speak and understand it."

"Why haven't you ever told me about the…this talisman?"

"Because it's embarrassing. And would you have believed me?"

"No. I'm still not sure I believe you. This sound like something out of a voodoo movie."

"It's real, Derri. I wished I'd never taken it."

"Would that have been better than never having met him?"

"No," she admitted. Her heart ached and she was miserable, but somehow she couldn't regret having met and fallen in love with Chandler.

"Oh shoot, you are in love with the knucklehead."

* * * * *

It was hard to go to work the next morning. But Cassy managed it because she was sure Chandler would make things as easy for her as possible by making himself scarce and he did. She didn't see him for the next two weeks. During the day, she didn't allow her thoughts to dwell on him, but at night, when she lay alone in bed listening to the soft, mournful sobs coming from her undies drawer, she knew history was repeating itself. Like Marie, she would no doubt go on to marry another man, but she would always love Chandler Raven, just as Marie had loved her Philippe.

"Are you all right, Cassy?" Deb, a programmer she worked most closely with asked her at the end of the second week.

She nodded. "Yeah. I'm just getting over a cold."

Deb looked skeptical and she wondered if everyone in the place knew she'd been foolish enough to sleep with the boss, who now wanted nothing to do with her.

"What to grab a bite after work?"

"Thanks, but I think I'll go home, take a long bath and hit the sack. But ask me again sometime?"

"Sure. Ah, if you need to talk…"

She forced a smile. "Thank you, Deb. I really appreciate that."

* * * * *

Chandler groaned, rolled over and looked at his bedside clock. Almost one a.m. He was bone weary, but thoughts of Cassy kept him awake. Several weeks had passed since he'd seen her, but his desire for her had only increased. He wanted her. He needed her. Of course standing at his office window watching her leave and arrive for work nearly every day didn't help.

He turned his head and looked at the spot on his nightstand where the Ebony Venus had sat. God, he missed it. The last time he'd seen the statuette, its features had no longer mirrored Cassy's. But he still wanted her — more now than ever before.

He closed his eyes and a picture of Cassy's beautiful face danced in his mind. What surprised him most was that when he watched her, he didn't always think in terms of sleeping with her. He found himself regretting that he'd never romanced her, never done any of the things that made a woman fall in love with a man.

Now lying on his back, he longed to have her in his arms. Granted he wanted to make love to her, but he also longed to just hold her. He wanted to caress her, kiss her and tell her how sorry he was that he'd hurt her. Make her feel needed and wanted, loved. Loved. Cassy, *je t'aime, ma chère*.

Jennifer was right. He was a coward. The last two months of avoiding Cassy had taught him that his interest in her was not strictly sexual nor was it bound so firmly in what Philippe had felt for his Marie. He did want to pursue a relationship with her that included romancing her and having her fall in love with him. Him, not Philippe. But unlike Steve, who was still seeing his Tia, despite Ellen's threat to toss him out of the house if he didn't give her up, he didn't have the balls to say to hell with everyone and openly romance Cassy. Served him right if Serge came back and booted him out of the picture. No. There was no way he was going to allow Serge to add her to his long list of women.

He felt himself hardening as he thought of her. She was so sweet. So warm. So giving. So willing to show him how much she wanted him. He groaned and slipping a hand into the slit in his briefs, he cupped his cock.

He closed his eyes and imagined the hand massaging his shaft and balls was feminine, soft, slender, golden brown. He kept up the movements of his hands on his cock and balls until he felt the pressure building inside him. When his climax hit him, he groaned, called out Cassy's name and collapsed onto his stomach. "Oh, Cassy! I miss you. I need you."

He buried his face in his pillow. Somehow, he had to do what Philippe had never done. He had to make things right with Cassy. *And with Marie.* He suddenly understood why he and Cassy had been drawn together and how they could be free of Philippe and Marie, free to live their lives the way they chose. Now if only he had the balls to pull it off. *You must find the strength, Chandler, for both our sakes.*

He nodded. "I know. I know and I promise I'll do my best to make it right for both of us, Philippe."

For the first time in weeks, he fell asleep and slept all night.

* * * * *

Slipping on her bathrobe, Cassy lifted the phone on her bedside table to her ear. "Yes?"

"Delivery for Ms. Thompson," a male voice announced.

She sank down on the side of the bed. Who would be sending her anything at seven in the morning? "I'm not expecting anything. Are you sure you have the right person?"

"Yes, ma'am. They're flowers are for a Ms. Cassy Thompson, apartment 1-B."

"Oh." She smiled. Derri must be trying to cheer her up. "Thank you," she said and released the lobby doorlock. She was waiting at her apartment door with a tip when the deliveryman rang her bell. She accepted the flowers, an elaborate mixed bouquet, offered a tip and closed the door.

She took the flowers back to her bedroom and sat them on her night table while she dressed. Smiling at Derri's thoughtfulness, she picked up her briefcase and left the apartment.

She arrived at work in a good mood. She was going to have to do something nice for Derri to make up for the flowers.

She called Derri during her morning break. "Derri, you shouldn't have."

"Shouldn't have what?"

"Sent the flowers. They must have cost a fortune. Being a big-time defense attorney must pay big-time dividends."

"It has it rewards, but what flowers? Cass, what are you talking about?"

She blinked in surprise. "The flowers. I got them before I left for work. They're beautiful, but you shouldn't have."

"Not to worry, I didn't. I have no idea what you're talking about."

"Then who sent them?"

"Beats me. Didn't you look at the card?"

"No. I was running a little late and I just assumed you'd sent them."

"Well, I didn't. But you know I ran into Frank last week. Maybe he sent them. He'd still like to get with you. Are you going to cooperate this time?"

She shook her head. "He's a nice guy, but I'm not ready to...I'm still feeling too raw to start seeing anyone else yet."

Derri sighed. "Oh Cass, are you still hankering for old knucklehead?"

She shrugged. "I guess I am, but don't worry. I'll be all right. In a month or two, I'll be ready to meet other men. I just need a little time."

"It's already been over two months."

"I know."

"Well, you holler if you need a shoulder to cry on."

She shook her head. She wasn't about to waste another tear on Chandler Raven. "I won't be crying over him anymore."

"Now that's what I'm talking about!" She could imagine Derri pumping her fist in the air. "Listen, I'm due in back in court in twenty minutes. I have to go, but we'll talk later."

"Okay. Later."

* * * * *

Chandler sat at his desk reading the monthly stats for what must have been the fifth time. As before, he reached the end of the reports without having absorbed any of the information. Swearing softly, he pushed the sheets away and went to look out the window behind his desk.

When he wasn't going through the motions of working, he jogged, played racquetball, worked out at the gym, but nothing seemed to relieve the tension building up inside him. His temper was almost completely out of control and he felt like he was about to explode.

He blew out a deep breath. What he wanted, what he needed was to make his peace with Cassy. He knew that his relationship with Ellen had already changed and would continue to change if he pursued a relationship with Cassy. Which meant that his relationship with Julie would probably change. He was uncertain how his brothers would react, but he no longer cared what anyone thought.

Of course there was the question of rather or not Cassy would even be interested in a relationship with him now. He hadn't given a very good account of himself the first time. Why would she risk being hurt by him a second time? The thought that she might not, sent a shudder through him. He might end up like Philippe, always longing for the one woman he'd been too cowardly to stand by.

There was only one way to find out how she felt about him. He turned and reached for the phone on his desk. It rang before he touched the receiver. He picked it up. "Yes?"

"Chandler, Steve has just arrived. He wants to see you."

The last time Steve had come to the office, it had been to tell him he'd been suspended from high school for fighting. This then would not be a social visit. He slipped into his chair. "Send him in."

Steve, who was usually clean-shaven, looked as if he hadn't shaved in a few days. His hair, short and spiked, appeared not to have been combed.

"Sit down and tell me what's wrong, Steve."

"Nothing's wrong, Uncle Chandler. I just wanted to ask you if I could store some things in your garage for a while."

"What kind of things?"

Steve shrugged. "My stereo, computer, television and VCR. Some clothes."

He leaned back in his chair, sighing. "Your mom put you out?"

He nodded. "Yeah."

"She caught you with Tia again?"

"No. I admit I was out of line letting her catch me with Tia. So we've been very careful lately. Tia hasn't even been over our house for a couple of weeks."

"You're not seeing her anymore?"

Steve's eyes widened. "Of course I'm seeing her. We've just been very discreet."

Chandler bit back the urge to say his discretion had come a little late. "So what happened?"

"I don't know. She just came home yesterday and insisted I agree to stop seeing Tia."

"And you said?"

"No! And she said I should plan on getting out of her house by the end of the month."

He looked in Steve's eyes and saw the anger, pain and defiance. "Steve, don't you think you should at least consider not seeing Tia again?"

"No! No! Why should I when we care about each other? I know Mom thinks Tia's a tramp, but she's not. She's just my woman and I'm her man. Mom doesn't like that? Too bad. No one is coming between me and Tia. Not her parents and not Mom. Uncle Chandler, we're in love."

"So what are you going to do?"

He shrugged. "Instead of going back to school full-time in January like I'd planned, I'll go part-time and get a full-time job. That way I can get an apartment where Tia will be welcome."

"Are you telling me you're not in school now, Steve?" he asked, surprised. "The semester started last month."

"I know, but I knew Mom would probably put me out, so I had to keep working so I could save enough money for an apartment when she did."

He was furious with Ellen. Jace would not have approved of Ellen misusing the college fund he had set up for Steven and Julie as a lever against Steve.

He was also proud because there no doubting Steve's resolve. He must really care for his Tia if he were willing to give up so much for her. While he applauded Steven's determination, he hated to think of all the extra grief giving up school full-time would bring him.

"Steve, are you sure you want to do that? Working full-time and going to school at night, isn't easy."

"I know that, but I have no choice, Uncle Chandler. I won't stop seeing Tia."

"Why not?"

"Because I love her!"

"Steve, you're nineteen and she's eighteen."

"Does that mean we can't be in love?"

"No. Of course not." He sighed. "Sorry, that was an asinine remark. Okay. But come January, you get your butt back in school full-time. You can move in with me and I'll cover your tuition."

Steve gave him a wary look. "Strings attached?"

"Absolutely. You have to keep up your grades."

"And? What about Tia? Will she be welcome?"

"Yes. All I ask is that you be discreet. I have no more desire to walk in on you and Tia making love than did your mom. Other than that, she's welcome."

Steve's shoulders slumped and he put a hand over his face. "Thanks, Uncle Chandler."

He got up and put a hand on Steve's shoulder. "Of course your mother is going to be furious with us both when she finds out."

Steve looked up at him. "But you won't change your mind?"

"No. Actually, I want to tell you how proud of you I am."

"For what?"

"For having the courage of your convictions and for being willing to put your feelings for Tia out in the open."

Steve shrugged. "What else can I do? At first I thought it was lust, but it's not. I love her, Uncle Chandler. I hate to disappoint Mom, but she just doesn't understand how I feel about Tia. But you understand. Don't you?"

The intensity of the question and Steven's gaze convinced him that his nephew knew of his own aborted relationship with Cassy. He returned to his seat. "I don't know."

"You don't? Mom said you were seeing a black woman."

"I was, for a while."

"What happened?"

He grimaced. "I wasn't as brave as you. The idea of being involved in a romance across racial lines was a bit unnerving." Then there had been the added complication of not being sure how much of what he felt were his feelings and how much were Philippe's.

"You're not seeing her now?"

"No."

"Are you all right with that?"

He shook his head. He'd been a bigger fool than poor Philippe. "No."

"So why don't you do something about it?"

"It's not that easy. There are obstacles."

"What's so hard? If you like her and she likes you, isn't that all that matters?"

But the big question was, did Cassy still like him? "I don't know that she feels the same way anymore. I didn't behave nearly as well as you have with your Tia."

"I couldn't behave any other way, Uncle Chandler. I love her. What else could I do but stick by her no matter what?"

Which is what Philippe should have done. What he should have done. It was too late for Philippe. Not, God willing, too late for him.

Chapter Eight

ഏ

When Cassy arrived home that night, she found Frank waiting in the lobby with a spray of red roses and a big smile. "Cassy, long time no see."

She smiled and accepted the roses. "Frank. This is a surprise."

"A nice one?"

"Yes. Of course. Are these for me? How sweet. Thanks."

"I know I should have called, but I really wanted to see you tonight. Will you have dinner with me?"

"Frank, I..." she stopped, gave herself a mental shake and smiled at him. "I'd love to, but I need you to understand that there's been another man in my life since we first met and I still have strong feelings for him."

"You mean you're in love with him?"

"Something like that."

"And he's not in love with you?"

She forced a smile. "Bam! Bam! You hit the nail right on its big ugly head."

"So you need a shoulder to cry on?"

"Big-time."

He sighed. "Damn. Oh well. What the hell. If it's meant to be, it'll be. No strings and no expectations but friendship, Cassy. At least for now."

"Good. Then would you like to come in and wait while I change?"

"Sure. Thanks."

They discussed the upcoming Jill Scott concert through her open bedroom door as she changed. "She puts on a great show."

"I know," he said. "Listen, if I can get tickets, would you like to go?"

"Ah…yes. That would be great, but I'd feel better if we went Dutch."

"That's not necessary."

"I know, but humor me."

"Okay. Dutch it is."

They went to a jazz club where they slow danced together after dinner. He held her close and she could feel his erection against her. When she turned her head, he kissed her. She closed her eyes and remembered another pair of lips brushing hers. Another pair of arms holding her close. Another shaft hardening against her.

But that was over and she needed to move on. And Frank could help her do that. Back at their table, he touched her knee before sliding his hand up her leg to her thigh. "I think it's time I took you home."

Her heart thudded. She knew what he was asking. She knew what Derri would say she should do. Maybe Derri was right. Maybe she should sleep with him. But how could she when every part of her body and heart ached for Chandler?

"That sounds very tempting, Frank."

His palm on her thigh stilled. "But?"

"But I'm a long way from being ready to sleep with another man."

"Damn!" He withdrew his hand and sat back in his chair. "I was afraid you'd say that. Okay. But I'll keep trying. Okay?"

She nodded. "Okay."

At her apartment door, he pressed a long, passionate kiss against her mouth. Despite her feelings for Chandler, she felt a rush of heat. The man knew how to kiss a woman. She felt warm and tingly when he lifted his head.

"I thought we were going to take it easy and slow...friendly like."

He widened his eyes. "That's what we're doing. That was a friendly kiss."

"Oh. And the hand on my leg at the club?"

"More signs of friendship."

"Oh."

He grinned and kissed her cheek. "I'll call you."

She nodded. "Oh, and thanks for the flowers."

He smiled at her. "I'm glad you like them, but you've already thanked me earlier."

"No. I mean for the ones you sent this morning. Having flowers delivered before work, was a great way to start the morning."

His smiled vanished. "It sounds like it. Wish I'd thought of it."

"You mean you didn't send them?"

"No."

"Oh. Well." She smiled. "Thanks for the roses." She stretched up to kiss his cheek. "Good night."

"Good night."

Without stopping to turn on the living room lights, she headed straight for her bedroom. With heart thumping, she eagerly plucked the small white envelope from the midst of the flowers and opened it. She swore slowly under her breath. The card was blank.

Who would send her flowers anonymously? For a moment, she toyed with the idea that they might be from Chandler. But that was crazy. He hadn't spoken to her in weeks. And after their last meeting, he wasn't likely to be sending her flowers.

The next morning another, more elaborate bouquet of flowers arrived. The accompanying card was blank. Annoyed, she tossed both bouquets into the trash on her way to shower, only to rescue them as she emerged from the bathroom.

The next morning a huge box of expensive chocolates and red balloons arrived with another blank card.

"Wow! Who's in love with you?" Derri asked, that night as they tried the chocolates after dinner.

"I wish I knew," she said.

"Hey these are exquisite." Derri closed her eyes and savored the small morsel. "And you know they cost a small fortune. Flowers. More flowers. Candy and balloons? You're doing something for some guy's libido."

"Well, I wish he's either stop sending this junk or sign the darn card already."

Derri stared at her. "What gives?"

"Nothing. It's just a little…weird to get stuff anonymously."

A shadow passed over Derri's face. About to question her, Cassy decided against it. Derri would tell her when the time was right. "Some women might fine anonymity…romantic."

"Yeah? Well, this one doesn't."

Derri shrugged and seemed to shake off whatever was bothering her, at least momentarily. She grinned, the dark eyes sparking in her pretty face. "I'll bet you would if you thought they were from your esteemed boss."

She started to shake her head. But what the hell. It was true. "Well, you might as well know…I have a thing for him."

"No kidding?" Derri rolled her eyes. "Thanks for the newsflash. I mean I'd never have known if you hadn't told me."

She laughed. "Okay, I guess it's pretty obvious."

"Yepper. So what are you going to do about it?"

"What can I do about it?"

"You can make him change his mind. You did it once you can do it again."

"That was before we slept together."

"Even better. Now he knows what he's missing."

She laughed, shaking her head. "Besides, I'm not so sure I did do it. I mean how do I know it was ever just me and not the damned talisman?"

Derri gave her an unblinking stare.

"Okay, I know you think I'm a little nuts."

Derri grinned and held her thumb and forefinger half an inch a part. "Maybe just a little. Let's face it, girl, that talisman of yours hasn't moved a muscle and I've looked in the dang blasted box at least ten times."

She nodded. "I know. I don't understand it. But I swear, Derri, they used to screw all the time."

"In the behind?"

"Yes. Sometimes he'd be going at her so hot and heavy, their moans would wake me up out of a sound sleep. A couple of times when I touched his butt, his cock came out of her and he came on my fingers."

"He came on your fingers? Ah huh."

She cast her eyes skyward. "Okay. I know you don't believe me and I don't blame you. I know it sounds wacky."

"Oh, big-time wacky."

She sighed. "What do you think I should do about Chandler?"

"That's easy. Ask the knucklehead out and seduce him."

"He's not interested."

"Ask him out and make him tell you that."

"And when he does?"

"*If* he does, you'll know it's time to move on. New day, new job, new man."

"That won't be so easy."

"It's plenty easy, Cass. Repeat after me — new day, new job, new man."

"New day, new job, new man."

Derri squeezed her hand. "And I'll be here every step of the way."

She nodded. "I'm going to need you. But I wish you'd let me be there for you."

"I will, Cass. I just need time to straighten it out in my mind. Bear with me."

* * * * *

"How dare you try to come between me and my son?"

Chandler stood in his office, his back to the window, his hands clenched into fists at his side. It really wouldn't do to give into the urge to tell Ellen to shut the hell up and get out of his office and his face. Not if he wanted to continue to see Julie.

"He needed a place to stay." He kept his voice level as he spoke. "Do you know he's not in school?"

Ellen looked shaken. "Not in school? What do you mean? Of course he's in school."

"No, Ellen, he is not. Instead of going back last month when the semester started he continued to work full-time with plans to go back part-time in January."

"And I suppose you're going to tell me that's my fault."

"Jace did leave sufficient money for his education and last time I looked, it wasn't tied to who he chose to date either. If I hadn't offered him a place to stay, he might never have gone back to school. And he would still be with her."

"He was bluffing. He wasn't going to continue to work full-time just so he could fuck her when he wants."

The urge to shout grew stronger. He swallowed it and sank into his chair. "Ellen, whether you like it or not, he's in love with her."

"It's not love, it's lust! And it'll run its course once he sees how hard it is on his own. Or at least he would have if you hadn't interfered."

"Whatever you chose to call it, he thinks it's love and he's willing to make sacrifices to keep her. Your insistence is only going to drive him away. He is not going to leave her."

"Why not? I hear you left yours after you'd had your fill of her. What's the matter, Chandler? The grass not so green after all?"

"For your information, Ellen, I haven't had nearly enough of her. And the grass is very green indeed."

He watched the surprise register on her face. "Are you saying you're still seeing her?"

"I'm saying it's none of your damned business who I chose to see. If I want to date a black woman, that's exactly what the hell I'll do. I don't need your approval or your permission to date who the hell I like. And what's more, neither does Steve. And I'm not going to listen to any more of your ignorant remarks about Tia or anyone I chose to date."

"So. The gloves are off. You're going to openly see a black woman?"

"I'm going to openly see who the hell I like. What part of that didn't you understand? If you don't like that, well, that's called too damned bad. Do I make myself clear, Ellen?"

"Crystal." She got up and moved across the room. At the door, she turned to face him. "Just don't count on seeing much of Julie."

He felt a knot of frustration in his gut. "If that's the way you want it, Ellen. So be it."

The color left her cheeks. "You mean you'll give up seeing her just so you can fuc—sleep with some black woman?"

"That's not my choice, Ellen. That's yours."

"She loves you!"

"I love her, but I am not going to let you use my feelings for her to dictate who I see."

"What is so almighty wonderful about these women that neither of you will give them up?"

"I told you, whether you like it or not, Steve is in love."

"And you? Are you in love too?"

He wasn't sure he could call what he felt for Cassy love. He just knew he couldn't forget her, didn't want to forget her, had to have her. "She's a very special woman. I've never met anyone who made me feel like she does."

Her face crumpled in disgust. "That's sex, not love, Chandler. There's a difference."

"Ellen, you know, I don't care what you or anyone else calls it. It doesn't matter. This is my life and I'm going to live it the way I want. Now if you're finished insulting me, get the hell out of my office and my life."

To his surprise, tears filled her eyes. "How can you do this Chandler, when you know how much I depend on your help with Steve and Julie?"

The tears softened his response. "Ellen, I love them and I'll always be there for them. And for you too, but on my terms. Who I see has nothing to do with you. Accept that and nothing needs to change between us."

"Do I have a choice?"

"No. No, you don't."

Chapter Nine

✲

"You look like you're in a good mood."

Cassy nodded at Deb and smiled as she checked the board for her assignments. Yet another lovely arrangements of flowers had arrived that morning—roses this time. And although the accompanying card was blank, she was beginning to find the thought of a secret admirer kind of romantic.

Trying to figure out who was admiring her from afar took a lot of her spare time. That was a good thing because it decreased the time she had to think about Chandler.

"I am in a very good mood."

"Good because Jennifer Johnson just called and you're wanted in the executive office pronto."

Her first irrational thought was one of delight, he finally wanted to see her again. Then reality set in. Whatever he wanted, it wasn't that.

She shrugged. "Okay. See you later."

Jennifer Johnson smiled when she presented herself. "He's expecting you. Go right in."

"Ah, thanks." She bit her lip. "You wouldn't happen to know what he wants with me, would you?"

Her smile was kind, but she shook her head firmly. "Go through and ask him."

"No one's complained about my work. Have they?"

"Not that I know of. I really don't think you have anything to worry about."

She nodded, squared her shoulders and went in.

He stood at the window. He turned and looked at her. Their eyes met and she remembered the first time she'd seen him, how breathless looking into his eyes had left her. It had that effect now.

She swallowed several times. "You wanted to see me, sir?"

He smiled suddenly. "Yes. Yes, I did…I do…want to see you."

She leaned against the closed door. "What about?"

He ran his hands through his hair. "About seeing you."

"About what?"

He blew out a breath. "Seeing you. Cassy, I'm sorry. I was such a fool. And I treated you badly. Can you forgive me?"

"Forgive you?" She shrugged. "Yes. I suppose I can."

"You can? You can! You forgive me?"

She nodded. "Yes."

He leaned his head back against the window, his eyes closing. "Oh, thank God! I wasn't sure you'd be willing to give me another chance after all this time."

A stab of excitement danced through her. "You mean…are you saying you want to see me again?"

"Yes!" He looked at her, an anxious look in his eyes. "Didn't I make that clear? But not like before. This time it'll be different. I'm not talking just sex. I'm talking a real relationship with romance."

"Romance?"

"Yes. You know with flowers and candy and dinner out…boring trips to the theater and whatever else you want. Whatever it takes. I'm sorry I didn't behave better before."

"Flowers and candy?"

"Yes. You do like them, don't you?"

"Yes."

"Good." He looked relieved. "I was hoping you did."

"You were? Oh, my God! It was you! You're the one who's been sending the flowers and candy and balloons and perfume!"

He nodded. "Yes."

"Why didn't you sign your name?"

"I wasn't sure how you felt. I thought if...I thought they might help soften you up. Did they?"

She thought of the long lonely weeks spent wanting him. Although he must have known how she felt, he'd done nothing to relieve her pain. Now he wanted to be relieved of his? As if he hadn't crushed her and tossed her away? Just as Philippe had crushed and deserted Marie.

"You know what, Chandler? You can take your flowers, your candy, and your romance, and go to hell! I wouldn't see you if you were the last man in the world!"

She had the satisfaction of seeing the dismay on his face before she stalked out of his office. She made it as far as the front exit before the reality of what she'd just done set in. After months of waiting for him to realize that they could be good together, she'd just tossed his overture back in his face. And told him to go to hell to boot.

It was a long frustrating day for Cassy. Every job took twice as long and at the end of the day, she had two calls pending. She and Derri met for a drink at their favorite café after work.

After playing with her drink for a few minutes, she told Derri about her conversation with Chandler that morning.

"You beat him down and kicked his sorry butt to the curb! You go, girl!"

She frowned. "Derri! How can you say that after telling me to win him back?"

"I only said that when I thought you couldn't get over him. Now that you have, you can move on."

She sipped her drink. "What if I don't want to move on?"

Derri leaned forward to clutch her free hand resting on the small round table, her lips parting. "Say *what*?"

She took a deep breath. "What if I want a real relationship with him? What if I want to have him romance me? Why would that be so bad?"

Derri gave her hand a squeeze. "Okay, girl. You've lost it. It's gone, girl. You want him? Why did you tell him to go to hell?"

She bit her lip, then giggled. "Oh, I don't know. It felt good at the time. For about five minutes. You should have seen the look on his face. He expected me to just welcome him back with open arms and forget all the grief he gave me. To hell with that plan."

"Okay. You've lost me. So what's the problem?"

"I wish I hadn't done it. What do I do now?"

Derri slowly lowered the lid of one eye. "Seduce him. Tell him you've changed your mind. You're an attractive woman. You're allowed to change your mind."

"What if he tells me to go to hell?"

"After the money he's spent showering you with gifts? I have two words for you—*not likely*. Obviously the man is as hot for you as you are for him." She leered at Cassy. "The two of you must be hot stuff in bed."

Remembering their lovemaking, she grinned. "You have no idea."

Derri lifted the menu and fanned herself in dramatic fashion. "Worse luck!" she exclaimed and they both laughed.

Derri sobered first. "Just one thing, Cass. Don't give it up so easy this time. Make him work hard to earn a spot in your bed. He'll appreciate it more."

She frowned. "Assuming of course, he's still interested."

"Go find out."

* * * * *

Buoyed by her conversation with Derri, Cassy headed home. She came to an abrupt halt when she rounded the corner of her street. Chandler's car was parked in front of her building.

Her heart thumped and she slowly resumed her stride as he got out of the car. They met in front of her building and he extended a bouquet of roses to her.

She looked up at him, her lips parting in surprise. "I didn't expect to see you here."

He nodded, looking weary. "I'm sure you didn't. I didn't expect to be here."

"Then why are you here?"

He extended the roses to her again. "I wanted to see you."

"After what I said?"

He shrugged. "I deserved that."

She accepted the flowers. "Well…what if I tell you I meant it?"

He sighed. "I hope you don't mean that."

"And if I do?"

He ran a hand through his hair. "I'm going to be a very unhappy camper. And I'll have to see what I can do to change your mind. Cassy, I really want another chance." He shook his head. "No. I *need* another chance."

She felt a sense of power as she looked at him. "I'll think about it."

As they were sizing each other up, Frank arrived. He joined them on the pavement, his dark gaze quickly moving over them before meeting Cassy's gaze.

"Everything all right?"

She nodded. "Yes." She clutched the roses against her chest. "This is my boss, Chandler Raven." She looked at Chandler, delighting in the narrowing of his gaze. "This is Frank Wilson. A friend of mine."

The two men shook hands. Chandler turned to look at her. "A friend, Cassy?"

"Who wants to be more," Frank added.

Chandler's lips tightened. "How much more?"

"A lot more, but I'm sure you know that already."

"Really? Well, I think you're going to find that a little difficult."

Frank's left brow rose. "And why is that?"

"Because I was here first and I don't plan to make room for you."

"That's my decision to make, Chandler, not yours," she reminded him.

He looked at her, his gray eyes bleak. "Cassy…"

"Actually, Cassy, I was hoping you'd have dinner with me tonight," Frank said. "I know it's short notice, but—"

"I'd love to have dinner with you." She slipped an arm through Frank's and looked at Chandler. "You'll excuse us?"

"Cassy…" Chandler spread his hands, looking helpless. "Don't do this. Please?"

"You had your chance, Chandler and you blew it. Thanks for the flowers." She looked at Frank. "I'm ready, if we go casual."

"Okay. Casual it is."

Chandler watched Cassy walk away with another man and strode back to his car. He slipped inside and slammed the door angrily. A feeling of despair overwhelmed him. Until he remembered how responsive she'd been when they made love. How miserable she'd looked when he'd told her sleeping with her had been a mistake. All that passion and misery couldn't have just disappeared.

He'd treated her badly and now she was going to make him eat crow and crawl on his hands and knees. She wanted him to eat crow? So be it. It was a small price to pay to win her back.

He thought of the man Cassy had left with and felt a rage like none he'd ever felt before. If he didn't back off, just maybe Chandler would have to take care of him, à la Serge. He shook his head. Okay, Chandler, calm down. You can not go around grabbing your competition by the throat and throttling the life out of them. He took a deep, calming breath. He was really going to have to stop hanging out with a short-tempered vampire.

* * * * *

Cassy and Deb were in the café two days later having lunch when Chandler walked in. She tensed as he stopped by her table. He nodded at Deb before looking at her. "Cassy. How are you?"

"I'm fine…sir."

"How did your date go?"

Rather badly. Frank had pushed to go to bed with her, she had refused, and they had parted in a cool silence. But he didn't need to know that. "Great." She smiled up at him. "We had a great time."

"I'm sorry to hear that."

She treated him to a cool smile. "I thought you might be."

"Are you busy tonight? If not, I wondered if you'd have dinner with me?"

"Dinner with you? Tonight?"

"Yes. Dinner tonight."

She hesitated. She wanted to shout yes, but she should probably play hard to get. "Thanks, but I have other plans."

He swore softly. "I'll call you?"

She shrugged. "If you like."

He sighed and nodded at them both before walking away.

"What was that?"

She took a long sip of her water before looking across the table at Deb. "What was what?"

"Cassy! The boss just asked you out!"

"Oh that." She shrugged and grinned. "I think he likes me."

When they returned to their workstations, there was a vase full of red roses on Cassy's desk. She lifted the card and read it:

Cassy,

Pardonnez-moi. Give me another chance. Please.

Chandler

Deb looked at her. "Who are they from?"

She grinned at Deb. "The boss."

"Wow! Way to go, Cassy!"

Way to go indeed. His need for her had forced him to openly acknowledge his feelings for her. *Pardonnez-moi*, indeed. Oh, she'd forgive him—eventually. After she'd made him suffer a little.

Chapter Ten

ॐ

As soon as Cassy walked into the lobby of her apartment building, her senses were overwhelmed with the fragrance of flowers. She saw why immediately. The desk where the doorman sat was covered with dozens of red roses.

He grinned, shaking his head when he saw her. "These, madam, are for you."

Her lips parted in a silent 'oh', "For me? All of them?"

"Every last one of them."

In her apartment, surrounded by the roses, she took a quick shower, covered the bed with rose petals, put on some soft music and sank naked amongst the roses. She closed her eyes and thought of Chandler.

"God, what a beautiful sight."

Startled, she gasped and sat up. Chandler stood in the doorway of her bedroom, holding a bottle of wine. "How...how did you get in here?"

Smiling, he held up a set of keys. "You gave these to me the last weekend we spent together." His gaze moved slowly down her body to center on her vagina.

She resisted the urge to cover herself. He'd already seen and kissed every part of her body. "You should have given them back."

"I would have, if you'd asked for them." He advanced slowly into the room. He placed the bottle of wine on her nightstand before sitting on the side of the bed. He brushed the back of his hand against her cheek. "Hello."

She needed to order him out of her apartment and take him back into her life and her bed on her terms. But one look into his eyes and she knew she wanted him in her life, in her bed and in her body—immediately. She turned her head and kissed his palm. "Hi."

"I need you, Cassy. Come back to me. Be mine?"

She lay back on the bed, leisurely spreading her legs so that he had a good view of her already heated passage. "Why would I want to be yours, Chandler? You didn't treat me very well before."

She watched in amused delight as he tried to keep his gaze from locking on her vagina. He failed and he took several deep gulping breaths. "I'll make it up to you, sweet. I promise."

"How?"

He reached out a trembling hand to touch her breasts, but she slapped it away and sat up in bed, glaring at him. "Oh, no you don't! You don't get to touch me unless and until I say you do."

He drew back his hand, clenching it into a fist at his side. He brought his gaze to hers. "Cassy, please. Don't do this. Don't torture me. *Reviens*."

"*Reviens*? Come back to you? Don't torture you, Chandler? You mean like you tortured me when I was the needy one? How does it feel, Chandler, to want someone who doesn't want you?"

"I want you! I've wanted you from the moment I set eyes on you! There was never a time since I met you that I haven't wanted and needed you, *chère*."

"*Chère*? Is that you talking, Chandler or Philippe?"

"It's me. It's always been me, *ma chère*."

"Then why was it so easy for you to hurt me?"

He shook his head, closing his eyes briefly. "It wasn't easy and I'm so sorry that I did." Although he didn't touch her, he leaned closer to her. "I need you to try to understand and forgive me. Please."

"Understand what? That you're sorry I'm not white?" She balled a hand into a fist and hit it against the bed. "Just as your great-grandfather was sorry my great-grandmother was Creole?"

"He wasn't sorry she wasn't white, Cassy. He was just sorry he wasn't strong enough to stand by her. He did love her. He never stopped loving her."

"Well his loving her didn't do her much good, Chandler. And neither does your being sorry and asking for forgiveness. I'm proud of who I am and what color I am, Chandler!"

"That is not what I meant!" he snapped. "I want *you* – just as you are. Okay, I'll admit there was a time when I...regretted that you weren't white. But that time is long past, sweet. It isn't your skin color that makes me feel as I do about you."

"And just how is it that you feel about me, Chandler? What is it that you feel? Lust? Desire? Passion?"

He looked directly into her eyes. "I feel all of that," he admitted. "But that's not all I feel. I feel tenderness, warmth, need...and love, Cassy."

"Love?" Her heart thumped in her chest. "Did you say love?"

"Yes. Love." He stroked her cheek. "*Je t'aime*, Cassy."

She swallowed quickly and licked her lips. "You...love me? You're in love with me?"

"Yes." His gaze was tender and he'd spoken without the slightest hesitation. He leaned forward until his lips were just a breath away from hers. "It's taken me awhile to realize that it is love, but that's what it is. I need and want you so much because I'm in love with you, *ma chère*. Love me too?"

Her heart beat so fast she could barely breathe. He loved her! Chandler Raven loved her too! Or did he?

She drew back and stared at him. "How do I know it's Chandler talking to me and not Philippe telling Marie he loves her?"

"He does still love her and he would like one last chance to tell her so. But I promise you, this is me talking."

"But how can we be sure?"

"I'm sure because there's a ritual attached to the Ebony Venus. While I admit that I did...occasionally touch and kiss her, I did not go through the ritual my grandfather told me about."

"What was that?"

"I was supposed to stroke her pussy until I could get my finger in her and eventually my cock. But there was no way I was sticking my cock into a lacquered statuette. What about you?"

She blushed. "I felt the pull, but it was a little too...much."

"Really? What were you supposed to do?"

"I was supposed to touch his behind until he came out of her and then I was supposed to..."

"To what? Cassy, after everything we've shared, how can you be embarrassed to tell me anything?"

"It's just...when he came out of her, I was supposed to put him...in me. And there was no way I was going to do that."

He stroked her hot cheeks. "There you see? Neither of us followed the ritual. What I feel are my feelings. I love you."

Her eyes welled with tears; tears for her and tears for Marie and Philippe who still loved each other after nearly a century of being apart. "Oh, Chandler. I do love you. I think I have from the moment I saw you."

He kissed her damp cheeks. "Don't cry, love. It's all right. As long as you want and love me, everything is all right." He slipped his hands on her shoulders and gently urged her back on the bed, amongst the rose petals.

As she lay with tears streaming down her cheeks, he rose and began to undress. Her heart began a painful thumping when he stood next to the bed, nude.

She stretched out a hand to gently caress the hard, muscled thigh nearest her before closing her fingers around his semi-erect cock. It pulsed warm and vibrant under her touch. She looked up at him. "Chandler, hold me...make love to me...*baise moi, mon amour.*"

He joined her on the bed, pulling her onto her side so that he could lay on his with his big body pressed warm and close against hers. He tipped up her chin and looked down into her eyes. "I'll hold you and I'll make love to you, but I won't fuck you." He brushed his mouth against hers, sending shivers of pleasure and desire through her. "Tonight I want to show you only the tender side of love. Later, when I've romanced you and you understand and fully believe how much I love you just because you're you, we can fuck until we're both senseless. Tonight, *ma chère*, we make love."

Every fiber of her body ached for this man with whom she'd fallen so deeply and utterly in love. "Oh, Chandler."

He urged her on her back and lay on top of her. He began kissing her slowly, softly; nibbling at her lips, stroking his hands down the sides of her body.

Her eyes fluttered closed and she surrendered her body and her senses to him. The tenderness of his kisses, his hands and body brought tears to her eyes.

He kissed them away, all the while whispering to her, "*Je t'aime.* I love you. I love you, sweet. Always."

Emotion choked her ability to talk or to think. But she could and did feel his cock hardening against her, the muscles of her stomach clenched in response. Her pussy pulsed and ached to be filled with his cock.

She thrust up her hips, moaning in a soft, mindless murmur. He responded by slipping his thighs between her legs and rubbing his cock against the outside of her cunt. Then he deliberately rubbed it against her clit.

A shock of pleasure and need shook her body and she gasped, clutching his shoulders. Her whole body burned with a need, a love and a lust that only he could fully satisfy.

Pressing his lips against hers in a warm, tender kiss, he slowly began to push the head of his cock into her channel.

Impatient, she shoved her hips upward. Deepening the kiss so that he could suck on her tongue, he propelled his hips down against her, driving his full length into her. Finally. Finally, he was one with her again. He was hers. And hers alone.

He lingered over their lovemaking, alternating between short, forceful thrusts and slow, languid slides into her vagina. Waves of delight rippled through every part of her body. Feelings, unimaginable and inexplicable cascaded over her, overwhelming her until the world and everything in it exploded in one delicious, incredible burst of joy and bliss.

"Sweet? Are you all right?"

She slowly opened her eyes. Although he lay above her, his cock still inside her, he rested most of his weight on his extended arms. She felt dazed, but completely happy. This wonderful sense of love and oneness was what Marie had spent the rest of her life longing for after Philippe left her. She blinked up at him. "Wow! What was that?"

He grinned and leaned down to kiss her lips gently. "That, my sweet, was love the way it was meant to be between a man and the woman he loves."

She linked her arms around his neck. "Are you sure, Chandler? I mean about us?"

He rolled onto his back, taking her with him so that she now lay on top of him. He threaded his fingers through her hair. "Yes. I want, need and love you. I have to have you."

She sighed and laid her cheek against his damp shoulder. "I'm yours, Chandler. I've been yours for the asking since we met."

He kissed her forehead. "Same here, sweet. I won't ever be foolish enough to risk losing you again, but I think you should know that there are people in my family who might not approve. I have associates and maybe some friends who won't approve and might try to make things harder than need be for us. But—"

She swallowed slowly, feeling joy seep into her heart. He was about to ask her to with him. And although she wanted more of a commitment, the thought of even a partial commitment was acceptable. In time, she was sure he'd want more. But maybe she was jumping to conclusions. Maybe he just meant people wouldn't approve of his openly dating her. "What are you talking about?"

His brows rose. "Marriage."

Her heart thumped and she jerked up to look down at him. "Marriage? Oh my God! Chandler! Are you...are you asking me to marry you?"

He hesitated before nodding slowly. "Yes. I was hoping you'd at least think about it. I mean I know I haven't given a good accounting of myself in the past. And I know we haven't know each other very long, but Cassy, there's a part of me that knows what's between us is good...it's right. I don't expect you to agree to marry me next week, but — "

"Good. Because I have no intentions of marrying you next week." She stroked her fingers down his cheeks. "In a couple of months? Probably. Oh Chandler, I do love you! Of course I'll marry you!" She threw herself on his chest and kissed his lips until she was breathless, then she sat up, reached over and turned on the lights and looked at him.

Lying on what was left of the rose petals, he looked good enough to eat. Her gaze shifted to his semi-erect cock. She licked her lips, wondering what he tasted like. But there would be time for that later. Right now there was something she wanted to do for Marie.

He moved to sit up, but she pushed against his shoulder and he readily subsided back on the bed. "You will? You'll marry me?"

She shrugged. "Well, to tell you the truth, although I love your cock, I'm not that crazy about you as a person. I mean I think you're rather a wimp, like that wimpy great-grandfather of yours, Philippe."

"A wimp?"

"Yes, Chandler, a wimp for letting other people keep us apart when you should have known from our first kiss that we belonged together." She saw his eyes narrow and went on, smiling. "But there's a part of me that's very vocal that finds you and your wimpy ways completely and totally irresistible."

The tension left his body and he smiled suddenly. "Really? And what part of you would that be?"

She took his hand in hers and guided it between her legs. "This part. It's small and totally unreasonable. No matter how much I tell it what a wimp you are, it wants to forgive you for anything and loves and wants you that much more."

His fingers moved in her. She closed her eyes. "Chandler, that feels so...good."

She didn't protest when he urged her onto her back and mounted her, quickly sliding his cock fully into her waiting pussy. "So I'm a wimp, am I?"

"Yes." She slipped her arms around his body to cup his hard, clenching buns in her hands. "But God, I love wimps!" she gasped as he began to move inside her. The movement of his cock along with her love for him, bolstered by the certainly that he loved her, combined to create a time and a place for just the two of them.

At least it would be just the two of them once they laid the memory of Marie and Philippe to rest. She pressed against his shoulders. "Chandler?"

He lifted his head and looked down at her with dark eyes. "Yes?"

"Marie wants to say a final goodbye to her beloved Philippe."

"He wants that too, but you know what he wants."

She nodded. "I know."

"And you're willing to do that for him?"

"Not for him. For her."

He gently withdrew from her body. "Are you sure, *ma chère?*"

She nodded, quickly, before she could change her mind.

He urged her onto her side. She closed her eyes and lay with her body curled into a slightly fetal position. She sighed softly when he began kissing and caressing her bottom. It felt nice. She sucked in a breath when she felt him gently insert one lubed finger into her tight, puckered butthole.

"Are you sure about this, Cassy?"

She nodded and made a conscious effort to relax. Still kissing and fondling her bottom, he inserted a second finger into her. When a third finger joined the other two, she gasped and bit down on her bottom lip. Oh God, she hated this. She couldn't do this.

Just this once, ma petite, a soft voice urged. *Let us be together like this just once more.*

She nodded and let her body go slack and released her control over her mind. Then she was in another time, another place. There was the smell of dank grass under her body and sycamore trees hanging overhead. And her lover, Philippe above her, waiting to love her one last time. "*Je t'aime*, Philippe," Marie whispered and turned onto her stomach, pushing her bare bottom up.

She felt warm, eager lips kiss her behind, then her cheeks were gently parted, a cool, soothing ointment pressed into her bottom. It felt nice and soothing and would ease his passage into her. Then finally, her lover, her Philippe placed his hard cock at her tight hole.

"*Je t'aime,*" he murmured and gently but firmly pushed into her other love hole.

"Hmm." His cock felt warm and hot as he feed it between her cheeks. She moaned and shuddered when she felt the last inch of him slide into her bottom. For a moment they lay on the bank of the river in the quiet night, enjoying their forbidden mating. It was like all the endless, painful years had never been. She was with her beloved Philippe.

Finally, he was inside her, where he belonged. Then she longed to feel him plowing deep inside her. "Fuck me, lover. *Baises moi, mon amour.*"

"*Pardonnez-moi m'amour,*" he whispered. "*Je t'aime.*"

"I forgive you, my Philippe, *mon cher.* For anything. For everything. *Baises moi. Prends mon cul, amour,*" she encouraged, shaking her behind against him. "Fuck me, lover. Fuck my ass, lover."

Gripping her hips and biting into her neck, her Philippe began thrusting his thick, hot cock in and out of her bottom. He moaned and lovingly cupped her aching breasts in his hands as he sank his full length within her tight hole.

Warm, sweet emotions washed over her. She gasped and shuddered, moving her bottom back against him, urging him to push deeper, stroke harder.

He gently rolled them onto their sides and slipped several fingers into her wet cunt as he fucked her firmly in her bottom. He filled her ears and heart with sweet, hot words of love as he filled her stuffed behind and her creaming pussy with his cock and his fingers.

Her bottom quivered and her thighs shook. Her Philippe was the only man whose cock in her butt ever gave her such sweet, spirit healing pleasure. There was nothing more natural or delicious than two people in love, making love and completely surrendering to the dark heat of their unmitigated desire and timeless passion for each other.

It had been so very long and she had missed having his cock buried deep in her ass. Moaning with long dreamed of pleasure, she turned her head.

Her Philippe, the love of her life, kissed her and the stars above their heads exploded behind her closed lids, sending her to paradise. Her pleasure set him off and she knew a sense of exquisite pride as he came in her bottom, filling her with his love juices.

"Oh Philippe, *mon cher, Je t'aime. Je t'aime.* Always."

"*Je t'aime*, my Marie. Forever!"

* * * * *

"Cassy? Sweet? Are you all right?"

Cassy opened her eyes and looked at Chandler, who lay on his side next to her in her semi-dark bedroom. She heard the anxiety for her in his voice. "Damn, Chandler! She must have been crazy to let him do that to her for so long." She pressed her face against his shoulder. "She might have enjoyed having her butt pounded by a jackhammer, but mine feels like it's on fire. Behinds weren't meant to be drilled by a cock as big as yours."

He kissed her cheek and caressed her sore bottom. "I'm sorry, love. I didn't intend to pound in you like that."

"Sure, buddy, tell me anything. I suppose you're going to tell me it was Philippe ravishing my bottom and not you?" she teased.

"Well, you know he was an ass man," he said, laughing. "And you know he wasn't usually so rough. It was just that he knew it was their last chance and he wanted to go out with a bang."

"Well, he did that all right."

"I am sorry, love."

"I thought there for a while you were going to split me open, but she thoroughly enjoyed it. So it's all right, as long as you don't expect to pound my behind on a regular basis."

"I don't expect to pound your behind at all. Philippe was into anal sex, not me." He tipped up her chin and kissed he gently. "Me? I'm a pussy man."

She sagged against him in relief. "Thank God. I know she enjoyed it, but it's definitely not my thing." She paused.

"Chandler, I think they're gone. At least she is. I can't feel her anymore."

He nodded. "He's gone too. They just wanted one more time together."

"Do you think they'll be at peace now?"

"I hope so. She forgave him and that's what he needed more than anything else." He slipped his body behind hers, spoon fashion, and cradled her against him. "Now there's just you and me, *ma chère*."

"Like Marie and Philippe? Always?"

"Almost like, them," he corrected. "They spent miserable lives apart from each other. You and I are going to spend the rest of our lives together."

She sighed and pressed back into his arms. "What shall we do with our talismans?"

He nuzzled her neck. "Philippe and Marie no longer need them to bring them back together forever. We'll give them away so they can work their magic for some other lucky couple or couples. I know just the man. In fact, I've already given mine to him."

"Who?"

"My friend, Serge."

She looked up at him. "Should we do that? I love you, Chandler and I am so happy we met, but should we just give them away and risk their influencing other people?"

He kissed her cheek. "Trust me, love, no one and nothing influences Serge. Besides, Serge's had a thing for black women ever since I've known him. He's already cherishing the Ebony Venus just as Philippe did."

"All right. If you're sure."

"I'm sure. Serge is…different."

"Different how?"

"Just…do you believe in vampires, *ma chère*?"

"Vamp…Chandler! Have you been drinking again?"

He laughed. "Our experiences with the talismans should have taught you not to be so skeptical, *ma chère*. There are such things as vampires. I'll introduce you sometime if you promise not to fall for him."

"Why would I want him or any other man when I have you, Chandler?"

"Right answer," he laughed and kissed her.

"What about my talisman?" she asked when they emerged from the long, sweet kiss.

"Why don't we give that to Serge too? I'm sure he knows someone who's looking for love."

"Whoever gets our charms is going to be in for the thrill of their lives."

He gently fondled her breasts. "So are we, *ma chère*. So are we."

She sighed softly.

"What?" he asked.

"Nothing. Well, I was just thinking that I'll miss my talisman. I've had it for so long."

"Where is it?"

She pointed to her dresser. "There in my undies drawer in a jewelry box. The bottom one."

He kissed her and climbed out of bed. She sat up, turned on the bedside light and watched him search through her drawer. A few moments later he returned to the bed with the box in his hand. He handed it to her. "Say goodbye, sweet."

She sighed again, took a deep breath and opened the box. The tiny couple was in their natural state, golden and lying on their sides with the female's back pressed against the male's front. The male's hand cupped her breasts.

Staring down at them, it seemed to Cassy that the couple's features bore smiles of contentment. She looked up at Chandler, her eyes welling with tears. "Oh, Chandler. I've never seen them look so peaceful. Everything is going to be all right with them now."

He leaned over and kissed her. "Everything is going to be all right with us too, Cassy. So you're all right with giving it to Serge?"

She nodded. "Yes."

He put the talisman back in the drawer and turned to look at her. "Hey, beautiful, how does a quick shower together sound?"

"You take a shower," she said grimacing. "I think I need a long soak."

He leaned over kissed he and lifted her in his arms. "How about we compromise? We'll both take a quick shower, then we'll soak together?"

She rubbed her cheek against his shoulder. "Sounds like a plan."

In the shower, he cleaned up quickly and soaped her up more slowly. Then, after running a tub of warm, soapy water, he lay in the low tub and pulled her down on top of him.

She smiled and turned her face against his shoulder. This was so nice. This was something Marie and Philippe had never been able to enjoy with each other. Knowing that was going to help her enjoy even the simplest pleasure with this handsome man. He held her, lightly caressing her and occasionally kissing her until the water cooled. Then they dried off and he carried her back to bed.

In the bedroom, he changed the bedding.

"Hey, you do housework?" she teased. "Now I know I'm going to marry you!"

He grinned at her. "If you marry me, I'll even do windows."

She laughed and linked her arms around his neck. "Not to worry, handsome. We're sharing everything, including the housework."

They slipped into bed and turned off the lights. She turned toward him. When he took her in his arms and held her close, she closed her eyes and knew that no matter how they had come together, she was with the man she planned to spend the rest of her life with. The idea was heady and exciting. Sometimes, a girl got lucky on her own, sometimes she got a little help. Either way, she'd got her man. She fell asleep in his arms.

BLOODLUST: CONQUERING MIKHEL DUMONT

୫ঌ

Prologue

ဆာ

Erica Kalai stood in front of the full-length mirror on the back of her closet door, staring at her reflection. She had poured herself into one of the skimpiest excuses she'd ever seen for a dress. It was short, she was not. The bodice had been designed to enhance the appearance of a modestly endowed female. Her breasts were large, firm, full, and in no need of external aids. The purpose of the material was to cling to the body of a female with slender curves. Her curves were very generous. If it was one thing James had loved about her, it was her full breasts, rounded behind, and what he had called "woman" hips. He'd loved to hold onto them as they went at each other. Thinking about what she'd lost, she frowned. These days, she didn't miss him as much as she missed the sex. Their love life had been fairly good and during their marriage, she'd developed quite an appetite for cock. Lord, she needed a good fucking.

She shook her head. *Okay, Rica. Don't get ahead of yourself. You'll be competing with a lot of younger females for male attention tonight. You might or might not score.* She considered the dress again. Overall, the dress had been made for a female who was young and daring. This party and her purpose in attending aside, she was neither.

She gave her reflection another longer, more critical look. Okay, maybe she wasn't so young, but tonight, given half a chance, she was going to be very daring. Hopefully, daring enough to get laid — again and again. If it was one thing she really needed it was to spend a few hours in bed with a real live man instead of the tiny little electronic "rabbit" or BOB (battery operated boyfriend, as she privately thought of her favorite sex toy) that had been her man since James had walked out on her.

While it filled some of her physical yearnings, nothing took the place of a real man with a hard shaft.

She shivered at the thought. It had been so long since she'd been plugged, she felt almost dizzy just thinking about the possibilities this dress, combined with a pair of sheer black stockings and three-inch heels would open up for her. She grinned. Of course when it was time to take care of business, she'd be hard-pressed to get out of the dress without busting it at the seams.

"Wow, Rica! You look great."

She jumped and turned to look at her younger sister, Meg, as she came into her bedroom. "Meg! I didn't hear you come in."

Meg grinned, holding up the set of spare keys Erica had given her. "I know. You were too busy admiring yourself." Meg looked her up and down. "Not that I blame you. Rica, you look...?"

"What? Like a tramp? Or as Mom would say, a trollop?"

Meg laughed. "Not that bad. You look good...just...so...uninhibited."

"And that's bad?"

"No! I think it's a good thing to look uninhibited."

Erica pursed her lips. Although Meg was much younger than her, she sometimes seemed so much wiser. "Maybe, but I feel as if I'm stuffed into this dress."

Meg's grin widened. "You look like it too, but it's a pleasing look. Your breasts are on display and so are your legs. Rica, I hope I look like you when I hit your age."

Erica frowned. "Hey, watch it, kid!" she said, pretending to be annoyed. But to the twenty-three-year-old Meg, she must seem almost over the proverbial hill. "Show a little respect for your elders."

Meg tilted her head, considering her. "I only meant you look so...hot."

She hoped she encountered a man who thought she was hot enough to take to bed and cool down. "Thanks…I think."

"Oh, it's definitely a compliment, Rica."

She nodded. "Then that settles it. I'll wear it."

Meg sighed, getting a faraway look in her eyes. "If James could only see you now…"

Erica shook her head. "He wouldn't be impressed. Why should he? He finally has his baby." She said, trying not to sound bitter. Even though she no longer loved him, it still hurt to remember how easily he'd walked away from their marriage and his vows of undying love.

"It's his loss, Rica," Meg said firmly. "I just know you'll meet a man who'll make everything that happened with him seem like a bad dream."

She shrugged. "Well, to be honest, Meg, I'm not really looking for a real relationship. I'm just sort of looking for…" she paused, frowning. How could she put it delicately?

"Love?" Meg suggested.

Actually, sex was more like it, but she nodded. "Yes…but of the casual variety."

Meg arched a brow, a rather surprised look on her pretty face.

She sighed. "I know…put like that it sounds a little sleazy, but Meg, I really need to be with a man, if you know what I mean."

Meg shrugged. "I'm not a nun. Of course I know what you mean and I think you have every right to find happiness wherever you like."

She wasn't exactly looking for happiness…at least not that night, but that was a story for another day. She smiled and held her arms open. "Hey kid, how about a hug?"

They hugged each other briefly before she glanced at her watch and started. "Hey, if I'm going to go partying in Salem, I'd better get a move on."

"Go give 'em hell, Rica."

What she really wanted was to give some hard-dicked man some pussy, but she thought that was better left unsaid. She nodded and quickly moved around her bedroom gathering her tiny evening bag and suitcase. She'd packed on the light side. Although she had a few days off, she hoped to spend most of that time on her back, in bed.

* * * * *

Mikhel Dumont looked at the tall, slender, dark-haired woman staring so insistently at him. "Why the hell should I waste my time driving to Salem to attend some asinine Halloween party, Katie?"

"Because I've seen a very good outcome for you if you do."

He loved and adored his younger sister, but sometimes she was a royal pain in the ass. "Katie, I am not driving to Salem."

"But Mik, it's only a half an hour drive at most and I know you'll have a great time. Go to the party. You won't be sorry."

He rose from the desk in his Boston office and turned to stare out the window. "Katie, we both know that not everything you *see* becomes reality."

She gave an impatient wave of her hand. "I'm not saying it does, but this will, Mik. If you don't go, you'll be sorry."

"I have things to do, Katie. I can't just drop everything and go running off on some wild—"

"It's Halloween, Mik…one of our special nights."

"It might be special for you, Katie, but to me, it's just a silly excuse for human and vampires alike to act like idiots."

She cast her eyes towards the ceiling. "Mik. Go to the party. Enjoy yourself."

Ever since Katie had been a small child, she'd had visions that were sometimes very accurate…sometimes not so accurate. He turned to face her. "What did you see that's made you so gung-ho?"

"Nothing specific, but very strong…"

He shook his head. "I can't go."

"Why not?"

"I half promised to spend the night with Deoctra. Like you, she seems to think Halloween is special."

Katie's blues eyes darkened and she crossed the room to clutch his arm. "You need to go to Salem and to the party tonight, Mikhel. Please. Promise me you'll go."

"What about Deoctra?"

Katie shrugged. "What about her? You don't love her."

Love was such an overrated word. "Love her? No, but—"

"She's waited this long, she can wait a little longer. Will you go? Please?"

He'd rarely seen Katie so insistent, and honestly, he wasn't really looking forward to spending the night, or any time, with Deoctra. Granted she sucked a mean cock, but she did nothing for him emotionally. He couldn't even work up enough interest to take advantage of the ass she was forever offering him. Although she'd made it clear to all in the vampire community that she had considered him hers for many years, he'd never even tried to fuck her. And she didn't seem to mind how many other women he fucked. "Okay. I'll go."

Katie's eyes lit up. "Great. I have something for you."

Her excitement piqued his curiosity. "What is it?"

"Your costume."

"My what?"

"Your costume. You can't go to a Halloween party without a costume. You'll love this one." She crossed the room to retrieve the garment bag she'd left hanging in his walk-in office closet and revealed a dark suit with a red cummerbund and white shirt. He stared at it for a moment and began laughing. "Don't be ridiculous. I am not wearing that getup."

"Mik! You have to go. It'll make everything fall into place."

"It's a Dracula outfit!"

Katie grinned. "Yeah. How appropriate is that? Ironic, huh? You showing up at a Halloween party dressed as Dracula. She won't know what hit her."

"She? She who?"

She smiled, shaking her head. "Oh no. If you want to find out who she is, you'll have to go to the party."

He shrugged. What the hell. He wasn't looking forward to spending the night with Deoctra and he hadn't been to a party in ages. It might be interesting. He nodded slowly. "Okay. That might be a way to kill an hour or two. What can I expect once I get there?"

She gave him an enigmatic smile. "Lots of pussy."

He was always up for lots of pussy, still... "I don't need to dress up like some movie Dracula and drive to Salem for a Halloween party to get pussy. I can get all I want right here in Boston."

"I know, but you'll be glad you went."

He shrugged. "Okay. You win, Katie. I'll go to the party and I'll even wear the suit, but this had better be worth my while."

"It will be, Mik," she promised.

He wasn't sure why, but suddenly he believed her. Maybe he would meet someone there who would make his life more than just an endless search for pussy. Of course that might create a bit of a problem if he did. But he'd worry about that when and if the need arose.

He kissed her cheek, took the ridiculous suit from her, and headed for the door.

"Mik?"

He glanced over his shoulder at her. "What now, Mother?"

She leered at him. "Nothing. I just thought you should know that I reserved a room for you." She mentioned an exclusive Salem hotel. "For a week."

She was sure of herself. "Have you now?" He grinned. "Then I'd better go get your money's worth."

"You do that. You'll have a good ol' time tonight, big brother."

For a moment, his thoughts turned towards Deoctra. He gave an inner shrug. He had an uneasy feeling she wouldn't be pleased, but he'd make it up to her later. He'd leave her a message telling her he'd see her in about a week.

Chapter One

ඔ

Erica somehow resisted the urge to tug at her short, tight, form-hugging dress in an effort to get it to cover more of her body. It was useless. The black dress she wore ended so far above her knees that nearly all her stocking-clad thighs were exposed. There just wasn't enough material to pull down and the dress was cut so low that anyone with half an eye would have an excellent view of her breasts. And at the time she'd bought the dress that had been the idea.

Now at the party, was a fine time to decide that coming as a hooker might not have been such a good idea. She *was* dressed as a hooker and she *was* there. She might as well make the best of it. She *would* make the best of it. After all, it wasn't every day a woman turned 40 and she meant to enjoy both her birthday and her night out.

Still, she hated to think what the teenage girls she taught at an exclusive private school just outside Boston would say if they could see their "respectable" instructor stalking around a renovated loft in spiked heels, blatantly looking as if she were on the prowl for cock. She thought about the condoms tucked in the tiny leather bag hanging off her shoulder and was thankful for the overall dark atmosphere of the interior. Her cheeks burned. She *was* on the prowl for cock.

After the breakup of her five-year marriage, she had spent so much time trying to fix up her friend Nancy that her own love life had suffered—a deliberate refusal to deal with her wariness, she knew, for she hadn't been all that eager to get out and start meeting men again. In fact, if not for her and Nancy's mutual friend Janna, she probably wouldn't even have come tonight. And just maybe coming here had been a complete waste of time.

She glanced around, taking a sip of the spiked apple cider. From what she could see all the men present appeared to be at least ten years her junior. She thought of the old woman she'd encountered in the alley as she arrived and tossed her head disdainfully. *Love would be hers indeed.* Forget love. After two years without a significant other to satisfy her almost constant cravings for sex, she would happily settle for a one-night stand with a man with a nice, stiff dick. It wouldn't even need to be large or thick—just hard. But unless she planned to rob the cradle, she wouldn't likely see any action tonight. Damn it!

Not that she had much to complain about. At least she didn't have to spend part of her Halloween night working like poor Janna. Because of the excessive hours Janna had been putting in lately, all their recent contact had been by phone.

She glanced around. Instead of spotting her pretty red-haired friend, her eyes locked with those of a man across the length of the warehouse. The breath caught in her throat and she found she couldn't look away. He was tall, dark and handsome with a capital H. Moreover, he didn't look quite as young as some of the other men there. Just looking at him made her mouth water and her desire flare. Oh damn, but he was a hunk!

Who was he? Where had he come from? He hadn't stood next to the jack-o'-lanterns just minutes before…

No way she wouldn't have noticed him. Not only was he dressed as her favorite antihero, Count Dracula, but more to the point, he stood there staring first at her exposed breasts and then into her eyes. While she was used to men staring, she'd never looked into a pair of eyes as dark or as compelling as this man's. Nor had she ever seen a man who oozed sex appeal from every pore in his body. Even sharing his gaze from across the room caused a stirring between her legs. Her need for sex increased tenfold.

Abruptly, almost as if he'd read her thoughts, the man casually tossed back the cape he wore and cast a quick look down. Her gaze followed his and she sucked in a breath, her heart suddenly thumping in her chest. Oh lord, help her! There, against the side of his leg, she saw the clear outline of a long, thick cock.

She stared at it, slowly and unthinkingly licking her lips, her cunt beginning to pulse with unbridled hunger. A lonely, sex-starved woman could surely enjoy a long, lustful one-night stand with a man packing that kind of piece.

But what was she thinking? She, who was always warning her students against the dangers of allowing teenage boys to talk them out of their clothes and into bed? She forced her gaze back to his face. He had the most sensual lips she'd ever seen on a man, she *knew* they would be honey sweet. And those eyes, so dark and magnetic. Someone had once said the eyes were the windows to the soul. She felt as if he were trying to drain the soul from her with his gaze alone. What was more, it was working, big-time.

But she was being ridiculous. The spiked cider, the incessant beat of the music, along with the raw sensuality of the handsome stranger dressed as Dracula, all combined to help loosen her grip on reality. Okay, she'd fantasized about meeting a man as forceful and compelling as The Count since she'd first read Dracula. However, she was no longer an impressionable fifteen-year-old. She had no reason to stand staring at a stranger's cock—a young stranger at that. She might be horny, but she still had her pride and her self-respect.

She wrenched her gaze away, looked across the room and then did a double take as she saw Janna walking away from a woman dressed as Xena. Could that be…no. It couldn't be Nancy.

She looked again, and this time her eyes met the woman's. It was Nancy! Even as she smiled in surprised delight and uttered a small, "wow," at the new Nancy, she was aware that the stranger still stared at her from across the room. She could feel his heated gaze on her.

Only he was no longer across the room. She felt a sudden tingling sensation down her neck and in her cunt and turned quickly to find him at her side. She looked up into his eyes. It must be the flickering flame from the jack-o'-lanterns that caused his eyes to glow and pulse with tiny, smoldering embers.

"Hello."

His voice was low and deep and danced along her nerve endings like a sweet, irresistible caress.

"Oh. Hello." Her voice came out in a breathless whisper that embarrassed her.

He smiled, revealing even white teeth, and extended his hand. "Mikhel Dumont."

"Erica Kalai." She placed her hand in his.

His fingers brushed across hers, sending tiny fires of desire dancing through her body. Talk about a magic touch. "It's a pleasure to meet you, Erica."

A feeling of utter delight permeated her as he locked his gaze with hers, then lifted her hand to his mouth and kissed it. Although his lips were gentle, she saw rampant lust blazing in his dark gaze. Of course she could be mistaken. She cast a quick look down at his leg.

She was not mistaken. The evidence of his arousal was still clearly visible. And lord what an arousal.

She glanced up again, blushing as she met his gaze. What would he think of a woman who couldn't keep her eyes off his cock? She might be a closet wanton, but she wasn't terribly bold in real life. So what was she doing there dressed as a hooker staring at the blatantly displayed cock of such a young, handsome hunk?

Feeling flustered, she tugged at her hand. Instead of releasing it, he captured the other one and gently urged her toward him. "Dance with me, Erica."

She hesitated. She didn't want to accept, but he wore an aura of power and authority as elegantly and as effortlessly as he did his costume. How, she thought on a mental sigh, could a woman resist all that in a handsome, well-hung man?

Not only did she readily allow him to draw her into his arms, but she shamelessly pressed her lower body forward until she could feel the beguiling outline of his cock. A ball of heat and desire tightened in her stomach and sent a shock of yearning careening straight down to her toes at the delicious contact.

God, she had to have him.

"That's right." He spoke softly. "Give in to your desires and passions. Press closer."

She did and felt him throbbing against her. Oh lord, she wanted to feel that long, thick cock sliding into her so badly she couldn't think straight. She shivered. *Fuck me, please.*

"The night is young, Erica. This is the night you will get everything you want."

She lifted her head and looked up at him, making no effort to hide her desire for his cock from him. "What? What did you say?"

"You will get everything you want," he repeated.

"Oh God, I hope so," she whispered.

He tightened his arms around her and they moved slowly around the room. They danced, not in time to the rhythm of the music, but rather in time to a primitive tattoo that seemed to envelop and isolate them in a world all their own. A small part of her mind was still aware that many other people surrounded them. But her heart, her desire, her physical need was aware of him only. She'd never met a man who could so easily mesmerize her and cause her to pulse with longing and lust. Who was this man? And how could he make her feel so lusty and uninhibited?

They danced slowly. Their feet barely moved, but their lower bodies brushed and ground against each other in a fashion that was positively indecent and oh-so wickedly delicious. She was being shameful, but she didn't care. As long as he kept his cock in close contact with her body, she didn't care about anything. As they danced, she wondered what her chances were of spending the night or at least a few hours with him.

Granted he looked very young, but she was so needy that she just didn't care. If he were willing to overlook the difference in their ages, she would gladly spend the night with him. Hell, as horny as she felt, she'd even pay for the privilege. She bit her lip, wondering if he would take a check. If not, she'd go to a cash machine and withdraw as much as she could.

He placed a finger under her chin and lifted her face to his. She reluctantly opened her eyes and looked up into his fiery gaze. "It's getting late," he said.

Oh no! He wasn't going to excite her passions and then take some young girl home for the night. "It's barely ten o'clock," she protested, trying to keep her voice from rising with her panic. "Surely you're not leaving already."

"My plans for the rest of the night do not include staying here much longer."

She sighed. Fine. If he wanted to go, fine. She wasn't going to beg. "Then don't let me keep you."

She attempted to draw away from him, but his arms remained tight around her. "You've misunderstood, Erica. I want you to leave with me."

"What? Leave with you? But I can't." Even as she spoke, she knew she was going to go with him. "I-I can't."

He brushed a big hand over her scantily covered ass and a shudder shot through her. "Why not?"

"Why not?" There was something about him that made it difficult for her to do anything but want him. She blinked and gave her head a little shake. This was ridiculous—he'd barely spoken two sentences to her and she was supposed to go off with him? Fantasizing about spending the night with him and actually doing it were two very different things.

"Yes. Why not?"

"Why not? I...don't even know you."

He caressed her cheek with a long finger. His eyes burned with intensity. "That's all the more reason to leave with me...to get to know me," he murmured. He ground his body against hers. "You will leave with me."

Lord, he felt good. How could she possibly deny her sex-starved body the opportunity to experience being fucked by the biggest cock she'd ever felt? Especially when the most fascinating man she'd ever met would wield it?

"You're too young," she hedged, glancing away. "You look about twenty-five."

He pressed his finger against her lips and a tingle ran through her. "Would it make you feel better if I were thirty?"

"That's still about ten years too young. Mikhel, I'm forty. Tonight."

"Tonight?" He smiled and suddenly twirled her around before spinning her back into his arms. "Happy birthday, Erica."

Laughing and feeling breathless despite herself, she looked up into his eyes. "Thank you, but that's about ten years too old to leave with you."

"Is it? Don't I have any say in the matter?"

She shook her head, breathless.

His eyes memorized her face. "No? Well, what if I tell you that I like older women, Erica?"

Oh boy, but she liked the way he spoke her name, letting it roll slowly off his tongue like the last drop of vintage wine he was both eager to consume while at the same time loath to finish. He made her feel like something rare and valuable being savored by a connoisseur. Damn, but it was a heady feeling. But did she dare leave with him?

She bit her lip. "You...you do?"

His smile was slow and warm. "Yes, I do. Come with me and I'll show you just how much I adore older women." He spoke in low tones. "I can promise you won't be sorry. I'll make you happy and satisfy all your needs and most lustful desires."

He bent so close to her that she felt his breath brush against her lips in a gesture that was as erotic as any kiss she'd ever enjoyed. She pressed closer, totally unable to resist him and the powerful sexual magnetism emanating from him. She felt...compelled...almost as if she had no choice but to go with him. And damn if she didn't like the feeling.

"Live a little. Forget caution and convention. Come with me, Erica," he murmured. "Come with me and experience a new and exciting level of pleasure. I will completely satisfy your every desire...over and over again."

She blinked, fighting for control of her senses, then took a deep breath. "I...I can't. I have friends here I haven't seen in weeks."

"What's your point, Erica?"

"My...point?" What was her point? She blinked, struggling to think clearly.

"Yes. Your point. If they're your friends, they'll understand that you have to come with me."

"I can't just leave with you and go off and..."

"And go off and what?"

She swallowed several times and looked directly into his dark, compelling eyes. "And be fucked senseless," she said boldly. For she knew that's exactly what would happen once he had her alone. And that was just fine with her.

"Why not? You came out tonight wanting to be fucked."

She blushed. "How...how could you know that?"

"Never mind how I know. The point is, I do know. And make no mistake, Erica, I fully intend to fuck you senseless...all night long. Just as you desire."

She went damp. "As I...how...how can you know what I desire?"

"Do you deny that's what you want?"

"No," she admitted, moistening her lips. "Is it the way I'm dressed?"

He shook his dark head. "Although I find your dress very provocative, that's not how I know what you want."

Then it was the way she kept pressing against his cock.

"No. That's not it either," he said.

She stared up at him. It was almost as if he'd known what she was thinking. "Then what is it? How do you know?"

"Come with me and you'll find out."

"I…I already told you I can't go with you."

"Why not? It's what we both want." His arm tightened around her waist, drawing her closer. The feel of his cock against her belly drove the last vestige of rational thought from her mind. Why not indeed? Nancy and Janna would understand. "Okay," she heard herself whisper, surrendering to the desire burning out of control in her.

"You won't be sorry," he promised in a soft, deep voice. "This will be a very special night for you…for us both. Delicious, unbelievable delights await us."

She hid a smile. She'd already agreed to go with him, he didn't need to pour it on so thick.

"I intend to fulfill your wildest fantasies, my lovely, lovely, Erica."

She believed him. She knew she was in for a long, deliciously wicked night. Later, when she was back in Boston, she would probably be ashamed and horrified that it had been this easy for a man to hop into bed with her for a one-night stand.

She looked up into the dark, mesmerizing eyes of the man holding her so closely. Forget that nonsense. No way she was going to regret a moment of her time spent with this man. She nodded. "I know."

He smiled, and an absolutely delicious warmth infused her. "I'll make this a very special night for you, Erica. This will be the most memorable birthday of your life."

She loved that he was so damned confident and sure of himself and his abilities as a lover.

He caressed her cheek. "Tonight will be a night neither of us will ever forget."

She tore her gaze away from him. Across the length of the warehouse, she spotted Janna. Her friend looked bored. She couldn't see Nancy among all the people now in the loft. Feeling guilty, she waved at Janna, sending a please-understand look.

"Don't worry about your friends," he said. "They will discover delights of their own. Tonight...this night belongs to you and me. Come with me, my lovely Erica and learn what it means to be fucked by a man who knows how to make love to a woman."

Oh lord, if he kept up that kind of talk, she'd come right on the spot before he could even get her alone and stick his big cock in her.

He laughed and gave her waist a squeeze. "Come with me, my lovely one."

"Oh yes." She nodded eagerly and allowed herself to be led from the party.

Outside in the cool air, he swept her off her feet and into his arms. She felt like a giddy teenager about to surrender her virginity on prom night. Oh damn, what a feeling. She slipped her arms around his neck, rubbing her cheek against his chest.

He carried her to his car with an ease that surprised and delighted her. If he could carry her more than a few feet without getting winded, he would hopefully be able to go on all night long as he'd promised. Hot damn, looked like she'd hit the proverbial jackpot.

Chapter Two

ഓ

Keeping his gaze on the road ahead of him, Mikhel was nevertheless very aware of the woman seated beside him in the dark interior of the car. He was more aware of her than he'd ever been of any other woman. The soft scent of her perfume tickled his nose enticingly. His nostrils flared slightly. The faint, but unmistaken aroma of her arousal inflamed his senses. There was nothing more intoxicating than the scent of an aroused woman eager to have him fuck her. His cock throbbed and swelled with need. The blood pounded through his veins. The hunger for her body and her blood threatened to overwhelm him. The desire to pull the car over on a dark stretch of the road and get a quick taste of her pussy was difficult to resist.

With any other woman he wouldn't even have made the attempt to resist his natural inclinations. When he wanted sex he wanted it now. But he knew this beautiful blonde woman was different...special. He didn't want their first time to be in the backseat of a car where he'd taken countless other women who had meant nothing to him.

Katie had been right. Coming to Salem had been the right move. Erica Kalai was special and their first taste of sex together must be special and memorable for them both. That meant bidding his time for a little while longer.

Still, eager to get her alone and into bed, he even begrudged the time it took to stop at her hotel for a change of clothing for the following day. Not that she'd have much need for clothes. He planned to keep her naked and full of his cock for as long as she could take it.

With her change of clothes in the suitcase on the back seat, he guided the car into the parking lot of the waterfront restaurant where he'd decided to take her for dinner. Although he hungered for sex with her, he wanted to woo her first. Rather to his surprise, he found he wanted to win her heart before he bedded her. When he took her, he wanted her to feel the same desperate level of lust for his cock and incisors as he felt for her pussy and her blood.

He turned to look at her, his thirst for her blood increasing. This was what was missing from his *relationship* with Deoctra. There was no passion there. No hunger. No lust. No desperate need. Nothing that made him think he couldn't live without her. Nothing about Deoctra made him feel as if he'd gladly face a horde of vampire hunters to be with her. Yet that's how he felt about Erica. Everything about this woman excited him—her tall voluptuous body, her big breasts, her blonde hair, the soft, sultry sound of her voice, the smell of her need for him, the unashamed way she looked at his cock...

Hell, she might even be hungry enough for it to take it all inside her. The thought alone nearly drove him crazy with lust. *Easy, Mikhel,* he tried to calm himself. *Romance first, endless pussy and passion later.*

Erica. Even her name fascinated him, feeding his hunger for her. He had to have her in his bed, feel her pussy accepting his cock, and taste her blood on his tongue and in his mouth. His hunger increasing with every passing second, he longed to skip dinner, take her straight to bed, and as he fucked her, slowly sink his teeth into her long, delicate neck. He would not hurt her. He couldn't hurt her. Nor would he let anyone else hurt her. He frowned, his thoughts turning briefly to the small, dark woman who would definitely not like the current turn of events. Because he already knew Erica was going to be more than a one-night stand. *No, Deoctra definitely was not going to like this.*

To hell with *her.* Full-blood or not, thoughts of her did not make his cock hard as did thoughts of the woman beside him. Hell, even when Deoctra sucked his cock, he didn't feel this level of excitement and pleasure as he felt just sitting next to this lovely woman. Erica. Erica. His Erica.

He thought of his mother's reaction when she learned about his new love. It was a pity Erica was human, but no one was perfect. He had a feeling that his long search was finally over.

He had spent the last twenty years searching for the one woman whose body and blood would create an insatiable need in him. The effect she had on him could only mean one thing—she was the one. The blood raced through his veins at the thought. Finally. He had met his bloodlust partner. He knew of at least two full-blood females who would not be happy, but this was his life and he would live it how he liked, with the bloodlust partner of his choice—Erica Kalai. His Erica Kalai.

Just for a moment, his thoughts turned to Deoctra again. He knew she had been waiting for him to want to settle down with her for a number of years. While he didn't want to hurt her, he knew Erica Kalai was the one woman he had to have.

He *would* have her. But he wanted her to come to him of her own accord, not because he'd subjugated her will with his…even marginally. Of course, if she showed no inclination to stay with him of her own free will, he would have to reevaluate his position.

"You're very quiet. What are you thinking?" she asked, as he held the restaurant door open for her.

"I'm thinking about how much I want you naked and aroused, under me in bed," he said and smiled in amusement as twin red spots raced up her cheeks.

"You're impossible," she murmured, averting her gaze.

"Is that your way of saying you want to be on top?"

He watched her face get rosier and suspected the idea of being on top of him, riding his cock at her own pace and controlling their fuck excited her.

But he saw she wasn't ready to admit it.

"That's not what I meant at all," she hissed, clearly embarrassed.

"Be my guest," he went on, as if she hadn't spoken. He found he liked teasing her and watching her blush. Red cheeks made her look even sexier. "I don't really care what position we use as long as I get my cock inside you soon and keep it there all night long."

"Lower your voice," she ordered, looking around as they stopped by the table the maitre d' directed them to. "Do you want everyone to know that you...we..."

"Are going to spend the night in bed together?" he suggested helpfully when she trailed off. "Fucking ourselves senseless?"

"We're not if you keep this up," she warned, her dark eyes stormy.

His smile vanished. While on some primitive level, he admired a woman with spirit, he was not prepared to be denied or dictated to by his woman...unless they were in bed. "Make no mistake, Erica. We are going to spend the night in bed together...regardless of what you say."

He watched her eyes widen. "Regardless of what I way?" She shook her head. "I wouldn't count on that if I were you, Mikhel!"

He studied her face. Her beautiful blue eyes swirled with angry lights and her cheeks flushed with agitation. She was lovely. He smiled. "You look delicious...good enough to eat when you're angry."

"You are impossible!"

"But you do plan to spend the night with me. Don't you?"

She tightened her lips.

He arched a brow and gave her a long, silent look. It was time to let her know he was used to getting his way with women.

After a long sigh, she inclined her head slightly, her eyes still glittering with a hint of defiance. He laughed and deliberately slapped her on her ass. Subduing her was going to be a real pleasure.

"Hey!" She threw him a warning look.

He decided he'd teased and provoked her enough for the moment. His schooled his features into a suitable look of contrition and pulled out chair. "Don't look at me like that. I apologize, although it's not really my fault."

"Oh really? Whose fault is it you don't know how to behave in a semicivilized fashion in public?"

He sat in the seat opposite her. "Yours."

"Mine? Just how did you arrive at that incredible conclusion?"

"Yours," he repeated. "I can't help myself. You go to my head and make me do foolish things."

He watched the play of emotions across her face — anger, surprise, hesitation, suspicion, and finally pleasure.

He knew she thought he was pulling her leg, but he really wasn't. She was making him behave in a new manner. He smiled at her. "Forgiven?"

She nodded quickly. "Yes...oh yes, Mikhel."

She spoke with a little shiver in her voice that made his cock harden. Sitting through dinner was going to be agony.

An hour later, still seated at their table overlooking the water, he fastened his gaze on her. He felt drunk with lust and anticipation. He found her face, and everything about her, intoxicating. Looking at her, talking to her — he loved it all...but he wanted more.

After several moments of silence, she put down her coffee cup and arched a brow at him. "Mikhel?"

"Yes?"

"You're staring...again...still."

He didn't apologize. "You're beautiful both in body and spirit. Of course I'm staring," he murmured. "How can I help myself? You are so utterly delicious."

She sucked in a deep breath. "I admit I like that you think that, but you make me sound like a dish you intend to eat."

"Oh, I do intend to eat you."

"Eat me? You mean…you don't mean…do you?"

"Oh, I think you know exactly that I mean, Erica. I am going to eat and enjoy you."

She took a long, steady breath. "Okay, I can accept and appreciate that you think I'm pretty in form, but in spirit also? How can you possibly know that after one dance and one dinner?"

Watching her, an unexpected tenderness welled inside him, something he'd never felt for any woman other than his mother and sister. He took a moment to delight in the feeling before smiling at her. "I can see the beauty of your spirit and soul in your lovely eyes."

"It's not my eyes you've been staring at or into, it's my breasts and neck."

"Your breasts are lovely. And your neck? Well, that's lovely too. Long and slender, and tender."

"Tender?" She laughed. "There you go again. I think you're letting that costume you're wearing go to your head. You make me sound like a piece of meat you plan to eat for dinner!"

So she thought he was letting his Dracula costume go to his head. He would need to go slowly so as not to frighten her too much. "Oh, make no mistake, Erica, I do plan to eat you for dinner or at least for dessert." His dark gaze flicked over her, his intentions obvious. "Your lips, your neck, your breasts, your pussy. I intend to eat and taste them all. I can't wait to get my tongue inside your pussy." And when he had, he intended to drink her warm blood. But he didn't mention that. She'd learn the truth about him soon enough.

He watched as a fresh surge of color stained her cheeks. She gulped. "Oh God," she muttered under her breath, "you are making me so hot and horny."

Laughing, he reached out and cradled one of her hands in his. Her blush turned impossibly deeper. He knew she'd realized that he had heard her thoughtlessly uttered words. She would soon learn just how acute his hearing was. "That's the plan, my Erica, to make you so hot and horny, that you're as hungry for me as I am for you."

She fanned herself with a hand. "Mission accomplished, buddy."

"In that case…" He lifted her hand to his mouth and brushed his lips across her fingers. His gaze never strayed from her face. "Tell me more about yourself."

She shook her head. "I've told you everything there is to know over dinner. I'm basically very dull. There's not much to tell beyond the fact that I'm divorced and a teacher, which you already know.

"Tell me about your husband."

"Ex," she said. "Very ex."

"Why?"

She shrugged. "He…we were married for five years and he got tired and discouraged."

"About what?" he asked, amazed that any man, once having won this beautiful woman, could bear to let her go. "Did he lose his mind?"

She smiled. "That's sweet, Mikhel."

"What happened?"

"He…we both wanted children."

"And?"

She shrugged again, a sad expression filling her eyes. "And we tried and tried." She sighed. "The doctor said there was nothing wrong with either of us and we should just relax and stop trying so hard and it would happen."

"And did it happen?"

"No, because he didn't buy it."

"Ah. He blamed you?"

She nodded, her eyes misting. "Yes…and maybe he was right."

"Why do you say that?" He compressed his lip. Should he look her ex up and kick his ass for hurting her? He quickly decided against the idea. After all, she was available and with him because her ex *had* hurt her. So in a way he had reason to be grateful to her ex.

"Three months after he left me, he got his new woman pregnant so I must have been the problem."

"So you think you can't have children?"

She nodded, then shook her head. "Oh, I don't know. The doctors all said I can, but let's face it, Mikhel, I'm now forty. So even if there is nothing wrong with me, forty is a little old to start having children."

"Is it? Do you still want children?"

She sighed. "I'm not married. I know it's old-fashioned and out of date, but I think a child should have a married mother and father...so sue me."

"So you're telling me that when I get you pregnant I'll have to marry you?" he teased.

She stared at him for a long moment, then laughed. "Oh Mikhel! You're getting more impossible by the minute. But I like it."

And he'd been serious. "I want children too," he said casually.

"And I'm sure you'll have as many as you like when you settle down with some lucky woman."

He sighed. She had no way of knowing how difficult fathering a child would be for him. Still, for the first time in years, he felt hopeful. Maybe fatherhood would not continue to elude him.

"You have no idea how much I'd like that."

She nodded. "No, I don't. Why don't you tell me? I want to know and talk about you."

His standard reply to such a line was to say he was single, headed a security firm in Boston, and then take the woman in question to bed. That wouldn't do this time. He smiled at her. "I talk much better in bed. Join me in my hotel room and I'll tell you everything you want to know."

Just for a moment he thought she would refuse, forcing him to decide between letting her exercise her free will and compelling her to accompany him. Suddenly, she averted her gaze and nodded. "All right."

He paid the check and they left the restaurant, fingers linked. They made the short drive to his hotel in silence. When he returned home, he would have to buy Katie an extra special dinner for convincing him to come to Salem for what he had termed an idiotic Halloween party. Instead, he had finally met the one woman for whom he'd spent years waiting.

In the hotel elevator, he realized he'd left her suitcase in the car. He shrugged. She wouldn't need it tonight anyway. Besides, he found it impossible to keep his hands off her any longer. As soon as the door closed, he stopped the elevator and swept her into the circle of his arms and buried his face against her neck. The feel of the blood pulsing through her veins made his cock so hard it ached. He licked and kissed her neck, repeatedly fighting the impulse to bare his incisors and sink them into her lovely, warm skin. The call of her blood was an irresistible force of nature. One he could only deny for so long before he had to respond.

She trembled in his arms and he felt her heart thudding against him. The thought that she might be just a little afraid of him helped cool his need to immediately taste her blood. He wanted her to freely bare her neck for him, inviting him to drink her blood. Although he didn't have much experience drinking blood, he'd heard that freely given blood was so much more refreshing and nourishing than that taken by force. Of course, having her just a little afraid of him was rather exciting. The conviction that she would not share his opinion, helped him control himself.

Shuddering with a combination of pussy and blood lust, he pulled his mouth from her neck, tipped up her chin, and looked down into her eyes. "Before we go to bed there's something I want to tell you."

"What...what is it? Are you married?" She wet her lips and cast a quick glance at his bare left hand. "Oh God, I didn't even ask before I came with you!" she cried, clearly horrified.

"No! No, I am not married," he quickly assured her.

"Then what is it? You have a girlfriend already?"

Deoctra, at a hundred plus, could hardly be called a girl. And although they'd been casually seeing each other lately, she meant nothing to him. "No, Erica, I have no steady or special woman in my life." Still, he felt a twinge of conscience, but dismissed it. Deoctra couldn't care for him any more than he cared for her, otherwise she wouldn't have stood by for years while he slept with other women. When he returned home, he would go see her and tell her he had found the one woman for him. His bloodlust.

"Then what is it?" The blood suddenly left her face. "Oh God, please don't tell me you're gay!"

"Gay?" He laughed. "If you only knew how much I love pussy, you would know how impossible that is."

"Then what is it? Tell me already."

"Erica, this is not just a costume."

She stared at him. "What do you mean?"

"Just what I said. It's not a costume."

The elevator beeped. He pushed a button and the ascent began.

"It has to be...unless you dress like this all the time. Oh!" She slapped a palm against her forehead and laughed. "You had me going there for a moment. You're an actor...well on the side when you're not working security."

He sighed. Why was it so hard to just tell her the truth? "I'm not an actor. I...do you know what I am, my Erica? Do you understand what I need from you tonight besides your beautiful body?"

Her forehead crinkled in confusion. "What do you mean, do I know what you are? You're a security consultant."

He stroked her cheek. "This isn't just a costume, my Erica, as you'll soon see."

"It's not just a...what...what do you mean?"

"Do you believe in the supernatural?"

"You mean like ghosts and witches?"

"Yes...and werewolves and...vampires."

"Vampires? You mean in real life? For real?"

"Yes, Erica...for real."

She laughed. "Come on. You're pulling my leg rather hard, aren't you?"

"I'm not pulling it at all. I'm serious."

"Oh come on, Mikhel! I know it's Halloween, but don't you think you're carrying this Dracula bit a little too far?"

Damn, but she was hard to convince. This was going to take a little time. He stopped the elevator again. He bared his teeth, allowing her to see his sharpened incisors.

She sucked in a breath. "Wow! They look..." She reached out a hand and touched one of his incisors. "They feel so real!"

"That's because they are real!"

"They can't be!" She touched his tooth again. "Where'd you get them?" She eased back his top lip. "How do they stay on?"

"I was born with them, Erica! What do I have to do to convince you that they are real? Sink them into your neck?" he demanded, exasperated. "This is not a damned joke. I'm just what you think I am, my Erica." To drive the point home, he allowed his eyes to glow.

"How...exactly how do you do that?"

"I don't know how I do it. I just can. I was born knowing how to do it," he said quietly. "I can't explain it."

She stared at him for several long moments. Then she pulled out of her arms and stumbled back against the elevator wall. "Oh God! You're frightening me. There are no such things as...as..."

"Vampires?" He closed the distance between them and touched her cheek. She gasped and recoiled, but there was nowhere for her to go, her back was already at the wall. "There are such things, my Erica, but you have no need to fear me. I will never hurt you. Never, my Erica."

She gulped in several deep breaths. "Okay. This is getting way too weird. Please. Let me go, Mikhel."

The elevator door opened behind them and he spun around. A man and a woman stood there, both dressed as vampires. He bared his incisors and growled low in his throat, "Take the next one!"

The couple gasped and stumbled back from the elevator and he pushed the button to close the door. When he turned back to face Erica, her face had lost nearly all its color, her eyes were wide and unblinking. He could hear her heart thumping in fear. Finally, she was convinced. And now wildly afraid of him.

He sighed, retracted his incisors, and stretched out a hand. Although she cringed, she allowed him to take her hand in his. "Don't be afraid, my Erica. Please." He drew her trembling body into his arms and held her tightly, rocking her. "I will never hurt you. Never." He cupped her face in his hands and stared down into her eyes. "I won't do anything to you that you don't want me to do. I promise. Trust me, my Erica."

"Trust a man I've just met who says he's a real-life vampire?"

The elevator opened at his floor and he urged her out into the hotel corridor with him. He held her hand as they walked down the hallway to his room. He paused and looked down at her. "I know it's a lot to take in, but I wanted you to know the truth about me before we went to bed."

To his amazement, she jerked away from him. "Are you crazy? You're out of your mind if you think I'm going to bed with a…a…with you!" she cried and fled down the hall toward the elevator.

Chapter Three

೧

He sighed. It was going to be a long night, he thought as he flashed down the hall after her. He caught her well before she reached the elevator and swung her around to face him.

He held her still, despite her struggles and allowed her to gaze in a combination of horror and fascination at his glowing eyes and bared incisors for several moments before he spoke. "Yes, you are going to bed with me, Erica. Tonight I intend to taste not only your pussy, but your blood as well. Resign yourself to that realization because it is going to happen…very soon now, my lovely Erica."

She shook her head and struggled to pull away. "Please. Oh God, please Mikhel, let me go!"

"It's too late for that," he warned. "You came with me of your own free will. I will get what you promised to give me."

"I've changed my mind. Please."

"That is not permissible. I will have you, but I will not hurt you."

"Please. Please. I've changed my mind."

"No, you haven't." He resisted the urge to try to shake some sense into her. He could still smell her desire for him. "You're just afraid and rightfully so, but I will not hurt you. Just trust me."

"There must be other women who'll want you…go get one of them."

"I want you… I have you…learn to deal with it."

"You…you're going to…force me…take me to bed against my will?" she demanded. "There's a word for that you know.

It's an ugly word the police use for men like you who can't take no for an answer."

His lips twitched. "I think the word you're looking for is rape," he said, trying to conceal his amusement.

She sucked in a breath. "Oh God! Not that! Please!'"

Why the hell were some women so damned melodramatic? While he knew on some level that she really was afraid of him, he also knew she didn't fear being raped by him. He stared down into her wide eyes. In fact, he sensed the mere idea of a pseudo-rape was something of a turn-on for her.

As if to confirm his theory, she buried her face against his shoulder. He could feel her heart thumping with a combination of fear and excitement. "Oh Mikhel! Part of me wants you, but another part of me is afraid. I…I don't want to be…forced."

The hell she didn't. Her need to be sexually dominated by him was almost palpable. But he decided to play along with her, while giving her what she really wanted. "Trust the part that wants me, my Erica and never, never fear me. I won't hurt you or let anyone else hurt you. Will you willingly come with me? If you really want, I'll take you back to the party, but I really need you to stay with me tonight. Will you?" There. If she really feared his forcing sex on her, she would take the opportunity he'd just handed her.

"And if I say no?"

"I'll take you back," he lied. There was no way in hell he was not going to spend the night with her.

She lifted her face and looked up at him.

He forced himself not to coerce her in any way. "So? Will you stay?"

His heart thumped in his chest and he experienced an incredible sense of joy when she nodded. "Yes. I'll stay," she whispered.

"Any conditions?" he asked softly.

She hesitated before nodding slowly "Just one very important condition. You have to promise not to...rape me."

Her voice caught on the word *rape* and he felt her heart thumping with excitement and anticipation. Oh, she definitely had a forced seduction fantasy. He liked the idea that she wanted him to dominate her sexually.

"Oh, I promise," he said dryly.

"You do?"

The unmistakable regret in her voice strengthened his resolve. Oh, he was definitely going to give just what she wanted.

* * * * *

Standing with Mikhel in the moonlight in front of the big floor to ceiling windows in his hotel room, Erica had never been more afraid in her life. And yet, she'd never felt more alive, more sensual and more lustful. She had never been more ready to have a man subjugate her will and forcefully take possession of her body. She had no desire to be held down or beaten and brutalized, but the thought of the handsome young stranger with the fangs and glowing eyes taking her without her full permission sent chills of lust and desire all through her. She had never shared her fantasy with anyone because it had always shamed and dismayed her, but she couldn't deny its existence. With this man she wanted it to become a reality-again and again.

The thought of this handsome man peppering her mouth with kisses, fondling her breasts and forcing her legs apart, and propelling his big cock into her body with one lusty thrust was the stuff of her wildest fantasies. Oh lord, it would probably be pure heaven to be forcibly subdued and taken by him.

Looking up into his dark, glowing eyes, she knew that he was, in fact, a vampire, that he intended to drink her blood. Nevertheless, the tenderness of his mouth as he kissed her lips and the gentleness of his hands as he carefully removed her shoes, her short, tight dress, her hose, and finally her lace underwear, lessened her fears. And heightened her need to live her fantasy for she suddenly knew that even while taking her against her will, he would not hurt her.

Maybe she was foolish to believe herself safe with him, but she couldn't quite believe he meant to hurt her. When she was naked, she stood with her heart beating wildly, her mouth dry as he slowly moved around her, frankly assessing her body.

She bit her lip. Although she'd managed to keep her weight under control, her body wasn't as firm or as supple as it used to be. Okay, so her breasts were still firm and her legs long. Surely he must have seen women with more buff bodies. Women with young, firm bodies and tight pussies. With his looks and those eyes and that cock, he could have any of them that he wanted. Yet, he clearly wanted her—at least for the night.

When he stepped in front of her, only moments after circling her body, she gasped. "Mikhel! How…how did you get your clothes off so fast?"

For he was naked and fully, gloriously aroused. He had an absolutely beautiful body, big and muscular with magazine hunk washboard abs, but once she looked at his cock, she couldn't look away. It was large and thick, and extended from a dark mass of curls in front of his big, sculptured body as he held his arms out to her. "Come. I need some pussy, my lovely Erica."

Sucking in her breath, she stumbled forward. His hard, hot cock pressed against her stomach. A rush of moisture trickled from her cunt and down her leg. Oh Lord! Oh Lord! This was going to be so good it would probably kill her, but she was going to die a very happy birthday gal. "Mikhel," she whimpered his name, her pussy pulsing with lust and need. "Oh Mikhel. I want your cock inside me so badly."

He tipped up her chin and looked down into her eyes. "Don't worry, my lovely Erica, I can smell your need for my cock." He bent his head and sensuously licked her neck. "And I am going to give it to you." He pressed closer, gripping her hips in his hands. He rotated his groin against her, letting her feel the heat and weight of his thick cock. "Feel my need for your pussy and your blood, my Erica."

She shuddered, her legs trembling. Nothing had ever felt as good as his hard length pressing against her body. She had to have that big, magnificent cock inside her cunt. "You can have them both, Mikhel. Just make love to me."

Slipping one arm around her waist, he reached between their bodies with his other hand and rubbed the big head of his cock along the length of her cunt, testing her readiness for him. She bit her lip, closed her eyes, and held on to his broad shoulders, her whole body hit by countless waves of pleasure. Forgetting the condoms in her discarded shoulder bag, she thrust her hips forward, hungry for the first feel of his rock-hard shaft. She wanted his cock and his cum—both deep in her cunt. "Please," she begged.

"Do you remember what I said about not forcing you, my lovely?"

She wiggled her hips, trying to maneuver the head of his shaft in her pussy. "Yes."

"Well, I lied. I think I will take you by force you after all."

"I don't care what you do," she cried wildly. "Just put your cock in my pussy! Please! Force me! Ravish me! I don't care! Tease me! Bruise me! Fuck me until I can't walk straight. I do not care! Just give me some cock!"

He lifted her left leg across his hip, buried his lips against her neck, and propelled his hips forward, sending the head of his hard length between the lips of her sex and into her already drenched channel.

She tensed her body, waiting for what would surely be pain when he speared her. There was no way having his entire cock forcefully driven into her pussy was not going to hurt like hell. But damn that's what she wanted. She wanted every inch of it pounding in her...hurting her, regardless of the pain.

But when he didn't immediately spear her, she realized he was not going to engage in a game of pseudo rape with her after all. Although slightly disappointed, she decided it didn't really matter. Just having her cunt invaded by the biggest cock she'd ever had made her legs buckle. She would have fallen, if not for the strong arm around her waist. Still kissing and licking her neck, he draped her other leg across his hip and slowly impaled her on the full length of his shaft. A jolt of heat and fire burned in her belly, quickly spreading to her stuffed pussy. Sucking in quick, almost painful breaths, she wrapped her legs around his body.

With his big cock halfway in her, he paused and looked into her eyes. "Are you all right? Should I stop?"

Young, vampire cock. Lord, it was so good. She could barely breathe, but... "If you stop or pull it out, I'll die," she wailed.

He laughed softly and slowly continued to push into her.

When she felt his pubic hair against hers, she let out a deep breath. Somehow she'd managed to take his entire cock inside her.

"Oh damn, you're tight." He closed his eyes briefly, touching his forehead against her and breathing deeply. "How does that feel?" he asked, after a moment, his voice, low and rough with lust, fondling her ass, as if its fullness pleased him.

Oh God, she'd never felt anything half as good. Her pussy had been made just to be stuffed full of this thick, delicious cock. "Oh...oh! I don't think I like it," she moaned, shuddering, in the grip of a near climax.

"Really? What a coincidence." He slid his hands along her ass, sending jolts down to her toes. "I was thinking the same thing about your pussy. While I admit it's wet and tight...baby, I know it's not very gallant to admit it, especially at a time like this, but frankly, my dear, I've had better pussy on many occasions."

"Liar!" she accused. "I'll bet you've never had any pussy half this hot and good," she surprised herself by saying. Hell, he wasn't the only one who could be arrogant.

She tightened herself around him and smiled with satisfaction when he groaned and shuddered. He bit into her neck without breaking the skin. "Since neither one of us likes this...shall I take my cock out of your pussy?"

"Yes. Please do," she said and tightened her pussy muscles to make sure he did no such thing.

"I think I will...as soon as I've fucked you once or twice...maybe three or four times. Oh God!" He scraped his teeth against her neck, holding her so tightly her breasts squashed against his chest.

"Oh God!" she echoed as he withdrew slightly before pushing back into her. She threw back her head with her arms linked around his neck, the beginnings of ecstasy danced through her as he took possession of her pussy again. He did that several times, teasing and exciting her passions until she was ready to burst. Every time he pulled out of her and slid back inside, her toes curled and she longed for a hard, furious fuck! The long, torturous movements were driving her nearly mad with hunger. Tired of being teased, she decided to take matters into her own hands. Gasping, she tightened her arms and legs around him and began sliding up and down the length of his thick, pussy-pleasing shaft.

She felt him struggling to hold on to a measure of control. She sensed that if he lost control, he might really hurt her physically. She could feel the leashed power in him...feel it in the muscles rippling under her caressing fingers and in the cock surging ever-so forcefully in and out of her, stretching her pussy, brushing untouched depths and unleashing deep-seated needs and passions.

Gasping for breath and moaning softly, she ground her pussy along his cock, luxuriating in the resultant bliss tightening her belly and filling her with lust.

"Please me harder," she moaned. "Please! Oh Mikhel! Fuck me harder!"

Gripping her ass in his hands, he obliged, thrust every thick, hard inch of his cock up into her pussy with a lust and power that nearly chased the breath from her body.

Lord, the pleasure was too intense to be borne. He was going to fuck her to an early grave and she was going to love every minutes of the dying. "That's it…do me…do me, Mikhel. Do it to me. Oh Lord, I've never had such a glorious fuck!"

She straightened her back and clenched her fingers in his hair, tore his mouth away from her neck, and greedily kissed his sweet lips. His tongue touched hers and oh Lord, she thought she would die! He withdrew his tongue from her mouth. When she cried out in protest, he shot it back in her mouth in time with his cock slamming back into her pussy.

"Ooooh lord! Oh lord, it's too good! Oooh!" She cried out and in just a matter of moments, she shuddered to a blistering orgasm, soaking his still-plunging cock.

"That's it, my love. Come for me, my Erica." As he whispered against her neck, he gripped her hips and began thrusting into her with rapid, powerful strokes that triggered another incredible climax. "That's it, my love. Cover my cock with your hot pussy juices. Come for me again and again. Cover my cock with sweet pussy nectar and I'll fill you with my cum."

"Oh God, Mikhel…it's so good…your cock is so good…*oooh*."

Her juices flowed over his cock until she felt weak. Moaning, she collapsed against him, burying her face against his shoulder, shaking with the aftermath of the absolutely blissful fucking she'd just received. Still on his feet, he held her in his arms, lightly kissing her hair. Although his cock was still buried to the hilt inside her, he no longer thrust into her.

Several moments passed while she lay against him, enjoying the realization that he was still steel hard before she lifted her head and looked up at him. "You didn't fall."

He kissed her neck. "What?"

She lifted her head and looked at him. "I've never had a man able to make love standing up without falling or leaning against something."

He kissed the tip of her nose. "You've never had a vampire make love to you."

"No." She leaned forward and kissed his lips. "I had no idea what I was missing, Mikhel." She sighed and drew her head back to look at him. "You are still so thick and hard. You haven't come."

"Not yet."

Their gazes met and locked and she sucked in a breath. "Is it true what they say about vampires?"

He lightly slapped her ass. "What do they say, my Erica?"

"That you never get enough pussy or blood?"

"I do have a rather large appetite for pussy, which I can't always control," he admitted. "However, it might surprise you to know that I don't have a particular need or thirst for blood...usually...but tonight I do, my beauty. I don't just want to fuck you, delicious though that was. I want to feel your warm blood running down my throat as I blast your sweet pussy full of my seed."

Her stomach muscles tightened and her pussy clenched impulsively around his thick, hard flesh. Oh Lord, help her. He had fucked her good and she would do almost anything for another fuck like the one she'd just had, but how far was she prepared to go? The moment of truth had arrived. She licked her lips and looked into his dark eyes. "I know you haven't come yet, but couldn't you just...fuck me some more? You can fuck me as hard as you like and have all the pussy you want."

"Oh, I intend to fuck you a lot more, but I need more."

"Oh Mikhel...do you have to have blood?"

He brushed his lips against hers. "Yes. I need to taste your blood."

"Oh God! I know I said you could have some, but I am so afraid."

"There's no need to be. I will not hurt you." He stoked her cheek. "Let me taste your blood and I will give you what you really want."

"What...what do you mean?"

His eyes glowed and he bared his teeth. "I'll take you by force...nicely, of course...or maybe not so nicely."

"I never said I wanted to be...where do you get the idea that I...I don't have a..." He arched a brow and she trailed off, blushing. "You're making me sound like a pervert saying I want to be taken by force."

He laughed softly. "Relax, Erica, I know it's just a fantasy. You don't have to be ashamed of it. I am fully aware that you have no desire for a man you don't know or want to force himself on you. But if you want to pretend that's what I'm about to do, knowing full well I would never hurt you, where's the harm?" He licked her neck and slapped her ass. "It's a fantasy we can both enjoy."

"Have you ever...raped anyone before, Mikhel?"

"No!" His answer was quick and abrupt. Looking into his eyes, she wasn't sure she believed him.

He looked down and she sucked in a quick breath. Had he really taken someone by force against her will? She touched his hair. "Mikhel?"

He reluctantly lifted his head and looked at her. "Erica, I'm not...when I was younger and high on the power that came with being what I am, I sometimes did things that I now regret."

When he was younger? He was still younger. She stared at him. "What kind of things?"

His jaw tightened. "Things I regret," he said.

"Is that a yes?"

"Not exactly...no."

She sighed, not sure she wanted to know more. "Then what have you done?"

"I've never raped anyone," he said.

But she decided he'd either come very close or had done something else which shamed him. "Well, whatever it was…it's okay," she said.

"You're…sure?"

She nodded. She had a feeling that nothing in his past could change how she felt about him…at least not now. Not now? Now was all they had. When she returned to Boston, both Mikhel and their night would be a delicious memory she would always cherish. "I trust you, Mikhel," she lied weakly. She wanted to give him everything he wanted, but she *was* afraid.

"That's my Erica." Holding her around her waist, he walked over to the big bed. Somehow he managed to lower them both to the mattress, while keeping his cock firmly inside her. She lay on the big bed with him on top of her, between her legs. His eyes glowed and he bared his incisors as he slowly began to move his cock in her pussy.

"Hmm." Oh nice. So nice.

Resting most of his weight on his extended arms, he rotated his hips. She gasped, feeling every inch of the thick, hot dick cleaving through her body, touching depths no man had ever touched before. The slow, controlled movement of his cock stirred glorious, indescribable feelings, not just in her cunt, but in every part of her body that could feel.

"Ooooh…God."

He used his knees to urge her legs further apart. He withdrew all but the big head of his cock from her clinging pussy, before lowering his weight onto her, crushing her breasts under his hard chest. Groaning softly, and burying his face against her neck, he shoved his entire shaft deep into her body with one hard, painful thrust.

She practically saw stars. Lord, she had never imagined sex could be so glorious…so liberating…all the while hurting like hell.

He made a small, harsh sound and remained still for several moments, with his cock throbbing inside her. He then began a relentless fucking that shattered her universe into a series of endless, cataclysmic earthquakes, all centered within her burning, cock-filled cunt.

Good…good…good! It was too good! She couldn't bear the pleasure flooding her whole body. Waves of pain and near bliss thundered through her. Her back arched, her stomach muscles tightened, and her toes curled. "Oh God! Oh God! Ooooh God!" God help her, she was about to lose her mind. She came and came until she thought the ecstasy would kill her.

"Get ready, my lovely, Erica. I have to taste your blood."

Just as she thought she couldn't bear any more, he sank his teeth into the side of her neck, cupped her butt in his big hands, and began drinking her blood. The combination of his cock and his teeth both assaulting her overwhelmed senses was too much. Shuddering with yet another orgasm, she moaned, and collapsed against the bed, feeling weak and exhausted. He clutched her to him, thrusting wildly, repeatedly into her until his seed overflowed her pussy and trickled down her leg. And still he fucked his cock deep into her cunt like a vampire possessed.

She lay, limp and sated, her senses overloaded with joy. She couldn't bear much more. He didn't stop, she'd come again, and burst into happy, microscopic pieces. Finally, he lifted his teeth from her neck and slowly eased his cock from her. When she muttered a soft protest, he rolled onto his back and cradled her body on top of his. He kissed her hair and stroked her shoulders. "Are you all right?"

"Oh God!" She shuddered and pressed close to his big, damp body. "Oh God, Mikhel! What was that?"

"Having been married for five years, I would have thought you'd recognize great sex when you had it," he teased, nipping at her shoulder. "What's the matter? Didn't your husband know how to please you?"

Although she'd never had any complaints with James' love making, there was no comparison between the sex they'd shared and what she and Mikhel had just experienced. "Not like that," she admitted. "But that was way more than just great sex."

"Yes, it was."

"What was it?"

"You're very perceptive, my lovely, Erica. What we just shared was bloodlust."

"I've never felt anything that good before."

"Neither have I."

She rubbed her cheek against his shoulder. "You haven't?"

"Not this good, no. "His voice sounded slurred. "Sleep now, my lovely Erica. When you wake, we'll love again. In the morning, we'll talk. Tonight, we make love again and again."

"Oh God! Yes. Please. Yes!"

He laughed softly and stroked his big hands down her ass. "We'll do it as often as you can take it, my lovely Erica."

"I can take a lot…even if it kills me!"

He licked her lips. "Killing you is definitely not in the game plan, my sweet, beautiful, Erica. Fucking you until you can barely walk? Yes. But never, never hurting you. I won't ever hurt you. You're too precious to me."

He had a way of making her feel sexy and irresistible and cherished at the same time. "Oh Mikhel! You're making me so hot! What are you going to do about it?"

He grinned up at her. "How about his?" He thrust his cock deep in her pussy.

"Oh yeah, baby! Yeah." She moaned, trembled, and eagerly pressed down against him. And they began another mindless fuck. This time he bit into her neck and breasts and slapped her ass so hard it stung.

Erica, who had never understood how any woman could enjoy having a lover beat her ass during sex, got hot and horny with each sharp blow he rained down on her butt.

Chapter Four

ဢ

Erica woke from a sweet dream of making love with a young, well-hung stud to find herself lying on her back with her legs sprayed open. Still feeling drowsy, she attempted to close them, but couldn't. It took her a moment to realize that she couldn't close her legs, because someone was lying between them, forcefully keeping them open.

Her eyes snapped open and she found herself looking up into a pair of eyes that appeared to glow. She gasped and shoved against the bare shoulders of the man lying on top of her, searching for the entrance of her pussy with the head of what felt like a very big and hard cock.

In the darkened room, she couldn't make out anything about him except that he was heavy and determined. "No!" she whispered and began to struggle with him, trying to close her legs.

He captured first one hand and the other in his and despite her resistance, he urged her hands up above her head. He held them there with one hand, while he continued to search for her pussy's opening. The head of his cock jabbed at her thighs on either side of her cunt and she shuddered. Part in revulsion, part in lust. Moisture flooded her pussy.

"What are you doing?"

What do you think I'm doing?

"No!" she pleaded again, her heart thumping. "Please don't."

"Pleading will not help," a deep, compelling voice hissed against her ear. "It turns me on and will only make me rougher."

Rougher? Oh lord, the very idea excited her. Still, she knew she should be afraid, but something deep inside her was coming alive as she realized nothing she could do would stop the man lying between her legs from stabbing his cock into her pussy against her will.

The thought of his hard shaft pushing its way uninvited into her pussy until he filled every inch of her, sent a surge of moisture flooding her cunt. Then he would fuck her hard and rough. Her pussy creamed in anticipation and she had to fight hard to keep from parting her legs. This would be more delicious if he took pussy against her will.

"I can smell your cunt," her tormenter taunted. "You want cock?"

"No," she moaned in an agony of lust.

"The hell you don't. I'll give you all you can handle."

"No!" She attempted to twist her body away. She only succeeded in helping the big head of his cock find its way to the opening of her pussy. She froze, her heart thumping, her legs trembling uncontrollably. She was about to have a strange man plunge his cock into her pussy without her permission.

A slow, insidious rush of lust washed over her. "No!" She moaned again, allowing her legs to gape open. Her body on fire with the thrill of what was about to happen, her hips jerked up and the big head of the stranger's cock quickly slid between her pussy lips and sank balls-deep into her vagina.

A wave of pain shuddered through her. "Oooh," she cried out. Under the pain, endless ripples of pleasure buffeted her pussy, setting her whole body on a slow, smoldering burn. Still holding her arms over her head, he fucked her hard and roughly. Damn! That hurt so good! Oh, the joys of having one's pussy pounded by a large, conquering cock.

"Stop it! You're hurting me!"

"I'll hurt you a lot more before this is over," he warned and shot his big shaft back into her.

The breath hissed between her lips as a sharp, sweet pain sliced through her. "Oh my God! Stop!"

"Not likely."

She pulled her hand free, balled her hands into fists, and rained punches on his shoulders. "You'll split me open!"

"Then you will die happy, little wanton," he said in a low, harsh voice and punished her by punching his cock in and out of her pussy at a furious pace that nearly made her see stars of absolute delight. Under the unrelenting pain, there was pure, white, delicious pleasure like nothing she'd ever experienced. She had to have more of this lovely domination.

"You like it, bitch!" he taunted and captured her hands again. Stabbing his cock into her, he forced them up over her head again.

"Oooh! No! That hurts! You'll leave bruises!"

"You love this. Admit it."

She again wrenched her hands free. "No!" she pummeled his shoulders with angry blows. "Get off me and take your big, hard cock out of my pussy or I'll scream."

He slapped her hands away and retaliated by pinching her breasts until her nipples hardened into aching peaks and she wailed in an ecstasy of pain. "Do and I'll just have to do this again! Now admit you love waking up to find yourself being taken by force!" he ordered.

She moaned with pain and shoved her hips upward as the big, thick shaft was withdrawn from her protesting cunt. Lord, how could anything that hurt like this be so sweet and addictive? "I like it!" she sobbed, searching for his mouth. When she found it, she curled her fingers in his hair and did her best to devour his lips and suck his tongue.

Through the pain, she couldn't stop her hips from lifting in a vain attempt to keep the conquering cock moving deep in her. It was a too sweet pain. "Hmm. Ooooh." She wrapped first one leg and then the other around the straining body pounding away at her. Now he'd have a harder time dragging his cock out of her.

Breaking off the French kiss to gulp in air, her senses were immediately assailed with a new delight when a pair of hot lips again fastened around one of her breasts and a firestorm of heat, lust, and delicious, unbelievably satisfying pain, caught fire in her and burned until it consumed her completely. Her pussy was consumed and she began sobbing. "Oh God! Please...don't...stop. Don't ever stop!" she moaned as a delicious and intense climax rolled over her. "Don't ever stop!"

"Silence, wanton bitch. Lie back and enjoy what will be the first of many forced seductions!" he threatened. "This pussy and you belong to me and I will take it as often and as roughly as I like."

He rammed his cock deep into her. Her pussy and her whole world burst into flames and consumed her. When her senses returned, she felt a prick on the side of her neck and memory of the preceding hours rushed back at her. "Oh. Mikhel," she whispered, just before a new explosion detonated in her.

Moaning and nearly senseless with pleasure and pain, she melted against the bed in an exhausted heap. Pressing his groin tight against hers, he continued to fuck her hard and furiously. Erica, her senses and her pussy having reached the end of their endurance, slipped reluctantly into unconsciousness.

When she woke some time later, he was again on top of her, thrusting into her pussy without her permission. The thought that this handsome stranger was ravishing her already sore pussy again sent a tingle of lust all through her. He rubbed against her swollen clit, and she dug her nails into him and raked them down his back.

He grunted and punished her with several hard thrusts of his dick into her very core. Everywhere his body touched hers, she burned with lust and desire. She dug her nails into his tight buns and fucked herself against him. She had lost the ability to think. But lord, she could still feel. She moaned and came again…and again. He pressed her against the bed and shot a load of seed in her unprotected pussy. She lay under him moaning with his cum seeping out of her bruised, but thoroughly satisfied pussy.

He held her, pressing soft kisses against her mouth as he gently stroked her body and whispered how sweet she was. Heaven.

* * * * *

As Erica lay sleeping, Mikhel rose from the bed and went to stare out into the moonlight night. His feelings confused him. Despite what Katie had said, he had not expected to find the one woman his heart as well as his body craved above all others at this point in his life. He had searched for her for at least twenty years.

As vampires went, he knew he was but an infant. Still the search for his bloodlust had seemed to encompass a lonely, empty eternity. He glanced over his shoulder. Erica lay on her side, her beautiful body curled up. He saw the outline of her behind. The lovely, twin cheeks were red from his slapping them as he fucked her.

Watching her sleep, his cock stirred. She was everything he'd ever wanted. Finally she was his. He turned from the window and walked over to the phone on the desk in the room. Without turning on the lights, he lifted the receiver and punched in a familiar number. He spoke softly so as not to awake Erica.

After he finished the call, eager to sleep with her in his arms, he stalked over to the bed and took her into his arms. Brushing his lips along her cheek, he drifted to sleep with her body cradled close to his. Yes. This was what had been missing from his relationship with Deoctra, he thought and surrendered to sleep.

As he drifted back to sleep, a small dark silhouette appeared in the shadows of the room and stood watching with glowing eyes and bared incisors for a long silence before being reclaimed by the shadows.

Senses alert, Mikhel came awake abruptly. Without rising, he lay on the bed, frowning, reaching out with his senses. He sat up and stared around the room, peering into the dark corners. When he sensed no other presence, he decided he'd had a bad dream. He and Erica were alone in the room. Still, it took a long time for him to fall asleep again. This time when he slept, his thoughts turned to Deoctra. He dreamed she was in the room with him and Erica, but knew he dreamed. He drew Erica closer within his embrace and fell into a deep, but restless slumber.

* * * * *

Erica studied her naked reflection in the bathroom mirror. Her hair looked wild and tangled, her eyes wide. Her body bore the bruises of a fair-skinned woman who had been on the receiving end of rough love. She moistened her lips and smiled, recalling the night before. Lord, what a glorious way to spend a birthday—in bed with a handsome, young stud with a hard, greedy cock, and a lust for her body and blood. She had lucked out but good.

But the night was over and it was time to get back to reality. She sighed and walked over to the shower. She turned the water on, adjusted it, and stepped in, closing the door after her.

Standing in the shower with cold water pouring over her, Erica closed her eyes and pressed her forehead against the wet tiles. Although she had thoroughly enjoyed her birthday night of passion, in the light of morning, her recklessness of the night before was difficult to accept. Not only had she left the party with a man who had turned out to be a real vampire, but she'd let him come in her unprotected pussy again and again. She frowned. Not that it mattered. James had come in her unprotected pussy for years and still she had not been able to get pregnant. True, she no longer missed James, but she would forever regret never having been a mother.

She turned her thoughts away from her failure to get pregnant and back to Mikhel and the night before. Lord, what a wonderful lover. He'd literally fucked her into unconsciousness several times. She flushed as she recalled waking in the early morning to find him fulfilling her forbidden fantasy. Lord, but that had been the most incredible feeling of her life. Recalling the pleasure she'd felt as he'd repeatedly pumped his big hot cock into her already battered pussy, she felt her desire stirring. Damn, but he knew how to make a woman nearly lose her mind. For the first time in her life, she understood how a woman could be driven to do crazy things to please a man.

Standing there reliving the pleasure Mikhel had given her, she reluctantly admitted she would have done anything he asked the night before, short of murder, to keep his big spewing cock pounding her pussy raw.

And now, instead of tearing out of his room while he slept, she lingered in the shower. She half hoped he'd wake up and join her for a last fuck, hesitant and pleased because she'd woken up that morning to find both nightstands covered with vases full of lovely, elegant red roses.

Thank you for sharing last night with me. I will always treasure the memory of our first night together, as I hope you will. Happy belated birthday, my lovely, lovely Erica.

Mikhel, your bloodlust.

Mikhel. Her bloodlust. Her anything. She sighed. How could she ever be content with another man after having been loved by Mikhel Dumont? How could she ever forget him? She ached all over and her pussy was sore. But how could she ever forget that big, delicious cock of his? How could she ever forget his hot, sweet lips devouring her breasts? Or his big, strong, muscular body crushing hers against the bed as he thrust her into one heavenly climax after another?

Oh Rica, don't be so dramatic. Okay, so he's a fantastic lover and made you feel like no other man ever has. What do you expect from a vampire, for God's sake. You'll get over it. Get your butt in gear and get out of here. Now. Before he wakes up and you lose your desire to leave. Run from him now — while you can. Run, Erica, run. She turned off the water, opened the shower door, and stepped right into Mikhel. "Oh!"

He stood just outside the shower door, naked and fully aroused.

What was he doing awake during the daylight hours? Looking up into his eyes and seeing his desire for her, her heartbeat quickened. How was she supposed to resist a man who looked at her forty year old body as if it was the most beautiful thing he'd ever seen? "Oh...Mikhel...I didn't expect to see you."

"Good morning, my beautiful Erica." Smiling, he slipped his arms around her and drew her close. "Let's say good morning properly — with a quick fuck."

His cock throbbed against her. Ignoring the twitching in her cunt, she pressed her hands against his shoulders. "Mikhel. Wait."

He muzzled her neck. "For what?"

"I didn't think...I mean don't you need to...sleep during the day or something?"

He lifted his head and smiled down at her. "You've been watching too many Dracula movies, my lovely Erica."

"I have?"

"You have. True, there are vampires who are of the nocturnal breed only, but I am not among that lot."

"Is that why I didn't see your coffin anywhere?"

He laughed. "Erica! Do not believe even half of what you've been told about us. I do not have a coffin."

She glanced towards the bedroom with the large floor to ceiling windows through which daylight must surely be pouring in. "Did you close the drapes?"

His firm, sensual lips twitched. "No to worry, my lovely. Neither sun nor daylight is harmful to me."

"Oh. Isn't any of what I've heard true?"

"I don't know." He grinned. "I don't know what you've heard, but right now I'm more interested in fucking than what you may or may not have heard about us."

"Oh no! We...we can't. Not again."

He licked her neck. "Why not? Didn't I please you last night?" He rubbed his groin against hers.

She gasped, her body infusing with heat and lust. It took all of her willpower not to part her legs and give him easy access to her suddenly aching cunt. "You know you did."

"Then?" He drew his body away enough to allow him to touch a finger against her clit. "Do you want me to stop?" He stroked his finger along the length of her pussy, sending shivers through her.

"No," she admitted. She never wanted him to stop.

"Good. Because I can't stop." Grasping her hips in his hands, he pressed insistently forward. The tip of his cock sank into her.

A shock of desire ricocheted through her. She moaned and leaned her forehead against his shoulder. How could she resist him when her body was consumed with lust and desire for him? Somehow she needed to find the strength to say and mean no to him. "Mikhel. Please. I can't afford to get pregnant." Even as she spoke, her hips jerked forward and she greedily enclosed several more inches of his warm cock within the depths of her pussy. Biting into his arm, she sank down onto him until his pubic hair meshed with hers. Lord, but he was thick and hard.

He tipped up her chin and looked down into her eyes. "It's a bit late to worry about that, my love."

"What...? What do you mean?"

He arched a dark brow. "Just what you think I mean."

She caught her breath. Hadn't she heard that vampires were sterile? Was that one of the things that was or wasn't true about him? She needed to know. Wanting to be pregnant was one thing. She couldn't get pregnant now. "I don't know what you mean, Mikhel!"

"We'll talk about it later, my lovely. Right now, I have to have you."

She knew she should insist on an immediate explanation, but it was impossible not to respond physically to his luscious cock and his obvious desire for her. Especially when he brushed his lips against hers. Whispering how beautiful and sexy she was, he slowly began moving inside her. He rotated his hips, taking care to rub against her clit with each incoming thrust. Warm, delicious eddies of ecstasy chased each other around in her pussy. But she could not afford to get pregnant.

"Please stop," she pleaded. "If you don't…you'll turn me into cock addict."

He laughed and thrust even deeper inside her. He cupped a hand over the back of her head. "Join me in my addiction, my lovely, lovely, Erica. Let it consume you as it does me."

Oh, what the hell! She hadn't managed to get pregnant in five years of trying. "Oh gladly, Mikhel!"

"I need you to do something for me, my Erica," he whispered against her lips.

"Anything," she promised recklessly.

Keeping his cock in her, he drew his upper body away from her. He bared his incisors.

She sucked in her breath, her fear of him returning. "Isn't it too soon for you to take more of my blood?" She was almost certain his drinking too much of her blood had caused her to pass out in the early morning.

His dark eyes glowed and flickered. He brushed his fingers against her neck in a soft caress. "It's not your blood I want this time, my Erica."

"It's not?" She breathed a sigh of relief. "Good. Then what…?"

"Let me show you." He put his right forefinger in his mouth. When he withdrew it, it was covered with blood.

"Oh Mikhel! You're bleeding!" She instinctively reached for his hand. She brought his finger to her mouth and kissed it.

"Hmm. That's nice."

Something in his voice forced her to look at him. He stared at her, his eyes glowing. "It...is?"

"Very nice. Will you do something for me?"

"What?"

"Will you suck it?" he asked softly.

She blinked at him. "What?"

"Taste my blood, my Erica. Taste me."

A shock of revulsion went through her. She dropped his hand and stared up at him. "Suck...you want me to...drink your blood?" She would have pulled away, but he clamped an arm around her waist, keeping her firmly impaled on his cock.

He rotated his hips and gently fucked her. "Yes. Taste me as I've tasted you."

"No! I can't!"

"Yes, you can."

"No, Mikhel! It's too...gross!"

His dark eyes glittered. "Gross? Never that. It's beautiful beyond anything you can possibly imagine. Share it with me, my lovely Erica. Suck me...taste me...become a part of me."

"No! There are limits, Mikhel and I've reached them. I can't...I won't suck...drink your blood."

She saw determination in his eyes and knew he wasn't prepared to take no for an answer. She shook her head. "I mean it, Mikhel...this is not like the seduction fantasy when I said no but really meant yes. I mean this...don't...please."

"It's something I need you to share with me, Erica."

"I can't! Don't you understand that there are limits?"

His eyes narrowed. "There are no limits between us. You are mine and you will do as I ask."

She bristled at his tone. Great cock or not, she was no man's lackey. "No, I will not!"

He bent his head and kissed her. Certain he meant to force his will on her, she tried to keep her lips pressed firmly together, but the feel of his mouth, moving against hers, stirred emotions and passions she couldn't control. Her lips parted, and before she could stop him, he'd lifted his head away and pushed his finger between her lips and into her mouth.

She felt several drops of his blood fall on her tongue. Instead of making her gag, the taste of his blood burning in her mouth created a new sensation in her. She shivered, her revulsion was quickly replaced by a need for more of his warm, sweet blood.

Satisfied her resistance had been overcome, he fucked her gently, almost tenderly. A cloud of joy enveloped her. This was what love, sex and lust was all about—being filled with a vampire's cock while he bled in her mouth, filling her with his essence. Without conscious thought, she grasped his hand in hers and began sucking at his finger as if it were his cock.

Releasing her waist, he stroked her hair while he continued his gentle fuck. "Oh yes. Yes. That's it, my Erica. Feel me. Suck me. Taste me. Share me. Become a part of me. Share my heat and passion, my lovely Erica."

His words, spoken in that warm, deep, almost hypnotic voice of his, rippled over her like a sweet, irresistible caress. She closed her eyes and sucked contently. Cupping one hand over his hard butt, she rotated her hips in time with his, eagerly matching him thrust for delicious thrust. His blood seemed to infuse a strange wildness in her. Her blood felt as if it were on fire. On some subconscious level she felt a sense of alarm, as if she were somehow being changed. She disregarded the slight sense of foreboding. Sucking his blood was too wonderful to be harmful if anyway. She sucked his finger and wildly fucked herself on his cock, shuddering with lust and need. God, help her, how had she ever lived without this wonderful man and his blood and cock?

When he suddenly withdrew his finger from her mouth, she cried out in protest and stared up at him. "Mikhel! What are you doing?"

He smiled down at her. "That's enough for now."

"No!"

"Yes. You're not used to ingesting blood."

She licked her lips to capture any traces of his blood there. "I want more!"

His dark eyes glowed. "Now you begin to see how addictive blood from the right person can be."

She caught his hand and struggled with him to bring it back to her mouth. "Yes. Please, give me just a little more."

"Not now, my love. Too much too soon and you'll get sick. In a day or two you can have just a little more."

"I won't wait that long! I want it now, damn you!"

"In a day or two." He gently, but firmly pulled his hand away from her and kissed her lips. "Let's go to bed."

She moaned in assent when he carried her back to the bedroom, never losing a beat of the piston-like rhythm of his pumping cock. Luscious waves buffeted her body. Oh God, the joys to be found on the receiving end of a big, skillfully wielded cock! Lying on the bed under his big body, with his cock plunging into her with the force and speed of an out of control jackhammer, she had one explosive orgasm after another. God almighty, she couldn't bear any more bliss.

Growling deep in his throat, he bit into her breast, slapped the sides of her thighs, and came. She clung to him like a limp doll as he pumped her full of lovely cum. For the first time in her life, she could actually feel a man coming inside her and damn but it was an incredibly erotic experience. When the world settled back on its axis, she sprawled on top of him, limp and happy. She buried her face against his shoulder, cupping a hand against his cock, which always seemed to be semi-erect. "Oh lord, Mikhel, but that was so good."

"Fantastic," he murmured against her hair.

"Delicious," she countered, flicking the tip of her tongue against his nipple.

He laughed and hugged her close. "If we keep talking about how delectable it was, I'm going to need to do it again," he warned.

"Oh no you don't, buddy!" She reluctantly pulled away. "I've never been so fucked in my life. I'll probably be walking bowlegged for the next few days."

He laughed again and she knew he liked the idea that she felt well and truly fucked to almost exhaustion. "What you need is a cold shower."

"I'd love to take a shower with you," he said, quickly, pinching her ass.

"Ouch!" She slapped his hand away from her still sore rear. "Oh no you don't," she told him. "I am not going into any close spaces with you naked. Take a cold shower alone. Now!"

Still laughing, he allowed her to push him off the bed. "Okay. No need to get violent. I'm going already."

"Take your tight ass in there and stand under a long, cold shower until your cock droops."

Standing near the bed, gloriously naked and still semi-erect, he leered at her. "You want my cock to droop?"

She locked her gaze on his cock, covered with their combined fluids and her stomach muscles tightened. "Yes," she lied shamelessly. "So take your ass into the shower, buddy."

He feigned dejection as he walked towards the bathroom. At the door, he turned, cupped his cock in his hand, and waved it at all. "Sure you don't want some more of the poor guy before I hose him down and he goes limp and unappealing?"

Even limp, his cock would probably make her pussy wet. "You've been given your orders, mister," she said.

With a last leer, he disappeared into the bathroom.

She slumped back against the bed, buried her face against the pillow that still bore his scent, and promptly fell asleep. She was in the midst of a nightmare where she was being chased by an invisible stalker, when Mikhel woke her with a gentle kiss on her lips.

She bolted into a sitting position, her heart thundering with fear, her eyes wide and frightened.

"Erica!" Showered and dressed in a dark suit, he sat on the side of the bed and took her into his arms. "What's wrong, love?"

She turned her face into his shoulder, clinging to him. "Nothing. Nothing. It was just a bad dream."

And yet it had felt so real.

He tipped up her chin and stared down at her. "Do you want to tell me about it?"

She shook her head. "I can't remember anything except I was very afraid. If you hadn't awakened me, I would have died, Mikhel!"

He shook his head. "No. I would never allow that."

"How could you prevent it?"

His eyes glowed. "There are many things you have yet to learn about vampires, my love. No one...even death will take you from me. You are mine forever."

She stared up at him, swallowing slowly. Some of her fears from the night before returned. What kind of power did he wield as a vampire? Had she made a mistake sleeping with him? What would happen when she told him she was heading back to her life in Boston?

He studied her face in silence for several moments before he kissed her lips. "You're safe now, my love. Go shower. The day awaits us."

A day she had not planned to share with him.

"Erica?"

She nodded and slipped out of his arms and rose. She smiled. "Give me half an hour."

She emerged from the bathroom forty minutes later to find him standing at the window, staring intently out, almost as if he were looking for someone...or, considering what he was...something. She could see from across the room that he seemed tense.

"Mikhel? Is something wrong?"

He turned and smiled at her, his shoulders relaxing. "How could anything be wrong when I'm about to spend the day with the most beautiful and enchanting woman in the world?"

Staring into his gaze, she saw his sincerity. Damn, but he knew how to make a woman glad she was female and forty. Hot damn!

Smiling, she waltzed across the room and into his arms.

He bent his head and pressed a tender kiss devoid of passion against her lips that made her eyes mist. She looked up at him. "Oh Mikhel!"

"Let's go eat, my lovely, Erica."

She wet her lips and reached for his hand. "How about an appetizer before breakfast?"

He laughed. "Nice try, but no go." He slapped her ass.

"Hey! That hurts!" she complained.

"Then get a move on, woman, or I'll put you over my knee and spank you until you can't sit down for a week without a cushion under your lovely ass."

She frowned at him. "Whoever thought a vampire would be so stingy with his blood."

He lifted his hand again and she scrambled away from him and ran across the room towards the door. Although he chased her, he allowed her to reach the door before he turned her into his arms and gave her a long, warm hug.

"Oh Mikhel, you are so sweet," she whispered, rubbing her cheek against his shoulder. Why couldn't he be older and human? Just her luck to meet and fall so hard for such a young vampire. How was she ever going to forget him when life returned to normal?

He smiled at her and they left the room, hand in hand. After eating a light breakfast, they spent the day sightseeing. Although Salem was only sixteen miles north of Boston, Erica had never visited The House of the Seven Gables or the enchanting Pickering Wharf. Strolling along the seaside harbor village, holding hands with Mikhel, she felt like a giddy teenager in love for the first time.

It didn't matter that the day was both cold and overcast. All that mattered was the fact that she was with the most exciting man she'd ever met. She knew in a day or two they'd part company and never see each other again. The thought left her feeling unsettled, but she fully expected to enjoy the time they had together. Life was going to be very dull after meeting and being loved by Mikhel Dumont.

To her delight, Mikhel seemed as love struck as she. His frequent sidelong gazes and quick kisses left her feeling happy and carefree. He couldn't seem to keep his hands or his lips off her. They couldn't take more than a few steps before he stopped to kiss or just hug her. She happily lost herself in his attention, refusing to consider the consequences of all the unprotected sex they'd had. Vampires were sterile. She had nothing to fear from his cum.

Still, all the doctors had said she was capable of having children. And she didn't know for a fact that vampires were sterile. After all, the bit about coffins and sunlight had been myths. What if their sterility was also a myth? She thought of all the sperm inside her body. For all she knew she might be pregnant. She caught her breath at the thought of the professional consequences of her turning up at work pregnant now that she was no longer married.

She could almost see the distaste on Dean Chapmen's face as he gave her her walking papers. She gave a mental shrug. She could always go back to teaching in the public schools. Anyway, what did anything matter as long as Mikhel was there, looking at her as if she were the most beautiful and desirable woman in the world? Besides, she was nearly half convinced she couldn't get pregnant. And since that was the case, she intended to continue to allow him to come in her as often as he liked until they went their separate ways.

She cast a sideways glance at him. Would he use a condom if she insisted? She turned against him and he immediately bent his head and pressed a lingering kiss against her lips.

Uncaring of who might be watching, she linked her arms around his neck and lost herself in the magic of his kiss.

"Hey, I'm hungry," he said suddenly, lifting his lips from hers. "Let's find something to eat before I undress you right here and eat your pussy instead."

She felt her face flush. Forgetting her own shamelessness just moments earlier, she pushed against his shoulder. "Hush," she hissed, glancing around to see if anyone was near enough to have heard him.

She saw a tall, slender, strikingly beautiful and young brunette looking at Mikhel with an unmistakable look of lust in her gaze.

Ignoring the woman's stare, he slipped his arm back around her shoulder and walked her slowly along the wharf. "How about some lunch, my lovely Erica?"

She nodded, although she wasn't really hungry…at least not for food. She flushed, realizing she'd rather go to bed than eat lunch, but she could hardly admit that without coming off like she was easy and cock-greedy. "Okay," she agreed. She smiled up at him and sucked in a breath at the knowing look in his eyes.

She frowned. Sometimes she got the feeling he could almost read her mind. But he couldn't do that. She dismissed the unease her suspicions created and allowed herself to just enjoy being with him.

The feeling of euphoria lasted until she and Mikhel parted after a late lunch. Standing alone in the ladies room of the restaurant, putting on fresh makeup, a sudden, abrupt chill ran up and down her spine. A feeling of menace seemed to envelop and surround her. Although she stood in front of the mirror and could clearly see that she was alone in the room, she turned quickly, looking over her shoulder. There was no one there.

Still, she bent and looked under all five-bathroom stalls. No feet were visible, but the feeling persisted. Taking a deep breath, she crossed the room and quickly jerked each and every stall door open. All were empty. "Get a grip, Rica. This is what comes of hanging out with a handsome, hunky vampire entirely too young for you," she scolded herself. "Halloween's over, so stop imaging things. Okay, there are such things as vampires, but they are not invisible."

She returned to the mirror, quickly applied her makeup, and hurried from the room, feeling as if some invisible danger pursued her.

Outside the ladies room, she paused, startled. A tall, dark man, dressed in all black, lounged against the opposite wall. For a moment, she relaxed, thinking it was Mikhel. "Damn but you look sexy as hell in black," she said. "Of course you look even sexier wearing nothing but your big, hard cock."

When the man straightened and looked directly at her, she found herself almost drowning in a pair of dark eyes that definitely did not belong to Mikhel. While she knew Mikhel could compel her with his liquid brown gaze if he chose to, she knew he wouldn't. This man seemed to have no such scruples. And his eyes were gray.

Man? If he were exerting his will on her, maybe she was looking at another vampire, one without Mikhel's scruples. She could feel him reaching out to her. She resisted angrily, but could feel him easily overcoming her will.

"Damn it, stop it!" she snapped. Then, when he showed no inclination to oblige, "Please. Stop." She bit her lip. She knew she could call out to Mikhel for help, but somehow she was reluctant to take that step. Why, she wasn't sure. Maybe it was because she didn't really feel threatened.

As abruptly as he'd begun to compel her, she felt him withdraw from her mind. Her shoulders slumped in relief and she stood frozen as he allowed his dark gray eyes to make a slow, thorough inspection of her body. His gaze lingered on her breasts long enough to make her nipples harden before moving down to linger on her groin area. He made no effort to hide the fact that he liked what he saw.

To her surprise, this stranger's frank approval of her body was neither unwelcome, nor unpleasant. In fact, her pussy pulsed and the breath caught in her throat. God, she was becoming such an exhibitionist. First, she slept with a vampire, allowing him to seduce her into sucking his blood, and now she was enjoying being ogled by a strange man who looked even younger than Mikhel. Was there no end to her current wave of shamelessness?

She cast a glance down at his leg and sucked in a deep breath. There was an unmistakable bulge of significant proportions lying against his leg. He looked as big and thick as Mikhel. How had she managed to meet two men of such enormous portions in such a short frame of time? She gave a mental headshake. It was no concern of hers how big this…boy's cock was or wasn't. Mikhel had already spoken for her day and hopefully her night.

Mikhel. Mikhel. She was no longer on the prowl. She was with Mikhel. She took a deep breath and started forward, her face hot with embarrassment.

For one moment, she thought the man would step in her path, but although he flashed her a knowing smile, he let her pass unmolested.

Despite herself and her desire for Mikhel, she turned to glance at the man. He stood staring at her, a knowing smile on his handsome face. Feeling shameless and horny, she glanced down. She wet her lips as her gaze drank in his gaze. When she looked up and encountered his amused smile, she turned and ran back towards the dining room. His laughter, warm and deep, echoed in her ears.

Chapter Five

ℬ

Still seated at the table they'd shared, Mikhel rose as when she approached. His dark gaze searched her face. "Erica? What's wrong?"

Ashamed of her response to the stranger, she shook her head and slipped into the chair he held out for her, feeling breathless and guilty. "Nothing."

To her surprise, he frowned and cast a swift gaze towards the exit leading to the ladies room, almost as if he knew what had happened outside the ladies room. "Nothing? Are you sure?"

She hesitated, bit her lip, and then decided to be truthful. Well, half truthful. The full truth would make her sound like a first-class tramp. "Actually, I'm a little rattled because there was a man waiting outside the ladies room when I came out."

He dark eyes flickered. "And?"

"And he stared at me."

"And? You're a beautiful woman. You must be used to men staring at you."

She smiled at the compliment. "His staring didn't disturb me as much as how it made me feel."

He raked a hand through his hair. "By that I suppose you mean he got you excited or aroused or both?"

"Yes," she admitted, in a low, barely audible voice. "Mikhel, I don't understand what's happening to me. I know you'll probably find this hard to believe, but I don't go around hopping into bed with strange men."

He sighed. "And that's what you wanted to do with the man outside the ladies room?"

Thoughts of the size of the stranger's cock seemed seared in her memory. She nodded. "Yes, but I don't understand why. You've more than fulfilled my wildest fantasies. How can I want someone else?" She watched the tightening of his lips. "I don't understand it. Please don't be angry."

He reached across the table and took her hands in his. "I'm not angry, but why you feel this way is something we're going to have to talk about—soon."

"Why not now?" she challenged. His air of knowing what was best for her was a little hard to swallow, especially when he was so much younger than her.

"Trust me to know when the time is right."

She shook off the feelings of dread and shame assailing her and nodded. "Okay. That's not my usual style, Mikhel, but I don't want to waste our time together disagreeing."

He squeezed her hand gently. "You know what I am."

She lifted a hand to feel the puncture marks on her neck. "It's difficult to believe, but yes. I don't understand how—"

"Actually, I'm not a full-blood."

"Not a full-blood?" She shrugged. "What does that mean?"

"My father is human, but my mother is a full-blood vampire. Both her parents were vampires, although she didn't know she was a vampire until she was an adult."

She stared at him. How could one not know she was a vampire?

"It's possible," he said quietly.

This reading her mind stuff was becoming a pain in the ass. "So how are you different from a full-blood?"

"In many ways. But for now, I'll just say I'm different in that I'm nowhere near as fast, or as strong as the physically smallest full-blood vampire."

She remembered how quickly he had taken his clothes off the night before. "Full-bloods are faster than you?"

"Much faster and stronger. But on the other hand, I am not as driven by a need for blood."

"Mikhel, you drank my blood. For a while there, I was afraid you weren't going to stop until…"

He sighed. "I'm sorry you were afraid. I never want you to be afraid of me. Did I hurt you?"

She shrugged. "I don't know if it hurt or not." She smiled suddenly, licking her lips slowly, suggestively. "If you remember, at the time, I was rather…preoccupied."

A brief smile touched his firm lips. "Believe it or not, I don't usually drink my lover's blood, no matter how aroused I become."

"But you have done it before?"

"Yes."

"Did you enjoy it?"

"No, not particularly. I'm not a full-blood so I don't usually hunger for my lover's blood."

"That's what I don't understand. If you didn't particularly enjoy it, why did I enjoy it so much last night?"

"I didn't enjoy it with the other women. With you, my enjoyment level went off the scale. But you and I are bloodlust partners. It makes all the difference. Any and everything we do together or for each other's pleasure, will be beyond sweet."

"So when you sucked your other lover's blood, have you ever gotten carried away and…?"

"Drained a woman while making love to her, thus killing her?"

She nodded, not sure she wanted to know the answer.

"No. I told you, I don't usually mix the two. I've only done it twice before last night with you. Both times happened years ago and neither time was particularly memorable. I don't lust or need to ingest blood to live."

"Should I be flattered?"

"Aren't you?" he asked with an arrogance she rather liked.

She smiled. "Yes."

"Good, because you should know that you are very special to me. And I will never hurt you, my Erica."

Her smile widened. "I like the way you say my name and call me your Erica. I like the way you look at me. I like everything about you, Mikhel." She paused, remembering how the man outside the ladies room had affected her. "Tell me, my tall, dark, handsome blood sucker, are there any more like you at home?"

There was a noticeable pause before he spoke. "I have a brother and a sister, Serge and Kattia, both younger and both apparent latents."

"Latents?"

"While they are undeniably stronger and faster than other humans, they have no other discernible vampire traits. Latents generally don't experience bloodlust."

"Bloodlust? You mean they don't drink blood?"

He hesitated. "They have the capacity to experience bloodlust, but for some reason, Mother says they generally don't. They also have sharpened incisors. As to whether or not they've used them…? Serge is very…sexual."

Serge. The name conquered an imagine of a dark, handsome boy. "What does that mean?"

"If he's awake, he wants sex. Lots of it. All the time. He has an unbelievable appetite for pussy."

She smiled, running the tip of her tongue along her top lip. "He sounds a lot like you. I'm amazed I can walk after last night."

He grinned. "I only want sex all the time with you."

Recalling his non-reaction to the stunning brunette earlier that day, she believed him.

He shrugged. "I'm much more restrained with other women."

Did that mean he still wanted other women? She hardly felt in a position to ask. "So your brother and sister don't drink blood?" she asked.

"That's not what I meant by bloodlust. Bloodlust occurs when a vampire meets the perfect mate who spawns a lust, desire and need, not only for blood, but for sex with that particular person. When the two desires are combined in the same person they create a need in the vampire to mate that overshadows everything else. "It's during bloodlust that vampires are most fertile."

She shivered. "Fertile? You mean women vampires. Right?"

"I mean all vampires. Female vampires are more likely to get pregnant with their bloodlust and males are more likely to get their mates pregnant."

"What?" She blinked at him. "How...how much more likely?"

"Highly likely." He shrugged. "Or so I'm told."

She bit her lip. "Mikhel...are you telling me I'm probably pregnant?"

She was annoyed to note the hesitation in him again. "God, I hope you are, but the truth is, I don't know. I'm not a full-blood and I've never gotten anyone pregnant."

She wet her lips. "And? I hear a but in your voice."

"But I've never been in bloodlust before."

She ran a hand through her hair. There was no need to panic. When she got back home, she'd go to her doctor and get a dose of morning after pills or something. "You could have told me all this *before* we had so much unprotected sex," she reproached him.

Tiny lights flickered in his eyes. "And risk your running away from me? I don't think so."

"I wouldn't have run away, Mikhel. I would simply have used the condoms I had with me."

He shook his head. "Condoms? I don't use condoms."

"Well, hot damn, Mikhel, that's fine for you but the last time I checked there was very little likelihood of your getting pregnant."

His eyes narrowed. She bit her lip and waited for him to remind her that there apparently wasn't much likelihood of her getting knocked up either.

"When I first saw you, I knew you were my bloodlust — the one woman who would create the perfect passion in me that all vampires live to experience."

The perfect passion? Okay. That explained what she felt for this man whose existence she hadn't even been aware of twenty-four hours earlier. One night spent with him and she found the thought of parting from him unbearable.

He lifted her hand to his lips and kissed her fingers. "Do you have any idea how good your pussy is?"

She flushed, but didn't look away. "I'm so glad you like it."

"Like it? I love it, Erica. I've never had any pussy that could even compare to it. There was no way I wanted anything between your pussy and my cock. I had to have full access to your pussy, my Erica."

"Oh Mikhel. You are so smooth." And she was a fool for sitting here being taken in by a load of rubbish.

"No! I mean it," he said with the uncanny knack for appearing to read her mind that made her increasingly uneasy.

She nodded. "I know. How is it that some lucky vampiress hasn't snatched you up and made off with you by now?"

She found his noticeable hesitation unnerving. "Mikhel? Is there someone special in your life?"

"From my prospective? No."

"That's a weasel statement if ever I heard one. Whose prospective are we talking about?"

"My mother's."

"Your mother? What does she have to do with this?"

"There's someone my mother would like me to mate with."

She sucked in a breath. Now he told her. "Why?"

He shrugged. "Because she's a full-blood. My mother loves my father dearly, but she regrets that my brother and sister are latents and that I'm only a half-blood."

"You mean she's ashamed of you and your siblings?"

"No! That's not what I meant at all. She just wishes we were full-blood vampires."

"If she's not ashamed of you, why is that so desirable for you to mate with a full-blood?"

"If I mated with the full-blood as she wants, the Walker–Dumont line of vampires will not die off. If, on the other hand, I father children with a human or even a latent, there's a high probability that our children would be latent or mere human."

Her lips tightened. "A mere human? And that would be a bad thing? You make being human sound like something I need to be ashamed of."

He shrugged. "As far as my mother is concerned, it is."

She resisted the urge to say his mother sounded like a first-class snob. "What about your brother and sister? Are they free to mate as they like or does your mother have mates lined up for them also?"

"Of course she has mates lined up for them. Will Kattia fall in line with Mother's plans? That remains to be seen."

"And your brother?"

"Serge is young with a lot of life to live. He will do just as he always has — whatever he likes, whenever he likes — with little regard for the resulting consequences. We all know Serge is not going to fall in line with Mother's plans."

"So how do you feel about this full-blood your mother wants you to mate with?"

He raked a hand through his hair. "What do you mean how do I feel about her?"

"It's a straightforward question, Mikhel. Answer it."

"She doesn't create a bloodlust in me."

While she believed him, she detected a reserve in him that gave her pause. "There's something you're not telling me. What is it? Are the two of you...lovers?"

"No!"

She studied his face. "But you have been?"

"No...well...not exactly."

"What the hell does not exactly mean? Either you're lovers or you're not." She leveled a finger at him. "And I am warning you, Mikhel, the answer had better be no because you told me there was no one special. If you just said that to get me into bed...you better had not have lied to me."

"I didn't...it's just that...a few times we...she..."

"What? You fucked her? What? Spit it out, Mikhel!"

"No! She...blew me."

The thought of another woman's lips wrapped around his cock angered her. "How many times?" she demanded.

"A...few."

"And you enjoyed it!" she accused.

"I...well..." he shrugged. "On a purely physical level...yes."

"What!"

"Don't give me that what. You enjoyed sex with your husband didn't you?"

"That's not the same thing, Mikhel."

"It's exactly the same thing. But at least for me with her there was no emotional involvement. It was just sex...she...she sucks a mean dick."

"Oh, does she? And just how do I know you didn't fuck her senseless too?"

His eyes narrowed and his lips tightened. "Because I told you I didn't. I've never had my cock in her pussy."

"Why not?"

"I've never wanted it there."

"And I'm supposed to accept it just because you said it?"

"Yes, God damn it, you are!"

She bit her lip and stared at him.

He stared back, his eyes cold. As she was about to avert her gaze, he suddenly shook his head. "You have no idea how much power a vampire-sucking can muster. It would be next to impossible not to enjoy it on a purely physical level, but she doesn't do anything for me emotionally. If she did, I wouldn't be here with you. You are the one woman for me. No matter who else I meet or care for, while we both live, there will never be another woman I care for as I do you."

That mollified her, but only somewhat. "But your mother won't approve of me."

"No, but then she doesn't have to. I approve of you. I want you. I need you. I won't give you up."

She smiled. "Oh Mikhel! I'm so glad to hear that. I was wondering how I was going to forget you once I headed back to Boston."

His dark eyes glittered. "What makes you think I have any intentions of letting you go? Remember, I live in Boston too, Erica."

Just for a moment, she considered asking where this full-blood lived. But what did it matter as long as he didn't want her? Except… "Mikhel, what about this full-blood? What will she say when you tell her you're not interested in her anymore? You'll do it kindly. Won't you?"

He shrugged. "She's not overly sensitive or devoted to me. I don't think it will matter much to her."

She sighed. "Good. I'd hate to think of myself as a woman who took another woman's man."

"I was never really hers."

She arched a brow. Men. The only man she'd ever blown, she'd married. She didn't know any woman who went around sucking cock without an emotional attachment. Maybe some women did…like this full-blood in question. "Oh. Good. Then everything will work out fine."

"Yes. It will. I promise. Just trust me."

"If I didn't, I wouldn't still be here."

Chapter Six

ဆ

They had dinner at a restaurant overlooking the water again. As they sat over coffee, he reached out and took her hand in his. "I'm taking you back to your hotel room so you can check out," he told her.

"Aren't you assuming a lot?" she teased.

He shook his head. "No. You're moving into my room with me."

"Just like that? Aren't you even going to ask if I want to?"

He grinned at her. "No. Got any complaints?"

He was rather overbearing. She liked it. She smiled. "None."

After finishing their coffee, he dropped her off at her hotel so she could pack her bag and check out. Alone in her room, Erica again felt an air of malice. As before, there was no one in the room with her. Remembering the incident at the restaurant that afternoon, she opened her hotel room door and looked out. She wouldn't have been surprised to see the stranger from the restaurant lounging in the hotel corridor, but it was empty. She closed the door and wedged a chair under the knob.

Moments after she finished packing the few items she'd brought with her, Mikhel called. "Are you ready?"

He sounded eager. She smiled. "Yes."

"I'll come up and get your bag."

Although her bag was very light, she'd been dreading walking down the long corridor alone. "Thank you."

When he arrived at her door, she threw her arms around his neck and kissed him. "Thank you!"

"For what? What's the matter, Erica?"

She rubbed her cheek against his shoulder. "Nothing... I'm just glad to see you again."

He grinned and kissed her cheek. "You can show me how glad you are later."

"Okay," she whispered.

It was a relief to get in her car and follow Mikhel back to his hotel. Still, she found herself frequently glancing over her shoulder. There were several SUVs behind her and somehow that increased her unease. It wasn't until they met outside the hotel and he took her hands in his that she felt safe again.

In his room, he tossed her bag aside and took her in his arms. "Dance with me, my Erica."

"There's no music."

He placed her hand over his heart. "Yes there is. Feel it?"

She smiled, linking her arms around his neck. "Yes."

They slow danced around the room to an inner music that played between her heart and his. She snuggled against him, wondering how she had ever been happy without him in her life.

"I wasn't happy without you, my Erica," he told her.

She lifted her head and looked up at him. "Oh Mikhel."

He brushed a hand along her cheek. "Make love to me, my Erica."

Recalling the one item in her suitcase she hadn't expected to be able to make use of, she nodded. "Yes, but I have something I want to try."

He tilted his head and looked at her. "What?"

"Let's undress and I'll show you."

They undressed quickly. She considered the beauty of his nude body for several moments before, heart thumping, she waved towards the bed. "Assume the position, Mikhel."

"Which position?"

"This time, I'll be in control," she told him.

His eyes glittering with excitement, he lay on his back with his legs spread, fully aroused. Lord, but his cock was a thing of beauty, long, thick and with a deliciously big, helmeted head. Feeling her cunt dripping just looking at him, Erica dimmed the lights and went to her bag. Her hands shook as she took out the handcuffs. Keeping them shielded with her body, she glanced over her shoulder at him. His eyes glowed. "Close your eyes," she ordered.

He did.

Taking a deep breath, she quickly crossed the room to the bed. "Extend your hands over your head."

His eyes snapped open and he glanced at her hands.

She nearly held her breath, praying he wouldn't object.

To her delight, he closed his eyes and extended his hands over his head. Straddling his hips, she leaned down and handcuffed his wrists together over his head. "Now," she told him, "we fuck."

He opened his eyes and looked up at her. "Then do it. Fuck me."

She grasped his hot flesh in one hand and slowly impaled herself on him until she felt his balls against her buns.

He sighed softly and shuddered.

Smiling, she reached back to caress his balls. Finding them warm and tight, she slowly began sliding her pussy up and down his hot cock, already slick with her juices. With her hands resting on his tight abs, she rose slowly, drawing her pussy off his cock. Feeling heat building in her pussy, she gradually lowered her hips until their pubic hairs touched. Then she ground her pussy on his cock, wanting to feel every inch of his big cock.

"Oooh." Lord that felt good.

He closed his eyes and parted his lips in a soft, wordless sigh of pleasure, thrusting his hips up against her to thrust deep in her body.

Watching the emotions ripple across his handsome face incited her own passion. Closing her eyes, she increased the speed and frequency of her plunging hips.

"Release me," he groaned, his body tense and straining as he thrust his way towards his climax.

"Oh no! I'm going to keep you captive," she said, not breaking her fucking rhythm.

"Remove the handcuffs!"

Rather than release him, she slid her hands down to grip his hips and rode him hard and fast, rapidly rising from his body only to slam her pussy back down on his cock, driving pain and pleasure into her pussy.

He growled deep in his throat and thrust hard at her. "Take them off, damn it!"

She laid her body on his, pressing her breasts against his chest, and claiming his lips in a hungry, desperate kiss.

His arms tensed, then she heard metal tearing. Moments later, he gripped her hips in his hands. She felt what was left of the handcuffs still around his wrists as he sat her up and began bouncing her quickly up and down on his body. "Faster," he hissed. "Faster! Ride me, my lovely Erica. Ride me. Take all my cock. Take it all, baby."

She gasped and gnawed at her lip as her pussy began pulsing and contracting wildly around his cock. Lord, it felt good. Too good for her not to explode soon. And she wanted it to last.

"Mikhel...please...not so fast or hard," she gasped. "Slow down."

"Too late. I want to feel you coming all over my cock. Cream me, baby. Cream me."

"Oooh!" She bit her lip and slammed herself down onto his cock, sending a jolt of pain spreading out from her pussy. Tendrils of pleasure quickly followed and erupted in her. Trembling, she fell against his chest, alternatively sucking his nipples and biting his neck as she came.

"That's it, baby. That's it." He held her as she gasped through her climax before he rolled her onto her stomach, drew her up onto her hands and knees. Bending over her back, he gripped her breasts in his hands.

"Hmmm," she moaned, loving the feel of his big hands on her. Even though she had already come, the beginnings of yet another climax began building in her.

Raking his teeth against her neck without breaking the skin, he fucked her roughly from behind. Sliding his cock between her shivering ass cheeks into her flooded cunt, he exploded, filling her full of his seed.

Falling just short of another orgasm, she collapsed onto her stomach. Turning her onto her back, he slid his big body on top of hers. He bit gently at her mouth.

"Oh Mikhel, if we keep this up without a rubber, I am definitely going to get pregnant," she moaned, kissing his lips.

He curled his fingers in her hair and used his knees to part her thighs. "Would that be such a bad thing?"

Still impaled on his thick cock, she pressed her face against his shoulder. "As I told you, I teach rich teenage girls at a very exclusive school. The parents expect me to be a role model for their daughters. Showing up pregnant while unmarried is not an option."

He responded by kissing her. "Make love to me again, my Erica."

She lifted her head and stared down at him. "Again? Now? Don't you ever get enough?"

"Have you had enough?"

"No," she admitted. They kissed and he ground his body against hers.

"Good, because I'm in the grip of bloodlust, my Erica. I need your pussy and your blood."

Raising his upper body and resting his weight on his extended arms, he began rapidly fucking his cock into her, pushing deep into her with each powerful thrust of his hips. Still teetering on the edge of release, she moaned and trembled as the most delicious climax she'd ever experienced detonated in her cunt. She tilted her head, exposing her neck.

She felt his hesitation. "Are you sure?"

"Yes, damn it! Take my pussy and my blood!"

She felt his teeth sink in. A jolt of electricity sizzled through her, as he fed at her neck while he came. She dissolved into a mindless haze. When rational thought returned, she wrapped her arms around him. "Oh Lord, Mikhel, I just know I'm going to get pregnant."

"Not to worry, my love. I'll take care of you both when you do."

She was too tired to point out that she was perfectly capable of taking care of herself and any child she was lucky enough to have. She bit into his shoulder instead. "Next time, no condom, no pussy, buster," she warned.

"Yeah? What if I bribe you by letting you suck my blood or by taking you by force again?"

She shuddered in anticipation of tasting his blood again...while he pried her legs apart and forced his big, pussy pleasing cock deep in her greedy cunt. "Let me suck your blood and you can have as much pussy as want, whenever you want it," she told him in a small, shameless voice.

"Erica, while I enjoy doing it to please you, it's not my fantasy," he told her. "Every time we fuck, I want you to be a full and willing participant. I want you to want my cock in you. I have no desire to force sex on you against your will. Part of your allure for me is your shameless lust for my cock."

Heat burned her face. His words made her feel even more like a pervert. "I know that, but...oh hell. I might as well admit that I love the idea of you wrestling me onto my back, prying my legs apart and then forcing your big, hard cock into my pussy. I'd love to be repeatedly *raped* by you, Mikhel."

He touched her cheek. "There's no need to be ashamed of anything we do with each other, my Erica. We can do it as often as you like…as long as it's what you want."

"It is."

"Then it's what I want too."

"And you don't think I'm weird for wanting it."

"Not if you don't think I'm weird for wanting your blood. Deal?"

"Deal."

"Good." He rolled away, sat up, and held up his hands, with the handcuffs still around his wrists. "Now you want to remove these?"

She sighed. "I just bought them. Did you have to break them?"

"Yes. Now take them off. Please."

She grinned suddenly. "I think I like you with them around your wrists."

He bared his incisors and twisted the metal until it fell away from his wrists. He tossed the ruined metal across the floor, took her in his arms, and kissed her until she drifted into a contented sleep.

* * * * *

Erica came abruptly awake. For several moments, she lay with her eyes closed. She savored the feel of Mikhel's warm nude body curled into her back, his big hands holding her as he slept. She frowned. She'd half expected to find Mikhel lying on top of her, "raping" the hell out of her, but that's not what had awakened her. Abruptly, she experienced the same sense of menace she'd felt earlier. She opened her eyes and lifted her head.

The moonlight shining in through the window provided the only source of illumination. She looked around the room, not really expecting to see anyone or anything there. After all, she'd been creeped out for most of the day with no just cause. Her eyes widened and a soundless scream rose in her throat as she saw a pair of eyes glaring at her from a darkened corner.

Oh god! It was the man from the restaurant. He was in the room with them. But it couldn't be. The eyes were too low. The man from the restaurant had been as tall as Mikhel. Besides he had excited rather than frightened her. She was imaging things.

She snapped her eyes shut. There was no one there. She opened her eyes again, half expecting to see the dark, magnetic stranger. Instead, a small, dark woman with glowing eyes emerged from the shadows.

Human whore! Mikhel is mine! You are about to learn the folly of tasting the cock that belongs to a full-blood!

The woman's lips didn't move and Erica didn't know if she'd actually spoken the words or just projected them into her mind. Either way, she knew this woman was a vampire…the full-blood Mikhel's mother wanted him to mate with. And she meant to kill her.

She wanted to scream, to wake Mikhel, but she couldn't move or look away from the dark eyes that glowed with malice. Oh God, she was about to die while Mikhel slept beside her.

Even as the thought formed in her mind, the woman became a dark blur, moving across the room so fast, Erica couldn't quite follow her movement. Now she stood over the bed, reaching for Erica's neck. And still she couldn't speak or move.

Before the small pale hands could close around her throat, she heard a low, angry growl. Mikhel's hands shot out and closed over the woman's wrists, wrenching her hands away from Erica's neck.

"Deoctra! Do not touch her!" Bounding up from the bed, he pushed out both hands, flinging the woman halfway across the room.

Erica watched in stunned amazement as the woman spun around in the air and landed lightly on her feet. "You belong to me, Mikhel. You have had ample time to stray and play with insignificant humans. I will no longer share what is mine with human whores. She has to die!"

Baring her incisors, she flashed back across the room, her malevolent gaze locked on Erica's throat. "Die whore!"

Mikhel leaped in front of Erica, crouching and growling. "Leave."

She cast an angry, contemptuous look at Erica. "You stood me up for this blonde bimbo?"

"I didn't stand you up and do not call her names."

She tossed her head angrily. "We will discuss your straying once too often after I've dealt with her. Now step aside, Mikhel."

"Never."

"This whore's ass is mine. Don't make me hurt you to get to her, Mikhel."

The woman's voice dripped with unmistakable venom and resolve. The sound of her voice, the confidence in her words, filled Erica with a sense of fear that nearly choked her. The woman was a full-blood and Mikhel had said even the smallest full-blood was stronger than he. So how could he possibly stop this woman from killing her?

"Before you can hurt her, you will have to kill me, Deoctra!"

"No Mikhel!" Erica reached out and touched his shoulder. "You don't have to fight for me. I'll go and I'll never come back."

"No! You are mine! I will never let you go. Never!" He hissed the words at her, without taking his gaze from the woman confronting him. "Stay back, Erica."

Stay back? While he risked his life trying to protect her in a fight she knew he couldn't win? Not likely. She looked around the room for something, anything she could use against this woman she was certain could and would kill them both if she desired. The only thing she could see that might likely serve as a weapon were the bedside lamps that looked heavy enough to cause some substantial damage.

She snatched the nearest lamp off the nightstand, ignoring the sparks that flew as the cord tore away from the socket. Jumping off the bed, she put her back to the wall. She pushed the shade off the lamp, wrapped the cord around it, and held the base in both of her hands like a baseball bat.

Mikhel shifted his stance so that he crouched in front of her. "Stay out of this, Erica."

"I can't!"

Erica's heart thumped in fear when the woman, who looked about five feet tall and weighed in at about a hundred pounds, reached out and grasped Mikhel by the throat. She watched in horror as the woman lifted him off his feet and tossed him across the room as if he were a child. His head hit the wall with a loud thump and he slid slowly down to the floor where he lay, unmoving.

"Mikhel! No!" Rushing forward, Erica swung the lamp as hard as she could at the woman's head. Hissing, the full-blood spun around and parried the blow with the side of a forearm. Then she ripped the lamp from Erica's hands and leaped at her, reaching for her throat.

Erica hit the carpet hard enough to jar her whole body. Before she could scramble to her feet, the woman's small, strong hands closed around her throat, immediately cutting off her air supply.

She rapidly overcame her first instinct—to try forcing the woman's hands from her throat. If Mikhel hadn't been able to do it with his superior strength, neither would she. Instead, she balled both hands into fists and slammed them against the woman's ears as hard as she could. At the same time, she jerked up her knee and rammed it between the woman's legs.

To her relief, the woman shrieked in rage and pain and released her. Gulping in deep, mouthfuls of air, Erica scrambled to her feet, snatched up the discarded lamp, placed her back at the wall and crouched.

"Whore! Out of deference to Mikhel, I was going to kill you quickly. Now I will slowly drain every drop of your blood from your body first! Your death will be very painful."

Thoughts of what this horror had done to Mikhel infuriated her. She knew she had no real hope of stopping this woman. She was going to die, but it was going to be *after* the damned fight. "Bitch! You want me? You come and get me!" she hissed.

The woman flew at her. Out of the corner of her eye, she saw a sudden blur of movement, then Mikhel stood in front of her. Clasping both hands together, he swung at the woman. Although the dark head jerked back at the impact of the powerful blow against the side of her jaw, the woman kept her balance. She leaped again and Mikhel reached out and grasped her throat in both hands.

Standing behind him, Erica saw the muscles in his back and shoulders tense as he lifted the woman off her feet and began shaking her. Erica sighed. It would be all right after all. She allowed her body to sag back against the wall. Her relief was short-lived. Bringing up her arms, the woman broke Mikhel's grip on her neck and spun away from him.

"Mikhel! Don't make me hurt you. You know you're not strong enough to stop me!"

"Don't count on that, Deoctra. I am not going to allow you to hurt her. I will find the strength to stop you…kill you if I must."

His words seemed to stun the woman. "After what we have meant to each other, you can speak of dispatching me?"

The hint of pain in the woman's voice was undeniable and Erica felt a momentary sympathy.

"I did not intend to hurt you, but she is my bloodlust."

"Bloodlust?" She spat. "What do you know of bloodlust? You are very young. That is why I have allowed you to chase human whores. But I have grown weary of watching lesser females fuck my man. Your whoring stops now, Mikhel. The human whore has to die!" The woman flew at Mikhel, her lips drawn back from her teeth. She slammed her body into him, knocking him off his feet, against the wall next to Erica.

Erica immediately lifted the lamp in an attempt to club the woman. But the woman was no longer standing next to her. She had pulled Erica away from the wall and sank her teeth into the side of her neck. Although she was aware that she was about to die, every nerve in Erica's body seemed to fuse, making movement impossible.

"No!" Mikhel roared. "Deoctra, if you hurt her, I will kill you." Erica saw a fury and horror in his eyes as he lashed out at their tormentor, grabbing her by her neck, and physically wrestling the woman away from her.

Released, Erica collapsed against the wall, weakly pressing a hand against her neck in an effort to stop the blood that flowed from her wounds.

She watched helplessly as Mikhel and the woman tumbled around on the carpet, each clutching the other's throat. Icy chills seized her when the woman suddenly pinned him to the floor.

"You are mine, Mikhel. My bloodlust. If you won't come to me willingly, then I will take you forcefully. Either way, I *will* have what is mine." She exposed his neck. She then reached back to fondle his cock as she sank her teeth into his flesh.

"No. Please don't hurt him." Too weak to stand, Erica grabbed the lamp, and began crawling towards the middle of the room, where the full-blood fed on Mikhel.

There was a ripping sound and Erica realized the full-blood had torn her dress and panties away and was repeatedly lifting her hips up and slamming them down in an effort to impale herself on Mikhel's big cock.

But he wouldn't cooperate, twisting his hips from side to side so quickly that Erica could barely follow his movements.

"Let me have your cock, Mikhel. It's mine. I've waited too long to feel it inside me. I will wait no longer. Shove it in deep and hard. Let me have it all, Mikhel and I'll show you the ecstasy of fucking a full-blood's pussy!"

"No!"

But she kept at him, twisting and moving her hips with unbelievable speed until Erica saw the woman's pussy find the big head of Mikhel's cock and slam all the way down until his thick shaft completely disappeared into her body. The woman was so tiny, Erica was sure the outline of Mikhel's big cock must be visible against her flat stomach.

"Oh yes! Ooooh yes!" The full-blood moaned and rammed her pussy furiously up and down on Mikhel's cock. "Finally! Finally I have you in me, Mikhel. My Mikhel. Finally."

Erica, watching helplessly, heard Mikhel moan softly and her heart felt like it was breaking. He was enjoying it! He was being raped and he was enjoying it…in front of her.

"Feel how hot, good, and delicious is the pussy of a full-blood, my handsome Mikhel. This is only a sample of the delights awaiting you once I claim you as my own, my love. Feel the heat and the tightness of my pussy around your big, luscious cock! Revel in it!"

His body shuddered and Erica saw his hips shoot up. He grabbed her tiny hips and pulled them down, shooting his cock up at the same time. Both vampires groaned with pleasure as his cock, glistening with her juice, again disappeared in and out of her cunt, several times, in rapid succession.

"That's it! That's it. Fuck me, my handsome, Mikhel! Fuck the cunt that belongs only to you! Always. Only to you, my handsome, Mikhel! Is it not the best pussy you've ever had? Tell me now that *she* is your bloodlust."

He shuddered again and Erica, with tears in her eyes, watched him jerk his hips down and several inches of cock came out of her pussy. "Yes! She is and always will be my bloodlust! Get the fuck off me!" Mikhel roared the words and Erica saw his hands flash upward and close around the woman's throat. His whole body tensed and he slowly, but steadily began to lift her off his cock. As he did, Erica saw his cock was coated with pussy juice and a trail of fluids trickled down to his balls. Oh God, no! Had he come in her already?

Erica froze in terror as yet another small, dark woman suddenly appeared from the shadows near the struggling couple. Without looking at Erica, the new arrival reached down, grabbed the full-blood by her hair, ripped her the rest of the way off Mikhel's cock, and tossed her across the room like a piece of fluff.

The full-blood hit the wall with a thud, but immediately bounded to her feet and spun to face the newcomer, her incisors bared. "Stay out of this, Palea."

The other woman bared her own incisors, her eyes gleaming with a fury that made Erica shudder. Oh Lord, was this yet another full-blood who wanted Mikhel and was prepared to kill her to get him? What had she gotten herself into?

Chapter Seven

ɛっ

"Deoctra! Hear me. No one takes my son by force."

Son? Relief washed over Erica. This was Mikhel's mother, a full-blood. Even if she didn't approve of Erica herself, she clearly would not allow Deoctra to hurt him.

"He's mine, Palea. I have a right to take what's mine. I have waited patiently and stood by while he took a succession of human whores. And I did not once complain. I let him have his fun. Well now it's time I had some fun. He's fertile now and he's mine. Surely you don't want him to mate with a human whore."

"Is it not obvious to you that he has already mated with her? Several times. Can you not see that her pussy is already full of his seed?" Her nostrils quivered as she cast lightning-fast gazes at Mikhel and then Erica. "Can you not detect the fragrant smell of their mating in the air?"

Cheeks burning, Erica cowered in the shadows.

"This is not as I would have wished it, Deoctra, but what is done can not be undone. He has chosen a different path than that I had hoped for, but I cannot allow you to take him by force."

Deoctra's eyes glowed and she screamed, touching her exposed cunt. "This is the pussy that should be full of his seed. Not some human whore. I will have what's mine, Palea. I have waited too long to lose him to some insignificant whore. I will have what is rightfully mine."

"No one takes a child of mine by force. No one. Anyone who tries will come to grief. We understand each other? Yes? Leave now."

"Not without him."

"I feel your pain, Deoctra. I, too, have lost one with whom I bloodlusted, but you must leave now and we will speak no more of this."

"How can you ask me to leave without him? He's my bloodlust! I will not allow her to take what is mine!"

"The choice is no longer yours, Deoctra Diniti! You have done things in the past for which you were freely forgiven. This will not be one of them unless you leave now. Leave now. Before I kill you. If he's hurt…if you have subjugated his will, I will seek you out and ensure you have a slow and exquisitely painful death. Yes? Now go."

Deoctra turned angry, glowing eyes on Erica. "I'll take the human whore with me."

Erica shuddered and bit her bottom lip to silence a scream of terror.

Palea Dumont shook her head. "You will not."

"Why not? Surely this human can mean nothing to you."

"She means enough to Mikhel for him to fight for her life at the risk of his free will. Leave now, Deoctra, or die now. The choice is yours. You choose to live a little longer. Yes?"

The air of authority and barely suppressed rage surrounding Mikhel's mother was almost palpable. Erica knew, without being told that this small, seemingly helpless female was more than a match for the other woman.

Nevertheless, she sent up a silent prayer of thanksgiving when Deoctra moved into the shadows and disappeared.

The other woman turned to Mikhel. "My little one. You are all right? No?"

Mikhel struggled to his feet, and Erica's heartbeat returned to normal. "I'm all right, Mother."

Palea Dumont rushed to her son and they embraced, kissing each other's cheeks.

Erica watched in amazement. Mikhel's nudity didn't seem to bother either one of them. Ashamed by her own lack of clothing, she pressed one hand over her mound and the other across her breasts.

Mikhel drew away from his mother and hurried across the room to kneel at her side. He touched her neck, then bent and kissed it tenderly. "My brave, beautiful, Erica! So ready to fight at my side. Are you all right?"

She nodded slowly, surprised. Other than being scared senseless and feeling weak, she seemed to be okay. She leaned forward and pressed her face against his shoulder. "What about you, Mikhel? Are you hurt? When she threw you across the room, I heard your head hit the wall and I thought…" Her eyes filled with tears and she shuddered. "Oh Mikhel, I thought she'd killed you!"

"Shhh. It's all right. I'm all right. There's no need for tears, my brave, beautiful Erica. I am not a full-blood, but I am not so easily hurt and harder still to kill."

"Now you tell me! Oh Mikhel. I was so afraid for you…"

"No fear for yourself, my lovely Erica?"

She shrugged. What would have been the point of surviving if he'd been killed? "If she'd killed you…it wouldn't have mattered what happened to me."

"Oh, my sweet, lovely, Erica. You feel it too?"

Although she wasn't sure what "it" was, she nodded.

"The moment I saw you, I knew you were the one." He leaned forward and kissed her. As he did, she felt his cock, damp and slick, rub against her. She shuddered and drew away.

"What is it?"

She bit her lip. "Mikhel…did she…hurt you when she…forced herself down on you?"

"Hurt me?" He sounded surprised. "No. Erica, I am very hard to hurt."

Aware of his mother standing, listening and watching them, she leaned forward and pressed her lips close to his ears.

"Did you...? You seemed to enjoy it." She bit her lip. "Did you enjoy it?"

He was silent for a moment, then he sighed. "On a purely physical level...maybe just a little. On an emotional one...not one damn bit." He curled his fingers in her hair and forced her to look at him. "You must not misunderstand what you saw. If I had wanted to fuck her, I could have done it right in front of you and then made you forget you ever saw it. If I were so inclined...I could have you both. I am not so inclined. I did not and do not want her...ever!"

"Then why does she say you're hers?"

"We had a relationship...one that was apparently more important to her than I'd thought. I regret that."

She couldn't help thinking he didn't sound all that regretful.

Almost as if he'd read her mind, he shrugged. "You are the woman I've spent my entire life searching for. You are the woman who completes me. You are the woman...my woman. Yes?"

"Oh yes, Mikhel!" she whispered. "Yes!" She pressed her cheek against his shoulder. "But she seems to really want you. Mikhel, is she is love with you?"

"I hope not. Honestly? I don't care. Before she tried to kill you, I had planned to go to her and explain I'd found you. I didn't think she was going to mind, but now I don't care how she feels. She meant to kill you."

"I know. I was so very afraid for us both."

He lifted her in his arms and carried her to the bed. He laid her on her back and pulled the sheet up to cover her breasts. "I know, but it's all right now."

She cast a quick look at his mother. "Cover yourself, Mikhel," she whispered. It was bad enough that the room reeked of sex and they were both naked. "Your cock is almost hard and your mother can see it!"

He shrugged. "It's not the first time she's seen it."

She gaped at him. "What? What do you mean it's not the first time? Are you saying? Mikhel! I—what are you saying? Surely you and your mother…?"

He glanced at her face and outraged her by laughing. "Oh, don't look at me like that, my Erica. I only meant that nudity is no big deal. We vampires are not bashful. My mother has seen my cock many times."

"Erect?"

"Yes."

"Since you've been an adult?"

"Yes. When we're home, it's not unusual for us all to be nude."

"All? Who's all?"

He shrugged. "Me, Serge, Kattia, my parents."

"You mean you all walk around naked and aroused in front of each other?"

"It's not a big deal, Erica." He turned to look at the woman who looked about twenty-five years old. "Mother, this beautiful, bashful woman is Erica Kalai…my bloodlust."

His mother emitted a low, soft sigh. "Oh my little one. You did not use protection. No?"

"Mother, I never use protection," he said, sounding amused.

"She's full of your seed."

"Yes, we've been fucking nearly all night," he said casually. "She has the most incredible pussy. It's so good."

Erica blushed and punched his arm. "Mikhel!"

He laughed unrepentantly. "Well, it's the truth."

"Oh my little one, she's not even a latent," his mother said. "This is going to complicate things."

"So be it. She is my choice, Mother."

"You are sure?"

"I'm very sure, Mother. I was sure the moment I saw her."

"Think seriously, Mikhel. Do not be led by lust alone. For all her faults, Dcoctra can easily take your cock all night long. That should have been obvious to you. Yes?"

"So can my Erica."

"She will surely squeal like the…how do you say it? A stuck pig when you try to fuck her fully and wiggle and cry until you have to take some of your cock out."

"No, she won't. Watch." Then to Erica's dismay, he pulled the cover off her.

"Mikhel!" She tried to snatch the cover back up over her body, but he tossed it across the room, leaving her body bare and fully revealed. "What do you think you're doing?"

"Can't you guess?" he challenged as he settled himself between her legs.

"Mikhel!" She shoved against his shoulders, trying to push him off her. "What are you doing? Your mother's watching!"

"I know," he said softly. "That's the point. She enjoys watching us make love."

"Well, she's not watching tonight!" she hissed angrily, shoving at his shoulders again. "Get the fuck off me! Now!"

"You don't really mean that," he said, easily subduing her.

"I do, damn you! Get off me!"

"After I fuck you," he said, sounding amused.

"You mean after you rape me!" she snapped, slapping his face.

He laughed. "Oh, but we both know how much you love having me rape you."

She continued to struggle. "Surely you don't intend to rape me in front of your mother."

"That's exactly what I intend to do. I'm afraid, my Erica, it will not be the first time she's seen that, either."

"Oh Mikhel! You told me you'd never raped anyone!" she cried.

"I should not have lied to you, Erica. I apologize for that. It will never happen again. But you should know that I am of vampire stock and I have done a lot of things of which you would not approve. Tonight…now…I intend to fuck you…with or without your permission."

To her everlasting shame, knowing he was serious turned her on. He was actually prepared to force sex on her…while his mother looked on. Her pussy moistened and her heart thumped at the idea. Still, she felt obligated to protest. "No, Mikhel," she pleaded. "Not like this."

"Just like this my lovely, Erica. I hope you're moist and ready for me because here I come." Holding her hands down at her sides, he sank his cock deep into her depths with one quick thrust.

"Oooh!" The breath hissed from her lungs. Her pussy caught fire and she pushed back against him, parting her thighs to give him easier assess. Even as she fought to keep from surrendering to the lust tightening her cunt, when he released her hands, she immediately clutched his butt. Lord, he felt so good inside her.

"That's it, my lovely Erica. Take my cock and fuck me back."

Oh, what the hell. So what if his mother was in the room watching? It was his mother. If he didn't mind her watching, why should she? She shuddered, surrendering completely to her desire, and began fucking back at him.

"Oh God, Mikhel. Please fuck me."

"As often as you like, my love," he promised.

"Fuck me…force me…"

"I'll do that as often as you like too." He eased his cock out of her, rose, and lifted her in his arms. She linked her arms around his neck and brushed her mouth against his chest, peppering his small nipples with kisses.

"Oh, my lovely Erica, that's very nice." He carried her to the writing desk in one corner of the room. He sat her on the end and bending his legs, he rubbed the big head of his cock up and down the length of her vagina.

She bit her lip. "Oh damn, Mikhel. That feels so good."

He laughed softly. "But not as good as this," he said and leisurely thrust into her.

"Oh no! Not as good as that," she agreed.

He lifted her legs over his shoulders. Slightly off balance, she pressed her arms back to support herself and shoved her hips back at him. "Oh Lord, your cock is so good."

"Then let me give you some more," he said and began fucking her with complete abandon.

"Ah, my little one. You are enjoying yourself. Yes? Her pussy is good. Yes?"

"Yes, Mother...very good. So good...better than any I've ever had."

The soft voiced exchanged, startled Erica back to an awareness that Mikhel's mother was still in the room, watching them. She flushed and tried to pull away from him, but he continued to fuck her quickly and rather roughly, overwhelming her senses.

"Mother, her pussy is incredible...hot...tight...and so very hungry for my cock."

Damn, she didn't care who was in the room watching. She couldn't get enough of his cock pounding her. Tossing her head back, she let the waves of bliss wash over her until they consumed her with the all the devastation of hungry flames. Absolute paradise.

* * * * *

"Wake up, sleepyhead."

Erica kept her eyes tightly closed and pulled the cover up over her face. She ached, she was tired, and she wanted to be left alone to consider the consequences of the mess she'd landed herself in. She still couldn't believe Mikhel had actually mounted her like that and fucked her while his mother watched with dark glowing eyes. Not that she was any better. She'd squirmed on his cock and bucked back at him like a five-dollar tramp on the prowl. She frowned. Or had his mother really been present? She was no longer sure. The night before was a blurred mixture of pleasure, terror and confusion. She wasn't sure what had been real and what was a nightmare.

If she'd only stayed at the party with Nancy and Janna, none of this would have happened.

"Hey. Aren't you tired of playing possum yet?" he demanded softly.

"Go away."

The cover was firmly pulled down from her face and a pair of warm lips brushed against her mouth. "You're angry with me?"

"Damn right, I'm angry with you! You took me without my permission!"

"But you enjoyed it," he said calmly. "And it *is* your fantasy. So where's the harm?"

"I should slap you until you see stars!" she threatened.

"Do and I'll be forced to force you again. Notice I didn't say rape," he pointed out.

Okay, so it hadn't been rape, and part of her gotten off knowing his mother was present. Still, she wasn't in the mood to be reasonable. "I hate you and everything that you let happen to me last night!" she snapped.

He sighed. "About that...I'm sorry about last night. Forgive me for not doing a better job of protecting you. I let my guard down but I promise it won't happen again. Forgive me?"

So now he was going to pull the woe-is-me routine on her. Men. You couldn't live with them, but who the hell wanted to try living without them? She opened her eyes and blinked up at him. He immediately pulled the cover completely away and spread his nude body on top of hers. As usual, his cock was hard as a rock and already leaking pre-cum

Despite all the horror of the night before, her body immediately responded to his. But she was through being ruled by lust, that had nearly gotten them both killed. She pushed against his shoulders. "No Mikhel. And this time I mean it."

"Ah…so you admit that you didn't mean your no last night!" he said triumphantly. "Of course, I knew that last night." He stared into her eyes. "If you had really meant it, I would not have taken you."

That was supposed to make her feel better? "Fuck you, Mikhel!"

"Oh baby! I wish you would."

"Get the fuck off me! Please!"

He stared down into her eyes for several long moments before he groaned and rolled off her. She sat up and held the sheet against her breasts. She felt her anger dissipating and tried in vain to hold onto it.

He sat up beside her. She sighed and reached over to touch his cheek, telling him without words that she forgave him.

He kissed her hand and stared at her with a grateful look in his warm dark eyes.

She stroked her hand through his dark, silky hair. "Is she going to come back, Mikhel?"

He extended silence was answer enough.

That was it. No matter how great a lover he was, she couldn't take this. She shook her head. "Mikhel, you are very special. I've never met anyone like you and I know I never will again."

His dark eyes narrowed. "That sounds strangely like the beginning of a *Dear Mikhel* speech."

She cleared her throat and nodded slowly. "It's been an incredible, memorable two days, Mikhel."

"But?"

"But…nothing…I'm never going to forget you."

He shook his head. "Erica, I know last night was frightening for you and I'm sorry, but—"

"Mikhel, I was scared to death, not only for my own life, but for yours as well. I can't go through another night like last night…I don't want to live like that."

He cupped his palm against her cheek. "You won't have to."

"How can I not when you can't guarantee that she won't come back?"

"She will come back," he admitted. "But you don't have to worry."

"Why not?"

His dark eyes began to glow. "Because I'm going to kill her when she does."

"Kill her? You mean…"

"I mean I'm going to kill her. What part of that don't you understand, Erica?"

"No! Mikhel, she nearly killed you last night. If your mother—"

"She never intended to kill me nor did she almost kill me. In the first place, I'm not so easy to kill. I'm not a full-blood, but I am my mother's son as well as my father's. Granted, Deoctra is a formidable opponent, but so am I."

"But you couldn't stop her."

"I would have," he said coldly. "I would not have allowed her to hurt you."

Granted, he'd seemed to be on the point of forcing Deoctra off him as his mother arrived, but would he have been able to keep her off him or Erica indefinitely? "She's very strong. And she looks like the if-I-can't-have-you-no-one-can type. Mikhel, she was really thrilled while she was…raping you. Now that she's had a taste of your cock, she won't be able to give it up."

"But you can?"

She nodded slowly. "Not very easily, but she looked like the type who kills rather than loses. She's not going to just let you go and I'd rather have you alive with her than dead with me."

"Without you by my side I might as well be dead!" he snapped. "Don't you understand that? Haven't I explained clearly enough to you what you mean to me?"

"I know I mean a lot to you...and you to me, but she's going to kill you if we keep seeing each other. I just know she will."

"I can take care of myself. She caught me at a weak moment when I let my guard down because I was with you, my Erica. But it will not happen again. There is no need for you to worry about me."

"How can I not? You can't take her alone, Mikhel."

"Do not underestimate me, Erica. You have no idea of the kind of power which I am capable of. She is stronger and a full-blood, but the force of bloodlust is stronger. I will not allow her to hurt you. I can take her alone if I have to. There is no way I'll allow her to hurt you while I live." He raked a hand through his hair. "Besides, I won't necessarily be facing her alone."

Oh Lord! He expected her to help him. She still wasn't sure what had possessed her the night before to try to battle a vampire, but she was not about to try that again. She shook her head. "Mikhel, I adore you more than you could possibly know, but I can't...help kill her."

"Help?" He leaned forward and kissed the tip of her nose. "I didn't mean you, my love."

"Then who? Your mother?" She glanced around the room. "Where is she?"

"She's home with my father."

"Then who?"

"If necessary, Serge will back me up."

"Your broth— But you said he was a latent with no real vampire tendencies!"

"Don't make the mistake of underestimating, Serge either, Erica. Latent or not, he too, is our mother's son. He is very skillful in anything and everything he undertakes. We're a close-knit family. Both he and Kattia will be there for me, if I need them. If necessary, Deoctra will die. She is powerful, but she cannot hope to stand against the three of us." He stared into her eyes. "You have to trust me."

"I do trust you!"

"Then stay with me."

She shook her head. "I want to, Mikhel, but I can't."

"I have no intention of letting you go."

She lifted her chin. "The choice is not yours, Mikhel. It's mine to make and I've made it. I'm leaving."

His eyes darkened. "You'll only leave if *I* allow you to leave. I could very easily force you to stay."

She sucked in a breath. "I know you could." She shook her head. "But I also know you won't."

He shook his head, his dark eyes twirling with angry lights. "Don't be so sure of that. Having found you, why should I let you go?"

"I am sure of it. You promised me you wouldn't hurt me. Well, I'd consider forcing me to stay against my will hurting me. Are you suggesting that you lied when you said I could trust you?"

"No." He closed his eyes and leaned his forehead against hers. "I am not like Deoctra. I want you to stay with me because you want to be with me."

She kissed his lips and pulled away. "I do want to be with you…more than you could possibly know, but I have to go."

"Erica. Don't. Please. You have no idea what you mean to me."

"I know what you mean to me, Mikhel, but I can't go around dodging a killer vampire who wants me out of the way so she can have you. I'm not equipped to deal with all this just to stay with you. Please try to understand." She climbed off the bed and began pulling on her clothes.

He watched her in silence, his dark eyes glowing, his jaw clenching. When she finished, he turned onto his stomach and buried his face in the pillow. "Please, Erica. I'll kill her. I promise."

"I don't want you to kill her. I just want not to be afraid. I have to go." She leaned over and kissed his hair. "Please don't make this any harder."

"Go."

She froze. "What?"

He suddenly spun around and stared at her, his eyes dark and cold. "I said go! If you're going, go! Now."

"Let's not part like this, Mikhel." She stretched out a hand to him.

He bared his incisors and sprang away from her. "Don't touch me. Just go!"

She snatched her hand back and lifted her chin angrily. "Oh, you're a real prince, Mikhel. One moment you're pretending you can't live without me, the next you're snarling at me as if you'd like to rip my throat out."

He leaped off the bed and confronted her, his eyes dark, forceful, and angry. "Trust me, Erica. You do not want to know what I'm feeling right now."

"If you are trying to frighten me, it won't work. I know you won't hurt me. I know—"

"Just get the hell out!"

There was undeniable menace in his voice and in the glowing eyes glaring down into hers. She was almost afraid of him, until she remembered his whispered promise that he would never hurt her. Even when he'd taken her without her full permission, she'd felt an underlying tenderness in him…a need to please her and fulfill her forced seduction fantasy.

She reached out a hand to caress his cheek. Although he bared his incisors, he didn't move away from her touch. "Please understand, Mikhel. Leaving you is the hardest thing I've ever had to do."

"I told you not to touch me." He pushed her hand away. "I have no wish to hear your pathetic human whining. If you're going, get out. Now!"

The words *while I'm prepared to let you go* hung unspoken in the air between them. She knew he walked a fine line between the need to force her to stay and the desire to allow her the freedom to make her own choice. Even as she backed away, she adored him even more for his refusal to force his will on her. Still, a small, irrational part of her wished he had refused to let her go. It was the same part of her that had enjoyed being taken without her full permission and then nearly fucked raw.

Chapter Eight

✇

"If she means so much to you, why did you let her go?"

Mikhel turned from the window of his hotel room to face the man who lounged casually on the unmade bed where he and Erica had made love the night before. "I let her go *because* she means so much to me."

"All the more reason for forcing her to stay, if you ask me."

He frowned. "You only say that because you don't know how powerful a force bloodlust is, Serge. How it drives and completely controls you."

"I'm inclined to think this bloodlust is more trouble than it's worth. When I meet a woman I want half as much as you want your Erica, I'll keep her using any means necessary."

He frowned. "You sound like Deoctra. You don't force your bloodlust to do anything. If you have to use force, then she's not your bloodlust."

"Really? What if only one of you is in bloodlust? Who's to say you will be your bloodlust's ideal partner? If it ever happens to me, I'm not taking any chances. I'll keep her by force if necessary."

He shook his head. "No you won't."

Serge picked up a pillow, held it close to his face and inhaled deeply. "I can smell her pussy on this pillow. She smells delicious."

"She is delicious."

Serge inhaled again before lying back, his face turned into the pillow. "What will you do if she doesn't come back?"

"I don't know," he said bleakly. He had never dreamed that, having found his bloodlust, he would ever lose her.

"Well, if you're not going to go after her and force her back, that means sooner or later she's going to get herself another man."

A low angry growl escaped his lips at the thought of his Erica with another man. He couldn't hurt her—no matter what she did. Any man foolish enough to touch her would be another story. Such a man would learn the hard way, the folly of daring to covet his woman.

Serge sat up, his eyes narrowing. "If she doesn't come back, I'll go after her and bring her back."

"No!"

"Yes. If you won't do what's necessary, I will."

He flashed across the room and stared down at his younger brother. "I won't have her hurt, Serge."

"Who's going to hurt her? Not me. Fuck her? Probably, but I'll bring her back to you unharmed otherwise."

"What do you mean otherwise?"

He shrugged. "She looks like the kind who likes it a little on the rough side. I'll bet you really pounded her and she enjoyed every second, didn't she?"

He reached out and grabbed Serge by the throat. "Don't you touch her."

Serge pushed his hand away and rose. "It'll be me or some other man. At least I won't fall in love with her. I'll fuck her hard, very hard and bring her back to you."

"Stay away from her."

Serge's eyes narrowed. "That's not what I said when you fucked Lisa."

A memory flashed across Mikhel's mind of a tiny, brunette with wide, deceptively innocent blues eyes, huge breasts and a tight, greedy pussy that had milked and sucked as much of his cock as she could take like he was her last fuck. And when her pussy could no longer take his cock, she had given him an incredible blow job. Hell, she'd even allowed him to ram her cute, tight little ass. And when that went raw, he had again invaded her mouth. After allowing her a few hours sleep, Serge had joined them and together, they had double fucked her in every conceivable position.

The three nights he had spent with her had been a decidedly pleasant experience. He still cherished memories of it.

"That was different."

"That's not what you said when you were fucking her."

He frowned. "She was not your bloodlust and you wanted to watch me fuck her. *She* wanted you to watch me fuck her."

"Yes, she did. And you did—until the poor woman could barely walk after that weekend with you. And I didn't complain. It's time to play fair, Mik."

"I am very fair, but Erica is mine."

"And she will continue to be yours. But fair is fair." Serge's dark eyes glinted. "Don't worry, Mikhel. I promise I won't fuck your Erica until she wants me to."

"She won't want you to."

"Has she sucked your blood?"

"Yes."

"And you can still say that?"

Mikhel took a deep, shuddering breath. He knew Serge had a point. But how was he supposed to share his Erica, his bloodlust with another man? Even Serge. Especially Serge. He tightened his lips. He had to get her back. Then he'd worry about how to keep Serge away from her.

"Serge, I am warning you!"

"I'll consider myself warned." Serge moved quickly across the room in time to avoid his half-hearted attempt to backhand him. "In the meantime, Katie and I will be next door if you need us."

Mikhel nodded. He supposed things could be worse. He could have Kattia threatening to go after her as well.

Serge paused at the door. "Don't worry, Mikhel. Even though I have every intention of fucking her, given the chance, I won't fall for her. Although she's very pretty, she's entirely too blonde and too fair for me. As you know, I like my women much darker. And gazing into a pair of blue eyes, no matter how deep, doesn't quite get it for me."

He nodded slightly. He'd known of Serge's preferences for quite a while, which was why the tiny brunette had surprised him. He dismissed the sudden, unexpected thought that he'd like the opportunity to spend a night or two with the woman Serge finally settled down with.

He frowned. Well, not really unexpected. After all, he and Serge had been sharing their women for years. And this sharing was a part of their culture he had always embraced. He just hadn't expected to think about it while he was trying to figure out how to get his woman back.

"Have you told Mother yet?" he asked.

Serge shook his head. "No."

"Why not?"

"She's already upset about you and your Erica. Why should I give her more grief, especially since there's no one special yet? Well, not exactly."

He noted the excited look in Serge's eyes. "You have someone in mind?"

Serge's eyes seemed to glaze over and Mikhel knew his mind was far away. "Yes. Oh yes."

"Who?"

"The woman from Philly."

"The woman from…? What woman from Philly?"

"As far as I'm concerned, there's only one woman in Philly."

He stared at Serge. For the last fifteen or so years, Serge generally had two or three women he slept with on a regular basis. And now he was saying there was only one woman in Philly? This one woman must be special indeed. "Who is she?"

Serge grinned. "You're not going to like the answer, Mik."

He frowned. "Why won't I like the answer? Who is she, Serge? And please do not tell me she's our client."

Serge arched a brow, a slight smile on his face. "Okay, I won't tell you that's who she is, but it won't change the fact that that's exactly who she is."

"No, damn it! We were hired to provide security for her, not romance her."

"I intend to do both."

"Why choose her?"

"I don't know about bloodlust, Mik, but the first time I saw her, I knew she was someone special who I wanted to spend a lot of time with. I don't really feel as if I chose her. I feel like I had no choice in the matter."

"And how does she feel?"

"I don't know. I haven't approached her yet."

That surprised him. He'd never known Serge not to go after a woman he wanted the moment he determined he wanted her. "What's the matter? Has she got a vampire boyfriend scaring you off?"

Serge's eyes glinted. "There's not a vampire born or made that I fear. The worst one can do is kill me and death doesn't really frighten me."

He nodded. Serge's lack of fear made him a formidable opponent. "Then what's the problem?"

Serge shrugged. "Unlike your delicious, uninhibited Erica, she is not likely to succumb so easily...unless I use coercion."

He leveled a finger at Serge. "Do not imply that Erica is easy."

Serge grinned. "Oh, but that's what I'm counting on. And she did let you fuck the shit out of her within hours of meeting you. In my book, that's easy. Hell, she didn't even pretend to play hard to get."

"I don't give a damn about your *book*, Serge. Watch how you talk about her."

"This from the man who called her a bitch and took her in front of Mother, despite her protests?"

"I didn't hurt her. And you just worry about your woman when you get another one."

Serge grinned. "Haven't I made myself clear? As soon as I find a way to introduce myself, the client in Philly will be my woman."

He arched a brow. "You are the last person I thought would have a problem with coercion."

"Normally I wouldn't and don't have a problem with it, but this woman is different."

"Different how?"

"She's not just another pretty face and a luscious body. She gives of herself. And I don't just mean pro bono legal work. She spends a lot of her free time volunteering in soup kitchens and shelters for the homeless. When she's not doing that, she's at alternative schools, giving motivational speeches. She's...different from any woman I've ever met." He shrugged. "I want her to want me."

"Ah. You begin to understand the allure of a woman who wants you."

"I suppose."

"Good. In the meantime, leave her alone. Business is business. Find your pleasure somewhere else."

Serge shook his head. "If you don't want to mix business with pleasure, don't. But don't try to dictate to me, Mik. You should know by now that it won't do any good. There is no way I'm going to stay away from her. I can't."

"So you intend to play around with a client and then just walk away?"

"Why not?"

"It's unprofessional. Besides, Mother won't be pleased."

Serge grinned. "I'm sure she'll understand. If a mere human is good enough for you, one is more than good enough for me. Besides, Mother knows I'm partial to human women. And there's always Katie."

"She's not likely to fall in line either," he pointed out. Their younger sister had never done what the Dumont males wanted or expected of her. Like Serge, she did exactly what she wanted, when she wanted, with little regard for the consequences.

Serge shrugged. "Not my problem. If you want someone to fall in line with Mother's plans, do it yourself."

He narrowed his gaze and considered flashing across the room to backhand Serge. Sometimes Serge seemed to have a hard time remembering who was the older of the two and whose position and blood status required respect. His friend, Aleksei, a centuries-old full-blood vampire was always admonishing him to slap Serge and Kattia into shape. Just to demonstrate how effective such discipline could be, Aleksei had slapped Mikhel around a time or two. Surprisingly, his mother hadn't interfered. Perhaps Aleksei was right.

Correctly interpreting his thoughts, Serge grinned. "Catch me if you can," he invited, then flashed out of the room, closing the door quietly behind him.

The door opened again almost immediately and Serge stood there, staring at him, a concerned look in his eyes. "Mik? Are you sure you don't want me to go after her?"

He nodded. "Yes."

"I won't hurt her, Mik."

"I know that, Serge."

"Hell, Mik, if you really don't want it, I won't even fuck her. Let me go after her and bring her back to you. I'll be very gentle and treat her with the utmost respect."

"I know, but…I can't force her to come back. She has to come back on her own… because she wants and needs to be with me."

"Okay. Are you going to be all right?"

He nodded, forcing a smile to his lips. "Yes." But how could he be all right without his bloodlust? For the first time, he began to understand some of what Deoctra must be feeling. Was this how his rejection of her left her hurting? No one should feel this bleak, utter despair just because they had loved or bloodlusted unwisely.

"Okay." Serge sighed. "If you need me…for anything at all…"

He widened his smile. "I know, Serge."

"Okay."

After Serge had gone, Mikhel turned back to the window. Where was his Erica? He closed his eyes, straining to "feel" her through the tenuous connection that had started to form between them.

Erica. Erica, my love. Come back to me.

Half an hour later, as he stood at the window, staring out into the city, a knock sounded on his hotel room door. He turned. "Come in."

The door opened and a tall man with dark hair and eyes entered.

Mikhel watched his friend cross the room. In addition to being a trusted employee, Cal Harris, was a close friend. "Cal. What are you doing here?"

Cal's gaze flickered over his face. "Serge called me. He said you might need to talk." They shook hands. "Is everything okay with you, Mikhel?"

"Yes," he nodded, then continued. "No…no it's not."

"Want to talk about it?"

"No." He turned away from Cal and stared out the window again. What was the point? Talking wouldn't help. Nothing short of having Erica back would help. "I really appreciate your coming, Cal, but talking won't help."

"How do you know if you don't try? You know I'm a good listener, Mik."

He glanced over his shoulder at Cal. "How is talking going to help, Cal? I found my bloodlust and she left me! How is talking going to change that?"

Cal sighed. "It was Deoctra, huh?"

"Yes! The silly, conceited bitch can't seem to get it through her thick skull that I don't want her!"

"I guess letting her blow you was a mistake."

He thought he heard a note of censure in Cal's voice that annoyed him. "How the hell was I supposed to know she'd go postal on me? At the time, it felt good and the thought that a full-blooded fem with her experience was waiting for me was a major turn-on. I didn't know she'd get so possessive and crazy if I found someone else.

"Hell, Cal, I didn't even intend to find anyone else. When Katie told me it was important for me to go to that stupid Halloween party I half expected to find Deoctra there. When I didn't see her there, I was on the point of leaving. Then I saw Erica and I knew the moment I saw her she was my bloodlust. And I had to have her."

"What are you going to do about Deoctra?"

"I'm going to have to kill her."

Cal sighed. "You're sure? How can I help?"

He shook his head. "I appreciate the offer, Cal, but this is something I need to do alone."

"Alone? You're going to take her on alone?"

"If I have to…if not…Serge will help, but I don't want you involved in case we have to kill her… I won't involve you in what the police will consider a murder."

"That doesn't worry me, Mikhel."

"It worries me, Cal. I want you to stay out of this and concentrate on running the firm while I work this out."

Cal hesitated and finally sighed and nodded. "Okay, but you know where I am if you want or need me."

He smiled and clamped a hand on Cal's shoulder. "Where you've always been—at my side. And I'll always be at yours, Cal."

Cal nodded. "I know."

He watched Cal leave before turning back to the window. He closed his eyes and reached out. *Erica...my Erica...come back to me.*

Chapter Nine

ജ

Erica fought back tears as she rode the elevator down to the ground floor. Every time the elevator door opened, she struggled off an almost overpowering need to run back to Mikhel. Leaving him had been the only practical thing she could do. She was not going to stay with him and spend what would undoubtedly be the rest of a very short life, trying to avoid being killed by the likes of Deoctra. And the Lord only knew how many other full-bloods might be lusting after him.

Tossing her suitcase into the trunk of her car, she drove out of the hotel parking lot, heading for home and sanity. Forgetting Mikhel would be impossible, but time would heal the newly self-inflicted wound in her aching heart. How dumb was she anyway to fall so hard for a man after spending just two nights with him?

So he was a fantastic lover who looked at her as if she were the only woman in the world. She'd found him and she'd find another handsome hunk with a big, hard cock that felt so very delicious inside her. In time, she might even meet a man like the one outside the ladies room. Hopefully, the man in question would be older.

She might meet a man with a big cock, she conceded. But no matter how big his cock, he wouldn't be Mikhel. And that was the problem, but she'd have to learn to settle for what she could get.

A scrumptious shiver of remembered pleasure rushed up and down her spine. It wasn't just that he was handsome and had a really large dick he wielded with a skill and passion that took her breath. Granted that had been the basis of the initial attraction. But it wasn't the size of his dick that made her heart feel as if it were breaking. It was the sense of wonder and belonging she felt when with him. The knowledge that he wanted her so badly that his desire for her kept his dick in a perpetual state of arousal, the certainty that he considered her his soul mate. No. His perfect mate. His bloodlust.

She shook her head. What good would being his bloodlust be if they were both dead? To take her mind off her troubles, she punched out a number on her car phone as she drove.

"Hey, how are you?" a warm voice demanded.

She smiled at the familiar tones. "Not so bad for a forty-year-old gal."

"Rica! I was just thinking about you," her young sister said. "I called your hotel room, but as you know, you weren't there."

"No...I...was out."

"All night."

"Ah...well, yeah. It was my birthday."

"Hmm. And what did you wear on your birthday...your birthday suit?"

Her lips twitched. Meg's perceptiveness always amazed her. "Part of the time," she admitted.

"Had a good time?"

"Yes."

"Got laid, huh?"

"Big-time."

"Still with him?"

"No...I...just left him."

Meg was silent for a moment before continuing. "Why? I can tell from your voice that you liked him a lot."

"There were reasons." She wondered what Meg would say if she told her she'd spent two nights with a vampire and been almost killed by his spurned lover.

"Married?"

The way that Deoctra had behaved, he might as well be married. "No."

"Gay and experimenting?"

She laughed. "Definitely not gay."

"Then why'd you leave him?"

"Meg, I can't really get into the reasons I left, but I had to leave him."

"Okay…what can I do to help?"

"Nothing. I just wanted to talk about him to someone who wouldn't ask too many questions."

"Rica, instead of talking about him, why don't you talk *to* him? Maybe you can work out your problems."

How could she work out his being a vampire? And no amount of talking in the world, would make Deoctra disappear. No, it was hopeless to want a relationship with him. And yet, despite all the reasons she shouldn't, she did.

And why not? Damn it. She was his bloodlust. And he was hers. What good would living to a ripe old age be if she did it without Mikhel? What good was anything without him? There was just no way she was going to be able to forget him. Honestly, she didn't want to forget him. Okay. So Deoctra might kill her before Mikhel could stop her. But that was a chance she was going to have to take, because damned if she'd let that full-blooded bitch stand between her and Mikhel.

While she felt for the other female, Mikhel had chosen her. *She* was his woman…his bloodlust. Damn if she'd let anyone come between them.

"Maybe we can," she said. "Meg…thanks, hon."

"For what?"

"Helping me work this out."

"I did? How?"

"By making the good sense you always do. I have to go."

"Where?"

"Back to Salem to talk to him."

"What's his name?"

"Mikhel. Mikhel Dumont."

"Mikhel Dumont. Nice name. Nice lover?"

"Oh hon, believe me when I tell you, you have no idea how much better than nice he is in bed."

"Oooh Rica, you go girl!"

She laughed. "I plan to…straight to his bed."

"You'll be in touch?"

"Yes…thanks, hon."

She broke the connection and turned her car around. The twenty minute return drive to Mikhel's hotel seemed to last an eternity. As she drove, she licked her lips, relishing the memories of their nights together. For the opportunity to be with him again, she would risk everything, including the loss of her job if she got pregnant.

She bit her lip. What if he were already gone? Or what if he didn't want her anymore? What if she walked in and found him fucking Deoctra? The devastation that thought caused was the surest indicator she needed that she had to go back. If she found him with Deoctra, then the bitch would have to die after all! She wasn't sharing him with that murderous bitch.

Her eyes filled with tears of relief when she spotted Mikhel's car in the hotel parking lot. He was still there. Barely taking the time to lock her car, she ran into the hotel.

She moved through the lobby and stopped at the elevator. Immediately, she felt that sense of menace. She glanced around. She could detect no one in the corridor with her, but she *knew* someone or something was there. *She* was there. Somewhere. Waiting to strike out at her.

She bit her lip, not sure what to do. Should she go up alone in the elevator and risk getting caught in there with a rampaging, vengeful vampire? Or should she retreat to the lobby and call Mikhel's room?

Before she could decide, the elevator doors glided open in front her. She paused, glanced around, and then dashed through the doors. She stabbed repeatedly at the door close button. A sigh of relief left her as the doors began to close.

She nearly jumped out of her skin when the tall, gray-eyed man she'd encountered outside the restaurant restroom a day earlier, slipped through the doors just as they slid closed.

He turned to look at her. After a brief glance, she determinedly stared ahead of her. She could feel his eyes on her and finally, was driven to turn to face him.

Their gaze met and she saw clear lust in his gray eyes. His lips parted slightly and she sucked in a breath, but she saw no signs of sharpened incisors. "What do you want?" she finally asked. She sounded confrontational and she paused and took a deep breath. She needed to be careful. The last thing she wanted was for him to leave her alone in the elevator...where Deoctra could and surely would attack and kill her.

Although the handsome stranger made her uneasy, she somehow felt safe with him. Without knowing why, she was certain that he would not allow Deoctra to hurt her.

He smiled slightly. "I want what most men want...a beautiful, willing woman in my bed to fuck all night long...again and again. You interested?"

"No! Of course not!"

He arched a brow and smiled at her. "Why not? Someone else have a claim on you?"

"Yes, and you won't like it if he finds out you've been annoying me."

He grinned. "Oh, I think I can take him, if need be."

"No! You couldn't. Save yourself some grief and leave me alone while you still can."

He laughed. "I'm not afraid of your boyfriend, but I suppose if he has your heart, I'll have to accept that."

He turned to stare ahead of him and she stared at his profile. That was it? He was taking no so easily?

The doors opened. A couple entered. The gray-eyes stranger suddenly cast her a wicked grin, winked at her, and slipped out the elevator a breath before the doors closed.

The couple who'd just entered the elevator stared at her in surprise…as if she could explain how the dark-haired stranger could possibly have managed to avoid being hit by the elevator doors.

But she dismissed him from her thoughts. She had other things to think about. Like how thrilled Mikhel would be by her unexpected return.

Outside his room door, she pushed the *Do Not Disturb* sign aside and fumbled in her shoulder bag until she found the keycard he'd given her. She swiped it through the lock, pushed the door open, and rushed into the room. "Mikhel!"

Still naked, Mikhel turned from the window, his incisors bared. Slightly startled, she closed the door and leaned back against it, swallowing several times to moisten her dry throat. She waited for him to smile and rush across the room to take her into his arms. He remained where he was, his lips pressed together in a grim line.

"I came back," she said after an extended silence.

"Why?" He glanced around the room. "Did you forget something?"

Cute. He was going to make her beg. Okay. She could do begging. She kicked off her shoes and started across the room, undressing as she went. She stopped in the middle of the floor, clad only in her silk underwear. "Yes. You."

Although his eyes began to glow and his cock stirred, he stayed where he was. "And what if I don't want you?"

She sighed. Bastard. He *was* definitely going to make her beg. "Can the shit," she said coolly. "I happen to know you do want me, Mikhel."

He shook his head, his dark eyes cold. "Do not make the mistake of overestimating your charms or my interest in you."

The heat rushed up her cheeks. "I'm not overestimating anything, Mikhel. You told me how special I am to you."

His dark eyes flickered with an emotion gone too quickly for her to interpret. "You're old enough to know better than to believe everything a man who is trying to get his cock in your pussy tells you, Erica."

She sucked in a breath. Damn him. He wanted his pound of flesh. He would get it, but she would make him work for it. She wasn't going to be the only one surrendering her pride. She shook here head. "That nasty little remark might sting, Mikhel, if I hadn't watched you battle so hard to protect me last night."

"Forget last night. This is here and now. You walked out on me when I begged you to stay. That changes everything…bitch."

She sucked in a breath. "You want your damned pound of flesh?" She tossed her head angrily. "Fine. What do you require of me, Mikhel?"

"Are you sure you want to know?"

She nodded slowly. "Let me guess. You want me to beg?"

He shrugged. "And what if I do? You made me beg when I asked you to stay and then you left anyway. Why don't you try it and see how it feels?"

She shook her head. "So you want to play tit for tat? How very mature of you."

"Don't talk to me about maturity!" he snapped. "You had no problem making me beg for something you knew you wouldn't give me. How mature was that, bit—"

She leveled a finger at him. "Hey you! You call me a bitch once more when we're not making love and I will slap you so hard you'll see stars for a week! I'm nobody's bitch…unless I want to be during sex. Is that clear?"

"Don't try to dictate to me, Erica. It won't work."

"The hell it won't! I did not intentionally make you beg."

"The hell you didn't and damn you, you know it! You loved having me beg! Well now I demand the same pleasure, Erica."

"So you really want me to beg?"

"Yes Erica. I really want you to beg."

"Well, I won't!"

"The hell you won't!"

She tossed her head angrily. "I don't need this grief from you."

"No one is keeping you here, Erica."

She stared at him, swallowing slowly. Was he serious? Would he really allow her to leave again? She couldn't read the expression in his dark gaze so she had no way to gauge how serious he might be. Damn him. She shook her head. Suddenly, she didn't care. She hadn't come back just to trade retorts with him. He wanted to prove he could dominate her? Fine. She'd never have a problem being dominated by a man who knew how to fully satisfy all her sexual needs.

If he wanted her to beg, so be it. "What do you want me to do?"

"Beg," he said coolly. "You do that and maybe I'll consider taking you back."

Despite her resolve, her temper rose. "What?" She lifted her chin. "You want me to beg? In your dreams, buddy!" She unhooked her bra and tossed it angrily at his head. At the last minute when she thought it would hit him in the face, he tilted his head slightly and it sailed past him.

Furious, she stepped out of her red bikini briefs. "I'm not begging for what's mine." She pointed to a spot in front of her. "If you know what's good for you, you'd better get your hard butt over here."

"Fuck you," he said coolly and remained where he was, staring at her with an arched brow that challenged her and her resolve.

She rubbed her fingers over her pussy, slowly rotating her hips. "I know you'd like to," she taunted. "So get your narrow, tight ass over here and I just might give you one or two quick fucks."

"If I decide I want to, I'll *take* as many fucks as I like with or without your permission." He stared into her eyes and then added, softly, deliberately. "Bitch."

Her heart thumped. Oh lord, she was but moments away from another delicious vampire fuck. "Dream on," she said coolly, enjoying the game they had begun. "And while you're doing it, move your ass over here."

When he didn't respond, she flung her panties at him, fully expecting him to dodge them too. Instead, he caught them in one hand and buried his face in them, breathing deeply. He then wrapped the briefs around his hard cock. Catching and holding her gaze again, he began to masturbate, moving her panties up and down his cock.

She tore her gaze away from his. Licking her lip, she watched with her gaze centered on his cock, her cunt convulsing. He rearranged the tiny piece of cloth so that the big head of his cock was encased in her silk panties. He rotated his powerful hips and slowly pumped his cock.

Oh God, what a turn-on. Erica gasped and began rubbing her burning pussy and clit with several fingers. There was something about watching a man pleasuring himself that always got her hot. She wasn't sure why. She just knew watching sent a flood of lust straight to her pussy.

With his free hand, he cupped his balls and began fondling them.

Oh Lord! Erica sucked in a breath and dipped first one finger and then a second into her cunt. Their gazes met and almost as if their souls had connected, they paused and then began to pleasure themselves in unison. As he pumped his cock, she thrust her fingers into her heated pussy and rubbed at her clit.

Keeping their gazes locked, they continued pumping and thrusting until Erica felt her stomach muscles tighten and her pussy begin to tingle. Then his lips parted and he shuddered and began coming on her panties.

Watching load after load of his thick, sticky seed shoot into the crotch of her briefs, she moaned and experienced a mini sensation of her own. But she needed more…she needed to feel his still hard cock tunneling into her hungry pussy instead of her panties. "I need you. Get your ass over here and give me some cock, Mikhel!"

When he showed no inclination to oblige, she decided to try her hand at aggression. "Bring that big dick of yours over here and give me some cock. Now," she demanded. "Don't make me come and get you. Get your tight ass over here now or I swear I'll handcuff you to the bed and ride you until your cock wilts," she threatened.

The words were barely out of her mouth before he flashed across the room and stood in front of her. "Why have you come back?"

His abrupt question startled her. After their mutual masturbation, she'd thought they'd developed a rapport. But apparently, he still wanted his pound of flesh. Handsome, stubborn, irresistible bastard. "I…" Oh what the hell. "I came back because I couldn't stay away." She bit her lip. "Don't you…want me?"

"Nothing's changed. I am who I am, Erica. I am what I am."

She nodded. "I know." She caressed his cheek. "And I adore who and what you are."

"Are you sure you know what you're doing, Erica, in coming back here?"

"Enough with the questions, already, Mikhel! I'm forty, not fourteen. I know exactly what I'm doing."

"Are you sure? Do you need more time to think this through? I won't rush you."

She shook her head. Normally she wasn't a person to make snap decisions. After all, it had taken her two weeks to decide to accept James' proposal. And that had happened only *after* they'd dated for two years. "I've made my decision."

"You need to be sure, because if you stay now, I can't guarantee that I'd be strong enough to let you leave again if you change your mind."

There was a definite air of menace in the warning. He stared into her eyes and she knew it was a warning. If she had half the sense she was always advising her students to exercise, she would turn around and get the hell out of there. But she couldn't leave him again. "Mikhel, I can't promise what I'll do in the future, but I'm here now. Isn't that enough?"

"For now. But like you, I can't promise I'll allow you to leave again should you change your mind. That's not true. I can guarantee that I won't allow you to leave. This is your one and only last chance to go. Stay now and you are mine for eternity."

Again the clear warning in his voice. She thought of Deoctra. "Now is all we have, Mikhel."

He surprised her by placing her saturated panties against her lips. "No, my Erica. We can have almost all the time we want together. There are things about us that you can't possibly imagine."

Therein lay part of her fear. How much of what she'd heard of vampire lore was correct? Granted, he wasn't all vampire, but he was more vampire than human. She inhaled and tasted the cum on her panties. Nice. Very nice. "I can't think beyond now. This moment, when I need you too much I can almost taste my need for you."

She tossed the panties aside and pressed her lips against the fine, dark hair on his chest. "I am *your* Erica, Mikhel. Your bloodlust, come back to you." She lifted her head and looked up at him. "And you are mine. Can't we just work with that for now?"

His chest expanded as he took a deep breath. He clasped her hands in his and held them against his chest. "Yes. You're back and that's enough for now. But there is much you will need to learn about us…about me."

She could feel his cock against her and her desires stirred. "Later," she agreed. "But now that I am here, what do you plan to do with me, my handsome vampire?"

"I plan to do plenty. I have waited my whole life to meet you."

She smiled as he lifted her in his arms and carried her across the room to the bed. "Your whole life? Don't be so dramatic, Mikhel, you're only thirty."

He sat on the side of the bed, staring down at her. "About that."

"What about it?"

"There's something I need to tell you about that."

"Tell me about what?"

He sighed. "Actually…I'm not thirty."

"Oh Lord." She sat up. "I knew it! Please don't tell me you're in your twenties."

"And if I were? What? Would you leave me now?"

"No," she whispered. "I couldn't." She sighed. "But why do you have to be so young? My baby sister is older than twenty."

Just her luck to meet a man who was everything she'd ever hoped for and have him turn out to be nearly young enough to be her son. Well, she was damned if she was going to give him up. "How much am I robbing the cradle by?"

He leaned forward and kissed her cheeks. "Actually, I'm a lot older than I look."

"Really? How much older?"

He drew back. "I'm sixty."

"Sixty? Did you say sixty?"

"Yes!"

"Oh Mikhel, don't lie to me! There's no way you're sixty!"

"But I am. As a half-blood, I age much slower than a normal man would."

"Even so you...oh damn!" She linked her arms around his neck. "I don't care how old or young you are. You are mine." She reached down and fondled his dick and balls. They felt warm and hard. "And I want what's mine."

She lay back on the bed and parted her thighs. "Give me some of that luscious cock of yours. Now before I have to get rough and take it."

Cupping her breasts in his big hands, he leaned forward and feathered her lips and neck with warm and tender, but insistent kisses. "My beautiful, adorable, Erica. I need your pussy and your blood. There's a hunger inside me...inside my soul, my heart...my cock, that only you can fully and truly satisfy."

She shuddered and buried her face against his neck. "Stop talking," she told him. "And put that big, lovely dong of yours where it belongs—in my aching cunt." She bit her lip and then laughed. "Lord, I've always wanted to call a cock a dong."

He pulled back and grinned down at her. "Oooh. Dirty talk. I love it. I love it when my bitch talks dirty to me."

"Fuck me and I'll talk as dirty as you like," she promised.

He spread his big body out against hers and slowly began to kiss her, running his hands over her body. He allowed just the tip of his short fingernails to brush against the sides of her thighs. Lifting himself slightly, he gently stroked her pussy and her clit.

Moaning, she pressed closer.

He laughed and stretched his big body back on top of hers. She loved feeling crushed by his weight. "Mikhel, please. I'm on fire and my pussy is already soaking wet. Skip the foreplay and give me some cock."

"Impatient little minx, aren't you?" He lightly nipped one of her breasts with his teeth.

"Please," she begged.

"Cock coming up, my lovely Erica." He turned her so that they were both on their sides, with his body curled against her back.

Although she regretted the loss of his weight on her, she felt amply compensated when his hard cock knocked against her buns. Hell yeah! She pushed back at him. Lifting one of her legs, he pressed forward, sending his entire length deep within her quivering pussy with one forceful stroke.

She moaned, shuddered, and closed her eyes as a thrill of delight spread out from her cock-stuffed pussy to surge through her whole body. He slipped one hand around her waist to rub against her clit, while the other one caressed and massaged her breasts. "You are mine. Forever."

"Oh yes, Mikhel."

He began to fuck her senseless, relentlessly pounding his big cock deep within the walls of her cunt. He seemed bigger and thicker than usual, stretching and filling every centimeter of space within her climaxing cunt. The sensations emanating from her pussy were absolutely incredible. Oh Lord. How could anything feel so wonderful? So devastating? So heavenly? How could she stand so much pleasure without losing her mind?

There was only one way this could get better. "Oh Mikhel. That's it. That's it. Fuck me! Fuck me! Fuck me! Fuck me hard! Oh...oh...oh yeah, lover! Take my pussy...you have it...you have it...it's yours. Take my pussy. Take all of me. And while you do, suck my blood. Fill me with your seed while I fill you with my blood."

She clutched at the arm across her waist and tilted her neck. Growling softly in his throat, he bit gently into her flesh. As she felt the blood flowing out of her body and into his mouth, her pussy...her body...the universe exploded around her.

Groaning and straining, he suddenly rolled them over so that she lay on her stomach. Lying on top of her with his incisors still buried in her flesh, he shuddered and came, pumping her so full of his seed that it overflowed her cunt and ran down her slit.

Even after he came, he held her still under him. Rotating his hips, he pumped his hard thick length deep in her, piston-like. She sank her teeth into the bed sheet, her hands clenched at her sides. His deep, hard thrusts hurt like hell, making her cunt burn. But Lord, it was such a sweet, sweet pain. She moaned and came again. Finally, he withdrew his teeth from her. Long after his body stopped shaking, he gradually pulled his cock out of her sore channel and lay behind her. He licked the last drops of blood from her neck and stroked her body, whispering to her in a soft, soothing voice. *She was beautiful. She was sexy. He couldn't get enough of her. She made him happy. He couldn't live without her. She was his. Always his.*

Always his. It had a very nice ring to it. She pressed against him, feeling happily and content. "I'll bet you say that to all your human whores," she teased drowsily.

He laughed softly. "Hardly. You are the first human woman I've met who could take all my cock without asking me to stop, slow down or take some of it out."

"I can sympathize." She rubbed her sore pussy. "I've never had such a large, hard cock in me before. For a while there I felt as if half a baseball bat was being rammed into me."

He stiffened behind her. "Half a baseball bat? Oh damn. That sounds unpleasant. I hurt you. I'm sorry. I—"

"Don't be. You really hurt me near the end."

"Damn!"

"Mikhel, be realistic. How could it not have hurt like hell at the speed you were shoving into me? I don't think you realize how much cock you're packing. For a while there, I thought you were going to poke a hole in me. But damn, I loved it."

"You loved it?"

"Oh yeah. Every pussy stretching second of it. Trust me, handsome, sometimes pain can be a very, very good thing."

He buried his lips against her neck. "I'm sorry," he said again. "I tried to hold back. I did, but you have no idea how good it feels to be able to slam my entire cock inside you. Just to be able to make love to you without holding back is so incredible.

"When we make love, I feel as if your pussy was custom-made for my cock. I love the way I have to push into your tight heat and then I get a charge out of the way your pussy squeezes and clings to my cock when I draw it out. You make me fight to get even an inch out of your hot hole. You have the best…the most incredible pussy in creation."

"Oh… Mikhel!" she whispered, thrilled silly by his declaration.

"You make it hard not to lose control with you, but I promise I'll be more careful next time."

"Don't you dare." She wiggled her buns against his thighs. "Seems I like it a little rough. At least I do with you. Lord, there's nothing as exquisite as feeling my pussy slowly being stretched to capacity by your big, thick cock. You're so hot and silky and man, I love your dong."

"Stretched to capacity, huh? And you like that? Sounds a little kinky to me."

"Oh yeah? You're a fine one to talk about kink. Sucking your lover's blood is the ultimate kink."

"Depends on what neck of the woods you hail from." He laughed. "Pun intended. Where I come from it's perfectly normal."

She turned her head and kissed his lips, stroking her hands over his tight, hard thighs. "Kinky or not, that was so good. Tell me, Mikhel, are all vampires as well-hung as you with big, thick, pussy pleasing cocks hanging between their legs?"

He nipped her neck. "For your information, the size of my cock has nothing to do with being a half-blood."

"Are you sure? I don't know that I've ever met a man with such a...big, thick cock." She dismissed an insistent memory of the man outside the ladies room.

"If you think I'm big, wait until you see my brother and father."

She pushed her elbow against his ribs. "Wait until I see you...? Are you nuts? I can imagine no occasion when I'll see your brother or your father's cock!" She bit her lip, then, letting her curiosity get the better of her, she asked, "You mean they're bigger than you are?"

"Yes. Serge is thicker and longer by an inch or two, but my father is what my mother calls 'hung like a horse'."

She shuddered, remembering his mother's tiny stature. "Your poor mother."

"On the contrary, from the way she cries out blissfully every time they make love, I think it's safe to assume that she loves every inch of my father's cock...especially when it's really ramming into her."

"Mikhel! How can you talk so casually about your father ramming his cock into your mother's...?"

"Pussy," he said when she trailed out. "And let me tell you, he really gives her a going over sometimes."

"Mikhel!"

"What? I told you. We're a very uninhibited lot."

"Just how uninhibited are you?"

He stirred against her. "I don't want to scare you off."

"Mikhel! I want to know what I'm getting into."

He sighed. "Okay. You promise to keep an open mind?"

"Maybe."

"Well, sometimes we make love together."

"We?" She half rose. "What do you mean by together?'"

He pulled her back down against him. "There's no need to sound so outraged. We don't practice incest, but we do sometimes watch each other make love."

She sat up and turned to look down at him. "You watch your parents making love?"

"Sometimes."

"You mean, you actually watch your father put his cock in your mother's...in her...?"

"I think the word you're looking for again is pussy," he said, sounding amused. "Work with me here. I've already told you that once. And the answer's yes. As you know, she's small and fragile-looking. He's big. It's an incredible turn-on to watch his huge cock disappear into her—"

"Okay." She sank back down against him. "We have reached the too much information stage."

"Oh, but there's so much more to tell you, my lovely Erica."

She blew out a deep breath. "Mikhel, how can you watch your parents make love?"

"We don't watch when they make love. That's private...well...some of the time it is. Mostly we only watch when they fuck during a Family Fuck Fest."

"A what?"

"A Fuck Fest. Vampires have them all the time. In addition, we have family-only ones. It's when we all get together and make love in one room. It's an incredible experience."

"And you actually call them Family Fuck Fests?"

"Why not? That's what we do during them."

"Is that all you do? I mean don't you eat?"

"Yeah...we eat—lots of pussy and drink lots of blood."

"And you called them Fuck Fests?"

"Yes. Why not? Years ago, when I was younger, we used to call them Love Fests, but Serge began calling them Fuck Fests and somehow the name stuck."

A Family Fuck Fest. Lord, something was happening to her because the idea of a Dumont Family Fuck Fest where pussy and cock was eaten and blood drank freely sounded so damned intriguing. "Make love…Fuck Fest…whatever you call it, Mikhel, watching your parents…together is beyond kinky."

He gently bit into her neck. "It's uninhibited and exciting. As you'll see."

A mental picture formed in her mind of a vampire orgy. Willing women having their pussies and other openings drilled by handsome, magnetic vampires with huge, thick cocks, wicked, glowing eyes, and erotic incisors bared. The idea of watching the couple responsible for Mikhel's birth fucking each other was extremely erotic. Her pussy tingled at the thought.

"I'll reserve my judgment." she said primly.

"No, you won't." He licked at her neck and slipped a finger inside her. "I know the thought excites you, my beautiful Erica. I can feel you creaming around my finger and I can smell your excitement."

"You vampires and your damned sense of smell." She laughed and kissed his arm.

He lazily rubbed his thumb against her clit. "There's a whole world of new experiences awaiting you, my lovely Erica."

Something in his tone gave her pause. Just maybe all the experiences wouldn't be pleasant. Like another encounter with Deoctra. Because she felt certain they hadn't seen the last of her. There was no way she was going to give him up so easily after having his big cock in her pussy. But she'd worry about that later. "Nothing too drastic, I hope."

"You might find some of our customs hard to understand at first, but please know that no matter what, you're my bloodlust and that makes you very important to me."

She was definitely not going to like everything ahead of her. But she was held hostage by her feelings for him. "Oh Mikhel, I was a fool to think I could ever bear to give you up."

He nuzzled her neck. "Never fear, my lovely Erica. I have no intentions of giving you up."

"What would you have done if I hadn't come back?"

"Come and gotten you. Whatever could I have done? No matter what happens, I can never be happy without you in my life. You are mine. Forever."

"Forever," she echoed.

She had no idea how she was going to explain him to her family and friends. But she'd worry about that later. It was as she drifted off to sleep that worries about Deoctra intruded on her thoughts again. The Lord only knew when that full-blooded bitch would turn up again or how they would handle her. Or if they could handle her.

Mikhel's arm tightened around her waist suddenly. "It's all right. Sleep without fear, my Erica," he whispered. "Deoctra won't catch me napping again."

His words startled her. She lifted her head and looked into his eyes. "She won't catch you...but...how did you know what I was thinking?"

He stared into her eyes. She felt as if he were looking into her soul, stripping away everything but her raw and unrelenting feelings for him. "You have a lot to learn about vampires, my Erica. I've tasted your blood and filled you with my seed. More importantly, you've ingested my blood. That's created an unbreakable bond between us. Over time, it was create physiological changes in you."

"Are you telling me you can read my mind?"

"Would it bother you if I could?"

"Yes! Mikhel, my thoughts are my own! I said I wanted you in my bed, not in my head."

He grinned at her. "Then I'm not telling you that."

"Mikhel! My mind is my own!"

"Okay. I can't read your mind, but I can...sense some of your feelings and it's only natural you should be worried about

Deoctra. But don't. I'll be ready for her. The next time she shows up, she won't like her reception. I will prepare you to defend yourself when I am not around."

She settled back against him, closing her eyes. She was probably going to need all the sleep she could get. With a vampire lover whose mother didn't approve of her, and a full-blood who wanted her dead, she had a feeling her future was going to be fraught with major surprises and danger. But with Mikhel as her bloodlust, it would also be filled with contentment and joy beyond compare. She had to trust that it would be an equal trade off.

"Let the bitch come," she told him with a bravado she didn't fully feel.

"I know you're afraid, my love, but I'd willingly die to protect you."

"I know and I trust you." She reached back and caressed his semihard flesh. "You are mine and I intend to keep you. She's not getting any more of this cock. My cock."

"Your cock, my Erica," he echoed, his voice a low, satisfied murmur.

"For how long?"

"Forever. You and I are going to be in love, bloodlust, and together forever."

Forever. It had a certain ring to it. "Forever," she echoed.

The End

Enjoy an excerpt from:
Bloodlust II — The Taming of Serge Dumont

Copyright © Marilyn Lee, 2002.

All Rights Reserved, Ellora's Cave, Inc.

Erica entered the last grade into her terminal, sent the file to the school's mainframe, and sat back in her chair. "At last," she said. She stretched and glanced at her watch. Six thirty-five. She'd made better time then she expected. She had plenty of time to head home, slip into something sexy, and wait for Mikhel to come spend the night with her. Ah, sweet, considerate, Mikhel.

Thoughts of him and their fairy tale relationship during the last few weeks brought a smile to her face. She'd been showered with flowers, champagne, jewelry, and long nights of love, during which they greedily drank each other's blood. Although a part of her was still dismayed by her behavior, she'd developed quite a taste for Mikhel's blood. There was no feeling in the world quite as wonderful as feeling his shaft surge deeply into her while she slurped his blood.

Still, there were things marring her happiness. First and foremost, she was in the process of making the most important decision of her life. If only she could confide in Mikhel. Mikhel. He was the last person from whom she could seek advice

Sighing deeply, she walked down the quiet, deserted corridors of Kennedy Hall. There were some lights in other offices, but she didn't look in any of the doors she passed. The few instructors that were still around were obviously working to get their grades uploaded before the midnight deadline.

She left the building by the side entrance and paused only long enough to pull the hood of her jacket up over her head before starting down the path that led to the rear parking lot. Halfway down the path, she felt a sudden, ominous chill run over her entire body—right through her down jacket.

She immediately knew the source of the chill. She darted a wild glance around. A hedge bound the path on one side and a high wall on the other side. The fact that she seemed to be on it alone, didn't reassure her. She knew she wasn't alone. *She* was there somewhere waiting for an opportunity to strike.

Oh, Mikhel. Where are you? Oh, get a grip, Rica. You can't expect him to sit around and guard you like a baby. He's taught you how to protect yourself better than you've ever been able to do before. So, do it. For now, you're on your own.

She glanced back at Kennedy Hall, trying to decide if she should turn back or make a run for her car. After the briefest of hesitations, she decided on the latter. The only people still around were nearing retirement and wouldn't be able to help her. If she went back, they might get hurt or worst. Clutching the small, but sturdy wooden spike Mikhel had given her, she quickened her pace. She was on her own, but she was far from helpless.

She had nearly reached the end of the long walkway when Deoctra stepped into the path. "Human whore, I've come to settle with you."

Damn. Some days it just didn't pay to get the hell outta bed. She dropped her briefcase and took the leather purse Mikhel had given her off her shoulder. With her back to the wall, she began swinging it slowly, letting it build momentum. The bottom of it was lined with a heavy metal that made it a formidable weapon.

"Discard the spike and come to me, whore and I will make this quick. Look at me."

She knew better than to look into the other woman's eyes. Nevertheless, the desire to do just as she directed was difficult to resist. "Oh, God, please help me."

"He can't help you, human whore."

"I wouldn't be too sure about that."

As if in answer to her prayer, a tall, dark man appeared on the path behind Deoctra. As the full-blood whipped around, the man wrapped one arm around her throat and the other behind her neck, gripping her in a headlock.

"Low breed! Let me go!" Deoctra snarled.

Struggling to hold on to Deoctra, the man looked at Erica.

Looking into the dark, smoky eyes, Erica recognized the stranger from Salem. "You! What are you doing here?"

"I am here to help you. So, leave me to do it. Go. Now."

"But you don't understand," she said. "She's a—"

"I know what she is," he said. As Deoctra tried to unbalance him, the man used one foot to kick her foot, lengthening her stride so that she herself was off balance. He transferred one hand across Deoctra's breasts and fondled her. "Hmm. Small, but nice."

"What do you think you're doing?!" Deoctra hissed.

"Can't you tell?" He dipped his head and licked the side of the full-blood's neck. "I'll bet you're a tasty little morsel." He lifted his head and looked at Erica. "Why are you still here? Go. I'll hold her here while you reach your car."

"But what about you?"

The big hand moved from Deoctra's breasts, to span her stomach. "I can take care of myself. Go! Now!"

Picking up her briefcase, she ran the rest of the way down the walkway. As she neared them, Deoctra hissed and struggled to reach out and grab her. Erica tore her jacket on the hedge avoiding her. Fear lending her speed, she cleared the path and raced across the dimly lit parking lot.

She could hear a series of growls and hisses behind her and she feared for the life of the stranger who had come to her rescue. She shouldn't have left him. She had to get to her car and call the police. Maybe the sound of the sirens would drive Deoctra off. In any case, she had to go back.

A few feet from her car, a small, dark woman appeared in her path. "Oh, God, not another one!"

She dropped her briefcase and gripped the spike like a knife. "Oh, God, Mikhel! Where are you?"

"Mikhel is not here, but we are."

It took Erica a moment to recognize the woman standing by her car, wearing a dark cape like coat with a fur-lined hood. When she did, her legs nearly gave out. "Mrs. Dumont." She ran forward, her breath coming in ragged gasps, and clutched the small, petite woman's arm.

"It's Deoctra." She stabbed a finger back towards the path. "She's going to hurt the man who tried to help me. Please. You have to help him."

Palea Dumont glanced towards the path, her dark eyes glowing. "Serge!" She looked at Erica. "Follow me."

Erica glanced around, expecting to see this Serge she'd heard so much about, but never met. She saw no one. Shrugging, she dropped her briefcase, clutched her shoulder bag and her spike. She had barely turned, albeit reluctantly, back the way she had come and already Palea Dumont had disappeared in a dark blur. Steeling herself, Erica quickly ran back towards Kennedy Hall. As she neared the path, low moans reached her ears. The sounds were unmistakable. Oh, no! Deoctra must be raping her would be rescuer, as she'd attempted to rape Mikhel.

"Mrs. Dumont! Please help him!"

She rounded the corner. Her heart thumped with fear when she realized that Palea Dumont was nowhere in sight. Then she turned her stunned gaze on the scene before her.

The man had somehow retained the upper hand on Deoctra, even though his pants were down around his legs, exposing a firm, hard masculine butt. He must have successfully fought off the rape attempt. The full-blood's small body was spread eagled against the wall. The man stood behind her, his groin pressed tight against her bare bottom, his hands holding her wrists, his face bent towards her neck.

He drew back his hips and shoved forward. Erica stood gaping in stunned amazement. For she could clearly see part of the man's shaft quickly disappearing into Deoctra's body. Moreover, not into her mount either. He was taking her in the behind!

The resultant shiver from the full-blood was unmistakable, as were the animal like growls coming from her throat. "Yes! Yes! For a low breed, you have a passable shaft. More! Give me more! More! Give it all to me. Fill me with your big shaft! Shove it in deep, hard, and fast. I can take it. I can take it all. Give it to me. Ooooh. Ooooh, yes!"

"You're a greedy little vamp, aren't you?" The man demanded as he slipped his hand down to cup Deoctra's small breasts. He quickly settled into a steady, hard rhythm, his butt clenching with every movement. The full-blood moaned, her small behind quivering with each thrust.

"Imagine a full-blood like you enjoying being taken by a low breed," he taunted.

"Shut up and do me!"

Heat rose up Erica's neck and flooded her cheeks. Her whole body felt hot. She pushed her hood back from her head so the cold air could cool her cheeks. The icy air didn't seem to bother either of the other two. They were clearly generating their own intimate heat.

Without warning, the man drew back, pulling out of Deoctra's rear end.

Erica, stared, biting her bottom lip. He was as large and as thick as Mikhel. No. Actually, he was bigger than Mikhel.

His condom-covered rod glistening with bodily juices, he rubbed the big head of his shaft against the woman's behind.

Even through the condom, she could see the man had a lovely piece of meat. She licked her lips. But how in God's name had the small woman managed to take that entire shaft up her rear end?

Deoctra meowed and shoved her butt back against the man's groin. "Put it back in! Now! Please!"

Reaching around Deoctra's body, the man thrust his fingers deep into her. She moaned and tossed her dark head back against his chest. "Oooooh. More. More. Moooore!"

The man suddenly turned his head and looked directly at Erica, a mocking smile on his face. She swallowed several times. She couldn't hide her reaction to the scene enfolding in front of her. He knew watching them fuck was arousing her.

"Put it back in me!" Deoctra screamed.

He fondled Deoctra's small behind and mouthed the words: "I'll be all right. Get out of here!"

"But…how can I repay you?"

He grinned at her, revealing a set of even white teeth to rival Mikhel's. "Easy. You owe me a long, slow night of loving. One night I'll show up in your bedroom to collect. Deal?"

The thought of this handsome young man turning up one night when Mikhel was away to collect on his debt, made her pulse and burn. "But. . .you don't. . .know who I am."

"Of course I know who you are and I assure you, I will collect."

"Stop talking to the human whore and do me!" Deoctra screamed. "Or I will kill you both."

"Kill me?" He laughed confidently and slapped her behind. "I doubt that. First off, I do not intend to be killed by you or anyone else. And second, you're too fond of my shaft for that." He looked at Erica again. "Remember. One of these nights, when you're lying in bed alone, I'll come for my night. Now go."

With one last, lustful gaze at the thick shaft sinking back into the other woman's body, Erica turned. She stumbled back to her car, aware of a disturbing sense of jealousy because the handsome stranger was with Deoctra. On a conscious level at least, she refused to allow herself to even think about letting him take her if he ever turned up. Still, to her shame, she allowed the thought to linger in her self-conscience, where it thrilled and titillated her.

Why an electronic book?

We live in the Information Age—an exciting time in the history of human civilization, in which technology rules supreme and continues to progress in leaps and bounds every minute of every day. For a multitude of reasons, more and more avid literary fans are opting to purchase e-books instead of paper books. The question from those not yet initiated into the world of electronic reading is simply: *Why?*

1. *Price.* An electronic title at Ellora's Cave Publishing and Cerridwen Press runs anywhere from 40% to 75% less than the cover price of the exact same title in paperback format. Why? Basic mathematics and cost. It is less expensive to publish an e-book (no paper and printing, no warehousing and shipping) than it is to publish a paperback, so the savings are passed along to the consumer.

2. *Space.* Running out of room in your house for your books? That is one worry you will never have with electronic books. For a low one-time cost, you can purchase a handheld device specifically designed for e-reading. Many e-readers have large, convenient screens for viewing. Better yet, hundreds of titles can be stored within your new library—on a single microchip. There are a variety of e-readers from different manufacturers. You can also read e-books on your PC or laptop computer. (Please note that Ellora's

Cave does not endorse any specific brands. You can check our websites at www.ellorascave.com or www.cerridwenpress.com for information we make available to new consumers.)

3. *Mobility.* Because your new e-library consists of only a microchip within a small, easily transportable e-reader, your entire cache of books can be taken with you wherever you go.

4. ***Personal Viewing Preferences.*** Are the words you are currently reading too small? Too large? Too... ANNOYING? Paperback books cannot be modified according to personal preferences, but e-books can.

5. ***Instant Gratification.*** Is it the middle of the night and all the bookstores near you are closed? Are you tired of waiting days, sometimes weeks, for bookstores to ship the novels you bought? Ellora's Cave Publishing sells instantaneous downloads twenty-four hours a day, seven days a week, every day of the year. Our webstore is never closed. Our e-book delivery system is 100% automated, meaning your order is filled as soon as you pay for it.

Those are a few of the top reasons why electronic books are replacing paperbacks for many avid readers.

As always, Ellora's Cave and Cerridwen Press welcome your questions and comments. We invite you to email us at Comments@ellorascave.com or write to us directly at Ellora's Cave Publishing Inc., 1056 Home Avenue, Akron, OH 44310-3502.

THE
☥ ELLORA'S CAVE ☥
LIBRARY

Stay up to date with Ellora's Cave Titles in
Print with our Quarterly Catalog.

TO RECIEVE A CATALOG,
SEND AN EMAIL WITH YOUR NAME
AND MAILING ADDRESS TO:

CATALOG@ELLORASCAVE.COM

OR SEND A LETTER OR POSTCARD
WITH YOUR MAILING ADDRESS TO:

CATALOG REQUEST
c/o ELLORA'S CAVE PUBLISHING, INC.
1056 HOME AVENUE
AKRON, OHIO 44310-3502

erridwen, the Celtic Goddess of wisdom, was the muse who brought inspiration to story-tellers and those in the creative arts. Cerridwen Press encompasses the best and most innovative stories in all genres of today's fiction. Visit our site and discover the newest titles by talented authors who still get inspired - much like the ancient storytellers did, once upon a time.

CERRIDWEN PRESS

www.cerridwenpress.com

Discover for yourself why readers can't get enough of the multiple award-winning publisher

Ellora's Cave.

Whether you prefer e-books or paperbacks,

be sure to visit EC on the web at
www.ellorascave.com

for an erotic reading experience that will leave you breathless.